Shado

By the same author:

Illusion and Reality
Horseman in the Snow (Warriors of Tibet)
The Performing Traditions of Tibet (Zlos-Gar)
The Mandala of Sherlock Holmes
Buying the Dragon's Teeth

Shadow Tibet
Selected Writings 1989 to 2004

Jamyang Norbu

BLUEJAY BOOKS
An imprint of Srishti Publishers & Distributors

BLUEJAY BOOKS
An imprint of Srishti Publishers & Distributors
64-A, Adhchini
Sri Aurobindo Marg
New Delhi 110 017
srishtipublishers@yahoo.com

First published by High Asia Press 2004
First published in India by BLUEJAY BOOKS 2006

Copyright © Jamyang Norbu 2004

ISBN 81-88575-81-X

This edition is for sale in India Sub-continent only

Printed and bound in India.

All rights reserved. No part of this publication may be reproduced, stored in a retrieval system, or transmitted, in any form or by any means, electronic, mechanical, photocopying, recording or otherwise, without the prior written permission of the Publishers.

This book is respectfully dedicated to the memory of my late uncle, Tethong Sonam Tomjor Wangchuk: scholar, patriot and reassuring moral and intellectual compass in an uncertain exile world.

Contents

Introduction   1

Opening of the Political Eye   11
TIBET'S LONG SEARCH FOR DEMOCRACY

Imperial Twilight   27
A TIBETAN PERSPECTIVE ON CHINA AFTER DENG XIAOPING

Atrocity and Amnesia   49
GOLDSTEIN AND THE REVISION OF TIBETAN HISTORY

Blowing the Sounds of Emptiness   63

From Tibet the Cry is "Rangzen!"   69

Songs of Independence   75

Broken Images   79
CULTURAL QUESTIONS FACING TIBETANS TODAY

The Heart of the Matter   97
SOME OBSERVATIONS ON THE INDEPENDENCE CONTROVERSY

Unquiet Memories   113
THE TIBETAN RESISTANCE AND THE ROLE OF THE CIA

Writer and Historian   131
K. DHONDUP (1952–1995)

Going for Broke   135
UNWAVERING ECONOMIC ACTION AGAINST CHINA

"Confucius Say..."   143
OLD VALUES FOR NEW TYRANNIES

Non-Violence or Non-Action?   151
SOME GANDHIAN TRUTHS ABOUT THE TIBETAN PEACE MOVEMENT

Dances with Yaks   161
TIBET IN FILM, FICTION AND FANTASY OF THE WEST

Scholar and Patriot   179
TETHONG SONAM TOMJOR (1924–1997)

Shadow Tibet   183
IMAGES OF CONTEMPORARY REALITY

Rite of Freedom   187
THE LIFE AND SACRIFICE OF THUPTEN NGODUP

Bungled Bombing   201
LETTER TO THE EDITOR

Silent Struggle   203
TSONGKHA LHAMO TSERING (1924–1999)

Body-Snatchers   215
ENDURING PHOBIAS AND SUPERSTITIONS IN TIBETAN SOCIETY (PART 1)

Oracle Bones   225
RANDOM SPECULATIONS ON CHINA'S FUTURE I

Return of the Referendum   243

Acme of Obscenity   253
TOM GRUNFELD AND THE MAKING OF MODERN TIBET

Ian Buruma–Jamyang Norbu: an Exchange   271

The Tibet–China Visit According to Peanuts   275

After the Dalai Lama   281

Back to the Future   285
ENDURING PHOBIAS AND SUPERSTITIONS IN TIBETAN SOCIETY (PART 2)

The Incredible Weariness of Hope   303
TIBET, TIBET: A PERSONAL HISTORY OF A LOST LAND
BY PATRICK FRENCH

Freedom Wind, Freedom Song   315
DISPELLING MODERN MYTHS ABOUT
THE TIBETAN NATIONAL FLAG AND NATIONAL ANTHEM

Tibetan Flag in 1934 National Geographic   333

Introduction

Every author is wise and forbearing in his own eyes
— Cicero

I NEVER IMAGINED I would end up in life — and a bit late at that too — a writer of sorts. For a considerable period in my youth I had regarded myself exclusively as a man of action. I was disabused of this conceit when I joined the Tibetan guerrilla force in Mustang in 1971. Lugging a rifle, few hundred rounds of ammunition, some grenades, a pistol and an unbelievably heavy pack — at altitudes where after every seven or eight steps I absolutely knew I was going to die — soon convinced me that I nowhere resembled the Hemingway character that I had, till then, persuaded myself I really was. In my last couple of years at school "Papa" had been the dominant literary influence on my life and I had taken all that "grace under pressure" stuff very seriously.

I was a voracious but a not very discriminating reader: devouring everything from Alistair Mclean to Tolstoy, from Robert Heinlein to Herman Melville — and everything else in between — easily averaging three or four books a week. Inspired by Robert Graves' *Count Belisarius* and Marguerite Yourcenar's *Memoirs of Hadrian*, I gravitated towards history, specifically ancient Roman and Byzantine history, starting with Procopius, moving backwards through Josephus, Seutonius, Tacitus, Livy, and then the Greek historians.

I had some skill in telling a story. So in 1970, the convenors of the First Tibetan Youth Conference got me to write them a play for the occasion. My first, *The Chinese Horse*, which I also directed, met with not inconsiderable success in the small refugee world, more for the novelty of the thing (it was the first proper modern Tibetan play) than for its debatable literary merits. The Dalai Lama got a command performance and he seemed to enjoy it. Since then I have written plays whenever I have had the chance to actually stage them — the last being a comedy, *Titanic II: A Drama of Romance, Immigration and the Freedom Struggle*.

But political writing, which makes up the bulk of my literary output, was something I was drawn to primarily out of frustration, or more precisely, an inarticulate rage. In the late sixties and seventies nearly everything one read on Tibet in the world press appeared negative, hostile and outrageously untrue. Not only were individual journalists and writers as Felix Green, Han Suyin, T. D. Allman, Neville Maxwell, Chris Mullin, Seymour and Audrey Topping and others, happily regurgitating Chinese propaganda, but even media institutions themselves: the *New York Times*, *Le Monde*, *The Guardian*, *Newsweek* and especially *Asahi Shimbum* and *The Far Eastern Economic Review*, often gave the appearance of being franchises of the Chinese Propaganda Ministry. Some of them still do.

Of course, one knew they were all lying through their teeth, or at the very least were allowing themselves to be deceived for a variety of self-serving reasons. Reading Han Suyin's offensively racist accounts of Tibetan imbecility — that we ploughed by making yaks butt plough handles from behind, till wise and infinitely patient Communist Party cadres explained to us how the yak had to go in the front and the plough at the back — made me tremble with anger. But what could you do? Even the few hippies in Dharamshala lured there by Manali hashish and Tibetan esoterica were more inclined to believe Maoist propaganda than anything a Tibetan refugee had to say about the tragic fate of his nation and people.

I am sure it was the moral indignation I felt, not just at the violence and the injustice Tibetans were enduring, but also the blatant efforts by Western admirers of Chairman Mao to represent the Chinese occupation of Tibet as beneficial, humanitarian and progressive, that eventually forced me to sit down and start putting down my thoughts and feelings on paper. I started off writing letters to the editor, only one of which even got published (in *Time* magazine sometime in 1973, if my memory serves me) and also articles. Frankly, they were painfully bad. I also tried my hand at short story writing and very optimistically submitted a few to *Playboy* (an American acquaintance told me they paid five thousand dollars apiece) *Harper's* and *Reader's Digest*, and received my first rejection slips. Nevertheless when these stories eventually saw publication in the *Illustrated Weekly of India*, *The Hindustan Times*, and *The Tibet Journal*, I was immensely proud and gratified.

But my political writing was getting nowhere. In fact, the harder I tried the more my prose seemed to degenerate into ranting and mush. In 1975, just after the death of Mao I wrote an article for the Tibetan Youth Congress magazine *Rangzen*, where in a straight stylistic borrowing from Zola's celebrated polemic, "J'accuse" in *L'Aurore*, I started every passage with the line "Mao is Dead." Though the prose was fairly excruciating, and the style, admittedly laboured, the charge against the Tibetan government of ignoring crucial developments in China and Tibet (even the death of Mao) while focusing on petty issues of exile politics, resettlements camps, religious rituals and the like, had substance — and it well and truly infuriated the Cabinet. I got into my first major scrap with the establishment. But that is another story.

Then one day, I think it was in the summer of 1976, I picked up a slim volume of essays by George Orwell. I had earlier read his novels but had only been impressed by *Animal Farm* and *Nineteen Eighty-Four*. I went through the oddly, even provocatively, titled first essay "The Decline of the English Murder" and then, like the cartoon character who has an electric bulb light up above his head, I got it. It was, more elegantly put, my one genuine road-to-Damascus moment, to date.

So, this was how it was done. You could take a serious topic, even a relatively dull one — in this case a comparison between the hypocrisy (but also probity) of pre-war English society and the casual amorality of wartime Britain, through a review of the famous murders of the period — and write about it in an interesting, amusing, sane and most importantly, convincing, manner.

I kept on reading. Another welcome revelation: Orwell's essay "Notes on Nationalism" assured me that I was bang on target at feeling anger and contempt for Western apologists of fascism and Stalinism (and by extension Maoism). Orwell explained the conduct of these intellectuals who, abandoning nationalism for real or fashionable reasons, could not genuinely give up the need for a Fatherland or a cause, and looked for it abroad. "Having found it" Orwell went on to further explain "he can wallow unrestrainedly in exactly those emotions from which he believes that he has emancipated himself." But this "transferred nationalism" Orwell believed, allowed the intellectual to be "more nationalistic, more vulgar, more silly, more malignant, more dishonest than he could ever be on behalf of his native country or any unit of which he had real knowledge."

In "Politics and the English Language" Orwell revealed to me how the corruption of language was crucial to the making and defending of bad, oppressive politics. That same year I managed to get hold of Orwell's *Collected Essays, Journalism and Letters*, in four Penguin paperback volumes, which affected me the most deeply among his works. Of course, my own writing didn't improve overnight, but that didn't matter. At least, I now knew how it had to be done. I had a road map, and I knew I would eventually get there.

I began to contribute articles (almost exclusively) to the *Tibetan Review*. This was the period when the Tibetan government was sending fact-finding tours to Tibet, and attempting to find some formula: "autonomy", "associate status", and so on, to persuade China to enter into negotiations. I commenced on my self-appointed mission of pouring cold water on the hopes of many in the Tibetan leadership, the Tibetan public and Western supporters that China was on the road to democracy and would come to some kind of positive understanding and arrangement with the Dalai Lama.

I have to be straight with the reader. I was not prolific; neither did my essays reach a wide Tibetan audience as they were written in English. To make matters worse, I could not resist throwing in the odd Latin tag I had retained from school. But however inadequate or limited in readership, these essays did somehow make an impression on the main players. The Tibetan government became hugely annoyed, and His Holiness once gave me a severe dressing down, and I daresay, I just might possibly have deserved it.

But it was the Chinese who convinced me that I was making a real impact as a writer. Tsultrim Tersey, one of the first exile-Tibetans to visit Tibet, reported in the *Tibetan Review* that at an official meeting in Lhasa he was told that my writings and the activism of the Tibetan Youth Congress were harming Chinese-Tibetan relations.[1] A few years later, I received, via the Tibetan Security Office, a personal message from the Chinese authorities in Lhasa: that my writings were as futile as the wings of a fly beating against a rock, and that as an educated Tibetan I should return to Tibet to join in the socialist reconstruction of Tibet.

I was hugely flattered by this attention, and began to get ideas quite above my station. "Wings of a fly", indeed. Did the Chinese know that in chaos theory there is a phenomenon called "sensitive dependence on initial conditions"; which in weather, for example, translates into what is only half-jokingly known as the Butterfly Effect — the notion that a butterfly stirring the air today in New York (or Dharamshala) can transform storm systems next month in Beijing?

But such brave and upbeat moments were, in Dharamshala, few and far between. The Tibetan capital-in-exile is an energy and confidence sapping place. The contradictions in our society, between our professed ideals of democracy and freedom-struggle, and the increasing predilection of exile-leaders, including the Dalai Lama himself, towards a kind of autocratic conservatism (sprinkled over with New Age rhetoric for Western consumption) became more glaring and irreconcilable every passing year. Why bother at all, one felt at times; but whether out of habit, stubbornness or residual hope, one somehow kept plodding on "like strolling east when the sun is setting. The distant places are already dark but there is still a little light just ahead of you so you take advantage of it to go on a little further."

---

1. Tsultrim Chhonphel Tersey, "One Month in Tibet", *Tibetan Review*, vol 14, no. 6, June 1979, pp. 12–27.

This observation is from *Loto Xiangzi* (translated into English as *Rickshaw*) by Lao She, one of China's great modern writers. A Manchu, born in Beijing in 1899, he greatly admired Dickens. He was "struggled" to death and drowned in Taiping lake near the Southwest corner of the old Manchu city in 1966. His best known work, *Rickshaw*, is the story of a Beijing rickshaw puller's tragic life. In a particularly poignant scene the rickshaw puller's dying wife makes the forlorn observation on life, quoted earlier.

Many writers at the time in China were deeply fatalistic about the future of their nation. Even Lu Xun, probably the greatest of them all, often felt the futility of his craft against the violence and venality of warlords, politicians and revolutionaries. This is how he put it in one of his most depressing pieces: "It seems to me that the spoken and written word are signs of failure. Whoever is truly measuring himself against fate has no time for such things. As to those who are strong and winning, most of the time they keep silent. Consider, for instance, the eagle when it swoops upon a rabbit: it is the rabbit that squeals, not the eagle. Similarly, when a cat catches a mouse, the mouse squeaks, but not the cat."

Yet, somehow, Lu Xun's writings have outlived the propaganda and ideology of his old nemesis, the Kuomintang, and will no doubt continue to be read and admired long after the disappearance of the Chinese Communist Party and its hacks and apologists. Good literature not only seems to be able to outlast tyranny, but further seems to have a regenerative effect on devastated political and psychological wastelands left behind by the likes of Hitler, Stalin or Mao.

So, Nietzsche was wrong and the apostle John right. "In the beginning was the word…"

After the war when Germany had been reduced to rubble its writers built it anew. Gunter Grass, Heinrich Boll, Siegfred Lenz, and others rewrote the destiny of their country. According to Salman

Rushdie "They tore down the language and created it anew. Hacking off the diseased parts, putting together, joining stitching, adding many things, but always humour, lots of humour."

I half-remember being lent a dog-eared paper-back copy of *The Tin Drum* in the summer of 1974. The adventures of the dwarf drummer Oscar Matzerath — who's screams broke window panes for miles around in war time Danzig, was so enthralling, so disturbing, and so maniacally profound, that I actually ran a slight fever during the course of the reading. Of course, it deeply affected my outlook on literature, though I find myself somewhat inadequate to the task of explaining exactly why. In his appreciation of the message of *The Tin Drum* Rushdie manages to give voice to the supreme lesson he derived from this great book:

> This is what Grass's great novel said to me in its drumbeats: Go for broke. Always try and do too much. Dispense with safety nets. Take a deep breath before you begin talking. Aim for the stars. Keep grinning. Be bloody-minded. Argue with the world. And never forget that writing is as close as we get to keeping a hold on the thousand and one things — childhood, certainties, cities, doubts, dreams, instants, phrases, parents, loves — that go on slipping, like sand, through our fingers.

Re-reading these pieces for this collection I can see I have, in a manner of speaking, somehow managed to keep a weather-ear cocked to the beat of the little drummer. Whatever else I may have failed to accomplish in my writings, I have at least kept on grinning and — as even my most severe detractor will attest — been absolutely bloody minded, argued with everyone, and gone for broke like there was no tomorrow.

About the title of the book — why *Shadow Tibet*? Well, one of my better pieces in this collection is so named. I also intended it as a tribute of sorts to the great Belgian sinologist and art historian,

Simon Leys, whose *Chinese Shadows*, was one of the first and most brilliant exposés of Maoist China that I came across. There is one other reason why this book is called *Shadow Tibet*.

Like alternate worlds in science fiction, two distinct Tibets appear to co-exist these days. One flourishes in the light of celebrity patronage, museum openings, career and academic opportunities, pop spirituality and New Age fashions. This is the Tibet that has captured the romantic fantasy of the West and which has drawn much of the interest that the Tibet issue receives at the moment. Here, Tibet is far more than the issue of Tibetan freedom and represents the unrealized aspirations of the affluent and the established for spiritual solace, ecological harmony and world peace. Here the problems of Tibet: the nation of the Tibetans, is nowhere as relevant or important as that of Tibet: the repository of a secret wisdom to save a materialistic and self-destructive West.

The other Tibet exists in the shadow of a cruel and relentless Darwinian reality. Under Chinese Communist occupation it is a world of paid informers, secret police, prison walls, torture, executions, unemployment, racism and overwhelming cultural loss; revealing itself in the lives of individual Tibetans (like sores on plague victims) in alcoholism, sexual degradation, broken families, violence and growing hopelessness. In the exile community this manifests itself, especially in the leadership, in intellectual confusion, loss of political direction, hypocrisy, cynicism and bitter religious and political strife.

Yet, this is also a world, unacknowledged perhaps, of selfless service, loyalty, love of country — and when called upon — of heroism and sacrifice. This is the world I have attempted to write about. This is Shadow Tibet.

Nalanda Cottage
Dharamshala

Opening of the Political Eye
Tibet's Long Search for Democracy

Lu Xun, China's greatest modern writer, occasionally had doubts about trying to open the eyes of the Chinese people to the reality of their situation. In a conversation with the editor of *New Youth* he put it:

> Imagine an iron house without windows, absolutely indestructible, with many people fast asleep inside who will soon die of suffocation. Since they will die in their sleep, they will not feel any of the pains of death. Now if you cry aloud to wake up a few of the lighter sleepers, making those unfortunate few suffer the agony of irrevocable death, do you think you are doing them a good turn?

Similar doubts have assailed me whenever I have attempted to write anything critical about Tibetan society or politics. I feel the doubts even more in writing today's article about events which have raised the hopes of many in the future of a democratic Tibetan government, as I cannot share their hopes entirely. Yet to remain silent is to accept despair, to accept that our government can never be reformed and that our society can never be regenerated. Lu Xun, in spite of his doubts, kept on producing those short, sharp, critical essays (*zawen*) that were his stock-in-trade until his death in 1936. So, perhaps the least I can do is finish this piece.

On hearing of the unprecedented election of Kashag (cabinet) ministers this May, I, like many other Tibetans who have long worried about the steady degeneration of the Tibetan government into muddle, defeatism and reaction, was initially elated to realise that some democratic reforms, however modest, had, at long last, come to Dharamshala. Yet the initial euphoria could not survive the depressing realisation that although, for the last thirty years the Tibetan government-in-exile had been based in the world's largest democracy, very little had been done to learn about it, or to promote any of its ideals and institutions within Tibetan society in exile.

Moreover, it does not say very much for the sincerity of our commitment to democratic ideals (which we have been espousing since the beginning of our exile in 1959) that we have only now begun to consider the actual election of cabinet ministers, some thirty years later. This is well after most Communist countries in Eastern Europe have become fully democratised and even Outer Mongolia, to which we considered ourselves to be a sort of cultural mentor, has had free elections. It is not as if we have not had the time and opportunity to bring about steady systematic reforms in our government and society in exile.

Our situation in India provided us with the ideal opportunity to experiment with democracy, since we did not have to worry about the basic problems that most governments face in running an actual country. The government of India was taking care of the defence of the area in which we lived, its public order, transport, electricity, communications, education, and the thousand and one other problems that usually frustrate the development of fledgling democracies. We had our problems, of course, but they were far from insurmountable.

Yet we did nothing, and only in May this year, absolutely out of the blue; in circumstances which I gather could even generously be described only as impromptu, were the first elections (of a kind) ever held for a Tibetan cabinet. Such hurried improvisations do not really inspire one with confidence in the long-term stability of the institution.

One other aspect of the new reforms caused me not only concern, but acute bewilderment as well. Revision of our present draft constitution of 1963 is certainly necessary, but I do not see the logic of entrusting this job to a committee headed by a reactionary ex-minister, Juchen Thupten Namgyal, who does not possess even primary school knowledge of modern political thought or jurisprudence, and who was the main inspiration in the previous Cabinet for the censorship of books. As bizarre appointments go, this is not quite in the class of Caligula's appointment of his horse Incitatus as consul, but it is close.

Still, one mustn't carp. At least some changes have come about, though only time will reveal how fundamental and permanent they are. Nonetheless, it would be beneficial to our understanding of the present state of affairs to review the brief history of democracy in Tibetan society in exile, and to reflect on the events that have shaped our political culture to this day.

After the revolt in 1959, it was driven home to any Tibetan with even a minimal appreciation of public affairs, that his old political system was clearly incapable of sustaining itself in a modern, and, what is more relevant, hostile world. For those who escaped into exile in 1959, it was abundantly clear that we had to learn from India and the West — one of the most important lessons being democracy. The Dalai Lama himself declared, "The very thought of democracy, though I couldn't put it in words, was with me in Tibet."

Just about one year after his arrival in India, in the summer of

1960, His Holiness called for the first free elections for the Assembly of Tibetan People's Deputies. A year later, he announced the outline of a constitution which was formally promulgated in March 1963. But there were limitations. Though popularly elected, the Assembly had no real legislative function, and since it was not influential in the appointment or removal of ministers of the Dalai Lama's cabinet, its role was essentially symbolic. Such gelded assemblies also existed in monarchist Nepal and Bhutan, and could in no way be said to be organs of representative governments. The constitution too had its limits. Executive power rested solely with the Dalai Lama and the Cabinet that he chose. Moreover, the powers of the elected legislature were severally circumscribed. But a provision for the impeachment of the Dalai Lama by the National Assembly presumably gave the document some bite. The constitution itself was considered to be a draft and only to be finalised and implemented when Tibet was independent. So no clear democratic principles were propounded nor a democratic framework constructed for the actual running of the government-in-exile.

Yet, however inadequate it was in practice, the inspiration of democracy and reform was a genuine one for many Tibetans in the first decade of their existence in exile. The feeling was pervasive that our old institutions had failed us, and that it was vital to learn from the outside world. Though people's faith in Buddhism had not diminished, it was felt that the ultra-conservatism of the church and the apathy of the aristocracy had been largely responsible for the disaster that had befallen Tibet. The Dalai Lama himself acknowledged how much Buddhism in Tibet had become mired in arid rituals and ceremonies, and set about trying to put his house in order. Symbolic of his intent was the design of the new temple in Dharamshala, which was simple to the point of starkness. A number of incarnate Lamas also disrobed to become laymen.

A premium was put on modern education, especially scientific. There was something of the spirit of turn-of-the-century China, with its "Mr. Democracy and Mr. Science". One Tibetan school started a children's parliament and permitted its elected representatives some responsibility in the administration of the school. Magazines and newspapers were published. *Sheja*, or "Knowledge", an informative and educational magazine, became popular with the Tibetan reading public, even though it was only mimeographed.

In spite of the enthusiasm, there was a pitiful dearth of knowledge about democracy, or, for that matter, any political system other than the traditional. The little that Tibetans, including the Dalai Lama, had learned politically, that could be termed modern, had come from the Communist Chinese. So right from the beginning there was an unfortunate distortion in our appreciation of such concepts as egalitarianism, freedom, free speech, reform and so on.

In Dharamshala "Behaviour Investigation" (*kunchue dhakter*) meetings were held for government officials, in the manner of the self-criticism sessions in Communist China. Children at the Mussoorie Tibetan school were addressed in the honorifics formerly reserved for aristocratic children. But where it mattered, in the accountability of government, or the safeguarding of the rights of individuals, there was little change.

Yet, out of this muddle, one of the most important events in the development of Tibetan democracy took place. The Tibetan Youth Congress (TYC), since its inception in 1970, has had an uneven history, but alone among all the various organisations in the Tibetan world, including even the government-in-exile, it is the only one that has been consistently democratic, and sometimes progressive. Its role in Tibetan politics was in the beginning a commanding one, and it saw itself as a kind of loyal opposition to the government. But the Tibetan government did not want any kind of opposition, loyal or otherwise, especially not one that was more aware than the government of the modern world, and loud in its criticism to boot.

The Cabinet gradually worked at undermining the TYC, and was for a time very successful. It managed to get compliant people elected into the leadership of the Congress. The Security Office of the Tibetan government once even attempted to dislodge a strong presidential candidate it did not like by offering money and support to one of his opponents. It did not help matters when a succession of youth leaders used the TYC as a springboard to a career in Tibetan government service, rather than working to transform the TYC into the kind of revolutionary organisation that would uncompromisingly struggle for its goal of an independent and democratic Tibet.

Gradually the novelty of modernism wore thin in Dharamshala. Everyone was unhappy with the elected representatives of the people, who invariably gave the impression that they were either opportunistic or stupid, sometimes both. It was difficult for even intelligent people to see that it was not the individuals but the system, with its built-in resistance to change or independent thinking, that was at fault. There was a sense of disillusionment with democracy before it had even been tried, or for that matter, even studied properly.

The arrival of Western travellers to Dharamshala did not help matters. They were, in the words of V. S. Naipaul, "The hippies, the people who wish themselves on societies more fragile than their own, all those people who in the end do no more than celebrate their own security." (*The Return of Eva Peron*). Democracy was, in their vocabulary, a "rip-off"; science: nuclear weapons and agent orange. It was the age of Aquarius and the One-Dimensional Man, and the fashionable *ennui* with nearly every development in the West that had till then been considered progressive.

The influence of such people on Tibetan society was essentially obscurantist. They patronized everything traditional; the more magical, superstitious and primitive, the better. The forces of reaction in Tibetan society in exile were given a new lease of life. I even know of an incarnate Lama who, having disrobed and married in the earlier novelty of modernism, now resuming his clerical activities because they were profitable with foreigners. Religious fundamentalism began to supersede any idea of learning from the West.

Great effort was expended at translating many hundreds of Tibetan religious texts into English and other languages. But, as far as I am aware, not a single book from the West, aside from the Bible, has been translated into Tibetan. A large number of Dharma centres were also set up to teach Tibetan Buddhism to Westerners (a particularly grand one is being constructed at the moment near Dharamshala by the Tibetan government). For many years now a number of people, including myself, have called for the establishment of a modern university in Dharamshala for Tibetans (to be founded and run on liberal humanist principles like Thomas Jefferson's University of Virginia) but nothing has happened.

I am on no account trying to put the entire blame for Tibetan political regression on our Western friends, but they did substantially contribute to it. Usually the presence of such tourists and visitors have only a marginal effect on the society they are passing through, especially in such large countries as India. But Tibetan society in exile was very small, poor, and because of the tremendous dislocation it had experienced, extremely impressionable. Through their constant disdain of Western rationalism, democracy and science, Western travellers effectively discouraged Tibetan curiosity about the West, and encouraged Tibetans to revert to their old and fatal way of dealing with reality by burying their heads in the sands of magic, ritual, and superstition.

Alexander Solzhenitsyn, in his recent visionary message to the Russian people, printed in *Komsomolskaya Pravda*, the Communist

Youth League daily, complained: "The Iron Curtain protected our country against all that the West has that is good: civic life without fetters, respect of the person, diversity of individual activities." In Tibetan society, too the purdah of religious fundamentalism has for some time now discouraged us from seeking "all that the West has that is good", and instead directed our vision backwards.

What little we did manage to pick up was, more often than not, the superficial and vulgar aspects of Western civilization as exemplified in the popularity of Rambo and Michael Jackson among many young Tibetans, even monks. Solzhenitsyn also mentions such "manure" seeping through the cracks in the Iron Curtain, "the manure of a straying and fallen mass culture and deeply vulgar fashions".

The decline in democracy was accompanied by a period of fascination with Communism. The Dalai Lama held forth on a number of occasions on the similarity between Mahayana Buddhism and Marxism. The formation of the first Communist Party of Tibet was actively encouraged and sponsored by the Dalai Lama. Lamas travelled to the Soviet Union and praised the achievements of the Communist Party. On a trip to Ulan Bator, one Tibetan geshe even denounced the unfairness of the old system in Mongolia, where monks and lamas had in the past lived in palatial monasteries while the common people lived in *yurts*.*

The strictly hierarchical nature of Communist society, the idea of a ruling élite formed of a specially initiated group of people, must certainly have appealed to many in a church which increasingly saw Western democracy as *go-shug mae-pa*, "without head or tail", i.e. disorderly and irreverent. It was especially hard for Tibetans to keep a clear ideological head at a time when everywhere in the world

---

1. A Tibetan overhearing the comment asked the geshe where else but in *yurts* did he expect the people to live since they were all nomads.

intellectuals and artists were embracing the vision of "revolutionary" societies, and even Westerners involved with Tibetans, mostly in Dharma circles, considered Maoist China to be a utopian, or at least a progressive, state. In fact, it is only in fairly recent times, with the Chinese leaders themselves acknowledging the excesses of their Maoist past, that such Westerners have involved themselves in any political activity on behalf of Tibet.

In the eighties things got worse in Tibetan exile society with organisations drawn along regional and factional lines gaining power and influence at the expense of genuine national organisations like the Tibetan Youth Congress. These regional and factional organisations were basically reactionary, and their influence on society unhealthy and divisive. There was practically no one with any modern education in their leadership, which tended to be made up of former monks, petty businessmen, mahjong players and the like.

In the early eighties a Tibetan Women's Association (TWA) was created, largely on His Holiness's insistence. An earlier women's organisation had fallen into decline and disbanded in the late sixties. But this fresh opportunity to create something forward-looking and liberating for Tibetan women was not taken up by the leaders of the Women's Association, who instead concerned themselves with such issues as the maintenance of traditional hair styles among Tibetan women.

As readers of *Tibetan Review* will know, association members also took to throwing rocks or assaulting Tibetans who met with their disapproval. The initial suspicion among Tibetan intellectuals that the TWA had been created by the establishment essentially as a loyalist pressure-group began to be confirmed.

The atmosphere of Tibetan politics became murky and unpleasant during these years, commencing with the political murder of the Amdowa leader, Gungthang Tsultrim (who opposed the Dalai

Lama's brother Gyalo Thondup) and the mysterious death of Mr. Gyalpo, husband of the Dalai Lama's sister. Known drug smugglers and gangster types were welcomed into the political scene by the Tibetan government, which wanted to use them against its critics. With the addition of some new arrivals from Tibet, who supplied the Chinese-style rabble-rousing and denunciation techniques, a period of unease and intimidation commenced in Dharamshala.

For a controversial letter in its journal, *Rangzen*, the Tibetan Youth Congress was denounced for having Chinese spies in its leadership. Any statement that in any way could be construed to be against the Dalai Lama was pounced upon, its author denounced, and, if physically available, violently assaulted. Intellectuals were the prime target. A well-organized and extensive official hate-mail campaign was launched against a Tibetan academic in Japan, who was alleged to have criticized the Dalai Lama in one of his books. Hundreds of death-threats were sent to him and letters to the Japanese government and to his university to expel him.

For a couple of my plays I was assaulted by a large Dharamshala mob (with the inevitable contingent from the TWA) and subjected to a "struggle", complete with experienced denunciators and the rhetoric of the Cultural Revolution. All these excessive displays of devotion to the Dalai Lama, of hysterical patriotism and religious fanaticism were actively promoted by the Tibetan government and eagerly taken up by the *lumpen* element in Tibetan society. Dr. Johnson's observation about patriotism being the last refuge of the scoundrel, could, in our case, certainly be extended to areas of religious devotion and leader worship.

The Cabinet took to censoring books, banning a number of important academic works on Tibetan history. Magazines like *Sheja* began to print nothing but hagiography, propaganda and official speeches (in their entirety). Even within government circles, criticism was not tolerated, and fault-finding officials were dealt with in a number of ways, one of the more lenient being a transfer to a remote and undesirable posting.

Then, in 1981, after a long squabble about election procedures, elections were suspended altogether, and it was decided to have the Dalai Lama select Deputies to the Assembly through a kind of divinatory process called *yeshe emche*; the word "emche" meaning to sort out and "yeshe" meaning either gnosis or primordial awareness, according to the dictionary.

I spoke out against this as being not only politically retrogressive, but also damaging to the Dalai Lama's credibility and prestige. It didn't work. The next batch of Deputies proved no better than their predecessors. In fact, some of them broke existing Dharamshala records for arrogance and stupidity. But worse was to follow. In 1987 a hitch developed in this novel system when everyone selected by the Dalai Lama for a new Assembly declined to serve. Tibetan democracy hit a depressingly all-time low.

Old-fashioned elections were called once again for the People's Assembly. Few Tibetans of any outstanding quality were now willing to stand for the elections. The lack of any real power in the Assembly to begin with, the years of the Cabinet cynically using the Assembly as an instrument for suppressing criticism and popular sentiment, and the selection of Deputies by the Dalai Lama, had completely eroded whatever little dignity and hope had been reposed in the Assembly at its inception.

Last year saw the political situation in Dharamshala degenerate to a depth never quite plumbed before. No doubt readers of the *Tibetan Review* will remember the "Taiwan Affair" that rocked Tibetan society. I will not go into it as it is a depressing tale, and marginal to the point I am trying to make. But the magnitude of the scandal, and the resultant loss of public confidence in the government probably prodded the Dalai Lama to take the steps he has taken: to suddenly calling for the elections of ministers this year, and fresh elections for the Assembly.

These are undoubtedly steps in the right direction. Tibetans, for all their pious and old-fashioned ways, are, on the whole, an individualistic lot, and the only way I can see to extricate everyone from the prevailing mood of cynicism and exhaustion is by genuinely and actively involving the people in the process of government. I have long felt that this would not only be a remedy for present ills within the system, but also a solution to the endemic problem of maintaining the loyalty of the people to the government, in the dangerously uncertain interregnum between the reign of one dalai lama and the next.

I am no trained political thinker, but for what they're worth, let me offer a few thoughts as my small contribution to the furtherance of the Dalai Lama's programme, and prepare the grounds for further discussion.

First of all, we must realise that it is not enough just to use democracy as a kind of emergency treatment for a political ailment, with the treatment being discontinued once the patient shows any sign of recovery. Democracy must become a way of life with us. There must be no turning back, even when democratic values come into conflict with religion, as they have done in the past, and will continue to do so on future occasions. On the whole, Buddhism, with its basis in egalitarianism, rationality, tolerance, and spirit of enquiry, may seem admirably suited to the temper of democracy, but the Tibetan version of it with its many magical elements, its political ideology of *Choe-sig ni-den* or "Religion and Politics in One", and its insistence on unquestioning obedience to the guru figure, certainly is not.

Therefore, we must have an absolute commitment by our leaders to democratic and humanist principles. Without that, the mere mechanical process of elections ensures nothing. Pakistan does, strictly speaking, now have free elections, but whether Benazir Bhutto or her opponents come into power, changes little in that country. Pakistani politics are basically feudal, elections being a concession to modernity whereby the Pakistani people are permitted to exchange one set of feudal land-owning chiefs for another, under the aegis of the generals and the mullahs.

For elections to have any meaning, for them to produce genuine representatives of the people and not the usual contingent of knaves and fools (at least in our case) they must be conducted in an atmosphere not only free from repression, but one charged with debate. People must be allowed full vent to express their opinions, hear those of others, criticise and discuss freely. Right at the moment this is not possible, for statements of any originality or boldness could quite easily be construed as seditious or against the Dalai Lama, and their authors vilified.

The principles of "separation of powers" and "checks and balances" no doubt serve to protect the integrity of representative government, but democracy can also be undermined when people are cowed and have no confidence in the future. One could not really call the Tibetans a "cowed" people, but because of their extraordinary devotion to the Dalai Lama, they easily lose heart when they feel they may cause him offence, even through no fault of their own. It is this weakness that the government has used very effectively till now to suppress dissent.

Therefore it is imperative that His Holiness ensure the freedom of speech of his subjects, if his experiment with democracy is to succeed. He must unequivocally and publicly announce that not only are Tibetans free to criticise his government but the Dalai Lama himself as well. He must also actively discourage and disown all vigilante groups professing to act in his name. Criticism must not only be tolerated, but welcomed as vital, fulfilling the same function as pain in the body, calling attention to the development of an unhealthy state of things. Debate must be encouraged at all levels of society, and also the publication of independent newspapers, journals, and books to inform and instruct the public.

If you discount the occasional scurrilous poster and the turgid and often mendacious government proclamations, all that the Tibetan public has in the way of a news service is rumour and gossip. More often than not, this tends to be wildly inaccurate as well as vindictive and pernicious. It is difficult for anyone who comes from a country with a free press (with all its drawbacks) to realise how deleterious it is to the social fabric not to have some kind of trustworthy source of regular and reliable news.

Vital, too, is the translation of literature of all kinds from the West, which as I mentioned earlier, has never been attempted, except for the limited contribution of Christian missionaries, and strangely enough, in Tibet itself, in spite of Communist Chinese control. Since Tibetan society in exile is too small to sustain any kind of publishing venture, other than religious, the Dalai Lama and the government must provide funding for such undertakings, without seeking to control them.

Another important factor in laying the foundation of democracy and developing the future leadership of Tibet is the creation of a University of Tibet, as mentioned earlier. This is not the place to go into details about the project; suffice to say that one of its spin-offs would be the presence of hundreds of highly argumentative and hopefully irreverent college students in Dharamshala, contributing generously to the surging volume of unrestrained debate and discussion in restaurants, tea-shops, *chang*-shops, homes and auditoriums, once the Dalai Lama has opened the floodgates of free speech.

It will certainly be noisy, probably even unsettling. At least it will be exciting. A lot of nonsense will be talked about and written, of course, but a great deal of positive ideas will also certainly be generated. Most important of all, it will be a process of learning for the people; and who knows what beneficial, inspiring and even profound contributions might come out of it all in the end? Whatever the drawbacks, and I am sure the die-hards and better-notters will see all too many, it will definitely be a vast improvement on the present political climate; something that can be described as sullen silence broken occasionally by sycophantic gibbering.

November 1990
Tibetan Review

Imperial Twilight
A Tibetan Perspective on China after Deng Xiaoping

SOMETIME IN SEVENTH CENTURY CHINA, at the Tang capital Chang'an, the Tibetan envoy to the court asked for copies of Chinese classics. A worried Chinese minister supplicated the throne saying:

> How can we give the contents of our classics to these barbarian enemies of the West? I have heard that these Tibetans have a fierce and warlike nature, yet are steadfast in purpose, intelligent and industrious, intent on learning undistractedly. If they were well read in the *Book of History* they would know about war-strategy. If they were well versed in the *Odes*, they would know how fighting men should be trained to defend their prince...

Whether the books they got improved Tibetan military acumen, the Tang annals do not tell us, but it is worth noting the curiosity of the Tibetans then in things Chinese, if only to contrast it with their later indifference. The Tibetan emperors not only sent students to India, as our own history books tell us, but also to China. Many of these students were as brilliant as those trained in India. In 672, the Tibetan minister known to us by his Chinese name of Zhong-Zong astonished the emperor of China with his profound knowledge of Chinese language and literature.

But since the end of the imperial age Tibetans have remained singularly ignorant about China and unconcerned about Chinese studies. Unlike our more astute ancestors, we did not bother to study an important principle laid down in one of the Chinese classics (the *Sunzi bingfa*) which the Tibetan minister probably took home with him: that a determining factor in the successful pursuit of war or statecraft is knowledge of your enemy. Although there are individual Tibetans these days well educated in Chinese language and culture, on a national and official level, this disturbing indifference for studying China is very much the norm.

Its effects are evident in the consistent failure of all the various China policies formulated by the Tibetan government for the past many years. Some attempts have been made to set up research offices to study China but these have been desultory, and no substantial interest or money has ever been committed to these projects.

Much of this indifference has been, of course, a product of resignation, stemming from a false perception of the permanence of Chinese power. In the sixties and seventies we shared an intellectual weakness with the West in assuming that what was not foreseeable in the immediate future was non-existent. Events in the Soviet Union and Eastern Europe, and even in China in the last couple of years, have shown us how wrong we were.

HISTORICAL FLUX

The Chinese themselves have traditionally never regarded the course of their history as static or linear. On the contrary, the opening line of the first and one of the most popular novels in the Chinese language, *The Romance of the Three Kingdoms* (*San guo yan yi*), now almost a proverbial saying, sums up the theme of the novel and also aptly epitomizes an abiding truth of Chinese history:

> Empires and dynasties when united tend towards dissolution, and when partitioned strive once more for unity.

But what is happening in China now, and what does it portend for the future? Will democracy emerge once Deng Xiaoping and the other Communist gerontocrats cease to breathe, as so many young Chinese dissidents in the West seem to believe, or is the PRC really tending towards dissolution in the inevitable manner of Chinese dynasties and empires preceding it, into chaos and civil war, with the accompanying famines, massacres and dislocations, on the usual mind-numbing, scales?

Traditional Chinese historiography holds that most dynasties collapse under the twin blows of "inside disorder" (*neiluan*) and "outside aggression" (*waihuan*). Although the latter has tended to appear unexpectedly, the former has often been heralded by natural disasters, celestial portents, and the appearance of millenarian faiths and messiahs.

In the remote villages of Sichuan province, a cult has sprung up promising a saviour in the form of a new emperor. It has the authorities worried, and in Neijiang, the administrative centre for villages and hamlets along the river Tuo, the police have arrested a number of "chieftains" and members of banned sects. The main target of the crackdown is a group calling itself the Yiguan Dao, "The Way of Basic Unity Society", a sect which also plagued Chiang Kai-shek's Nationalist government before 1949. Though the authorities claim to have crushed the organisation, its roots remain deeply embedded in rural life. Its emergence is just a small indication of a new nationwide craze for all kinds of religious beliefs, ancient cults and bizarre traditional arts.

In Chinese history the emergence of such quasi-religious movements has often come about at a time of crisis in the dynasty, and sometimes even caused or contributed to its downfall: the Red Eyebrows at the end of the first Han dynasty, the Yellow Turbans at the end of the later Han, the White Lotus and the Red Turbans who rebelled against the Yuan dynasty, the White Lotus again in the declining years of the Ming, the Taiping and the Boxers during the decline of the Manchu dynasty, to name but a few. Even aside from these notable historic uprisings, Chinese history is so full of countless peasant revolts animated by strange cults, that the Communist Party has good reason to take such phenomena seriously.

Mystical sects and secret societies were ruthlessly proscribed in 1951, to be replaced by the exclusive cult of Maoism. But now, with the obvious moral and ideological bankruptcy of the Chinese Communist Party, it is not difficult to see why, in spite of strenuous official attempts to combat "counter-revolutionary feudal superstition", the craze for cults and religions among the Chinese people will probably increase, with unpredictable results.[1]

LIMITS OF MODERNISATION

Popular disenchantment with the Party has increased with the leadership's attempts at modernisation, and the partial opening up of China to the West. Comparison with the West and Japan has provided the Chinese people with a point of reference for their discontent and sharpened their grievances. It has also underlined to them,

---

1. In April 1999 hundreds of thousands of members of the Falun Gong sect held a peaceful demonstration before Communist Party headquarters in Beijing. The Party reacted some months later, in July, with large scale arrests of sect leaders.

as nothing else could have done, the enormity of the Party's failure, and the heartbreaking price in suffering, violence and moral degradation that the people have had to pay.

The modernisation programmes have also forced the Party into a profound and seemingly irreconcilable dichotomy with its present decision to forbid the free passage of ideas and innovations from the West into China, while at the same time constructing an economic structure that is essentially dependent on the unimpeded flow of ideas of all kinds. But an ideological resolution, of sorts, has been concocted for this paradox whereby technological knowledge from the West, becomes acceptable whereas political and cultural influences have to be resisted. Although, on the face of it, it may sound workable, it ignores the fact that Western science emerged from Western philosophy and that there is a fundamental interrelatedness between the two.

The great advances in modern scientific thought took place in the West in an atmosphere of political and cultural freedom. Therefore in a society like the PRC where the truth has always had a "class character" (or whatever character was required of it by the reigning ideology), it is not surprising that the sine qua non of Western science, the objectivity of truth, takes on the attributes of a dangerous virus. It may not be entirely by chance that an eminent scientist like Fang Li Zhi should have emerged as a champion of human rights in China. With every advance in technology, especially communications, this dilemma will probably become more acute. The use of fax machines in China to spread dissident propaganda from Hong Kong after the Tiananmen Square massacre may be just a hint of things to come.

China faced a similar dilemma in the last century when Western colonial powers used their superior military and technical knowledge to force concessions from a relatively backward China. Certain

Confucian scholar-officials as Zhang Zhidong, and the utopian reformist Kang Youwei, were attracted to a widespread philosophy of the time that attempted to tackle this problem with the formulation: "Chinese learning for essence, Western learning for utility" (*zhong xue wei ti, xi xue wei yong*). Generally abbreviated as the *ti-yong* idea (from the Chinese words for "essence" and "practical use"), this was a culturally reassuring position in a time of ambiguous, often painful change. It affirmed that there was indeed a fundamental structure of Chinese moral and philosophical values that gave continuity and meaning to the civilization, upon which the necessary Western technical and scientific developments could be grafted.

But it didn't work then, and it is difficult to see how it will work now, especially when the basis of Chinese philosophy and culture, the "essence", seems to have been violated beyond redemption. For the past forty years, the energy of the Communist Party, and to a considerable extent that of the nation itself, has been expended in savage campaigns to "destroy the four olds" (*po si jiu*) — old ideas, old culture, old customs and old habits — and to replace them with one of the most unrelentingly sterile and soul-destroying versions of Stalinism, never quite achieved by Stalin himself. Is this the "national essence" (*guo jing*) that present-day leaders of China are seeking to protect from decadent Western influence?

SOCIAL AND ECONOMIC BREAKDOWN

Present attempts by the leadership to force the nation back to purer ideological ways are doomed to failure. In the past, the hold of the Party on the people came largely from a simple idealism in the people themselves, and their willingness to believe whatever the Party told them, no matter how obviously untrue. But this mental bamboo curtain is gone forever. The Chinese people have seen through the lies of the Party and cannot be fooled as they were before, when their patriotism, and hope for some kind of decent future were exploited by the Party to enslave them.

Cynicism is now the order of the day, and the Party's control over society is slipping away slowly. A dramatic and telling example of this was, of course, the students' and workers' defiance of authority at Tiananmen Square in May 1989, and the subsequent massacre in June. But even on a less dramatic scale, the appearance of vast numbers of mobile casual workers all over China, in clear contravention of Party dictates on illegal movement, is indicative of a breakdown in the *danwei* "work unit" system. A communist refinement of the traditional *baojia* "mutual security" system, and structured into groups within communes, neighbourhoods, offices, factories and universities, it was a sophisticated and near-perfectly effective system of policing and regulating the lives of every Chinese. The *danwei* not only controlled physical movement beyond a permitted locality, and such things as job assignments, housing, education and travel opportunities, but even the right to marry and to have a child. Manned by forty-eight million Party members, it was the world's most pervasive network of social control.

The escape of such activists such as Chai Ling, who managed to hide out in various places in China for nearly a year before managing to leave the country altogether, is another indicator of how this near-perfect system of mutual surveillance and control has broken down, though to what extent we cannot yet be certain.

Even in the countryside, strong indications of a new attitude of defiance towards officialdom is emerging, seen in recent physical assaults on tax collectors. A year ago five were murdered and more than three thousand wounded in the line of duty. So violent were the attacks that 353 of those injured were permanently disabled. Even the authorities are having to admit to incidents that betray a growing conflict and tension throughout the countryside. *The People's Public Security Journal* recently reported a violent battle between two villages in Fujian province over a stolen dog, but that appears to be only the visible tip of a larger, unreported breakdown of party bureaucracy and threat of chaos, appearing everywhere in the Chinese countryside. The apolitical and often petty nature of the causes of all these conflicts (a riot in Sichuan over water-melons, for example), seems to indicate not only the erosion of party authority but loss of the individual's sense of social order as well.

China's economy, too, is in a fairly grim situation, even by the admission of the Finance minister, Wang Binqian, last year; and is still reeling from the impact of an austerity programme launched in late 1988 in an attempt to tame inflation. Even the relative economic success of the coastal regions has caused disturbing rifts between these areas and the centre, and poorer inland provinces. Embarrassing and previously unthinkable delays were caused in the drafting of the five-year plan last autumn, when certain provincial leaders rejected proposals for richer regions to subsidise massive failures in the state-owned industrial sector, and prevent the centre itself from going broke. This division can only widen as the leadership's attempts to control power, and inevitably the economy, intensify with every perceived hint of challenge to its authority, no matter how insignificant.

In comparison to its moribund Soviet counterpart, the Chinese economy may dazzle at the moment, but its advantages are essentially short-term, as events during the end of the eighties effectively demonstrated. In the long term, economic progress can only come with the stability and confidence generated by fundamental and substantial political and social reforms, and that is where the Soviets may have made the correct decision, even at the very stiff price they are paying now.

THE CRISIS IN LEADERSHIP SUCCESSION

Contrary to the expectations of many Chinese dissidents, China's problems will probably be compounded by the death of Deng Xiaoping, for the political system in China has an endemic inability to effect an orderly succession of power. This failure has deep roots in the CCP's practice of leadership by "lines", whereby the top leadership group is divided into those of the "first lines," who are the designated successors and who manage the day-to-day work of the party, including some policy formulation, and the "second line" leaders, who are the paramount leaders who never really retire, but for reasons of age and health are involved only in major issues of strategy and policy. The concept originated in part from Mao's concern over the succession issue in the early 1950s and in part as a result of the failure of the Great Leap Forward.

Such an arrangement must obviously create constant friction between the two lines, as members of the first line, who are expected to do most of the work, are not granted sufficient power to meet their responsibilities, while second-line leaders, in semi-retirement, enjoy the real authority and frequently interfere in the decision making of the first line. Such a system also places tremendous and sometimes intolerable strains on new leaders who, in order to survive, must build independent power bases, but who in so doing nearly always run the real risk of offending and alienating second line leaders who were their patrons previously.

This is why planned attempts at leadership succession in the history of the CCP have invariably failed, and failed under remarkably identical circumstances. For instance, Mao's first two officially designated heirs, Liu Shaoqi, and later Lin Biao, were not only unsuccessful in taking over the leadership, but were removed from their positions under circumstances involving humiliation, incarceration, and even death. Deng Xiaoping's two *protégés*, Hu Yaobang and then Zhao Ziyang, also experienced similar misfortunes, though Zhao has been luckier than his predecessors and is still alive. Even more ironically, Deng Xiaoping selected a relative unknown in Jiang Zemin at the eleventh hour, much as Mao finally settled on another nobody, Hua Guofeng, from his deathbed.

POLITICS OF REVENGE

This crisis in China's political future is not solely limited to the question of leadership succession. It has its origins in a range of institutional problems that, although sometimes masked by the very personal nature of political power in China, have been building to a head since the death of Mao.

Yet the one crucial predicament, the resolution of which I am convinced is imperative for any progress in Chinese political conduct, is of a cultural and psychological nature, and was festering in the national and individual psyche long before Mao Zedong came into power. It is unfortunately a condition of which, as far as I know, most Chinese people do not readily admit to. Yet their thinking and behaviour are rooted in its subtle, all-pervasiveness and central role in Chinese political culture.

In January this year, for three nights running, Beijing's main opera house, a drab and draughty concrete auditorium on Protect the Nation Street, once again echoed to the strident revolutionary arias of *The Red Lantern*, one of a handful of "model operas" promoted by Jiang Qing during her heyday as China's supreme cultural commissar. Officials who ordered its production, however, got more than they bargained for. Rather than a lesson in revolutionary zeal and obedience, it seemed to many in the audience to contain a more subversive message, one calling for revenge. "You can't kill all the Chinese people", sang the hero, "a debt of blood must be paid in blood." The crowd cheered.

An endemic cancer in Chinese political culture has been an obsession with revenge. It has prevented the leadership and people from utilising any opportunities for reforming society or redressing injustices without concomitantly laying claim to an exclusivity of virtue, hence justifying violent revenge against previous wrongdoers and oppressors, real or imagined. A never-ending cycle of revolution following repression following revolution is thus perpetuated where compromise and common sense are the first victims.

This characteristic of Chinese political culture has been commented on by a number of distinguished Sinologists as Merle Goldman, Geremie Barme, and Lucian W. Pye, to name but a few.[2] Pye feels that everybody in present-day China has "scores to settle". Within the leadership, the hardliners wanted revenge against the reformers who, for the last few years, had been insulting them, saying that they did not understand how to manage China's economy. The reformers, in turn, must seek revenge against the hardliners for pushing them aside and saying that they had brought China to chaos. The dissidents, of course, also need revenge, and the officials who were humiliated will be out to settle their scores too.

Geremie Barme points out that the rampancy of revenge in Chinese public life today will certainly damage the country's social fabric. He notes that the Beijing Public Security Bureau reported that by the end of July 1989 it had received some sixteen thousand

---

2. Merle Goldman, "Vengeance in China", *New York Review of Books*, 36;17 (9 November 1989); Geremie Barme, "The Politics of Revenge", *The Independent Monthly*, Sydney, (14 Septembre 1989); Lucian W. Pye, "Tiananmen and Chinese Political Culture", *Asian Survey* (4 April 1989)

calls on its informer "hot line" denouncing "Counter-Revolutionaries," of which four thousand turned out to involve neighbours, husbands or wives hoping to use the police to settle scores with each other. People who had lost out during the decade of private money-making sought revenge against those who had prospered under the reforms. Indeed, in offices, factories, schools and universities, the men and women who thrived in the atmosphere of the political campaigns of the Mao era were becoming the watchdogs of the new morality, for they were "the mediocrities who are inept at everything but betrayal".

CYCLES OF TERROR

It would be an error to see all these forces threatening to tear apart the empire as recent phenomena, a reaction to the Tiananmen Massacre, or even the upheavals of the Cultural Revolution. They have their origins in the policies of the Communist Party right from its coming to power, and even earlier. Those who only know of (or profess only to know of) the Tiananmen Massacre and the Cultural Revolution should be aware that these were only two incidents in the long and tragic catalogue of terror and mass-murder perpetrated by the Communists on the Chinese people.

Large scale massacres commenced right from 1949, with the "Land Reforms" after which came the "Suppression of Counter Revolutionaries" campaign in 1950, the "Three Antis" (*san fan*), and the "Five Antis" (*wu fan*) campaigns from 1949 to 1952, the Sufan purges in 1955, the "Anti-rightist" campaigns in 1957, the aftermath of the Hundred Flowers campaign, the Great Leap Forward and the establishment of communes in 1958, the Cultural Revolution (1966–76), the "Anti-Lin Biao and Anti-Confucius" campaign

(1973–75), the campaign for the denunciation of the "Gang of Four" (1976–78), and so on, all of which entailed the killing of tens, even hundreds of thousands of people, the true extent of which will probably never be known.

One estimate, *The Walker Report*, published by the US Senate Committee of the Judiciary in July 1971, placed the total death toll since 1949 between 32.25 and 61.7 million. The astronomical scale of the killings makes even such infamous events as the Nazi Holocaust and Cambodia's "Killing Fields" seem minor, at least in scale. At a time of relative peace with no real challenge to its rule, the Communist Party of China murdered more of its own citizens than everyone — civilians and soldiers — who were killed in World War II.

"REFORMERS" AND "HARDLINERS"

In spite of the leadership's efforts to demonstrate that nothing untoward has actually occurred in China, it is difficult to see how long present attempts at maintaining a Potemkin facade, even with such skilfully engineered public relations extravaganzas as the Asian Games can be successful. The sophistication of Communist leaders at manipulating Chinese public thinking and Western perceptions of China are impressive, but, as events of 1989 revealed, they are not without limits.

Yet Chinese cultural abhorrence of individual expression, their idealisation of the collective will, and their overriding need to maintain face, will probably prevent the kind of noisy, chaotic and unembarrassed airing of dirty linen now taking place in the Soviet Union, and more's the pity. No such therapeutic release will mitigate the gigantic and certainly violent outburst of rage and despair when the Chinese people finally break their silence to "Speak Bitterness" (*su-ku*) and "Sever the Mandate" (*geming*).

However much the Chinese people desire it, a gradual movement towards reform and change, even in the uncertain and chaotic Soviet fashion, is difficult to envision happening in China. No Chinese Gorbachev has yet appeared on the political horizon, and I do not expect one to show up for a long time yet. Many Western analysts have nominated such "reformists" as "One-chop Zhu" Rongji, the mayor of Shanghai, and Li Ruihan, the Politburo member in charge of propaganda, for the role, but in China the track record of "reformists", once ensconced in power, is far from reassuring.

Until very recently, Mao Zedong was considered a great reformer, even by eminent scholars as John King Fairbank, who should have known better. And though we now cannot view Deng Xiaoping as anything other than a poisonous old dwarf, we must remember the days when Deng the outspoken "reformist" was removed from office in disgrace after the previous Tiananmen incident of April 1976, where "tens of thousands of police and militiamen" violently cracked down on a peaceful crowd paying homage to the dead Zhou Enlai. Just thirteen years later Deng was doing the same to another "reformist", Zhao Ziyang, and cracking down with far more deadly force on another crowd of peaceful demonstrators at Tiananmen.

But no tears should be wasted on Zhao Ziyang either. Though he wept with the demonstrators and was removed from office in disgrace, it is fairly certain that had he been in power and challenged in the same way by demonstrators, he would have reacted in like manner. The massacre in Lhasa in March 1989 was directly ordered by Zhao Ziyang himself, then Party secretary. After the killings he sent a message to Lhasa praising the Armed Police as "brave and persistent". Friends of China, and indeed, the Chinese people themselves, looking for reformers, should bear in mind what Lu Xun said about such types: "Whoever was in power wishes for a restoration."

Whoever is now in power is in favour of the status quo. Whoever is not yet in power calls for reforms. The situation is generally such".

THE NATIONAL CHARACTER

Lu Xun's despair at such shortcomings in the Chinese political character has been echoed in recent times by the Taiwan-Chinese writer, Bo Yang. In his pamphlet, *The Ugly Chinaman* (1986), he decries what he sees as the cruelty and narrow-mindedness of the Chinese, whose unbalanced personality he believes functions only at two extremes. "In his inferiority, a Chinese person is a slave; in his arrogance, he is a tyrant. The result of these extremes is a strange animal with a split personality." Even Chinese democrats in the West seem to suffer from this. They want freedom and justice for themselves, but are unwilling to extend it to others, such as the Tibetans.

Last year a friend, Lhasang Tsering and I talked to a large number of Chinese students in the USA, all of whom were unequivocally opposed to the Communist regime. When the discussion turned to Tibet the "split personality" clearly came to the fore. Where one minute the Party's lies about events at Tiananmen were being vehemently denounced, the next minute Communist propaganda of the crudest kind was being coolly trotted out to justify China's occupation of Tibet. Gross racial and cultural misrepresentations about Tibet and Tibetans, that would have caused apoplexy if applied to Jews or Blacks, were aired before us by the Chinese students without a hint of embarrassment or self-consciousness.

When Soviet troops invaded Czechoslovakia in 1968, a young Russian, Pavel Litvinov, and a number of his friends, unfurled a banner in Red Square expressing their shame at the oppression of a small nation by a large one. Andrei Sakharov also denounced the Czech invasion and suffered for his courage as Litvinov and his friends did. No Chinese in China has ever protested the invasion of Tibet, much less gone to jail for it.

Of the many million Chinese living outside China, none has expressed any moral concern at this crime committed by the mother country; many in fact have tacitly approved of it, and regimes like the Kuomintang in Taiwan have sought to take advantage of the tragedy in Tibet for their own ends. This failure of the Chinese people to speak out against injustice was pointed out by the alleged mastermind of China's crushed democracy movement, Wang Juntao. In a letter recently smuggled out of Biejing's maximum security Qincheng prison he said that it reflected a spiritual malaise for which all Chinese, not just the Communist Party leadership, must bear responsibility.

Until I heard him speak to Chinese students at Edinburgh University, I had always accepted the media's comparison of China's best-known dissident and astrophysicist, Fang Lizhi, to Sakharov. Fang was an impressive speaker with a sardonic yet attractive sense of humour that probably did him no good in his own country. His sincerity was obvious, and his energetic denunciation of the Chinese leadership contained none of the mealy-mouthed qualifications so usual in the statements of many Chinese dissidents with distorted notions of face or patriotism. But when someone asked him a question about Tibet, Fang replied that he knew very little about Tibet but he thought that the Tibetans ought to negotiate with the Central government. Just that. His answer surprised me. If the Chinese government was so amenable to negotiations, why hadn't he negotiated some settlement for himself with the authorities instead of fleeing to the West?

Somewhere in its recent history the Chinese psyche has undergone a peculiar kind of moral lobotomy, whereby no pain, humiliation or suffering, except for that experienced by itself, could ever be real. Unless this morbid condition is corrected in the Chinese "national character" (*minzuxing*) it is hard to see how any genuine peace, freedom or happiness will ever take root in China.

ENDING THE EMPIRE

Since Chinese insensitivity towards such basic human rights' issues is rooted in their veneration of the collective will, as is usually pointed out, I believe that a moral and cultural regeneration of China can only come about with the dissolution of the super-collective, the Empire. Solzhenitsyn's exhortation to the Russians (in his recent message in the *Komsomolskaya Pravda*, "How we must Rebuild Russia") to let the Baltic republics, Armenia, Georgia, Moldavia and four of the Central Asians republics go, is one that has equal relevance to the Chinese. "We have no need for empire, for it destroys us," said Solzhenitsyn.

Never in its history have China's frontiers extended as far as they do now, and never has social, moral and cultural life in the "Middle Kingdom" sunk to such depths of sterility and brutality either. Is it simplistic to postulate some kind of connection in China between imperial ambition and inhumanity, between size and happiness?

The Song dynasty is unique in Chinese history not only for its conscious renunciation of imperialism, but also for the consistent humanity and efficiency of its rule. Song rule was based on general acquiescence and constitutional to an extent never before and since achieved in Chinese history. It never made any attempt to extend its borders beyond the Great Wall, and was never threatened by internal rebellions of any importance. And the many buffer states on its frontiers that Song diplomacy consciously encouraged and sometimes even subsidised, fended off the irresistible advance on China of Ghengis Khan's Mongol hordes for over half a century. Chinese civilisation reached an apogee in these years, with many arts, especially painting, never since being equalled. It was also the time of the greatest development in science and technology. Chinese traditional medicine seems to have attained its highest point then. Another important and significant field of development in Song time was jurisprudence. In the realm of philosophical development it was the most active period China had ever experienced, apart from the feudal age.

China's feudal age, the Spring and Autumn Period (*Chun qiu*), 770–476 B.C., and the Period of the Warring States (*Zhan guo*), 475–221 B.C., was an era of many disparate states, small duchies and kingdoms. Yet it was the most glorious age in the history of Chinese thought, a period when ethical and philosophical systems arose which have exercised a lasting influence on the culture of the Far East, similar to the influence of classical Greece on European civilisation. It was the age of the "Hundred Schools of Thought" (*Zhuzi baijia*) when such philosophers and sages as Confucius, Mencius, Lao Tzu, Mo Tzu and others attained such rarefied heights of moral and political speculation that all later intellectual achievements, right up to this century, appear to be mere footnotes. Even Beijing's current chosen intellectual hack, He Xin, waxes lyrical about the Spring and Autumn and the Warring States periods, as times in China's history "that were full of vigour and democratic spirit". (*Beijing Review*, 20–26 Aug. 1990)

UNDERSTANDING THE FUTURE

There can be no doubt that China is on the verge of a great crisis. We can see the cracks in the facade of the Empire, though when that vast edifice will crumble and break up is difficult to predict. The vastness of the country and its immense age gives its history a rhythm very different to that of other nations. A follower of Confucius once asked the sage whether it was possible to predict the future ten generations. Confucius replied that the careful study of China's past would reveal truths about life under future dynasties, "even a hundred generations hence".

It must be admitted that "China Experts" in the main have not been too successful in forecasting anything about China that has remotely resembled subsequent events. But where a few exceptions, as Miriam and Ivan London, Simon Leys, and the late Laszlo Ladany, have conscientiously observed the Confucian dictum on "careful study", we have been rewarded with valuable insights into possible courses of events in China.

It is vital to be rigorously discerning about information concerning China. Aside from the cupidity of "experts", reality in the "Middle Kingdom" too often succumbs to the sophisticated manipulative skills of Chinese leaders and the national obsession with keeping up appearances.

The Cultural Revolution brought China to the brink of absolute catastrophe, but we failed to see it then. It may serve as a sop to the Tibetan authorities that most countries in the world were equally ignorant of events in China, but their survival did not depend on that knowledge as ours did. Not only was virtual civil war breaking out in many areas of China, even in the capital of Mao's birthplace, Changsha; but the dangers of recrudescent warlordism were becoming very real. China's largest province, Sichuan, showed alarming signs of separating from the centre. Li Jingchuan, who was not only Party boss there, but directed the Party's South-West Regional Bureau and controlled Guizhou, Yunnan, and Tibet, was accused by Maoists of running an "independent kingdom". After tremendous bloodshed and manoeuvrings he was finally replaced with another equivocal figure, Zhang Guohua, who until then had been running Tibet, virtually as a personal domain. The "Gang of Four" accused him of this and of controlling all sources of power in Tibet.

I have often heard Tibetans with personal experience of the anarchy of the Cultural Revolution in Tibet, bemoaning the failure of the Tibetan exile leadership to exploit the situation then. What might have happened if we had, is difficult to say, and such conjecture is best left to armchair strategists. My only regret is not that we failed to take advantage of the chaos of the Cultural Revolution, but that we didn't even bother to study China seriously enough to realise what was really going on there at the time.[3]

This disturbing indifference in Dharamshala to Chinese affairs reached a scandalous climax in 1976, when even after the death of Mao Zedong, the Kashag did not bother to meet for some weeks, to discuss the consequences of this monumental event for the Tibetan cause. I remember writing a somewhat histrionic denunciation of the Cabinet's negligence in the Tibetan Youth Congress journal *Rangzen*. The Cabinet reacted to the piece like a bull to a red rag and a regrettably bitter clash ensued between the Youth Congress and the Tibetan government.

My hope is that our current leadership will undertake a thorough appreciation of events in China, not just with the intention

---

3. In *Surviving the Killing Fields*, Haing S. Ngor, the Cambodian doctor who also acted in the film *The Killing Fields*, writes: "Except for their dark skins, everything about the Khmer Rouge was alien, from China. They had borrowed their ideology from Mao ... like the concept of the Great Leap Forward. Sending the intellectuals to the countryside to learn from the peasants was an idea of the Chinese Cultural Revolution. Their AK-47s and their olive green caps and their trucks were Chinese. Even the music they played from the loudspeakers was Chinese, with Khmer words."

of locating bits of information to prop up official dogma on the merits of "Associate Status" or "Genuine Autonomy", but to discover a realistic basis on which a positive plan of action, no matter how modest, could be drawn up. It is just possible, even at this most desolate moment in our history, that destiny, or *karma* or whatever you want to call it, is preparing one last chance for us to save our nation and civilisation from extinction.

June 1991
Tibetan Review

Atrocity and Amnesia
Goldstein and the Revision of Tibetan History

INTELLECTUALS ARE, I suppose, no more dishonest than other people. On the other hand, they can call upon far greater resources to sustain a lie than the average person, who, when confronted with the obvious truth, generally has no other recourse than to accept it, even if with bad grace. The naivety and dishonesty of many Western intellectuals in their dealings with leftist totalitarian regimes, especially China, have now been pretty well exposed. Such books as Stephen Mosher's *China Misperceived* and Paul Hollander's *Political Pilgrims*, are profoundly disturbing records of this unfortunate phenomenon, providing a lamentable catalogue of the folly and cupidity of those who, by their very calling, should have been most proof against such failings.

Among the many incidents recounted in these books two in particular still rankle, for I once admired the particular intellectuals mentioned in them. In one, a well-banqueted George Bernard Shaw is travelling across a famine-struck Russia and blithely dismissing the horrors around him. In the other, John Kenneth Galbraith (equally well-dined) sings the praises of Maoism while touring a country bled white by famine and the Cultural Revolution.

Yet at a time when Communism is fast disappearing, and Maoist-inclined academics become a near extinct species, the reader may well ask what value, other than as records of more unenlightened times, do these two volumes hold for us? Well, for one thing they provide an unexpected psychological dimension to certain very contemporary questions in the Tibetan world. Take, for instance, the row we've had in the *Tibetan Review* over Melvyn Goldstein's controversial article, "On the Dragon's Side of the Tibet Question". The two books not only ought to help one to appreciate the issues in this particular debate in a wider and less personal context, but also serve as useful references for anyone trying to make sense of the strange dichotomy of academics like Goldstein, whose accomplishments in the field of Tibetan Studies stand uneasily alongside a self-serving political naiveté regarding Communist China's crimes in Tibet.

Lively as it has been, the debate over Goldstein's article is not, I feel, as important as it would once have been. World opinion has reversed from a position of gushing idealisation of Communist China to the present state of moribund scepticism, which though far from ideal is, without doubt, a definite improvement. And at least for the present, the objectivity of intellectuals trying to portray the CCP as a congenial institution open to dialogue and compromise is not entirely unquestioned. In such a relatively rigorous intellectual and moral climate, *apologias* for China have naturally become rare commodities, and even those, half-hearted and hardly worth the effort of refuting.

Yet I found that certain aspects of Goldstein's article could not be so easily ignored. They had an immediate relevance (though probably not in the way the writer had intended) to certain disturbing developments in contemporary events: namely the resurgence of neo-Nazism, the ascendancy of far right-wing political parties in many parts of Europe and the emergence of "revisionist historians" attempting to "prove" that events like the Holocaust had never taken place.

Of the many provocative assertions made by Goldstein in his article, the one that disturbed me profoundly was his claim that "there was never any Chinese policy aimed at eradicating Tibetans by singling them out and murdering them, as was the case in Nazi Germany with Jews". This brought to mind what I had read about the unbelieving and derisory reaction of politicians, academics and journalists in the West when first confronted with evidence of Nazi persecution of Jews in the thirties. There was a widespread belief at the time that Jewish propaganda was exaggerating, out of all proportion, random acts of brutality committed by a small section of the Nazi Party (Rohm and SA thugs) that was certainly not representative of the views and policies of Adolf Hitler and the mainstream of the party. To many it was inconceivable that a nation and a culture that had produced Beethoven, Goethe and Wagner could be capable of such acts of barbarity as Jewish "refugee accounts" were claiming. It was only after the war, when allied troops entered concentration camps and extermination centres, and when Nazi archives were captured and studied, that the full extent of the Holocaust was revealed to the world.

More recently the accounts of mass killings in Cambodia by the Khmer Rouge were disparaged by many in the West. Only when the Vietnamese army threw out Pol Pot and brought to light overwhelming and incontrovertible physical evidence of the "killing fields" did many Western intellectuals belatedly acknowledge the terrible reality of a carnage they had deliberately ignored or played down. Before Vietnam's ouster of the Khmer Rouge the eminent linguistician, Noam Chomsky, had pooh-poohed reports of genocide in Cambodia, dismissing with vehement scorn and certainty "tales" of Communist atrocities, and declaring refugee accounts to be "extremely unreliable".

In any discussion on mass-murder in Tibet, it is important to constantly bear in mind that, unlike Nazi Germany or Pol Pot's Cambodia, Communist China has not lost a major war. In fact, this last totalitarian state has so grown and prospered that it has become respectable in the eyes of Western governments, which have consistently viewed the policies and deeds of the regime in Beijing with calculated and cost-free high-mindedness. Though some lip service is paid to the question of human rights in China, thousands of slave labour camps still exist all over China and Tibet, the unremitting and bone-grinding toil of millions of its wretched inmates providing Goldstein and other Americans with cheap cotton underwear, shoes, toys, and steel pipes, among a host of other things. In fact, according to a *Newsweek* article of 23 September 1991, prison labour has become a mainstay of the Chinese economy in a number of regions and a very important source of foreign exchange. According to Harry Wu, a Hoover Institute scholar: "The labour reform camps are the reason China is so stable."

Since the Chinese government is ultra-secretive about official information, especially that concerning its massacre of its own citizens, and is furthermore under no pressure from any source, domestic or foreign, to open its records, our knowledge of the true extent of the great killings in China is necessarily limited. Yet a number of China experts and institutions have, through extensive and laborious research, managed to put forward possible figures on the number of people exterminated by the Chinese Communist Party (CCP) since its accession to power. Jean-Pierre Deyardin published in *Le Figaro* of 19–25 November 1978, a figure of 63.7 million killed.

The Walker Report, published by the US Senate Committee of the Judiciary in July 1971, placed the total death toll since 1949 between 32.25 and 61.7 million. At a time of relative peace and no real challenge to its rule, the Communist Party of China murdered more of its own citizens than the total number of people killed in every theatre of action during World War II, soldiers, civilians as well as the victims of the Holocaust.

Goldstein buttresses his initial statement with a supplementary line of quite extraordinary mendacity, that: "Those Tibetans who died unnaturally in Tibet during this period did so through revolts and famines, not through a deliberate policy of genocide." Even a cursory knowledge of modern Chinese history shows us that though the CCP may not have had a program to exterminate people on purely racial lines, it definitely had a clear policy of wiping out entire groups of people, entire strata in society, such as landlords, feudal elements, counter-revolutionaries and so on.

We know that in 1950–51, when the Party launched the "Land Reform" program, it insisted that landlords not only be "struggled" but also executed, though in many areas peasants were reluctant to do so. Millions of so-called landlords were killed. Mao himself admitted in 1957 that 750,000 people were killed in the campaign. One of the most brilliant and discerning China watchers, the late Laszlo Ladany was absolutely clear about this in his last book on the history of the Communist Party of China. The investigative reporter for *People's Daily*, Liu Binyan, one of China's top journalists and dissidents in exile, gives a personal account of participation in a local "land reform" campaign in his book, *A Higher Kind of Loyalty*, and stresses the official involvement in the persecution and killings of the accused, whom the poor peasants were for the most part reluctant to "struggle" or execute.

The "Land Reforms" were only the beginning of a continual

series of various campaigns where invariably large scale-killings took place. The Cultural Revolution is the only one most of us have heard about, as that is the only one the Chinese government finds it convenient to own up to.

Tibetans may not have been specifically killed because of their race (though Chinese xenophobia and racism would preclude us from ruling this factor out altogether) but they were killed nonetheless because of their unsatisfactory class backgrounds, ideological unreliability, counterrevolutionary crimes and so on — for, as Simon Leys point out in *Broken Images* "you can be a counterrevolutionary in Maoist China in the same way you could be a Jew in Nazi Germany". Such reasons were, incidentally, much the same for the murder of a couple of million Cambodians. The Khmer Rouge did not kill to exterminate a race, just to remove certain undesirable classes in society.

The great killings that took place in China and Tibet were not mere fleeting episodes of random brutality, as Goldstein tries to imply, but the direct result of a systematic application of Maoist theories of social engineering. These were, incidentally, a major source of inspiration for the development of Pol Pot's own ideas on "transforming society".[1] But going by the kind of political philosophy that Goldstein probably subscribes to, it would seem less reprehensible to murder people for theories of class-struggle than for eugenics.

---

1. One of the least examined, and hence, least known consequences of the Cultural Revolution and the factional fighting in Tibet is the growth of a national consciousness among Tibetans which resulted in violent uprisings all over Tibet around 1967–69, and which became so serious that the Chinese authorities dubbed it the "Second Tibetan Rebellion". In a conference hosted by the Amnye Machen Institute in Dharamshala on October 29 & 30, 1996, "The Sea of Inhumanity: Tibet in the Great Proleteration Cultural Revolution", among the papers presented and opinions expressed, what came across was that the extent of the factional fighting, which later developed into anti-Chinese uprisings, was nearly on a scale of the national uprising of the fifties.

The deaths of many Tibetans through starvation, especially in the concentration camps, were not just caused by natural events like famine, but were rather the result of a deliberate policy of the Chinese authorities to control prisoners and their productivity through slow starvation. According to Jean Pasqualini, who wrote the classic account on Maoist prisons, *Prisoner of Mao*, the Chinese authorities had developed the system to such a degree of efficiency and sophistication that Stalinist gulags and Nazi concentration camps were crude and unproductive by comparison. The Chinese did not have to resort to such primitive and wasteful ways of getting rid of people as gas-chambers or bullets. Instead they simply starved a person to death, and during the time it took him to die, used the powerful incentives of slight variations in the wretched farce of a daily ration to extract the maximum amount of labour and submission from him. It is probably as horrible a way to die as being gassed to death — and it takes a much longer time to accomplish.

Furthermore, the fact that the Tibetans revolted against the Chinese in no way diminishes the enormity of China's crimes in Tibet. The Tibetans revolted for the same reasons that the Jews of the Warsaw ghetto rose up against the German occupation army in 1943. The extermination of those courageous Jewish fighters is no less a part of the overall genocide as the murder of Jews who entered the gas chambers without offering any resistance.

Yet while Goldstein's insinuations that the violent deaths of people in Tibet were largely the result of legitimate military operations conducted by the PLA (the suppression of revolts and civil disorder) or the consequence of natural disasters like famine, can be largely discredited, it must be acknowledged that accurate figures on the killings in Tibet are difficult to come by. The Tibetan government's figures of over a million people killed in Tibet is not unquestionable and probably obtained by methodology less than absolutely scientific. On the other hand the weight of anecdotal evidence thus collected has been overwhelming, and disturbing enough not to be casually disregarded. Bearing in mind that the very same regime that committed the crimes is still in power, it would be wise, especially for someone laying claims to academic objectivity, to refrain from cocksure pronouncements of Chinese innocence, until such a time, and it may come sooner than we think, when official records can be opened and mass-graves disinterred.

The Panchen Lama, in his address to the Tibet Autonomous Region Standing Committee Meeting of the National People's Congress held in Beijing on 28 March 1987, was quite clear as to the mass killings of people in Amdo. A part of the address reads:

> In Qinghai (Amdo), for example, there are between three to four thousand villages and towns, each having between three to four thousand families with four to five thousand people. From each town and village, about eight hundred to one thousand people were imprisoned. Out of this, at least three to four hundred people of them [*sic*] died in prison. This means almost half of the prison population perished. Last year, we discovered that only a handful of people had participated in the rebellion. Most of these people were completely innocent. In my seventy thousand-character petition, I mentioned that about five per cent of the population had been imprisoned. According to my information at that time, it was between ten and fifteen per cent. But I did not have the courage to state such a huge figure. I would have died under *thamzing* (public struggle session) if I had stated the real figure.

A couple of years ago, at a conference "Forty Years On: Tibet 1950–1990", at the School of Oriental and African Studies in London, Goldstein presented a paper on the nomads of Phala. Based on his study of this nomad community, he concluded that nomads in Tibet had not faced tremendous upheavals in their lives, as other sections of Tibetan society may have done. He did acknowledge that they had faced difficulties during the Cultural Revolution (he makes the same claim in the article under discussion). I was present at the conference and astonished at Goldstein's statement, coming as it did from a scholar of his considerable reputation. When I got an opportunity, I asked him if he was not aware that the nomads of Phala were part of the estate of the Panchen Lama's monastery, Tashilhunpo, which had actively collaborated with the Chinese, and therefore not only been treated exceptionally well, but had this privilege extended to communities that belonged to it. Goldstein did not give me a straight answer.

Phala was no more representative of the nomadic communities of Tibet than the Maoist Disneyland of Dazhai was representative of China's agricultural communes, or Daqing of its industries. The experiences of the people of Phala before the Cultural Revolution were, without doubt, very different to those of most other nomad communities throughout Tibet. Many nomad tribes in Amdo, Kham and Central Tibet revolted violently against the Chinese and paid for their presumptions. One of the earliest and largest uprisings against the Chinese was led in 1956 by Yuru Pon, the paramount chief of the nomadic tribes of Lithang. In Central Tibet too, the nomadic tribes of Sog, Naktsang, Namru and other areas rose up against the Chinese and many were wiped out. The Panchen Lama, in his address of 1987, makes particular mention of the fate of the Golok nomadic tribes:

> If there was a film made on all the atrocities perpetrated in Qinghai province, it would shock the viewers. In Golok area, many people were killed and their dead bodies were rolled down the hill into a big ditch. The soldiers told the family members and relatives of the dead people that they should all celebrate since the rebels had been wiped out. They were even forced to dance on the dead bodies. Soon after, they were also massacred with machine guns. They were all buried there.

When I first thought of writing this article a couple of months ago, a book appeared in London which made a declaration similar to Goldstein's — not about Tibetans, but Jews. The gist of it was that the Holocaust had never happened, that the gas chambers had never existed, but were invented for British propaganda purposes and then picked up by Jews to extort German and American finance for Israel.

What surprised me about the book, *Hitler's War*, was that it did not seem to be the usual anti-Semitic rantings of the loony right, but a well-selling book marketed in London's main bookshops. The writer, David Irving, is a bona-fide historian, who shot to fame some years ago through his exposé of the phony "Hitler Diaries" that the popular German magazine *Stern* had not only published but even sold rights to *The Times* (London) and *Newsweek*. The "Diaries" had even duped the respected English historian, Hugh Trevor Roper.

David Irving's books have been published by major publishing houses in Sweden and Germany, and Macmillan in Britain. Irving has extensive knowledge of Germany and its history, and speaks, reads and writes German with native proficiency. Goldstein, whose Tibetan though good, is not on the same level. Irving is well acquainted with many Germans, including some of those very close to Hitler, as Christa Schroeder, the Fuhrer's second senior secretary, and his aide, Nicolas von Bulow. Some of these Germans later bitterly regretted confiding in Irving. Goldstein, too, has been on intimate terms with many Tibetans, including prominent aristocrats. In fact, he even married the niece of a former Tibetan cabinet minister.

Irving is getting a fair bit of publicity in Britain, his opinions being reported in many of the major papers like *The Sunday Telegraph* and *The Independent*. He has also had a number of TV and radio interviews and appeared on Thames TV's *This Week*. In Germany, Irving attracts crowds shouting "Sieg Heil!", with his lectures extolling the heroism of Rudolf Hess and condemning the war crimes of the British. In one lecture in the East German city of Halle, before a mob of flag-waving youths, he announced that as an Englishman and an historian, he declined to have any part in the victor's refusal to give the Germans justice and truth. "I want people still to be reading my books hundred years from now," he said, "so that they will say: 'Well, through people like David Irving, we got closer to the truth.'"

Other "revisionist historians" and "experts" I have read about are Robert Faurisson of France, and "the gas chamber specialist", Fred Leuchter of the United States. Three years ago Leuchter was commissioned by a German-Canadian neo-Nazi, Ernst Zundel, to conduct "scientific" tests in the former gas chambers in Auschwitz and Majdanek. Leuchter found no traces of Zyklon B gas there, which is hardly surprising after forty-three years.

Thirty-five years have passed since the murder of the Tibetans first began in the villages, monasteries, grasslands and slave-labour camps throughout the Tibetan plateau. Though hard physical evidence of what happened in these places may be as difficult to detect now as traces of Zyklon B at Majdanek, what happened, did happen. The ubiquitous control of information by a totalitarian state and the disingenuity of perverted scholarship may have been able to gloss over the truth till now; but if international events in the last few years are anything to go by, there is hope that such a state of affairs cannot be sustained for long. Indeed, in order to bring about such a positive conclusion sooner it is important that such falsification of history, especially when perpetrated by someone of Goldstein's reputation, be constantly and promptly challenged in print as has been done on this particular issue first by Phintso Thonden, and later by others.

Goldstein is not another obviously Maoist propagandist as Tom Grunfield or the early Chris Mullin, but an acknowledged Tibet expert, whose opinions on the subject are solicited by UN committees, US government departments and the like. He is therefore in a position to do considerable damage to the Tibetan cause when he bruits about his "ethnic solution" to the Tibetan problem, which requires for its realisation that the West not "continue to talk about a Tibetan 'Holocaust'", to use Goldstein's own words.

What he really means is that the West should not take China to task for any of its crimes in Tibet, including human rights' violations. That if the West kept absolutely silent regardless of what China did in Tibet, then eventually the Chinese leaders would come around of their own accord to endorsing Goldstein's "ethnic solution". This, by the way, being a rather ingenious scheme to marginalise the role of the Dalai Lama, play down the voice of Tibetans in Tibet calling for independence, and to legitimise, in the eyes of the world, those Tibetans (some, friends of Goldstein's) collaborating with the Chinese in the continued enslavement of their own people.

Yet, after all's said and done, I find it difficult to condemn Goldstein, even when he is being particularly annoying, striking statesmanlike attitudes as "Melvyn of Tibet" (as he has been dubbed by another Tibetologist). For right here in Dharamshala we have the senior-most minister of the Dalai Lama (and older brother), Gyalo Thondup, now openly urging Tibetans to give up independence and live under Chinese rule. Gyalo Thondup has also reprimanded Tibetans in Canada and the United States for campaigning against MFN status for China and for organising boycotts of Chinese goods manufactured in slave-labour camps. Goldstein at his self-seeking and arrogant worst is a less reprehensible figure.

Before concluding, I would like to say that though the subject of this article has obliged me to discuss the opinions of David Irving alongside those of Goldstein, maybe too substantial a comparison should not be drawn between the two. Irving, however monstrous and hateful his political views, is admittedly a genuine and accomplished historian. Goldstein, on the other hand, is an anthropologist attempting to write history, and his works clearly demonstrate the limits of such a fundamental perspective shift.

History is the first of the humanist disciplines while "Of all the modern social sciences, anthropology is", according to Edward Said, "the one historically most closely tied to colonialism" (since it was often the case that anthropologists and ethnologists advised colonial rulers on the manners and mores of native peoples). The structural-anthropologist, Claude Lévi-Strauss referred to his chosen profession as "the handmaiden of colonialism".

Of course anthropology has come a long way since sahibs in pith helmets disdainfully measured (with oversize callipers) the skulls of "Hottentots", but in Goldstein's rationalisations of Chinese colonial rule in Tibet one gets a sense of what the real purpose of anthropology had been, not so very long ago. Yet it must certainly be recognized that Goldstein is a scholar of substantial accomplishment, probably leading the field in Tibetan studies in quantity of research work, though lacking breadth of vision, sensitivity and moral integrity for original and insightful interpretation.

Whenever a victorious Roman general was permitted a public triumph by the Senate, a slave held a jewelled Etruscan crown over his head during the procession and occasionally whispered in his ear a warning against hubris. I feel that a similar arrangement would be beneficial to Prof. Goldstein whenever he felt tempted to dismiss, in speech or in print, the truth of China's crimes in Tibet. The message of the whispered admonition could, of course, be one more germane to the occasion, perhaps in Goldstein's case the somewhat manifest observation that "suffering is not the exclusive preserve of one people".

May 1992
Tibetan Review

Blowing the Sounds of Emptiness

Sounds of Peace
Rhythms of Peace
Sounds of Inner Peace
— composed and performed by Nawang Khechog

In an interview in *India Today*, the great Indian flautist, Hari Prasad Chaurasia made a remark about his simple instrument that struck me at the time for its poetic imagination. I regrettably don't recollect his exact words, and my copy of the magazine has long since passed on to the local rag-picker, but I think it went something like this: that the flute was the instrument whose music was the most purely spiritual, the one that took him closest to God. It did not require strings, reeds, or membranes to produce its melodies, just holes — emptiness.

It seems to me that Nawang Khechog is attempting such a symbiosis of instrument and spiritual expression in his music. Not only is he a specialist in the transverse flute, but he also plays a number of wind instruments from all corners of the world. He has mastered the didgeridoo of his present home in Australia, and also pan-pipes and ocarinas from South America; all instruments that depend on "voids" of one sort or the other for the source of their resonance.

But the spiritual claims made by Nawang Khechog for his music do not stop at just this particular quality of his instruments. By his art he seeks to achieve one of the primary objective of Buddhism: a peaceful state of mind. "I try to create a mood of peace and harmony that frees the mind of anger jealousy and greediness." A tall order? Well, Shakespeare didn't think so. What worked in his days on "savage breasts" and "restless spirits", could certainly be capable of assuaging the more pliable souls of New Age folk.

Though I have not had the pleasure of hearing Nawang Khechog live, I am assured by someone who did, at a rock concert at Bondai beach in Australia, that after the first few notes from his flute a rather frenzied audience of many thousands calmed down to listen to his music in relative silence. It also seemed that this pacific mood was not just confined to the sort who, at such events, invariably comport themselves in full lotus position and go into deep meditation, but also spilled over to the more raucous realm of heavy-duty yobs clutching litre cans of Fosters.

A music critic for the *Erie Showcase Entertainment Guide* wrote that: "His (Khechog's) flute playing mirrors a common experience I've had in meditation over the years. When I ascend into the space between thoughts or breaths, I feel more peaceful, joyful, and expansive. This inner state is expressed with integrity and purity by Khechog." Khechog seems to have received a uniformly friendly press wherever he has performed, though unfortunately most of the write-ups seem to be just variations on the outpourings of our *Erie* reviewer; more revealing of the emotional and spiritual confusion of the writer, than of the actual music of Nawang Khechog.

So what is his music really like? I falter at providing an answer. Music is one of the most subjective of arts, sublime harmonies for some being intolerable cacophony for others. But probably the best way to understand his work is to first strip it of all the accretion of New Age verbiage that has grown over it like barnacles, in the last few years. A Tang dynasty artist once complained that people were judging paintings with their ears. In our day and age such shabby deceptions are perpetrated, at least in the case of music, with the eyes, or, to be specific, through reading review columns.

But even having accomplished a decent de-barnacling job of Khechog's music in my head, I cannot emphasize enough how ill-qualified I feel to say anything definite about his work, except to make a very personal and subjective interpretation, which, I do not hesitate to state, could be equally and justifiably held up to ridicule and castigation. But since Khechog is the first Tibetan musician I know, creating and performing this kind of experimental music, I would like to pay him the highest compliment I can, by discussing his music seriously as music, and not as anything else.

I enjoyed listening to his three albums and was intrigued by the quality of the sounds, not least for the very Tibetan, sometimes autobiographical undertones present in them. The influence of Tibetan ecclesiastical music was clearly apparent throughout his works, though subtly altered to remove the more dissonant and "primordial" (Anagarika Govinda) qualities of that tradition, especially the thunderous clatter and roar of drums and cymbals.

Khechog's flute compositions evoked on one level the tonal qualities of *gyaling* (double reed oboe) music. As I was listening to *The Sounds of Inner Peace*, this sensation was reinforced by the sounds of actual *gyalings* that drifted over to my house from the nearby Namgyal Monastery. Nawang was a monk at Dharamshala for eleven years and such sounds must have constantly been around him. At other times, his flute music veered off into long plaintive melodies that harked at Khampa *lu* songs, perhaps drawn from childhood memories of a free nomadic life in Eastern Tibet.

They were the most fleeting of impressions, but once or twice I thought I heard the trills of *pahari*, or Indian hill music, weaving into his compositions. Did Nawang take his flute and wander about the mountains in Dharamshala, listening to the music of the Gaddi shepherds? One of his compositions on the pan-pipes, a wonderfully flowing, rippling and bubbling impression of the course of some Himalayan cataract, also left me wondering about the many hours he had spent by the waterfall and river at Dharamshala, unconsciously absorbing its movements and resonance.

With the didgeridoo of the Australian aborigine, Nawang reproduces the deep bass sounds and thunderous blasts of the *dungchen*, the Tibetan giant horn, though once again his interpretation, though seemingly derived from a Tibetan monastic tradition, is clearly and uniquely his own. I suspect this magnificent instrument, with its other-worldly roar and its roots in the dream-world of the native Australian, of being the show-stopper in his performances. Clearly children love the sound of the didgeridoo, as a write-up in the *Hartford Courant* reports of Khechog's concert at a school at West Hartford, Connecticut.

Besides schools, Nawang has played at a range of venues from a zoo in Sydney to the UN General Assembly Hall, and also at various concerts with other musicians such as Philip Glass and Joan Baez. Clearly Nawang is beginning to make his mark on the "alternative" music scene, and his tour of the United States last year (one of his sponsors being Richard Gere) has provided him with a wider international audience than before, when he just performed in Australia.

The New Age treacle is well and truly smothering everything of value in Tibetan culture at present, from the highest tantric initiations to the lowest bass register of Gyuto chants, and it is perhaps asking too much of one lone Tibetan musician out in the West, not to sink into it, especially when lamas are happily diving head-first into the stuff. But it is nonetheless a pity, for Khechog's seems to me one of the most original of all contemporary Tibetan music. Because of its experimental form and its attachment to the idea of peace and mental harmony, it does, on occasions, tend to become repetitive and uncertain of its direction; but all music of this kind faces such problems. How many Kitaro albums can you listen to without yawning? An excessive use of the reverb blurs the intention of Khechog's compositions on a number of occasions.

Khechog is one of the most interesting of contemporary Tibetan musicians not only because his work is created on the cultural and spiritual structures derived from his own traditions, but also because it is genuinely innovative. These innovations have substance and, to use a favourite Tibetan diorism, *khung-lung*, meaning that they have definite sources as well as continuing traditions; such, to a Tibetan way of thinking, being fundamental requirements for the successful pursuit of any worthwhile human activity, cultural or spiritual. Western obsession with novelty, self-expression (but does the self really exist?), and "creativity" have yet to substantially influence Tibetan society and is still greeted by many of its members with incredulity and mild derision. As Khechog's innovations are, in the main, derived from the threatened cultures of native Australians and South American Indians, people with ancient, yet not classically formal, musical traditions, the sympathetic vibrations running through these diverse traditions do lend to a satisfying unity and wholeness with the Tibetan elements of Khechog's compositions.

Currently, Hong Kong–Taiwan pop influence of the most whiny and tinkly sort seems to have taken over the development of modern music in Tibet. Unfortunately, this craze does not seem to have adversely affected the dominance of the pseudo-classical, pretentious, boring but ideologically correct sound exemplified in the compositions of Aram Khachaturian (*Ode to Stalin*), Xian Xinghai (*Yellow River Cantata*), and Nie Er (*March of the Volunteers*), that still permeates Chinese music in the PRC, and which has considerable influence on Tibetan music in Tibet as well as in exile.

New Tibetan composers in exile, namely in Germany, Switzerland and India, have made the beginnings of an effort to create a popular new music form, often basing it on old Lhasaen tunes and folk songs from different parts of Tibet, but adding new lyrics, modern instruments and fresh arrangements. Though certainly very well received by the Tibetan public, the results of these efforts somehow seem to me insipid, possessing neither the energy of good Western popular music nor the charm of the old Tibetan traditions. But, of course, these are the merest of beginnings of this new movement, and I for one, certainly look forward to more exciting musical fare in the near future. Khechog could provide a crucial direction to the course of modern Tibetan music, but for that he would have to work within the Tibetan musical world, which at the moment is splintered, confused, and lacking in confidence and energy.

I would like to see a "Year of Tibet" for Tibetans, where among other cultural and artistic events, Tibetan singers and musicians from all over the world, including Nawang Khechog, could gather to swap tunes and ideas, and where they could perform together to entertain, move and inspire an audience of ordinary Tibetan "black-headed people" (the laity) from where it all came in the first place.

May–June 1992
Tibetan Bulletin

From Tibet the Cry is "Rangzen!"[1]

THE WORD "RANGZEN" (INDEPENDENCE) is the most constant and powerful refrain in nearly all protest documents that have come out from Tibet in the last few years, whether it be lengthy petitions to the United Nations, humble scraps of paper surreptitiously passed on to tourists, or wall posters hurriedly pasted up in the night (sometimes upside down) on the walls of Lhasa city. In fact, every political demonstration and protest has had as its essential demand, independence for Tibet; followed by a demand for human rights, and expressions of loyalty to the Dalai Lama as the sovereign ruler of Tibet. Hundreds of such posters, leaflets, pamphlets and manifestos have made their way out of Tibet. A representative few are discussed below.

The most recent of such documents is a copy of a poster that

---

1. I wrote this and the following short piece "Songs of Independence" sometime in 1993 for distribution at a conference of various Tibet support groups in the USA. The International Campaign for Tibet was, at the time, making a big effort to sideline the issue of independence in favour of "genuine autonomy".

was pasted up in the centre of Rongbo town (on the wall of the official guesthouse) in Rebkong, Amdo (Qinghai province). Another copy of the poster was also pasted in another section of the town. The poster is essentially a warning to Tibetan people not to believe in the *White Paper* issued by the Chinese government, and it assures the people that Tibetan independence will come soon. It also warns all Chinese to return to China. The document claims to be issued by the Rebkong branch of the Committee for Independence (*Rangzen tsok-chung*). It is dated 26 (?) 1992.

A poster dated 1 August 1992, and acquired by a Swiss-Tibetan visitor to Lhasa last year, carries a warning to those Tibetans "working against the struggle for the rightful cause of independence". Interestingly enough, the warning is not only directed at those collaborating with the Communist Chinese, but extends to those in the pay of Taiwan. Tibetans in exile visiting Tibet are also warned against doing business in sacred images, as also are such dealers in Tibet. The poster concludes on a stern note of warning to all malefactors: "We the people, know who you are. You are following the wrong path. You must change your ways. Otherwise you will soon have to exchange your ill-gotten money with your life. The nation of Tibet belongs to the Dalai Lama and the Tibetan people. The Three Regions (*Cholka sum*) Amity Society."

A nine page petition to the "leaders of the United Nations", describing human rights abuses in Tibet and the many guises (economic reforms etc.) under which Chinese immigration to Tibet was taking place, concludes with these lines, "Though the Tibetans at the moment cannot show their gratitude to the UN, as our nation is under the oppression of the enemy, one day, when Tibet gains its independence, the people will surely do so. Jointly from the people of the three regions of Tibet (*Cholka sum thunmong*), on the twenty-fifth day of the sixth moon of the Fire Rabbit year."

Another memorandum, dated 4 October 1987, from the same group is addressed to the United States Senate and the House of Representatives. It thanks the 150-odd congressmen for sending a message to the Chinese government in 1985, protesting against the oppression of the Tibetan people, and also stating that Chinese claims to Tibet are unfounded and false. The memorandum also mentions that on the 22 October 1986, the American Federal Reserve Bank(?) passed a regulation wherein was mentioned that Tibet was an independent nation(?).

The memorandum concludes, "When we Tibetans heard this we became very happy. Our sun of happiness has risen from the West. Furthermore, the statement that Tibet is completely independent has been like food to a starving man and water to a man dying of thirst. It has made us drunk with joy. From the people of the Three Regions (*Cholka sum*)."

A mimeographed list of slogans is dated 10 December 1988. The slogans were probably meant for a demonstration, maybe the one to commemorate the United Nations Human Right's Day, which is mentioned at the head of the list. The slogans are uniform in structure, and somewhat Chinese in character with the cry "Ten thousand years to...," (Tibetan: *ku-tse tri-drak*, Chinese: *wan-sui*) preceding all the slogans:

> Ten thousand years to the "historically significant Tibetan nation!"
> Ten thousand years to the struggle for Tibetan independence!
> Ten thousand years to the memory of the Tibetan people who struggled against China for forty years!

There are also separate slogans praising the demonstrations of 27 September 1987, 1 October 1987 and 5 March 1988.

One unusual document is a leaflet distributed during a demonstration in Lhasa on 10 December 1988. The first declaration in the leaflet, in Tibetan and English, is unequivocal: TIBET IS AN INDEPENDENT COUNTRY. This is not only one of the few documents where an English translation is provided, but where the document has been printed off a hand-carved woodblock, exactly in the way traditional Tibetan books were printed.

Perhaps the most important political document to come out of Tibet since the last wave of protests began is the "Drepung Manifesto" in 1988, published by Drepung monks who had all taken part in the first demonstration in Lhasa on 27 September 1987. Printed as an eleven page pamphlet using wooden blocks (as the above mentioned handbill), the text is a manifesto for an independent democratic Tibet. (For an interesting analysis of this text see: Ronald Schwartz's "Democracy, Tibetan Independence and Protest under Chinese Rule", *The Tibet Journal*, Vol. XVII, No.2, Summer 1992.)

But the most expressive — especially in their brevity — of such documents must be the short messages on scraps of paper slipped into the pockets of tourists or palmed off into the hand of some visitor. One such, written almost certainly by a person from Amdo, with the distinctive spelling and syntactical differences from standard Tibetan literary form, states bluntly: "You Chinese must not remain on Tibetan soil. The three provinces of Tibet are independent. From five hundred people of Gansu." (Parts of Amdo have been incorporated into Gansu province.) No date.

Another brief appeal (undated), this time to the world: "You people from the outside, please help the Dalai Lama to get Tibetan independence (*Bod-jong rangzen*). We pray for His long life. In this peaceful land surrounded by high snowy mountains, the source of all benefits and happiness is the Dalai Lama." (This last sentence is a direct quote from the old Tibetan national hymn.)

The saddest of these appeals is one directed to His Holiness:

> Gongsa Kyapgon Gyalwa Rinpoche, please, we entreat you, all Tibetans want independence. We are all in great sorrow as we do not have independence. Independence, please, please.

Spring 1993
USTC Newsletter

Songs of Independence

TIBETANS HAVE TRADITIONALLY expressed political dissent and criticism through song and verse. Totalitarian control of Tibetan society and even individual minds, has put a halt to this vehicle of witty free expression — though not quite entirely. Even in the bleak sixties and seventies the walls of prison cells have sometimes seen defiant anti-Chinese verses scratched on them. Even toilet walls, especially in Lhasa, I have been informed, were covered with scatological verses and insults, often directed against local party functionaries and leaders, and sometimes against the Party itself. In between unmentionable obscenities, there is often a bold *Rangzen* (independence).

The last few years have not only seen a more open singing of anti-Chinese songs, but the verses of these songs now speak outright of *Rangzen*, where before indirect allusions like "the sun of happiness" etc., were prevalent. One of the most popular songs in Lhasa at present was first heard in 1989 during a religious festival, Peley Ritoe,[1] especially observed by women. A rough translation:

> He has not bought India,
> He has not sold Lhasa.
> The Dalai Lama is not without a place to stay.
> The Joyous Palace (the Tibetan government) is greater than ever.
> I went on a pilgrimage to Dharamshala,
> The Dalai Lama was sitting on his Golden Throne
> On either side Lotus flowers had bloomed.
> Rangzen will surely come soon.

Another popular song from Lhasa.

> Each of us has to travel our own road,
> But Tibetan brothers and sisters unite and rise up!
> Old Tibet was violently stolen by the Chinese,
> Tibetans are beaten and tortured every day,
> They eat our food and steal the clothes off our backs
> By force they stole our Rangzen.
> Brothers and sisters be vigilant!
> Look at all the prison camps,
> Where we are beaten and tortured like beasts,
> Where we eat a few rotten vegetables with no oil
> But even if I have no food at all for a week,
> I will never forget the Dalai Lama's kindness.

Another song in the same style:

> Though each has to travel his own road,
> All Tibetans unite,
> Together we will struggle for Rangzen.
> We cannot make all that is bitter sweet.
> Don't listen to them, listen to me,
> I have a tale to tell.

---

1. A festival to honour the goddess Palden Lhamo (Sanskrit: Sri Devi), which in Lhasa is especially observed by the women of the city who dress in their best, sing songs and offer libations of chang at the chapel of the goddess in the Jokhang Temple.

Listen carefully, it is about Tibet.
Before we were free,
Now we are crushed under Chinese oppression.
Before Tibet was the land of the Dharma,
Now it is a Chinese prison.
Tibet is full of Chinese barbarians,
All our youths are locked up in prison.
But even the cruellest torture
Will never alter the courage of our youths.
I pray once again for *Rangzen*.

These songs, especially the first, are sung openly by Tibetans. Quite a few Chinese beggars and street entertainers have come to Lhasa. Some recite Buddhist mantras in front of the Jokhang. One old mendicant has a monkey that he has taught to prostrate in the manner of Tibetan pilgrims outside the temple, and is a great favourite with pious old women. It also appears that one Chinese street-minstrel has learnt the popular song "He has not bought India, He has not sold Lhasa", and has profited from singing it before Tibetan *chang*-drinkers who gather at the Naga Temple park (Dzonggyab Lukhang) behind the Potala, where the Sixth Dalai Lama used to practise his archery and carouse, some centuries ago.

Spring 1993
USTC Newsletter

Broken Images
Cultural Questions Facing Tibetans Today[1]

SOME YEARS AGO I attended a conference on Tibet at the School of Oriental and African Studies, in London, where the eminent Norwegian Tibetologist Professor Per Kvaerne presented, through slides, examples of socialist realism in thangka painting as formulated and encouraged by the Chinese authorities in Tibet. The centrepiece of his collection was a representation of the Commander-in-chief of the Red Army, Marshal Zhu De, giving "teachings", as it were, to Geda tulku, the left-leaning lama of Bheru Monastery — whom the Chinese claimed was murdered in 1949 by the English radio operator, Robert Ford.

Certain basic conventions of thangka painting had been observed in the execution of the painting, especially in the relative positions occupied by the figures — the guru and the disciple —

---

1. Based on a talk given at the Royal Academy of Arts, London, 13 October 1992. The title "Broken Images" has been borrowed from Simon Leys' collection of essays on Chinese culture and politics (1979).

and also in the heights of their respective seats. Besides Tibetan artistic conventions, strictures of a more ideological kind — first pronounced by Mao Zedong at Yanan in 1942 in his famous "Talk on Arts and Letters", and later developed to their extreme during the Great Proletarian Cultural Revolution — had also been observed in the spirit and execution of this painting.

The revelations in Professor Kvaerne's presentation understandably raised some concern among participants at the conference on the debasement of thangka art, but such apprehensions were quickly swept aside by Dr. Graham Clarke of Oxford and Professor Melvyn Goldstein of Case Western University. They declared that this reflexive show of concern was merely another, and typical, instance of Westerners getting precious about ethnic culture. Furthermore, they declared that this unthinking reaction in wanting to see such traditions preserved sprang more from unfulfilled needs in the Westerner's own emotional and psychological make-up, than from genuine concern. In their opinion, this attitude did not give due consideration to the role of natural evolution in traditional culture and art.

Dr. Clarke recounted his own unhappy experience in Nepal observing the rapid disappearance of Nepalese folk songs before the inroads of Bombay film music. As a cultured person he was, of course, saddened by the loss of Nepali folk songs, but consoled himself with the reflection that this was a universal phenomenon, and the price one paid for becoming a part of the modern world. Professor Goldstein too, contributed to this plea for pragmatism and acceptance of change. Commenting on a "thangka" where one of the subsidiary proletarian "deities" is depicted joyfully manoeuvring a motor-cycle with one hand and carrying a boom-box in the other, Goldstein cried out, "What's wrong with motor-bikes?"

Now, much as I agree with our two academics about the

need for natural development in the arts, they are, in this instance, being quite disingenuous. The advent of socialist realism in thangka painting is not a natural process; nor is it even an incidental and unplanned commercial contagion like the Hindi-movie song epidemic in Nepal. It is instead the deliberate and organised misuse and debasement of an art form by a centralised totalitarian power, not only for the eradication of a separate Tibetan cultural identity but also for the propagation of a crudely materialistic and violent ideology.

Cultural change in Tibet is far from "normal", as academics like Goldstein and Clarke (who see nothing particularly wrong with Chinese rule in Tibet) like to represent it. They have also adopted the Chinese assumption that sinicization is tantamount to modernisation. It is this prejudice that is at the root of the problem, since Tibetans do not have a choice of sources for formulating their own cultural development as even people in a poor and remote country like Nepal do.

I have not recounted this anecdote merely to vent my spleen at left-leaning academics in Tibetan studies, but because two issues vital to the future of Tibetan culture are raised in it: one, the deliberate and well-planned programme of the Chinese to sinicize Tibetan language and culture; and two, the very static and backward-looking view of cultural preservation held by Tibetan leaders in exile. The latter has, it must be admitted, been much influenced, encouraged and supported in its blinkered conservatism by the emotional needs of many Westerners for an unchanging, mythic Tibet.

The conspicuous symbols of Chinese misrule in Tibet are the stark ruins of the thousands of monasteries, temples and historical buildings looming jaggedly in the desolate Tibetan landscape. But cultural genocide in Tibet has not been confined to the physical destruction of buildings and artefacts, the burning of books, nor to the imprisonment and killing of religious teachers and members of the intelligentsia. There is another and more indeterminate area where the Chinese occupation authorities have effectively lobotomized culture by excising it of any real tradition or genuine spontaneity, and transforming it into a cultural noodle-machine for cranking out endless political and racist propaganda.

In Tibetan language, literature, performing arts, sculpture and painting, the harm China has done, though less dramatically apparent than the ruins of Ganden Monastery, has had an equal, if not a more profoundly negative influence on the Tibetan collective psyche.

One of Beijing's systematic machinations in this regard has been in the attempted sinicization of the Tibetan language. All radio broadcasters and TV announcers in Tibet have been trained to sound tonally Chinese; more precisely — to enunciate Tibetan tones in such a way that it resembles Chinese, thus violating the phonological rules of Tibetan. I am no expert on linguistics but someone who is, told me that from the linguistic point of view, what the Chinese are doing is absurd. Mandarin has no tone or vowel harmony — i.e. the previous (or following) vowel tone cannot affect adjacent vowel tones. This gives it a staccato sound peculiar to Chinese. Tibetan has both tone and vowel harmony. By altering the tone of Tibetan to make it sound like Mandarin, the Chinese are in effect making it incomprehensible.

The uniformity of this sinicized diction and accent of Tibetan TV and radio announcers belies any other explanation than systematic training. I have also been told by a Tibetan who worked at the Lhasa TV station that trainee announcers spend more than a year just listening and attempting to acquire the standard sinicized tone before being allowed to broadcast. The tone of this official Tibetan is now so Chinese that it is nearly incomprehensible to listeners like myself in exile, and it takes a great deal of getting used to, even for a fluent

Tibetan speaker, to understand what is actually being said. My informant maintains that Lhasa radio broadcasts are often not understood in neighbouring districts of Phembo, Lhokha and Nyemo. The situation in Kham and Amdo is less extreme. Interestingly, it appears that among the general Tibetan populace, this sinicized way of speaking has not caught on and is only fashionable with those few who admire Chinese ways.

The Chinese, since their invasion of Tibet, have also worked on the creation of a new political and social vocabulary in Tibetan. There certainly was need for innovation in this area, but the new words created under the aegis of the Chinese occupation force were invariably ill-conceived and crude translations of Chinese terms, in turn derived to a large extent from Japanese and Russian translations of Western terms.

But more than just the issue of linguistic unwieldiness, the political consequences resulting from this radical overhauling of the Tibetan language appear to have had a negative effect on political thinking. Neither questions have so far been addressed by Tibetans in exile who, generally oblivious to the subtleties of totalitarian machinations, have blithely accepted a great deal the new language in the spirit of reform and progress. Professor Goldstein has enthusiastically embraced China's restructuring of Tibetan language in his dictionaries and language study books, though an incisive and scientific study of this ideological linguistic manipulation is yet non-existent.

It requires no great linguistic or political insight to see that what the Chinese have done is introduce an Orwellian kind of "Newspeak", where the Tibetan and Chinese equivalents of words like democracy, freedom, socialism, revolution and egalitarianism, have meanings very different, in some cases even opposite, to the accepted sense of the words. They have become, in both the Tibetan and Chinese context, fluid, *mantraic* terms whose uses are essentially ceremonial — props in the sustenance and legitimisation of the powers that be. This perversion of language for political advantage is, of course, not just a Chinese offense; many governments and politicians resort to it, though generally in a clumsy ad hoc manner.

The uniqueness of the Chinese approach is in the creation of a planned and much-tested system for its realisation, which has not only been thoroughly implemented throughout the length and breadth of China for well over three decades, but appears to still retain an inexorable hold on the minds of the people. A friend of mine who is a recent arrival from Amdo, showed me a sample issue of a new Tibetan magazine (which never got started) meant to educate people on democracy. The lead article was unabashed in declaring that Tibetans must create a "United Front" to bring about "Democratic Reforms".

The effect of this linguistic cretinization is still visible in the absolute dearth of any great contemporary literature in China, more than twenty years after the Cultural Revolution. Even during the bleakest period of Stalin's rule, Bulgakov was writing *The Master and Margarita* and Pasternak *Doctor Zhivago*.

The ineffectiveness of the Chinese Democracy Movement can probably be explained, to some extent, by the residual effects of this linguistic conditioning. What exactly does democracy mean to a leader of the Chinese Democracy Movement — even if he is at present living and studying in the United States? I have met a few such dissidents, and when we discussed the subject I did not get the feeling that we were talking about the same thing. The burden of linguistic perversion is a heavy one; pushing down, immobilising, distorting thoughts and concepts long after the heavy hand that imposed it may have been removed.

The apparent failure of the exile-Tibetan experiment with democracy, can be interpreted — I am generously overlooking many other causes here — as a failure of political language. Nothing really wrong is seen in setting up a democratic government for the apparent objective of making members of the Dalai Lama's family into cabinet ministers or members of Parliament; or in having the constitution drafted by a committee chaired by a former minister who lacks even a primary school knowledge of democracy; someone who has been the main instigator of the previous government's programme to censor all Tibetan publications, and control all artistic and intellectual life in Dharamshala.

However vulgar and corrupt present-day American politics may appear, democracy and freedom as once interpreted by a Jefferson or a Lincoln are words still vibrant with inspiration and hope. All we Tibetans have consulted so far for our political direction is this Chinese-created glossary, and the only definitions we can find in it for those noble words are euphemisms for sycophancy, cynicism, demagoguery, nepotism and intellectual laziness.

It is not only language that the Chinese have attempted to distort; sinicization has taken place in every sphere of Tibetan life and culture: as mentioned earlier in painting, and more so in the performing arts, which are regarded as invaluable propaganda weapons. But more on these later.

Ever since their departure from their homeland, the Tibetan government and community in exile have made a conscious effort to preserve their religion and culture, both of which are under real threat back home. In the preservation of religious literature and certain religious institutions, the success of this effort is clearly visible. In other aspects of Tibetan culture, the results have at best been mixed, if not unsatisfactory.

The disproportionate concentration of attention and resources on religion cannot be explained solely by the well known piety of the Tibetan people, but must be attributed partly to the attraction it holds for the West. The sixties and seventies were very lonely periods for the Tibetan cause, with leftist ideas and theories, especially Maoism, holding centre stage in Western intellectual and political attention, so that even the interest of a few hippies in Tibetan Buddhism was seen as a welcome development, and disproportionate energy and resources were poured into encouraging it.

Institutions such as the Library of Tibetan Works and Archives in Dharamshala, primarily set up to research Tibetan history and culture became (much against the will of the Director and staff) something resembling a Dharma centre. Hundreds of Tibetan Buddhists texts were translated into Western languages, especially English, while nothing from the West, with the exception of the Bible, was translated into the Tibetan language.

One of the few non-religious institutions set up in Dharamshala for the preservation of culture was the Tibetan Institute of Performing Arts (TIPA). But even there the reasons had more to do with politics than culture. TIPA was initially conceived of as a vehicle for Tibetan propaganda, and for the entertainment of visiting foreign patrons. There was nothing sinister about this development. In Tibet, the modern concept of the performing arts, of the proscenium stage and "cultural shows", had been introduced by the Communists, who viewed this art wholly as a propaganda tool. One of Red China's warmest admirers, Edgar Snow, has explained why in *Red Star Over China*:

> There was no more powerful weapon of propaganda in the Communist movement than the Red's dramatic troupes, and none more subtly manipulated ... When the Reds occupied new areas, it was the Red Theatre that calmed the fears of the people, gave them rudimentary ideas of the Red programme, and dispensed great quantities of revolutionary thoughts, to win the people's confidence.

Many Tibetans, especially the young, were impressed by it — overwhelmed in some cases. A number of Tibetans were trained as performers and musicians in the various Minorities Institutes, as well as in conservatories in Beijing.

Unfortunately, when TIPA (or the Tibetan Dance and Drama Party, as it was first called) was set up in Dharamshala quite a few of its members were such Chinese trained artistes. TIPA's early performances were therefore considerably influenced by Communist Chinese "aesthetics". Ersatz folk dances were choreographed to a degree where, except for the costumes, they could well have been dances from Hangzhou or Xinjiang. Crude propaganda plays which derived their artistic inspiration from the early Red Army propaganda skits — the forerunners of Madame Mao's revolutionary operas — served to inflame the nationalistic passions of the Dharamshala refugees.

New historical dance dramas were produced, which though based on pious versions of imperial Tibetan history, appeared, in execution, to derive their inspiration from Beijing opera.

Many of the new songs composed at that time were essentially Chinese tunes with obscure classical lyrics composed by Tibetan religious scholars. One of the directors of TIPA did try to counter this by removing some of the more obvious Chinese influences and reintroducing the traditional opera. But he had a difficult time of it, as by then not only had this Chinese influence permeated the minds of the performers but the taste of the general public as well; so much so that this glitzy sinicized pseudo-art form was regarded as genuine Tibetan culture.

In Tibet itself, the Chinese have, over the years, managed to make the Tibetans not only accept but even like and admire a hideous kind of singing, somewhere between the nasal falsetto of Beijing opera, and an exaggerated "European classical" style, introduced by the Russians to China.

Traditional scripts of Tibetan opera have been rewritten in order to conform not only with Communist ideology but also Chinese interpretations of Tibetan history. A good example of this can be seen in the changes made to the traditional Tibetan opera, *The Chinese Princess and the Nepalese Princess* (*Gyasa Bhelsa*), now called *Princess Wen Cheng*, after the excision from the story of the inconvenient Nepalese Princess.

Ideological changes can also be observed in the play Nangsa, traditionally the story of a beautiful but pious maiden of Gyantse district forced to marry the son of a powerful lord. She is badly abused in her new home and dies, but because of her piety is sent back again to the world of the living by the Lord of Death, Yama. At the end of the story Nangsa attains enlightenment and, forgiving her husband and family, shows them the true path to the Dharma.

A Chinese dramatist, Hu Jin'an, changed the story to one of class conflict. Nangsa returns from the dead with a large sword and proceeds to murder her husband and in-laws. The acting and dancing style have been so speeded up and "modernised" that it seems to be a deliberate parody of Tibetan opera dancing. The title of the play has also been changed to *Maiden Langsha*, probably to make it sound more Chinese.

My efforts as Director of TIPA, from 1980 to 1985, to remove such Chinese influences, and to make the institution less a vehicle for propaganda than a genuine artistic and cultural centre, were more successful than those of previous directors, but they were not long lived. In fact, I was forced to leave TIPA for some of my productions, which were deemed ideologically incorrect. TIPA has now been put under the control of the Religious Department of the exile government.

Right now, the performing world in exile is in considerable disarray. Not only has the Communist Chinese influence managed to make some inroads, but because of China's so-called liberalisation a new Hong Kong–Taiwan pop influence has not only taken over the development of modern music inside Tibet but has spilled over into the exile world. I know of a few Tibetan musicians and performers who are trying hard to fight this influence but the situation does at present seem rather discouraging.

Things appear to be comparatively better in the plastic arts, especially in painting. I do not want to deal at length with thangka painting. Suffice to say, that in spite of many problems, the art is managing to survive in exile. Thangka painters earn good commissions, and demand for their work is high enough that sufficient young Tibetans are being trained and will maintain the tradition for some years to come. There are, of course, major difficulties to be overcome, the primary one being that since many of these painters do commission work, generally of standard deities, aspects of the tradition that are not in general demand are being lost. Inside Tibet, things are very different and, as I mentioned at the beginning of my talk, thangka painting has suffered such indignities as being used a vehicle for Communist propaganda. But, on the other hand, a lively modern movement has appeared which seems to hold some promise for the future of Tibetan art.

Beginning with the painter Amdo Jampa, who painted the murals in the Kelsang Palace in the Norbulingka, a number of young Tibetans with artistic talents were trained in the fifties, sixties and seventies in art schools in Beijing and other parts of China. By and large, they appear to have been trained not only in Western art techniques but also in the traditional Chinese style with its delicate landscapes: winding mountain paths, and mist covered crags. On returning to Tibet, some of these painters found what they had studied to be inappropriate to a country that was anything but delicate or artificial. This year I met a young artist from Lhasa, Gongkar

Gyatso, who talked to me at length on the development of contemporary art in Tibet. He said that, after taking one look at the oceanic expanse of the Changthang, the northern plains, and the frighteningly huge and unbelievably deep blue Tibetan sky, he tossed aside the art education he had received in Beijing and began to look in other directions for inspiration. He and others seem to have found it in the Western tradition. There is little time for me to discuss this phenomenon in detail but I will provide a couple of examples.

Ngawang Dakpa is a young Khampa painter presently living in Lhasa. In his works he has consciously attempted to depict the strength and, one could say, the love of freedom of the Khampa people. Most of his works seem to be influenced by the Mexican muralist, Diego Rivera.

Another painter of an earlier generation is Tsedor, trained in China in the early seventies. Most of his life was spent in producing works of socialist realism for the state. He now paints landscapes and portraits that are tortured and brooding, with the heavy lines and vivid colours of Van Gogh. In fact, a couple of his paintings, one of a distorted Tibetan monastery, and another similar study of the Jokhang at Lhasa, prompted in me the memory of Van Gogh's *View of the Cathedral at Arles* which I had seen at the Jeu de Paume in Paris some twenty years ago.

Gongkar Gyatso considers himself essentially an abstract painter, but he is also the only Tibetan to have executed a mural (in the sino socialist-realist style) for the Great Hall of the People in Beijing. He was one of the founders of the *Cha Ngarmo Remoe Tsokpa*, the "Sweet Tea House" group of modern Tibetan painters that from 1985 held exhibitions of their works in a Lhasa tea house where Tibetan youths gathered to talk. Gyatso told me that aside from the fact that the tea house was a natural gathering place for the Lhasa youth, the artists could have been influenced in their choice by romantic notions of the cafe life of Parisian artists.

Monet, Courbet and other impressionists had gathered at cafes, and Gauguin even exhibited in one, during the Universal Exposition in Paris of 1888, when his pictures were excluded from the Official Art section.

What motivates these Tibetan painters seems to be a sense of their national identity. This feeling is probably heightened in the face of undisguised Chinese contempt for Tibetan culture and values. Many of these artists regularly take trips out to the Changthang and to other remote areas of Tibet not only to find subjects for their paintings, but to locate a source of identification with Tibet, through its mountains, lakes, rivers and sky. In a limited sense, the works of these artists could be described as "nationalistic". Though no overt political message is present in their works, a distinct, even overpowering sense of Tibetanness, quite removed from anything Chinese, is immediately obvious in nearly every one of the paintings I have seen so far.

The Sweet Tea House group disbanded in 1987 when, after a very successful exhibition covered by Lhasa radio and television, and attended by TAR bigwigs, the artists were badgered by the authorities to accept official support, and also to allow party-approved Chinese painters into the group. Besides this, a number of Sweet Tea House artists did not like the idea of being tied down to a permanent organisation.

Even traditional thangka painters inside Tibet have been moved to explore and re-discover their roots; or so an article in *China's Tibet* (Summer 1991) reports. Traditional thangka painters from Gyantse, spurred by the competition of new and modern artistic movements, have travelled all along the Yarlung Tsangpo river searching for the earliest signs of Tibetan art in such places as Yambulagang, Samye Monastery and the tombs of the ancient Tibetan emperors. These artists also made the long trip to the Caves of the Thousand Buddhas at Dunhuang to seek inspiration from the ancient murals painted by Tibetan artists in the eighth to the tenth century when Dunhuang was a Tibetan imperial possession.

Young writers and poets in Tibet, frustrated by the sterility of Communist Chinese literary culture, are also reaching into the distant historical past of their nation in search of fresh directions. A Tibetan writer of my acquaintance from Amdo, Pema Bhum, (Associate Professor of Tibetan literature at the Minorities Institute at Lanzhou) has visited every historical site in Central Tibet and the Caves of Dunhuang, not just once, but on a number of occasions, sometimes with his students.

One of the directions in Tibetan poetry and literature seems to be coming from the past, and a much older past than the *1300* years of Tibetan Buddhist history. The classical Tibeto-Indic literary form emerged from this later period, which not only produced the bulk of Tibetan Buddhist writings but other related literature as well.

Classical Tibetan is also the standard official literary form at present in exile, taught at schools and monasteries, and maintained by an unofficial academy, not only of doctors of divinity but officials and educated lay people as well. However profound or ancient, the drawbacks of such a literature are patently obvious in exile, where Tibetan schoolchildren read Enid Blyton, Biggles, and Nancy Drew, and avoid Tibetan literature because it bores them to tears. It is not difficult to see why. Tibeto-Indic literature has very little, especially in imagery and inspiration, that is Tibetan. One does not read of a hero possessing the strength of a wild yak but rather that of Nalagiri the elephant. How many Tibetan nomads have seen an elephant, much less one with a Sanskrit name? The list continues, with peacocks, lotuses and the *utpal* flower being used as metaphors rather than Tibetan plants, birds or animals. The Sanscritic literary conventions pervading official literature seem in this day and age extremely formal and contrived.

But Tibetans are traditionalists if anything, and young writers who are crying out for a vital living language are looking even further back into the past for their inspiration — before the advent of Buddhism and Buddhist literature. The ancient Tibetan texts discovered in the Dunhuang Caves and other places in Central Asia by Sir Aurel Stein and Paul Pelliot are the lodestones which are transforming Tibetan prosody and literature.

Of these many and varied documents the main inspirations are being derived from ancient song-verses of the *glu*, *mgur* and *mchid* forms, that were not only widespread in imperial times but vital for the maintenance of the royal chronicles, the history of the nation, maintaining imperial administrative records in song/verse, and also the sending of coded messages through verse riddles.

This more naturalistic and genuinely Tibetan literary form of ancient times, as represented by the *glu*, *mgur* and *mchid* has survived in various folk traditions all over Tibet, as in the songs of Milarepa, the *Gesar epics*, various wedding songs and certain declamatory traditions of the Tibetan people. So, in a sense, this movement towards a new poetic and literary form is a continuation, or maybe more appropriately, the reawakening of the ancient voice of the Tibet's glorious imperial past.

One of the pioneers of the new Tibetan poetry was Dhondup Gyal of Amdo, who is said to have committed suicide in November 1985 at the age of thirty-five. It is also possible that he may have died accidentally like Emile Zola, suffocated by the fumes from a coal fire. Dhondup Gyal's pioneering efforts have opened the doors to a new literary form, not only inside Tibet but in exile as well. All over Tibet literary/academic journals and reviews are being published. These publications are all official or semi-official, and at the last count there were over forty of them. In spite of Chinese censorship, many of them manage to often produce work of interest and value.

Nevertheless, it must be admitted that no great modern literature has as yet emerged from Tibet.

The best known Tibetan author in China is Tashi Dawa, whose writings are trite, posturing and derivative. He appeals to Chinese readers, as he essentially confirms age-old Chinese racist notions of Tibetan savagery and superstition. Furthermore, he only writes in Chinese. *Tsug-Yu* by Langdun Paljor is probably the first novel in the Tibetan language but it is also unfortunately little more than an exercise in socialist realism. I am informed by experts in Tibetan literature that it is nonetheless a more convincing work than Bapa Jampel Gyatso's *Kelsang Metok*, which was an earlier socialist realist novel, but originally written in Chinese.

In exile, projects to preserve traditional literature have met with far more success than attempts to bring out new or original works. Efforts have been made to start modern literary journals and movements but somehow these have never quite succeeded in getting off the ground. For such ventures a certain critical mass is probably required, not only of writers, but reviewers, editors, publishers, and of course, readers as well. Refugee society seems just too small to sustain such ventures.

But right now, the beginnings of a convergence of talents from inside and outside Tibet is taking place. And one of the positive results of this has been the establishment in mid-1992 of the Amnye Machen Institute. Named after the great mountain range in North-Eastern Tibet, this institute is an independent centre for research, publication and dissemination of information and knowledge on the literature, history, art, society and politics of the Tibetan people, with emphasis on the neglected, the contemporary and the lay aspects of these subjects. It is the first such institute set up in exile that is non-religious, liberal and humanist in direction but also aimed directly at informing the Tibetan people, primarily those inside Tibet, and raising their cultural and intellectual awareness.

Two months ago, the institute launched the only independent Tibetan language newspaper. *Mang-tso* ("Democracy") has been a terrific success, every issue selling over five hundred copies in Dharamshala alone — which is a record of sorts. *Jang-zhon* ("Young Shoots"), a journal of new writing, is creating fresh awareness not only among writers in exile, but inside Tibet as well, from where we have received contributions. The Institute's journal of Tibetan Women's Studies, *Yum-tso*, ("Turquoise Lake") is the only one of its kind both outside and inside Tibet, and will go a little way to redressing the existing lack of awareness of the contribution of Tibetan women to Tibetan spiritual, cultural and national life.

Besides newspaper and journals, the institute has published academic works and original writings of contemporary Tibetan writers. A volume of the selected works of Dhondup Gyal is now being published. The Institute has also undertaken the translation into Tibetan of important books from the West and East. Four books are ready to go to press, while ten other translations have been commissioned from various Tibetan translators. A number of lectures on art, literature, philosophy and politics have been organised in Dharamshala, for schools as well as the general public. The first exhibition of contemporary Tibetan art has also been organised by the Institute.

But in spite of the creation of such an institution, and the efforts of artists, writers and academics inside and outside Tibet, the survival of Tibetan culture in Tibet as a living and viable entity is far from being assured. In addition to the perennial problems of official proscription and perversion, Tibetan culture must further deal with additional complexities created by the tremendous social and economic changes in China. For instance the single-minded materialism dominating life in China now — plus a whacking thirty per cent inflation rate — has driven many artists and writers in Tibet to give up their professions. In exile, on the other hand, unexpected problems have been created by the otherwise not unwelcome attention from the West.

In quantum theory, according to Heisenberg's uncertainty principle, the very act of observing a subatomic particle or quantum object changes the entire nature of that quantum world. The size, wealth and power of the West when compared with that of Tibetan exile society is in some ways the difference between a macro and a micro world; and Western interest in Tibetan culture does, even unintentionally, affect the direction and equilibrium of traditional Tibetan life. The effect of this can be discerned to a degree in what I think may be called the "New Aging" of Tibetan culture, where beliefs and mysteries that once gave beauty and power to ritual and art, are in real danger of becoming enfeebled and trivialised because of commercialisation, excessive exposure and the unrelenting demand of modern society for entertainment and novelty.

December 1993–January 1994
Tibetan Review

The Heart of the Matter
Some Observations on the Independence Controversy

*If one does not know to which port one is sailing,
no wind is favourable.*
— Seneca

THE WORD "REALISTIC", whenever introduced into any discussion on Tibetan politics, never fails to set my teeth on edge. It invariably signals the opening of the argument that if the Tibetans compromised on the question of independence and accepted some form of autonomous status within China, then the Chinese authorities would reciprocate with concessions; which though not as preferable as independence, would make life inside Tibet more tolerable, and hence ensure the survival of the Tibetan people.

On the face of it, yes, a reasonable argument. So what's the catch? Well, for one, the Chinese have never evinced any desire to discuss a compromise solution — not even the most pathetically watered down one proffered by Dharamshala. But certain Tibetan ministers, officials and some foreign friends will insist that there have been positive signals from the Chinese, at least on occasions, indicating their readiness to talk. So who's being untruthful here? No one really — at least not wilfully so.

Early this century astronomers world-wide saw through their telescopes intricate networks of canals radiating all over the surface of Mars. On the strength of this evidence, the theory was put forward of a great Martian civilisation that had once built this monumental system of waterways. There were two main causes for this mass delusion: one, everybody wanted to believe that there were canals, hence civilised life-forms on Mars; two, there was a linguistic misunderstanding. The astronomer who first made the discovery was an Italian, Giovanni Schiaparelli, who reported the sighting of "canali", which in Italian means channels, not man-made "canals".

Our delusion, which eventually fossilised into a full-fledged and official *idée fixe*, began with the introduction of Deng Xiaoping's Four Modernisations and the announcement of the first fact-finding delegation to Tibet in 1979. I recall the excitement and hopes these events generated in Dharamshala at the time. Going back to Tibet suddenly appeared to become an immediate possibility. There was even a mild panic among building owners in McLeod Ganj. I went around deliberately pouring cold water on these expectations and did not particularly endear myself to those who had most need to subscribe to such fantasies, namely, the naive and those in power.

Everyone talked of the Four Modernisations but no one, except for myself, seemed to have heard of the Four Absolutes — which was essentially Deng's way of saying that aside from economic liberalisation, he would tolerate no criticism of, nor challenge to, the Party's absolute power. I am sure that, even now, many Tibetans and friends have not heard of this disturbing obverse to the Four Modernisations.

Furthermore, everyone at the time seemed to assume that Deng Xiaoping was a fresh entrant on the Communist political scene, like Gorbachev, and not that he was one of the oldest Chinese Communist Party leaders, someone who had even opposed Mao for initiating the Hundred Flowers Campaign to allow some criticism of the Party. Later, when Mao reversed his line, Deng was put in charge of the anti-rightist campaign to take care of "stinking" intellectuals and critics of the Party. About 2.9 million people were accused of rightism. About five hundred thousand, by Deng's own estimate (offered in 1980) were condemned. The campaign was marked by great brutality.

No great intellectual perspicacity was required to see that the cause of Tibetan independence would soon become a bargaining chip in our futile bid to elicit some concessions from China. I mentioned these misgivings in a number of articles in the *Tibetan Review*, but, like most things I wrote at the time, they had as much impact on actual events as "a fly beating its wings against a boulder", which was how Chinese authorities in Tibet, betraying an unexpected penchant for colourful imagery, disparaged my writings.

Whenever the Tibetan issue has received any substantial attention in the world, be it with the demonstrations in Lhasa or the awarding of the Nobel Peace Prize to the Dalai Lama, the Chinese have nearly always succeeded in side-tracking international concern by making titillating press announcements soon after the event, declaring their willingness to sit down and talk with the Dalai Lama or his representatives. Those sympathetic to Tibet naturally heave a huge sigh of relief on hearing this, and the situation is then effectively defused.

At Dharamshala a delegation to Beijing is announced and fierce intrigues are conducted by various political factions to get their man on the team. It all comes to nothing, of course. Once in a while, though, the delegation does actually get to go to Beijing. They invariably return to Dharamshala in a daze, with a look on their faces not unlike that on Charlie Brown's when he is lying flat on his back, after having been persuaded by Lucy, for the umpteenth time, to take a running kick at a football that she never fails to yank away at the last moment. "Isn't trust a wonderful thing, Charlie Brown?"

Aside from Deng Xiaoping and Li Peng, another and equally unpleasant politician who has been successfully pulling off something like this has been the Bosnian Serb leader Radovan Karadzic. For the last few years, every time a US president began to talk seriously of using force to halt the bloodshed in Bosnia, Karadzic has at once cooed sweet reason, talking of getting all the warring parties to a conference, and what not — keeping up the patter long enough till Western resolve invariably became deflated.

To be fair to Chinese leaders, it wasn't a lie, at least not an outright one, when they said that they would be willing to sit down and talk with Tibetans. Whenever Beijing declared its readiness to discuss "all other issues" if Tibetans gave up their demand for independence, we never asked ourselves what exactly Beijing meant by that wonderfully vague phrase. We always assumed that this would either be the question of autonomy, or some other special status within China.

But if one carefully goes through all that the Chinese have actually said concerning dialogue with Dharamshala, there is absolutely nothing to indicate their willingness to make even the tiniest of concessions. So what do the Chinese really want to talk to Dharamshala about? I think they made that clear in the only statement they issued where they specifically mentioned what they were prepared to discuss. This statement was made by Hu Yaobang in 1984 and laid down five points for discussion; these essentially dealt with knotty details that would arise from the Dalai Lama's return to the "motherland" — after he had given up his demand for Tibetan independence: questions like his political rank (would he be restored to his vice-chairmanship in the National People's Congress?), whether he would be allowed to live in Lhasa or maintain a ménage in Beijing; by what route he would make his journey, and so on. That is the furthest extent to which Beijing has been willing to enter into discussions with Dharamshala.

The main proponent of giving up independence and cutting a deal with China is the Dalai Lama's brother, Gyalo Thondup, who is a minister in the Kashag. He has been energetic in spreading his message that Tibetans in exile should give up the hopeless cause of independence and return to Tibet. He is not one of those leaders conspicuous for leading by example. So far neither he nor any of his immediate family have shown any inclination of abandoning their relatively comfortable lifestyles in exile to return to Tibet. But what GT (as he is known to the less reverent) lacks in this respect he makes up for in the intensity with which he has been conducting his campaign. There has been a large demonstration by a rent-a-crowd contingent of naive students from the school for new arrivals, at Bir, especially trucked in to Dharamshala, carrying placards and banners, some even wearing headbands declaring "We love Gyalo".

Threats of violence and arson were made to the Tibetan Youth Congress which, in an issue of their magazine, *Rangzen*, carried letters from Tibetans in North America, Europe and Japan protesting against speeches made by Gyalo Thondup when he visited North America in 1992. In these speeches, GT had reprimanded Tibetans living in the US and Canada for hurting the Chinese economy by organising boycotts of Chinese goods, and campaigning against MFN status for China. He voiced a personal concern that if China lost MFN status hundreds of thousands of Chinese would lose their jobs in Guangdong province alone. All of this was in addition to his usual message on the impossibility of achieving Tibetan independence and the need to cut a deal quickly with the present leadership in China.

Through threats and intimidation, an ugly climate of fear and suspicion has been created in Dharamshala where you could be accused of "being against the Dalai Lama" for merely stating your desire for Tibetan independence. One of the unfortunate consequences of all this has been the outbreak of large-scale fighting at the school for new arrivals from Tibet at Bir, where pro and anti-Gyalo Thondup factions, involving a few hundred students, battled it out with knives, rocks, sticks and axes. The school was effectively closed down for a number of months, adversely affecting the studies and lives of hundreds of innocent students from Tibet. The school has only reopened recently, but residual violence remains. The principal was assaulted violently by two students, some months ago. The school had about 750 students before the outbreak of trouble, now it is down to 400.

A writer friend of mine, a new arrival from Amdo, Pema Bhum, has been constantly harassed and threatened with violence, even murder, for allegedly "insulting the Dharma" in an academic paper on modern Tibetan literature that he presented at a Tibetology conference in Italy last year. The real reason for his unpopularity with a section of politicians here has probably more to do with his attempts to dissuade the students at Bir school from getting involved in Dharamshala factional politics. He also offended many supporters of GT at a large meeting of Amdowas, where he raised a sole dissenting voice when everyone else voted to withdraw from the Tibetan democratic process if the parliamentary committee investigating GT's controversial statements was not called off. Right at the moment a fatwa of two hundred thousand rupees has been placed on this young writer's head by Ngawang Tempa, a leader of the

Tibetan Cholsum United Association (*Chigdril tsokpa*), a Gyalo Thondup front organisation.

Gyalo Thondup affects a somewhat Olympian attitude in matters of statecraft, coolly making public statements absolutely contrary to Tibetan government policies — and getting away with it too. A rather craven parliamentary investigating committee cleared him on this matter, justifying his controversial statements on the grounds that they were only "personal opinions". There is more than a touch of the late Chiang Kai-shek in GT's political make-up, which is not at all surprising seeing he was educated at a Kuomintang school in Nanjing just after World War II, and was reputedly close to the Generalissimo's family. Nothing sinister about that, of course. However, such an influence, especially during one's formative years, is probably not conducive to the flowering of any democratic sentiments in one's later political development. GT likes to operate only at the highest levels of polity, and claims to be on close terms with Deng Xiaoping and other top Chinese leaders. GT once lectured to me, in his slightly Chinese-accented English, on how he had reproached Chinese leaders in Beijing for their heavy-handed tactics in Tibet. "I thole them, I thole them, why?"

I would probably once have been flattered by such a sharing of confidences, and impressed by this anecdotal, yet nevertheless heady, proximity to great people and events; but I had read of Neville Chamberlain being "firm" with Hitler, while Goring and Ribbentrop were killing themselves laughing in the ante-room. These days, it is a political rule-of-thumb with me that an accurate perspective on monsters can only be obtained at a distance. You get too close and all you see are rather ordinary people, asking for understanding, sympathy or even admiration. "The banality of evil", I think was how Hannah Arendt described it, in a reference to the revelations of the Eichmann trial in Jerusalem. Dictators, and hence politicians by extension, must be judged solely by their deeds, not by what they say or promise; nor by their "friendship" with one, no matter how close or seemingly genuine.

We have to be particularly wary of Chinese leaders. Over and above the usual set of treacherous vices that seem to be standard issue to modern despots, Chinese leaders are the inheritors of an ancient tradition of "barbarian control" that has been used in the past with an impressive degree of success against Tibetan, Uighur, and Mongol *fan guan* (barbarian officials). Such distinguished visitors from the West to the Middle Kingdom as John Kenneth Galbraith, Edward Heath, Richard Nixon, Margaret Thatcher, George Bush and others, have been courteously subjected to the same, and have all dutifully gone through their paces with the eager compliance of performing poodles.

In the last few months, Gyalo Thondup has had talks with Chinese leaders at Taipei, and, more recently, Beijing. In view of his previous indiscretions, GT has been, seemingly, encumbered with official minders — two on his Taipei visit and one for Beijing. The peculiar thing about this arrangement is that none of the officials accompanying GT spoke Chinese, and the negotiations have all been conducted in that language. This has raised the suspicion among many, including, I understand, the aides themselves, that their participation was nothing more than window-dressing for Tibetan public opinion, behind which GT, once again, did exactly as he pleased.

Like American Indian chiefs going to see the "Great White Father" in Washington, Tibetan politicians have vied with each other to get a berth on delegations to Beijing. Whether this "one sided infatuation" (*dan xiang si*) as the Chinese so aptly put it, serves any national purpose, is debatable, but it provides our politicians with an illusion of playing at the big table, and like most power drugs of this kind, produces an irresistible addiction.

I think His Holiness now realises how misplaced his efforts to initiate a dialogue with the Chinese have been. The first indication came on the 17 April 1993, at the Institute of Performing Arts. After watching a Lhamo performance the Dalai Lama made an unexpected political statement in which he mentioned that all the many efforts made by him and the Tibetan government to negotiate with the Chinese had made no headway. He also expressed his fears that Chinese overtures concealed a darkly insidious and long-term plan for ensuring the end of Tibetans as a nation and people. He concluded that Tibet now faced its greatest danger in the ever-increasing immigration of Chinese settlers. He called on all Tibetans and friends to do everything they could to fight this threat.

*

One of the latest arguments of the anti-independence lobby has been on this issue of Chinese immigration to Tibet. What is claimed is that the question of the survival of the Tibetan people is now so acute that even the cause of independence must be sacrificed in order to ensure racial survival. But where on earth is the connection? Have the Chinese leaders even hinted that if Tibetans gave up their claims to independence they would halt Chinese immigration? Of course not. Giving up the cause of a free Tibet and having everyone in exile returning quietly to Tibet would ensure an even quicker end to the existence of the Tibetan people.

Anyhow, I mistrust this sudden discovery by some of the dangers of Chinese immigration. Right from the mid-eighties it was obvious to all but the most wilfully stupid, what the Chinese were doing. I wrote a detailed two-part article on this subject six years ago in the *Tibetan Review*. Even earlier, I know of a number of concerned Tibetans who, after visiting Tibet, had warned the Tibetan government of the growing threat of Chinese immigration to Tibet. But some of the people who now claim to be desperately worried by Chinese immigration were often those very people who were pooh-poohing reports of Chinese immigration six years ago, preferring then to believe that a wonderful deal with China was just around the corner.

For a number of years now, the few Tibetans who have vocally insisted on maintaining the cause of an independent Tibet have often been seen by non-Tibetan supporters of Tibet as dangerous extremists, undermining the good work of all those working towards the far nobler goals of establishing Tibet as a "Zone of Ahimsa" or a Buddhist environmental theme park; and promoting the Dalai Lama as a global New Age super-guru.

Nationalism has always been a dirty word for those Westerners who have been interested in Buddhism and Tibet; and with the present murder and mayhem in the Balkans let loose, in part, by unbridled nationalistic passions, who can say that they are entirely in the wrong. At the same time, I cannot but help note that the critics of nationalism are invariably those who have *pukka* passports, and a nation of their own to return to when Dharamshala or Lhasa could get too depressing or dangerous. The internationalist may find the idea of nation states old-fashioned and limiting, but at the moment that's all we've got (and some of us haven't got it). People who have it can afford to speculate on alternatives, but they should not, like Marie Antoinette, push their preferences on more unfortunate people. Cake may be exciting but bread sustains life. Tibetans would like a loaf, please.

Some years ago, when my friend Lhasang Tsering and I were giving a talk at the University of Calgary, a Chinese student asked a question which I had previously encountered in the writings of certain "experts" on China (David Bonavia) and Tibet (Mel Goldstein). The thrust of it was that: Yes, the Tibetan case for independence was not entirely without cause or merit, but the reality was that they would never get it. So why shouldn't they reconcile themselves to Chinese rule and attempt to benefit from it? After all even China, a former victim of Western imperialism, had benefited from that humiliating experience, in the sense of having been forced to learn about science, technology and modern politics from its oppressors, as had other countries in Asia and Africa.

Not only is such an outlook historically ill-informed on the character of old-style colonialism and imperialism, it is dangerously naive on the nature of modern totalitarian states, especially when the state in question has the chameleon ability to change everything about itself in order to survive — everything, that is, except its permanent core of violence, lies and repression.

Churchill, in his *History of the English-Speaking Peoples*, relates the fate of Britain as a Roman colony, after British resistance had been overcome:

> For nearly three hundred years Britain, reconciled to the Roman system, enjoyed in many respects the happiest, most comfortable, and most enlightened times its inhabitants have ever had. In culture and learning the land was a pale reflection of the Roman scene, not so lively as the Gallic. But there was law; there was peace; there was warmth; there was food, and a long-established custom of life. The population was free from barbarism without being sunk in sloth of luxury. Some culture spread even to the villages. Roman habits percolated; the use of Roman utensils and even of Roman speech steadily grew. The British thought of themselves as good Romans as any ... There was a sense of pride in sharing in so noble and widespread a system. To be a citizen of Rome was to be a citizen of the world raised upon a pedestal of unquestioned superiority above barbarians or slaves.

The celebrated Indian writer Nirad C. Chaudhuri dedicated his *Biography of an Unknown Indian* to the memory of the British

Empire, saying "all that was good and living within us was made, shaped and quickened by the same British rule".

But if Chaudhuri is too much the Anglophile, let us hear the view of an Indian less enthusiastic of British rule. Gandhi, in his autobiography *The Story of My Experiments with Truth*, says: "Hardly ever have I known anybody to cherish such loyalty as I did to the British Constitution. I can see now that my love of truth was at the root of this loyalty. It has never been possible for me to simulate loyalty or, for that matter any other virtue ... Not that I was unaware of the defects in British rule, but I thought it was on the whole acceptable. In those days I believed that British rule was on the whole beneficial to the ruled."

I am not trying to justify Roman, British, or any other kind of imperialism here. Gandhi was right, of course, to later change his mind and fight for independence. Whatever benefits imperial rule may confer on its colonial subjects, in the end it makes them lesser people. The costs outweigh the benefits.

How much more so under Chinese rule, where such benefits are non-existent. I do not think it necessary to go into detailed comparisons here, but let us take one of the most important foundations of any society — law. Nearly all the legal systems of present-day European nations are based, in one form or another, on Roman law — on the *Codex Justiniani*, the Emperor Justinian's great legal code. Transcending even its legal function, Roman law, in the end, became one of the profoundest intellectual forces in the history of European civilisation.

The British Empire's greatest legacy to India is constitutional government and the rule of law. Imperfect as the system is often criticized of being, it is still the lifeblood which powers this great democracy, and the sinews which bind its disparate people together as a nation.

I think it can be said without exaggeration that nothing remotely similar has taken place in Tibet. Instead, the lessons we have learned from the Chinese, legal and otherwise, have not only been negative, but pernicious in the extreme. Taking into account the constant lies, violence, famines, "struggles", mutual surveillance, denunciations, "Reform through Labour", and varieties of cultural revolutions that have been inflicted on the Tibetan people for over four decades, it is surely a miracle that they have not all regressed into hopeless depravity, cynicism, drunkenness, brutality and madness.

A triumph of the Tibetan character? One would think so from reading accounts of "smiling, friendly" natives in recent travel books on Tibet. Complementary certainly, but not too discerning of the fearful bashing the Tibetan spirit has taken. No psychological study has been conducted of the people living inside Tibet, but I have the very uneasy feeling (I hope I'm wrong here) that the damage inflicted on the mental health of the Tibetan people, far outweighs the destruction of the monasteries and temples. Even now, with the liberalisation in the economy and social lifestyle, the law in China is no more than just an instrument of state repression.

In the final reckoning, I am convinced that Tibetans must have independence if only for survival as a people. With every passing year we are getting closer to extinction. Aside from the deliberate Chinese government policies to erase Tibetan identity, by sending Tibetan children to schools in China, or possibly making Tibet a special economic zone, the sheer relentless pressure of China's exploding population will eventually push Tibetans to extinction. No autonomy, or any kind of understanding or accommodation with China will prevent it. One cannot accommodate an avalanche, neither can one stop it half-way. Only independence holds out some hope for Tibetan survival — and even that is touch and go.

I am in no way claiming that achieving independence will be easy — or even possible, in the near future. All I am saying is that in the cold clear light of all the evidence we have before us, the struggle for independence, no matter how desperately hopeless it may appear, holds out at least a chance for Tibetan survival.

The various fantasies being espoused in the name of compromise, understanding and realism serve only to divide Tibetan society, and provide legitimacy to all manner of dubious self-styled experts, "honest" brokers, pocket Kissingers, "friends" of Chinese leaders, even well-meaning imbeciles — all eagerly contributing to the production of an effectively disorienting smokescreen of policy confusion (Do the Tibetans want associate status, a zone of peace, human rights, some help with the environment, freedom, a Vatican for the Dalai Lama, emigration to America... what on earth do these guys want?) behind which the Chinese are going about the business of resolving the issue once and for all.

THE LATEST ON SINO-TIBETAN NEGOTIATIONS
A POSTSCRIPT

I wrote the above article last April for a book of essays, *Tibet: the Issue is Independence*, conceived and edited by Ed Lazar. But since then a number of critical developments, not mentioned in my article, have taken place. I covered these events for the independent Tibetan language newspaper, *Mang-tso* ("Democracy"), published by the Amnye Machen Institute. My first story on the Sino-Tibetan negotiations came out on 15 September 1993. It essentially, reported that on 5 August this year, Gyalo Thondup admitted to the Tibetan Parliament that all his discussions with the Chinese for the past fourteen years had achieved nothing. Furthermore, he added that he had been constantly scolded and browbeaten by Chinese officials, who never listened to anything he had to say.

Inside Tibet, rumours of GT's negotiations with Chinese leaders raised, unduly, the hopes of many Tibetans, and in some cases dissuaded activists from further protest against the Chinese. New arrivals from Lhasa told me that after hearing of the negotiations, people have been advising activists not to provoke the Chinese as a deal for some kind of Tibetan self-rule was imminent.

Shortly afterwards, the Tibetan government released a number of documents relating to its relations with China since 1979, including texts of the Dalai Lama's letters to Chinese leaders — some of which were published in the *Tibetan Review* and *Sheja*. The Dalai Lama also released a statement, and in no uncertain terms, stated that all the efforts by him and his government to negotiate with China had failed.

In addition, Beijing's diplomatic mask has slipped on a couple of occasions recently. We now know that in a recent inner circle meeting, the Chinese premier Li Peng spelt out the "Three No Concessions" policy. Li said that no concessions should be made on the issues of Hong Kong, Taiwan and Tibet. As far as Tibet was concerned, not even the minimum ("half a step") was to be conceded as it could cause a chain reaction within China. (*World Journal*, 8 December 1993.) Furthermore, secret documents leaked from Beijing some months ago detail Chinese strategy to "Divide and Destroy" Tibetan supporters. The documents also reveal that China considers negotiations with the Dalai Lama to be an exercise to resolve the problem of his "reparation", rather than any genuine discussion on the issue of Tibet.

March 1994
Tibetan Review

Unquiet Memories
The Tibetan Resistance and the Role of the CIA[1]

FREUD'S FAVOURITE IMAGE of the mind was as an archaeological site, filled, layer by layer, with the buried strata of the past (but one where these layers could rise into consciousness at any time). However the Tibetan national mind, or at least that part of our collective memory which deals with our recent and violent history could perhaps be best compared to an iceberg. A small part of it floats in our view, mostly during the annual Tenth of March commemorations, while the far greater mass moves silently unseen beneath the surface of our hypocrisy and indifference. Yet history abhors such disregard, and the past may yet one day surface to upset the cherished fiction of our official non-violent history and ideology.

In marked contrast to developments in other areas of Tibetan studies, very little attention has been paid to modern Tibetan history,

---

1. This essay started off as an "extempore" presentation at the conference "Fourty Years On: Tibet 1950–90", held at the School for Oriental and African Studies, London on April 1990, and was subsequently published in *Resistance and Reform in Tibet*, edited by Robert Barnett and Shirin Akiner, Hurst & Co., London, 1994.

and within that, even less to the violent and cataclysmic period in the 1950s and 1960s when the Tibetan people, especially the tribesmen from Eastern and North-Eastern Tibet, took up arms against Chinese domination. What few published accounts of the Tibetan Resistance movement exist are on the whole vague about figures, place-names and details of the people involved.

Such books as *Tibet in Revolt* by George Patterson, *From the Land of Lost Content* by Noel Barber, *The Cavaliers of Kham* by Michel Peissel and *The Secret War in Tibet* by Lowell Thomas Jr. are good reads, supportive of the Tibetan cause and probably the best that could be done at the time with the limited information available, but they are on the whole rather nebulous works. In a couple of them the authors make no mention of the real leaders and participants in the uprising, while glorifying as heroes and resistance leaders, people who were not only nothing of the sort, but often well-known collaborators.

There has also been a singular lack of inquiry into the Resistance movement on the part of the exile Tibetan government. The government has always had an uneasy relationship with the Resistance. The wide extent and popularity of the Resistance highlighted the failure of the government's policy of co-operation with the Chinese occupation forces. Traditional prejudices between Khampas and the Lhasa government also played their part. Early in the 1960s the exile Tibetan government did attempt to gather statements from as many refugees as it could and collected a number of accounts from people involved in the Resistance. These accounts were never very extensive or detailed, and only a few of them were ever published. A number of these records seem to have been lost or misplaced, but an attempt is being made to put them back together as far as possible.

The Resistance itself did not go in for documenting its activities in any systematic or extensive way, and was suspicious of other people's attempts to do so. With the establishment of connections with the CIA there was an almost obsessive insistence on secrecy that was carried to a degree where it did more harm than good. No real attempt was made to publicise the activities of the Resistance to the world. Even within Tibetan exile society, little attempt was made to inform the public of its activities. Secrecy was also maintained so as not to embarrass the governments of India or Nepal where the Resistance maintained bases and agencies.

After the closure of the last guerrilla bases in Mustang in 1974, the Four Rivers, Six Ranges organisation in India, mainly composed of former Resistance members, made attempts to gather and record detailed histories of every guerrilla group or *dmag-sgar* that had belonged to the Resistance movement. This project has apparently suffered considerable setbacks and it does not seem that it will be possible for these records to be published in the near future. A posthumous biography of the leader of the resistance, Gompo Tashi Andrugtsang, was published in India in 1973, but it was sketchy and badly translated.[2]

Lhamo Tsering, a leader of the Mustang guerrilla force and the assistant to Gyalo Thondup, one of the Dalai Lama's elder brothers (who was a kind of overall leader of the Resistance for some years), has also written his memoirs. The book has not been published at the time of writing, but it promises to shed light on many aspects of Resistance history, probably focusing on Resistance activities in the 1960s and 1970s when he was involved in a position of responsibility.

Another person closely linked to anti-Chinese activities in Lhasa, especially in the mid and late 1950s, is the controversial Alo Chonze.

---

2. Gompo Tashi Andrugtsang. *Four Rivers, Six Ranges: A True Account of Khampa Resistance to Chinese in Tibet*, Dharamshala: Information Office of His Holiness the Dalai Lama, 1973.

He was one of the leaders of an underground Lhasa-based nationalist organisation, the Mimang (the "People"). He is publishing, in instalments, a semi-historical, semi-autobiographical account of the Tibetan Uprising and of the politics of exile. Two volumes have been released of which the first provides interesting information on the Lithang Uprising (1956) and the formation of the underground Mimang organisation in Lhasa.3

My contribution to the subject has been a play *Yuru* (1981) about the uprising in Lithang and the tragic death of the resistance leader Yuru Pon. I also wrote *Horseman in the Snow* (1979) about the life and struggle of a Khampa warrior, Aten Dogyaltsang, and an account of the resistance in Nyarong and surrounding areas. The book was subsequently reissued as *Warriors of Tibet* in 1986.

Although many Resistance leaders and fighters have died, a number are still alive in Nepal, India and Switzerland. Many of them, these days, seem willing to be interviewed and to talk freely about their past. In a recent French television documentary on the Tibetan Resistance,4 Khampas spoke openly about their activities, their old CIA connections and even their connections with the Indian intelligence and military.

Washington still regards American support for the Tibetan Resistance as a sensitive issue, and the appropriate records remain classified. A few obscure newspaper articles 5 and some references in

---

3. Alo Chonze (Alo Chos-mdzed), *Bod kyi gnas-lugs bden-'dzin sgo-phye ba'i ldenmig zhes bya-ba* (*The key that opens the door of truth to the Tibetan situation*), self-published.

4. Marie de Louville and Michel de Castelverd, "Tibet. L'armée des ombres", broadcast in the series *Resistance* by the TV channel Antenne 2, Paris, 2 September 1991.

5. Jeff Long, "Going after Wangdu: The Search for a Tibetan Guerrilla Leads to Colorado's Secret CIA Camp", *Rocky Mountain Magazine*, July–Aug. 1981.

certain books on the CIA[6] are all that is available to the public on one of the few long-term and successful operations conducted by the American secret service. According to Fletcher Prouty, a colonel in the US Air Force who managed secret air missions for General Erskine's Office of Special Operations, Tibet is "buried in the lore of the CIA as one of those successes that are not talked about".[7]

Such lack of information on the Tibetan Uprising has enabled the Tibetan leadership to successfully rewrite history, playing down the role of the armed revolt and fostering the fiction that popular resistance was non-violent. Though unhesitatingly subscribed to by many friends of Tibet, this story is patently untrue. There was never a non-violent campaign against the Chinese. Even the few public demonstrations before the uprising of March 1959 were not a display of the public's commitment to non-violence; quite the reverse. They were a signal to the Chinese that the Tibetans were prepared to act violently to protect their leader and their religion.

This non-violent interpretation of modern Tibetan history has accorded only a minor role to the Resistance movement. It has even given rise to two very misleading assumptions, both of which we shall examine: first, that the overall scale of the uprisings against the Chinese had not been significant; and secondly, that the uprisings had been fomented by the CIA.

MAGNITUDE OF THE TIBETAN UPRISING

From anecdotal evidence provided by surviving Resistance fighters, refugees and recent escapees from Tibet, it would seem that during

---

6. Victor Marchetti and John D. Marks, *The CIA and the Cult of Intelligence*, New York: Dell, 1980.
7. Fletcher L. Prouty, "Colorado to Koko Nor: The Amazing True Story of the CIA's Secret War Against Red China", *Denver Post*, 6 February 1972.

the uprisings the scale of the fighting and the consequent deaths and dislocation in Eastern Tibet were enormous, and comparable in magnitude to the events in Afghanistan following the Soviet invasion. Yet the consequences of the Tibetan uprisings have not been as great for China as that of the Afghan conflict for the Soviet Union, especially since official propaganda ensured that the Chinese people remained largely ignorant of it. Still the Tibetan Uprising has remained the one persistent running sore that has tainted China's otherwise successful efforts at keeping up appearances before the eyes of the world. Roderick MacFarquhar considered that the Tibetan Resistance produced "the gravest episode of internal disorder (in the People's Republic of China) prior to the Cultural Revolution"[8]

Even if we were to discount the anecdotal evidence, the scale of demographic dislocation in Eastern and North-Eastern Tibet, where most of the fighting took place, provides sufficient evidence to substantiate the claim of many refugees as to the massive extent of the fighting and casualties in these areas. One of the standard corroboration of this provided by the refugees is the claim that, subsequent to the crushing of the uprisings, all or most of the ploughing in the villages and districts were being done by women (unthinkable in the past) as there were no men left in the area.

Chinese figures taken from their 1982 census[9], fifteen to twenty years after the revolt had been crushed, indicate a much larger ratio of women to men in Eastern and North-Eastern Tibet. Such disparate sex-ratio figures do not appear in other parts of Tibet or even China, although vast numbers of people died in these places too, for other reasons, such as the 1960–63 famine (probably the worst in human

---

8. Roderick MacFarquhar, *The Origins of the Cultural Revolution*, New York: Columbia University Press, 1983.

9. *The Population Atlas of China*, Oxford University Press, 1987.

history), which affected both sexes equally. We must also bear in mind that the majority of the Tibetan people lived in Eastern and North-Eastern Tibet, where much of the fighting had taken place.

No substantive effort has been made by any person or organisation, not even in the exile Tibetan government, to find out the number of people killed in the uprisings in Eastern Tibet, or in the rest of Tibet and Lhasa. In fact the only published figure we have for Tibetans killed in the Lhasa Uprising and its aftermath is from official Chinese sources. A booklet marked "secret" and published in Lhasa on 1 October 1960 by the political department of the Tibetan Military District, says of the aftermath of the Lhasa Uprising: "From last March up to now we have already wiped out (*xiaomie*) over 87,000 of the enemy."[10]

EARLIEST RESISTANCE TO THE CHINESE

Prevalent at one time among journalists and academics sympathetic to China was the idea that the Tibetan revolt was essentially a conspiracy of the Tibetan church, the aristocracy and the CIA, and that even the Dalai Lama's flight to India was engineered by the CIA.[11] Vestiges of such notions still prevail today.

Popular resistance in Eastern and North-Eastern Tibet began long before any American involvement in Tibet. In fact there is evidence to prove that sporadic resistance to Communist Chinese advances occurred in these areas even as early as 1949. We need not go into accounts here of earlier clashes between Tibetans and

---

10. *Xizang xingshi wenwu jiaoyu di jiben jiaocai*, Lhasa: Political Department of the Tibetan Military District, 1960.

11. Chris Mullin, "The CIA–Tibetan Conspiracy", *Far Eastern Economic Review*, 5 September 1975.

Communist forces, especially in 1934–35 during the Long March,[12] as these clashes were not related to the actual invasion and occupation of Tibet in later years.

In interviews with tribesmen from Gyalthang in South-Eastern Tibet, now part of Yunnan province, I learned that they had resisted the Red Army when it first advanced into their territory in 1949. Their claims are, to some extent, confirmed by the accounts of Peter Goullart,[13] a White Russian employee of the Kuomintang government, who served in the late 1940s as an agricultural expert in the Nakhi (Naxi) town of Lijiang in Yunnan province. Goullart states that in 1949, after the fall of Kunming, the provincial capital, and the Red Army push towards the west, Khampas from Gyalthang, which bordered Nakhi territory, came to Lijiang and, helped by local Nakhis, managed to inflict an initial defeat on an advance guard of the Red Army. Later, the Communists used more subtle tactics and infiltrated agents among the younger Nakhis, which led to their demoralisation and the fall of Lijiang to the Communists. Goullart also mentions that the Gyalthangwas were a more warlike and formidable people than the Nakhis.

Gyalthang's resistance probably explain why it was one of the first places in Eastern Tibet where "democratic reforms" were carried out from as early as 1953. Gompo Tashi Andrugtsang mentions the event in his autobiography: "In the area of Gyalthang Anthena Kham, the following year [1953] the local population was divided into five strata and a terror campaign of selective arrest launched by the Chinese. People belonging to the first three strata were either publicly humiliated or condemned to the firing squad."[14]

---

12. Edgar Snow, *Red Star Over China*, New York, 1938.

13. Peter Goullart, *Forgotten Kingdom*, London: Readers Union, 1957.

14. Andrugtsang, op. cit.

Another area of early resistance to the Red Army came from somewhere geographically very distant to Gyalthang, namely Hormukha and Nangra in Amdo, or North-Eastern Tibet. Here, the fight against the Communist had been going on for a considerable time with Ma Bufang, the Kuomintang governor (in reality a semi-independent Muslim warlord) of Qinghai province, who led his Hui cavalry allied (sometimes) with Amdowa and Mongol tribesmen.[15] But when Communist victory seemed imminent in 1949, Ma Bufang fled with his wives and treasure on two DC–10s. The Red Army reached Nangra and Hormukha in September 1949, according to an eyewitness, Rinzin,[16] who later also participated in the fighting.

In December of the same year, the two chiefs of Nangra, Pon Wangchen and Pon Choje, led their men in the battle against the Chinese. There were a number of encounters, in one of which the son of Pon Wangchen was killed. Rinzin claims that the initial contingent of Chinese troops with whom they fought consisted of around six thousand men, who were later reinforced by an additional ten thousand troops from Rebkong after the outbreak of fighting.

The people of Hormukha joined in the fighting in February 1950, but by then it was too late to affect the outcome of the conflict as the Chinese had many more troops in the area. All the major Amdowa forces were destroyed. In one disastrous encounter Pon Choje was nearly captured but managed to escape by faking death. Nearly all the tribesmen were forced to leave their homes and take to the mountains from where they began hit-and-run guerrilla operations against Chinese supply lines and patrols. These operations proved more

---

15. Leonard Clark, *The Marching Wind*, London: Hutchinson, 1957.

16. *Tibet Under Chinese Communist Rule*, Dharamshala: Information Office of His Holiness the Dalai Lama, 1976.

successful than the pitched battles they had been conducting till then. The Amdowas of Nangra claimed that, because of their determined resistance, the Chinese referred to Nangra as "Little Taiwan".

In 1952 a truce was arranged by some Lamas of Dechen Monastery. Pon Wangchen was taken to Xining and then to Beijing, where he is said to have met Mao Zedong. There was a brief period of peace between 1952 and 1953, but once again the Chinese began denunciations, struggles, arrests and executions, and renewed fighting broke out all over the territory. The Chinese had by now built up an overwhelming superiority in numbers and in quality of arms, and there was no doubt as to the final outcome of the conflict. Many thousands of Amdowas were killed in the fighting, executed or sent to labour camps. Many also committed suicide. Some escaped to Lhasa. In the words of Rinzin, "only a few blind men, cripples, fools and some children were left".[17]

Such resistance against invading Chinese forces in the late 1940s and early 1950s was not a common phenomenon in Eastern and North-Eastern Tibet at the time. Nor did the Tibetan government forces receive much help from local Khampas when Communist troops attacked in October 1959. A considerable degree of the Tibetan government's prestige and authority had waned in Eastern Tibet since 1918 when, under Kalon Jampa Tendar, Governor General of Eastern Tibet, Tibetan power and influence in that entire area had been at its pinnacle.[18]

Before the Chinese invasion of 1950, the Tibetan government had attempted to rouse the people of the frontier regions to resist the Red Army, but without much success. Taktser Rinpoche, one of the Dalai Lama's elder brothers and abbot of Kumbum Monastery in

---

17. Ibid.

18. Eric Teichman, *Travels of a Consular Officer in Eastern Tibet*, Cambridge, 1922

Amdo, told me that his monastery had received a letter from Lhalu *zhabs-pad* (minister), the governor of Eastern Tibet and Commander of the Tibetan army there, a year before the invasion, instructing the monks of Taktser to resist Chinese forces. But Lhalu's efforts to rouse Amdowa and Khampa loyalty were not very successful, except in a few cases, as at the monastery at Chamdo.[19]

Isolated though they were, the outbreaks of fighting in Gyalthang, Nangra and Hormukha and certain other areas were of sufficient scale and ferocity to be indicative of the coming course of events in Eastern Tibet. Soon Chinese policies in Eastern Tibet began to create a new wave of hostility against the occupation forces that became particularly violent around the winter of 1955–56, one of the most immediate causes being the implementation by the Chinese of a set of programmes labelled "Democratic Reforms". The Chinese called this uprising the "Kangding Rebellion"[20] after the Chinese name for the Tibetan frontier town of Dartsedo, which was the Chinese headquarters for the whole of Eastern Tibet. The revolt spread like wildfire all over Eastern Tibet, and soon tribal chiefs from diverse areas tried to organise a joint effort to defeat the Chinese.

Yuru Pon, the paramount chieftain of the Lithang nomads, sent messengers all over Eastern Tibet calling for attacks on Chinese positions on the eighteenth day of the first Tibetan month of 1956. Monasteries and tribes in Nyarong, Kanze, Bathang, Drango, Linkashi and other areas responded to this call to action. Yuru Pon later died in the bombed ruins of the Great Monastery of Lithang in the aftermath of a fake surrender where he killed two senior Chinese officers with a concealed pistol.[21]

---

19. Robert Ford, *Wind Between the Worlds*, New York: David McKay, 1957.
20. Anna Louise Strong, *When Serfs Stood up in Tibet*, Beijing, 1960.
21. Alo Chonze, op. cit.

Dorje Yudon (Dorgee Eudon), the younger wife of the chieftain of Nyarong, Gyari Nima, stated in an interview [22] that the Gyaritsang family received a letter from the Lithang chieftain asking them to revolt on the eighteenth day of the first moon of 1956. He also wrote that he would send them another message confirming the date of the revolt as soon as he received answers from all the chiefs in Eastern Tibet.

Since Gyari Nima had been summoned by the Chinese authorities to Dartsedo for a meeting, Dorje Yudon took up the leadership of the Gyaritsang clan and other tribes of Nyarong. When she organised meetings in various parts of Nyarong to persuade people to join her revolt, the Chinese authorities realised what she was up to and attempted to have her assassinated at her home by two Nyarongwa collaborators, aided by two Chinese soldiers.

The attempt failed, as did other attempts to arrest Dorje's uncle and other leaders of the revolt in Nyarong. She was therefore forced to call the revolt four days earlier than the date agreed upon with Yuru Pon. The Nyarongwas were initially successful in destroying various small Chinese garrisons in the region and also in killing and capturing many collaborators. Surviving Chinese troops fell back on the Chinese administrative centre for Nyarong which was located at Drugmo Dzong, the Fortress of the Female Dragon. The surviving Chinese soldiers barricaded themselves behind the massive walls of the ancient fort and prepared to hold out. The Nyarongwas tried to storm the place a number of times but were unsuccessful.

The Chinese sent relief forces from Kanze which the Nyarongwas tried to intercept and ambush. Initially Dorje Yudon's forces were successful but, after a month, larger Chinese forces from Drango

---

22. Holly Elwood, "Dorgee Yudon: The Leaders of the Rebels", unpublished interview, 21 May 1989.

and Tawu managed to break the siege of the Fortress of the Female Dragon. Dorje Yudon recalls that twenty-three tribal chieftains in Kham first responded to Yuru Pon's call to revolt, and that they called their loose-knit alliance *Tensung dhanglang magar* or "the Volunteer Army to Defend Buddhism".

THE CHARACTER OF THE REVOLT

Though there were obvious limits to which military action could be co-ordinated among the various tribes of Eastern Tibet, the general uprising in 1956 did succeed in clearing the Chinese out of nearly all of Eastern Tibet for a brief period. The Red Army soon returned in greater strength and numbers, but that sad conclusion need not concern us here. Yet it is worth noting that, despite long-standing tribal animosities and differences, a fairly successful attempt was made to unite the efforts of Eastern Tibetans in fighting the Chinese. When one considers that this attempt at co-ordination had to cover many hundreds of miles of mountain wilderness, without even basic communication equipment, roads or motorised transport, it is remarkable that such a widespread rebellion should have successfully taken place, more or less around the date agreed upon.

The name that the Khampas gave to their Resistance movement, "the Volunteer Army to Defend Buddhism", reflects what may be called the ideological nature of the uprising, and thus the support it gained all over Eastern Tibet and later in Central Tibet. Dawa Norbu, in an article on the *Tibetan Revolt*, considered that the Khampa Uprising was in defence of Tibetan Buddhist values, and of the political and sacred institutions founded upon such values. "As long as the Chinese did not tamper with the objectively functioning social system and the value systems still considered sacred by members of that society, as happened in Outer Tibet, there was no revolt, although the unprecedented Chinese presence in the country caused great resentment and anxiety. But the moment the Chinese tried to alter the functioning and sacred social system in Inner Tibet which they considered de jure China proper, the revolt began."[23]

This traditional ideology on which the revolt was based gave it sufficient popular appeal to transcend the borders of Eastern Tibet and to ignite passions and violence even in Central Tibet, where the Chinese had caused no disruption in the social system, and where the aristocracy and clergy were being actively courted by the Chinese authorities. Hence many Tibetans have considered the Uprising a national one[24], in the sense that the sentiment of the majority of the Tibetan people were involved.

Yet the leaders and members of the resistance movement, mainly composed of Khampas and Amdowas, were too often unable to transcend narrow tribal loyalties, for the movement to take on a fully national and dynamic character. The traditional Lhasa-Khampa divide, though bridged on a number of occasions during the revolt, was also never reconciled satisfactorily. The other name of the resistance movement, *Chushi Gangdrug*, "Four Rivers, Six Ranges" — an ancient term for Eastern Tibet — might be seen as underlining the narrower and divided character of the movement.

With the savage suppression of the Uprising in Eastern Tibet and the large-scale movement of refugees to Lhasa, the focus of the Resistance shifted to Central Tibet, where, under the leadership of the Lithangwa merchant-chief, Gompo Tashi Andrugtsang, the earlier

---

23. Dawa Norbu, "The 1959 Tibetan Rebellion: An Interpretation", *China Quarterly*, no. 77, March 1979, pp.74–93.

24. Phuntsok Wangyal, "The Revolt of 1959", *Tibetan Review*, July–August 1974.

very loose-knit confederacy of guerrilla bands was re-organised, and a single Resistance army formally created on 16 June 1958, in the district of Lhokha, south of Lhasa. Weapons were purchased secretly from India.

Dawa Norbu points out that "the vast majority of the twenty-three Khampa leaders of the Tibet Revolt were merchants who had made their fortunes since the 'Liberation', as China kept pouring silver coins called *dao-yuan* into Tibet to pay the Tibetan ruling class and the road workers. But instead of making more money or running away to India safely with their silver fortunes, Khampas spent the Chinese money on the purchase of arms and ammunitions for the revolt."[25]

The Resistance also received information from sympathetic ministers and officials of the Tibetan government on the location and content of secret government arsenals. From these they removed substantial quantities of arms and ammunition[26], which enabled the guerrillas to cut off the three strategic highways south of Lhasa and near paralyse Chinese army operations in that area.

LIMITS OF AMERICAN INVOLVEMENT

It is from these tumultuous and far-ranging events that the Tibetan Resistance movement takes its origins. It was only after these events and other successes, reports of which reached the ears of the American government in due course[27], that the United States actually sent assistance to the Resistance forces in Tibet, although this aid

---

25. Dawa Norbu, op. cit.

26. Andrugtsang, op. cit.

27. US Department of State, Office of Intelligence Research, Division of Research for Far East, *Intelligence Report no. 7341*, "Unrest in Tibet", 1 November 1956.

only began to reach the hands of the fighters in 1958. By all accounts, during the crucial period of the Resistance in Eastern Tibet and during its greatest successes, no American arms or assistance of any kind were received by any Resistance group.

Accounts of the CIA engineering the Dalai Lama's escape [28] seem to be mostly the result of creative journalistic imagination. The only agents the CIA had in Lhasa who attempted to make some kind of connection with the Dalai Lama and the Tibetan government were two Lithangwas, Athar and Lotse, who had been parachuted near Samye some time before the outbreak of the revolt in Lhasa. Lotse died a few years ago but Athar is still alive, in New Delhi. He told me that he and his partner secretly managed to see Phala, the Dalai Lama's Lord Chamberlain (*mgron-nyer chen-mo*), who with Surkhang *zhabs-pad*, was the leader of the nationalist faction in the Tibetan government, and sympathetic to the Resistance.

Athar gave Phala a message from the American government asking for an official letter from the Tibetan government requesting American military aid. Phala told Athar that it was too late and that it would be impossible to trust the entire Cabinet or the Assembly with such a sensitive and potentially compromising message. Phala confirmed this story of his meeting with Athar in a conversation I had with him some years ago before his death. Phala planned and organised the Dalai Lama's escape using Athar and Lotse with their radio transmitter to keep the Americans informed of developments in the escape plan, and later during the actual escape itself.

The true extent and implications of the Tibetan Resistance have never been studied systematically. [29] From the little understanding

---

28. Mullin, op. cit.

29. The situation has improved with the publication of four volumes of Lhamo Tsering's *Resistance* series by Amnye Machen Institute, though eight volumes remain

I have managed to gain through conversations and interviews with people who were involved, I have come to realise that the amount and the quality of information on these events are frustratingly inadequate. The far greater mass of historical knowledge and memory floats undiscovered beneath the surface of our indifference and neglect.

It is my hope that the present ridiculous attitude of Tibetan officials, Western dharma practitioners and New Age type supporters who regard the Resistance movement as an embarrassment — either because it somehow detracts from the preferred peace-loving image of Tibet as a Shangri-La, or because the Resistance committed the ultimate sin (for lefties at least) of accepting money and arms from the CIA — will change and a more realistic and inquiring attitude take its place.

1994
Tibetan Review

---

to be published. The release of White Crane's documentary on the CIA in Tibet, *Shadow Circus*, has made a considerable change in the Tibetan public and supporter's appreciation of this important period of Tibetan history. Even two former CIA personnel connected to the Resistance have come out with their own books: Roger McCarthy's *Tears of the Lotus*, and Ken Knaus' *Orphans of the Cold War*. The latest book on the subject is Conboy and Morrison's *The CIA's Secret War in Tibet*.

Writer and Historian
K. Dhondup (1952–1995)

IN 1979, when the Communist Party of Tibet was founded in exile, I wrote a long essay for the *Tibetan Review* — a critical study of Communism in general preceeded by a somewhat dismissive analysis of our new political party. Some months later I came across a newsletter published by the Regional Tibetan Youth Congress of Chandigarh in which the chairman of the Communist Party, K. Dhondup, was interviewed. When asked about my attack, Dhondup replied that though he did not agree with what I had written, he welcomed the fact that I was the only person who had come out openly and criticized it in print.

Dhondup-la had a quality that is rare among Tibetans, especially those having anything to do with politics. He had a "large interior" (*khogpa chenpo*). Even his enthusiasm for Communism, in a society that is near exclusively conservative, reflected this quality of the man, and also his ability to see both sides of a question. Of course, I felt his advocacy of Communism to be wrong (in later years he described his enthusiasm for Communism to being "an error of youth"[1]) but people who do things make mistakes.

I feel that Dhondup-la's largeness of heart and mind grew out of the many books he had read. He was that rarity among Tibetans, a person who read books. I don't mean religious texts. He was one of the few Tibetans with whom you could have an intelligent discussion on Western literature, movies, art and Tibetan history. He was himself a writer and historian, having published two works on Tibetan history. A third, on the history of the Imperial age, unfortunately remains incomplete. He was also the editor of the *Tibet Journal*, the primier academic journal on Tibet. He wrote many articles in the *Tibetan Review* and, as *Review* readers will know, countless letters reflecting his genuine concern for the Tibetan cause and people. He was also a poet[2] and edited the first literary journal in exile, *Pema Thang* ("Lotus Fields").

Disillusioned with Dharamshala, Dhondup settled in New Delhi and became a successful businessman. But whenever there was something to be done for the Tibetan cause he did not hesitate to come forward. He used his location in Delhi to make many friends with Indian leaders and intellectuals. Last year, when there was a politically instigated riot against Tibetans in Dharamshala, Dhondup-la, though very ill, worked tirelessly, spending his own money unstintingly to bring to Dharamshala eminent Indian academics, jurists and political leaders from Delhi.

---

1. K. Dhondup, "Mumbo-jumbo in the Tibetan Society" (review of Civilized Shamans by Geoffrey Samuel), *Tibetan Review*, vol. 29, no. 3, March 1994, pp. 20–21.

2. One evening Dhondup-la asked me what I thought of Robert Graves' belief in the "White Goddess" as a kind of primordial muse of poetry. I could see that the idea appealed to him hugely. I didn't tell him that I thought his charming wife being named Dolkar or "White Tara" might have had something to do with his enthusiasm for Graves' theory.

Dhondup-la was born in the tenth month of the Tibetan year (1952) in the village of Rupingang in the Upper Dromo Valley. His father, the late Kalsang Dhondup, was popularly known as "Acho Kay", or Elder Brother Kay. His mother, Kalsang Dolma, was born in 1919–20. The family belonged to one of the four "*tso*" or clans of Upper Dromo.

As a child Dhondup-la studied at the Central School for Tibetans in Darjeeling, and later received his bachelor's degree from Saint Joseph's College, also in Darjeeling. He worked for the Library of Tibetan Works and Archives from 1975 to 1985, and was a member of the Governing Body of the Amnye Machen Institute.

He married Dr. Tsewang Dolkar Khangkar (the daughter of the well known Tibetan physician, Mrs. Lobsang Dolma Khangkar of Dharamshala) in 1977. Their eldest child Tsering Yangchen, born in March 1978, died in the same year. Their second daughter, Sonam Peldon, was born on 26 September 1980. Their third daughter, Dechen Dolma, was born on 31 October 1982.

Dhondup-la died on 7 May 1995 at 6 A.M. at his home in Delhi. He is survived by his mother, wife, daughters, and his sister Yangkee Yatung Angontsang.

15 May 1995
Mang-tso (Democracy)

Going for Broke
Unwavering Economic Action Against China

I UNDERSTAND FROM A FRIEND who has just returned from a Caribbean holiday that the manner in which turtle meat is sold in the markets there is not a sight for the faint of heart. The creature is not butchered outright. Instead it is flipped over on its shell and the amount of meat required by each customer is sliced off and sold, thus ensuring that the remaining meat stayed fresh. The wretched turtle grimly hangs on to life till practically every bit of his flesh has been removed. John Steinbeck and his marine biologist friend Ed Ricketts once removed a turtle's heart and kept it in a jar of salt water. It went on beating for several hours.

The cause of Tibetan independence has for over forty years now evinced such a *chelonian* tenacity of survival. This is indeed a very fortuitous thing, since it has regularly had large slices of its ideals and aspirations removed in order to accommodate various political as well as personal conveniences and interests. The largest chunk of all was cut way back in 1951 with the signing of the 17-Point Agreement, but since then — especially since the early eighties — much has been sliced off for this, that or the other. There seems to be little meat left now, and with "Referendum", "Middle Way Approach" and "Truth Insistence" we are cutting very close to the bone.

The latest carving job I've noticed was just a couple of months ago and appeared on the *World Tibet Network News*. In a release from the president of the International Campaign for Tibet (ICT), Lodi G. Gyari, dated 13 June and entitled "MFN for China Alert", there were three points that struck me as strange, even bizarre, and which have since then bothered me like a bad tooth.

1. "ICT has been consistent in its position: while not calling for total revocation, we have supported bills to condition renewal of MFN."

What on earth is wrong with calling for total revocation of MFN for China? After all, revocation of MFN merely means denying China certain trading privileges that it has with the USA. It does not mean cutting off trade with China or even imposing economic sanctions. India, the world's largest democracy, has not been granted MFN status by the United States. I must also point out that ICT's position on MFN has been anything but "consistent". In May 1990, I was in Washington DC when a major Congressional hearing on MFN was taking place. At the time ICT was so gung-ho for "complete revocation" that even someone like myself was immediately drafted to fight the good fight. Michelle Bohana, then ICT's leading lobbyist, took me around to the offices of a number of congressmen and senators where, as a "visiting Tibetan writer", I had to articulate the non-official argument, as it were, for full revocation of MFN for China.

2. "Supporting complete revocation of MFN would not send a constructive message to China and would not give them a reason to improve their treatment of the Tibetan people."

Why wouldn't it? There is conclusive evidence, even in some of ICT's own reports, that repression in Tibet has intensified to an appalling degree since China was extended MFN status. Furthermore, if the supposed representatives of the immediate victims of China's oppression have watered down their position to an extent where they are now calling on the US government not to revoke China's MFN status completely, then we certainly have no right to act indignant when Clinton de-links human rights and MFN. What is sauce for the ICT goose is sauce for the administration gander as well.

> 3. "In a way, ICT's quiet diplomacy and consistent position on MFN has paid off in that we have come to be regarded as one of the voices of reason in the debate."

I am really curious about who regards ICT as the "voice of reason" on the MFN debate? The US-China business lobby?

In 1992, the Kashag minister and brother of the Dalai Lama, Gyalo Thondup, visited North America. In a lecture hosted by the ICT he reprimanded Tibetans in the US and Canada for hurting the Chinese economy by organising boycotts of Chinese goods and by campaigning for revocation of MFN status for China. He voiced a personal concern that if China lost MFN status it would affect hundreds of thousands of jobs in Guangdong province alone. He succeeded in thoroughly confusing the issue among our supporters in Washington and in demoralising the US Tibet Committee and the Canada Tibet Committee who were then successfully organising a boycott of Chinese made toys. Also, for some years now, I have been hearing bitter complaints from some US Tibet Committee members that ICT sidelined their campaign to revoke MFN for China.

Right now the Students for a Free Tibet, the Milarepa Fund and the Tibet Freedom Movement in Bloomington, Indiana have launched a campaign to boycott Chinese products. It seems to have had a positive start and we are informed by the Tibetan Rights Campaign in Seattle, that a department store in that city has promised not to carry any goods made in China. The climate for such a campaign is just about right. Americans seem to have gotten over the initial euphoria for cheap Chinese goods, and are beginning to feel their damaging effect on American manufacturing, and with it the loss of decent jobs.

China's increasing military threat in the Pacific region in the last few years is also a plus factor for the campaign. But however favourable the climate I am afraid that if the Tibetan side once again knuckles under to pressure from Beijing or the US-China Trade Lobby (or even ICT) then we are going to see a repetition of the same sorry situation we had a few years ago when the spirited campaign of the US Tibet Committee and the Canada Tibet Committee to boycott Chinese made toys and deny MFN status to China was effectively derailed.

What can be done to prevent another *débâcle*? To kick things off I will offer three suggestions. They are so commonplace that they certainly must have occurred to the reader at one time or the other. My rationale for offering them at all, is that their very ordinariness often causes them to be overlooked, and that is precisely when confusion and demoralisation could set in. I am aware that the headings sound like maxims out of a social worker's training manual but the explanatory passages are reasonably simple and straightforward.

ROLE RECOGNITION

This is stating the obvious, but in an age of power worship, victim bashing and revisionist historiography, there cannot be a surfeit of repeating such an obvious truth as that *China invaded Tibet and not the other way around*. Tibet is the victim and China the oppressor. It is Tibet, not China, that has been completely isolated and excluded from the family of nations.

China is not only in the UN but has a permanent seat in the Security Council. In fact, it has so much support from other nations that for five years now it has effectively managed to quash any discussion in the UN of its human rights' abuses. Whatever little in the way of censure or pressure China gets from a few Western countries is entirely the result of its own blatant human rights abuses, its outrageous disregard for international conventions as copyright regulations, and its routine sabre-rattling and nuclear testing. In fact the international response to even the most atrocious of Chinese misdeeds has been extremely muted, no doubt conditioned by concerns of trade and fear of China's retribution.

Tibetans leaders should not shy away from representing themselves in their true role as representatives of victims, even though their own personal circumstances in Dharamshala or Washington DC, may be infinitely more secure and comfortable than that of their unfortunate fellow-countrymen in Tibet. No doubt it is a far more attractive and dignified proposition to play the role of the "honest broker" or "the man of reason who can see both sides of the question", but it is a dishonest pose. Our leaders must represent the victims, the Tibetan people.

RECOGNITION OF HISTORICAL ANTECEDENTS

Another factor to be borne in mind is the fact that economic sanctions and boycotts, though not immediately capable of results, are generally effective in the long run. Gandhi's Swadeshi campaign to boycott English textiles was the first effective demonstration of the untenability of British rule in India. Gandhi's campaign caused much suffering in Britain. A large number of mills in Lancashire were closed and many thousands rendered jobless. But the moral righteousness of Gandhi's action was so evident that, when he visited Britain in 1931, he was given a rousing welcome in Lancashire by unemployed workers.

The power of economic sanctions was most clearly demonstrated in South Africa in the struggle against apartheid. The sanctions hurt the black community the most, since it was the poorest and had the least economic cushion against outright penury and hunger. Nevertheless, the resolve of South African blacks and their leaders never wavered. In fact, even after Nelson Mandela was released and a number of important reforms put into place by President de Klerk, the ANC called for the continuation of international sanctions till apartheid was completely dismantled and a transitional government was in place.

Pro-democracy forces in Burma have been unequivocal in calling on all countries of the world for the imposition of an overall "South Africa-style economic sanction against the ruling military government in Burma". A worldwide campaign for consumer boycotts and shareholder pressure has forced companies like Amoco, Eddie Bauer, Liz Claiborne, Macy's and Petro Canada to withdraw from Burma. Last year three cities in the United States, Berkeley, Madison, and Santa Monica, passed laws boycotting companies which were doing business in Burma. On 22 April this year Pepsico announced its plans to sell its forty per cent stake in a joint venture in Burma. Of course, the way ahead is far from evident or easy, but at least the pro-democracy activists and their leader Aung San Suu Kyi have no doubt as to the soundness and integrity of their strategy.

ANTICIPATING CHINA'S REACTION

We must always bear in mind that even a fractional success of the boycott would translate into billions of dollars in losses for China. Therefore a strong Chinese reaction should definitely be expected; not just the usual direct and abusive one, but an indirect and almost certainly insidious one as well. Chinese efforts to subvert the integrity of the boycott campaign will probably best be countered by financial probity. It is vital that there be complete transparency in the workings of campaign organisers and in their raising and disbursement of funds.

A sound guide in this matter is Mahatma Gandhi. In his autobiography, he provides a detailed and very useful account of how the organisers of such public campaigns and movements ought to go about managing their finances, collect dues and so on. Based on his own experiences as the secretary of the Natal Indian Congress in South Africa, it not only reflects his high moral standards, but reveals a shrewd insight into people, and also a sound grasp of money matters, the last no doubt inherited from his *Bania* (merchant and banking caste) forebears.

August 1996
Tibetan Review

"Confucius Say..."
Old Values for New Tyrannies

MOST OF US are not at our cerebral best first thing in the morning. Stimulants like coffee and tea do help, but around this time of the year with MFN business in Washington (plus the hoo-hah of the Hong Kong handover), an unusually high degree of alertness is required to guard oneself against the China Business Lobby's subtle persuasions lurking within the contents of the morning paper.

I must confess that I have, on an occasion or two, been somewhat swept away by the skilful prose of those who tell us that in order to help the people of China we must ignore the Chinese government's human rights' violations — concepts like human rights and democracy anyway being Western inventions which should not be insensitively foisted on an ancient Confucian culture of obedience, loyalty and reverence for hierarchy.

But then I brew myself another mug of strong, mahogany-brown tea, sit back and ask myself what the probability is of the journalist or columnist in question ever having dipped into the *Analects*, the *Odes*, or any other Confucian classics for that matter. Reason is restored.

Even President Clinton was moved to make a reference to Confucius around this time last year, when explaining why he felt it necessary to de-link trade and human rights "a proud Confucian culture that prizes order over liberty is specially reluctant to take a step that is perceived as kowtowing to the US".

Actually, the sage is on record as saying, "Let humanity be your highest standard". Confucius may not exactly have been a democrat by present-day standards but he believed in the rule of law and accountability in government. Though Confucius was convinced that hierarchy and ritual were vital to the running of a state, he was very clear that princes should rule through moral authority and not through violence and oppression. An even more humanist and democratic development of Confucianism is represented by Mencius, who not only put the interests of the people above that of the ruler, but even vindicated tyrannicide.

In his book *The Burning Forest*, the Belgian art historian and China scholar Simon Leys tell us that: "In traditional China, 'morality' (which means essentially Confucianism) was the main bulwark against incipient totalitarianism." He refers to the Chinese historian Yu Ying-shih, schematically summarizing an article by him on this question as follows: "Confucianism described the world in terms of a dualism; on the one hand there is the concrete, changing realm of actual politics, on the other hand there is the realm of abstract, permanent principles. The duty of the scholar-politician is to serve the ruler insofar as the ruler's behaviour and policies harmonise with the unchanging moral principles, which provide a stable reference by which to judge them. In case of a clash between the two realms, the Confucian scholar must, in the strong and unambiguous words of Xun Zi, 'follow the principles and disobey the Prince.'"[1]

---

1. "Anti-Intellectualism in Chinese Traditional Politics," *Ming Pao Monthly*, February and March 1976.

At the end of the last century, the neo-Confucian scholar Kang Yu Wei (1858–1927), who was also China's first great modern reformer, came up with a radical interpretation of Confucius' teaching which shook the intellectual world of the Chinese gentry-literati. In Kang's view, Confucius was a forward-looking "sage king" who saw history as a progressive unilinear development from an age of disorder where kings and emperors ruled over people, through an age of approaching peace guided by constitutional monarchies, eventually to an age of universal peace and republican government.

Kang had been the main inspiration behind the extraordinary but shortlived reform movement of 1898 by the Manchu Emperor Guangxu. The emperor's aunt, the ruthless, reactionary Dowager Empress Cixi, had the young emperor arrested, and six of the main reformers beheaded. Kang just managed to flee China in a British warship. In exile in Darjeeling (my old hometown) in British India, he completed a synthesis of Confucian, Buddhist and Western Utopian ideas, which he explained in his astonishing *Book of the Great Community* (*Datongshu*).

Beside such standard utopian prescriptions as the abolition of nation states, the creation of a world government, and the ending of all wars, class and economic distinctions, Kang's most original reflections concerned the problems of abolishing the two other "boundaries" in the Great Community, the boundaries of the family and boundaries of gender. Such ideas were at the time revolutionary not only for a Confucian scholar but even for a Western one.

Long before the seeds of Communism were first planted in China, there was a broad intellectual movement embracing democracy. "Mr. Democracy and Mr. Science" represented, for the youth and intelligentsia of turn-of-the-century China, the two fundamental requisites for a modern Chinese state. The founding father of the modern Chinese state, Dr. Sun Yatsen, was a democrat.

His widow, Song Meiling, together with Cai Yuanpei, chancellor of Beijing National University and the writer Lu Xun, founded the Chinese League for the Protection of Human Rights as early as 1930.

It cannot be over-emphasised that democracy and human rights do not merely represent foreign values now being forced on a reluctant Chinese society. They existed in China's political debate since the end of the last century. They now appear never to have existed only because of the effectiveness of totalitarian propaganda in erasing the political memory of an entire nation, and in blurring the historical perception of the rest of the world.

The notion of a set of "Asian values" (as Confucian values are referred to in a larger context) of hierarchy, order and tradition that places little value on freedom and democracy can be dismissed outright if we take into account a large chunk of Asia which is oddly, but invariably, overlooked in this debate. I mean, of course, the world's largest and, arguably, liveliest democracy — India. If anyone from the West were to have the temerity to suggest to an Indian that he or she give up democracy and embrace "Asian values", I definitely think that hard words would ensue.

Of course, there are other Asians, besides Indians who do not feel the necessity of limiting themselves to observing "Asian values". Malaysia's young deputy prime minister, Anwar Ibrahim, in a *Newsweek* interview (2 September 1996) said:

> Does Sun Yatsen represent Asian values? Of course he does. He was a democrat and he believed in freedom of the press. And the media played a role in Sun's revolutionary era. The Philippines, Indonesia, Malaysia, Vietnam, Thailand — they all had similar experiences. The founding fathers always subscribed to moral fervour and traditional values — very Asian at that — but certainly they were great democrats.

He also has some choice word for "old values" describing them as "feudal" and "corrupt". At a meeting of South East Asian leaders in Singapore he offered this advice to those proponents of "Asian values" facing criticism from the West. "If you don't want the West to be condescending, don't be condescending to your own people." The remark so annoyed Lee Kuan Yew, dictator of Singapore, that he began rustling a copy of the *Asian Wall Street Journal* as Anwar spoke.

Lee Kuan Yew (Harry Lee) has been one of the leading advocates of Asian and Confucian values. He has developed his own effective methods of silencing political opponents and outspoken journalists, while avoiding the more conspicuous excesses of dictatorial rule which could possibly embarrass his supporters and friends in the West. Right-wing dictators of the post World War II era have generally had a negative militarist image (dark glasses and army uniforms) that has prevented them from spreading their political message outside the immediate areas of their own control. But Singapore's civilian exterior, clean-cut orderly economy and anti-democratic politics make up a dangerous "model", not just for the likes of China and Burma, but possibly even for shaky new democracies in Asia and Africa with economic problems and over-ambitious leaders.

Henry Kissinger and James Schlesinger have honoured Lee Kuan Yew as Singapore's "architect of the next century". They and other members of the Nixon Center for Peace and Prosperity probably find the idea of a successful capitalist/fascist country with good golf courses and a muzzled press, secretly attractive. Others of more democratic bent are troubled. In a recent essay in the *New York Times*, William Safire warned that "The Singapore virus — the notion that capitalist prosperity can be abetted by political repression — could infect the global economy with its strain of fascism."

In Dharamshala, where democracy and the free press have yet to feel fully welcome, a mutant strain of the Singapore virus has seriously infected our freedom struggle. For instance, in the sixties and seventies Tibetans firmly believed that the whole purpose of having a government-in-exile and keeping together a united exile community was to fight for freedom. The official version of our *raison d'être* as refugees, oft repeated in the speeches of the Dalai Lama and his ministers, was that Tibetans had not left Tibet because of economic hardships but to continue the struggle for Tibetan independence from a more advantageous location.

But last year the Dalai Lama stated in a couple of interviews that since Tibet was economically an underdeveloped country it would be beneficial for it to be part of China and its booming economy. He also added that as Tibet was a landlocked country it would need to be part of China which had access to the sea. It is not the place here to debate His Holiness's views on economics and geo-politics, but it can most certainly be said that his recent utterances have thoroughly confused and demoralised many of his followers.

So we have now sunk to a nadir where Tibetan offices as the International Campaign for Tibet (ICT) no longer call for revocation of MFN for China. Instead its Director, Lodi Gyari, announced some months ago in a New York Chinese language newspaper that though he had formerly been a nationalist, he had now seen the light and was no longer an advocate of Tibetan independence. Nawang Khechog, the Tibetan New Age flautist, also seems to have been affected by this virus, for, before a recital at a public ceremony in New York to commemorate the Tiananmen Massacre, he announced his newfound belief that Tibetans must give up their struggle for independence.

But a few Western supporters of Tibet and a some die-hard Tibetans, are still firmly rooting for freedom: organising trade boycotts and marches to promote the cause of an independent Tibet. Their untiring enthusiasm and idealism, in spite of the enormous contradictions between their position and that of the Dalai Lama's, under whose leadership they are ostensibly operating, is not only cause for admiration, but for someone as cynical as myself, cause for a little bewilderment as well.

Still, one must toast their efforts, even if right at this moment it can only be done with a mug of strong tea.

August 1997
Tibetan Review

Non-Violence or Non-Action?
Some Gandhian Truths
About the Tibetan Peace Movement

IN THE TIRELESS DRIVE of the Dalai Lama and his admirers to promote the Tibetan struggle as a wholly non-violent affair conducted by a race of uniquely spiritual people (who would rather give up their country than commit any act of violence) truth has, unfortunately, become the first of casualties. However pious and arguably necessary, this mission to project Tibetan history and contemporary events through the rose-tinted lens of official pacifist ideology ignores the sacrifice and courage of the many thousands of Tibetan freedom fighters (monks and lamas included) who took up arms for the freedom of their country. But I have commented on this at length, in a couple of previous articles, and it is perhaps unnecessary to go into it again.

I touch on the subject here primarily to bring to the reader's attention some observations on "truth" and "non-violence" by a person eminently qualified to pronounce on them. Mahatma Gandhi believed that the love of truth was a more important human quality than non-violence. He called his methods *satyagraha* or "firmness in truth", and felt that terms like "pacifism" or "non-violence" did not fully convey the essential spirit of his philosophy of action.

Gandhi's ideas on *ahimsa* or non-violence were not simplistic. He acknowledged that the very fact of living involved some *himsa*, destruction of life, be it ever so minute. Gandhi himself served as a stretcher-bearer in the Boer War, the Zulu Rebellion and in the Great War, and later explained his actions: "It was quite clear to me that participation in war could never be consistent with *ahimsa*. But it is not always given to one to be equally clear about one's duty. A votary of truth is often obliged to grope in the dark."

He did not attempt to excuse his personal role in these wars merely because that role was a limited one. "I make no distinction, from the point of *ahimsa*," Gandhi argued, "between combatants and non-combatants. Those who confine themselves to attending to the wounded in battle cannot be absolved from the guilt of war. The question is subtle. It admits of differences of opinion, and therefore I have submitted my argument as clearly as possible to those who believe in *ahimsa* and who are making serious efforts to practise it in every walk of life."

At the beginning of World War II, Gandhi supported a resolution for recruiting Indians into the war effort. He even went around raising recruits himself, though many people were upset by this. "You are a votary of *ahimsa*," some of his followers protested. "How can you ask us to take up arms?"

Gandhi's reply reveals how he considered a person's social responsibility and his duty to his country to sometimes override even a powerful moral conviction as non-violence. He said: "I recognize that in the hour of its danger we must give, as we have decided to give, ungrudging and unequivocal support to the Empire of which we aspire in the near future to be partners in the same sense as the

Dominions overseas ... I would make India offer all her able-bodied sons as a sacrifice to the Empire at its critical moment, and I know that India by this very act, would become the most favoured partner in the Empire, and racial distinctions would become a thing of the past."

One of Gandhi's arguments when recruiting Indians to join the army was not too well received by the British. "Among the many misdeeds of the British rule in India," Gandhi claimed, "history will look upon the act of depriving a whole nation of arms as the blackest. If we want the Arms Act to be repealed, if we want to learn the use of arms, here is a golden opportunity."

When Pakistani raiders invaded Kashmir and began to approach Srinagar — after Kashmir's accession to India on 26 October 1947 — appeals were made to Prime Minister Nehru by leaders of Kashmir, including the Maharajah and the popular Muslim leader, Sheikh Abdullah, but Nehru dithered. Finally, at the insistence of Patel, Nehru ordered military help to proceed. Patel, through a broadcast over All India Radio commandeered all aircraft available in India and started air operations.

A relieved Gandhi told Patel, "At one time I was feeling very miserable and oppressed when I heard this (the Pakistan invasion). But when the Kashmir operation began, I began to feel proud of them, and every aeroplane that goes with materials and arms and ammunition and requirements of the Army, I feel proud." Gandhi justified his view, "Any injustice on our land, any encroachment on our land should be defended by violence, if not by non-violence ... If you can defend by non-violence, by all means do it; that is the first thing I should like. If it is for me to do, I would not touch anything, either a pistol or revolver or anything. But I would not see India degrading itself to be feeling helpless."[1]

---

1. *Sardar Vallabhbhai Patel; India's Iron Man*, B.Krishna, Harper Collins India, 1996.

But whatever exception Gandhi may have considered allowable to nations and individuals in the matter of self defence, he was himself, of course, a committed and unwavering adherent of *ahimsa*. He died by an assassin's bullet because he considered having a bodyguard as condoning violence for one's personal safety. The point I am trying to make here is that though Gandhi was himself unwaveringly committed to his non-violent ideology he did not allow it to blind him to reality, nor lead him into dishonesty in its propagation. He did not hesitate to state that recourse to violence was not something that could be entirely avoided in the course of human affairs.

Whether one admires Gandhi for his non-violence, his spirituality, or his love of truth and courage (the last two qualities are what I find most appealing about the man), I do not think there can be any argument that Tibetans and friends can learn much from his life and mission for our own struggle. In Tibetan exile society, routine and somewhat ritual accolade is paid to Gandhi by leaders and politicians but little serious effort is expended in studying his works, which is a real pity. However one may disagree with some of Gandhi's ideas (I have problems with his views on celibacy and his obsession with his bowels), the clarity and honesty of his thinking are what shines through in all his books and articles.

Tibetan ideas on non-violence are, by comparison, confused, naive, and in certain cases seem to derive from magical beliefs inherent in traditional Tibetan thinking. For instance, the speaker of the Tibetan People's Assembly, Samdhong Rinpoche, who has come out with his own version of Gandhi's *satyagraha* doctrine (but which Rinpoche has translated somewhat awkwardly as "Truth Insistence"), once made the somewhat fantastic pronouncement that if fifty per cent of the Tibetan people were able to comprehend Rinpoche's doctrine of "Truth Insistence", the Chinese would be compelled to leave Tibet in less than three months. The Dalai Lama does not make as extravagant a claim for the efficacy of his Middle Way doctrine. Both views, however, reflect their roots in traditional metaphysical thinking and clearly reveal an imperfect understanding of the politics of nation states and the Darwinian reality of our modern world. Gandhi, with his legal training in London, his subsequent practice and activism in South Africa, and his reading of Western thinkers of his time, certainly seems to have had a better grasp of the realities of his day. As such, he was capable of developing a non-violent strategy that, whatever its shortcomings as viewed by some Indian intellectuals today, was able to achieve its main task of freeing India of British rule.

Though Gandhi tried to represent himself as the product of his own ancient culture — even in externals with his loin-cloth, bamboo staff and wooden slippers — his political and social thinking owed more to nineteenth century European liberalism than to anything indigenous or traditional. His faith in non-violence was by no means typical of Hinduism. By his own admission, Gandhi's pacifism was inspired primarily by the "Sermon on the Mount" and Tolstoy. His championing of women's rights and his antipathy to caste are also certainly derived from contemporary Western thinking. Even his first deep insight into Buddhism seems to have come from reading Edwin Arnold's *Light of Asia*.

In South Africa, Gandhi used British methods of political agitation: writing letters to the newspapers, leading a petition drive, founding a political organisation with membership drives, carefully-kept accounts, a small library, and regular meetings for lectures, debates and group decisions. He also wrote two pamphlets.

Three thinkers of his time impressed Gandhi profoundly. His ideas on civil disobedience and non-cooperation came from Thoreau. His belief in pacifism, as mentioned earlier, came in part from

Tolstoy — especially Tolstoy's book, *The Kingdom of God is Within You*. Gandhi's social philosophy was certainly inspired by Ruskin's *Unto This Last*. Gandhi was tremendously impressed by this book. He read it on a train journey from Johannesburg to Durban in one sitting, not getting any sleep that night, and became determined to change his life accordingly. "Of these books, the one that brought about an instantaneous and practical transformation in my life was *Unto This Last*. I translated it later into Gujurati, entitling it *Sarvodaya* (*The Welfare of All*)."

In the course of human history other "votaries of truth", besides Gandhi, have, at some time or the other in their lives, probably had to "grope in the dark" when attempting to reconcile duty to nation and people with love of peace. Not all great leaders, of course, made the Gandhian choice, yet do we regard them as any lesser than the Mahatma in moral stature?

The closest thing American democracy has to a saint is Abraham Lincoln. He presided over the most bloody war in American history. That he fought the war for democracy, to preserve the Union and to end slavery, does not easily cancel out the terrible price paid by the American people for Lincoln's refusal to accept a separate Confederate nation. We must also bear in mind that Lincoln was not tricked or bulldozed into the war by politicians and aggressive generals around him. In fact, during the first years of the war, Lincoln had considerable difficulty trying to get his overcautious generals to pit the Union army in any serious battle against Confederate forces.

Joan of Arc would, by pacifist lights, no doubt be regarded as a violent woman. Before her arrival on the scene the conflict between the French and the English was, to borrow from American military parlance, "a low intensity conflict", primarily because of French disunity and the weakness of their king, Charles VI. Joan's leadership and inspiration escalated the violence dramatically, but it also eventually freed France from the English yoke.

Certainly, peace is preferable to war, and non-violence to violence. Only someone with serious mental or moral shortcomings would dispute the general rightness, even righteousness, of the proposition. But people and nations are sometimes confronted with problems where violent action seems to be not only the sole possible solution but the heroic and wise one as well. Was the illusory peace that Chamberlain and Daladier bartered from Hitler at Munich worth the price of betraying Czechoslovakia? On the other hand, were President Roosevelt's efforts to push a reluctant America into World War II the evil machinations of a Jew-loving warmonger, as the German propaganda ministry might have put it, or an act that probably saved mankind from Nazi domination?

Or closer home, was it wrong for the people of Lhasa to rise up in armed rebellion to protect the life of the Dalai Lama? Was it wrong of the Dalai Lama to use the armed escort of resistance fighters to escape from Lhasa? What would have happened had he remained? He might have been killed in the fighting, or suffered imprisonment, torture and public humiliation like the Panchen Lama. In the opinion of the Dalai Lama's youngest brother, Tendzin Choegyal, had the Dalai Lama remained in Tibet "they (the Chinese) would have used His Holiness just as the Japanese used poor Pu Yi (the last Manchu emperor). That's what he would have become, another Pu Yi."[2]

So, in a sense, the Dalai Lama owes his freedom, his present international stature and maybe even his Nobel Peace Prize to violent men who rescued him not only from physical danger but from a situation that was politically and morally compromising. They also

---

2. *Kundun*, Mary Craig, Harper Collins, London, 1997.

freed him from a relationship with the Communist Chinese that was not only hopeless but unhealthy as well.

This article does not seek to advocate that Tibetans take up arms here and now, but to point out to our leaders and friends that the complexities of human affairs call for a more eclectic and robust approach to the Tibetan problem than the current pacifist inertia. Even if, let us say, we eventually adopt a non-violent strategy by consensus, this decision should come about through study, discussion and appreciation of realities, not merely as an article of mystical faith nor because it is being applauded by celebrities and world leaders for whom peace, trade with China, and maintenance of the status quo, is definitely more important than Tibetan freedom.

But getting back to Gandhi. When all's said and done, the Mahatma's brand of non-violence towers above ours because his was a doctrine of sacrifice, courage and above all, action; qualities, which in the Tibetan non-violent movement are conspicuous only by their absence — unless one counts the heroic courage of some lone activist inside Tibet. Otherwise, in the rank and leadership of the movement in exile, non-violent activism seems to have become entirely an affair of celebrities, rock concerts, Hollywood movies, conferences, careers and conveniences. The ultimate convenience being the giving up of our main goal of independence in order to save "Tibetan Buddhist culture" — a euphemism, if I have ever heard one, for the power of the theocracy.

We should also remember that Gandhi led by example. The genuine simplicity of the Mahatma's lifestyle (Sarojini Naidu's crack about the cost of supporting the Mahatma's poverty is more witty than substantial), his readiness to face police batons, endure imprisonment, even face death for his convictions were doubtless more inspirational to his followers than just teachings and initiations.

Such fearlessness and integrity is, to be brutally frank, non-existent in our leadership circles.

But the Tibetan "Truth Insistence" movement seems to have discovered a substitute. In a document I have received, which seems to be a manifesto of the movement, Samdhong Rinpoche expresses the conviction of being able to instil the requisite qualities of courage, endurance, forbearance and compassion in his followers through the wonderfully vague yet impressive sounding method of "philosophical understanding". If I know anything about how things are done in Dharamshala we are definitely in for more nebulous, "feel-good" conferences (with silk-lined folders and expensive colour souvenir magazines for delegates), seminars and workshops, all of which will probably be underwritten by some well-meaning foreign foundation with more enthusiasm and money than awareness of the real and frightening dangers assailing Tibetan society.

Inside Tibet courageous souls still defy Chinese might with courage worthy of Gandhi. Still the question must be asked whether any of those brave activists are, in any true sense, non-violent activists. In conversations with a number of new arrivals in Dharamshala, I received the definite impression that nearly all of the demonstrators and activists in Tibet adopted non-violent methods (up to a point, they threw stones and burnt down a police station) because they were not in a position to do anything else; and that if the time came where violent insurrection were possible against the Chinese they would welcome it. Orville Schell, who secretly interviewed a number of activists inside Tibet for the Frontline film *Red Flag Over Tibet*, told me that an important Tibetan Lama he interviewed had said that the only way to stop the Chinese was through violence.

And this is beginning to happen, albeit in a modest way. Judging by the few bombs that went off in Tibet in recent years, some stubborn Tibetans definitely seem to lack appreciation of our official non-violent philosophy. If Gandhi were still around, one might suppose that he would, as a matter of course, condemn our bombers and applaud the exile peace movement. But I am not sure. In the 11 August 1920 issue of *Young India* he wrote:

> I do believe that where there is only a choice between cowardice and violence, I could advise violence. I would rather have India resort to arms than she should become a helpless witness to her own dishonour.

*

(I had earlier ended the article here but a friend, after reading the draft, suggested I include the opinion of another "great soul" in this discussion. The Thirteenth Dalai Lama, in the conclusion of his Political Testament, did not mince words on the question of defending Tibetan sovereignty against Chinese aggression: "We should make every effort to safeguard ourselves against this impending disaster. Use peaceful means where they are appropriate; but where they are not appropriate, do not hesitate to resort to more forceful means.")

September 1997
Tibetan Review

Dances with Yaks
Tibet in Film, Fiction and Fantasy of the West[1]

JEAN JACQUES ANNAUD'S *Seven Years in Tibet* may not have met with much critical acclaim, but its makers can console themselves that they have come up with the first feature film where, I am given to understand (for I have not seen it yet), Tibet is represented as a real place. And that is, at least from the Tibetan point of view, a definite improvement on things. In all previous films having to do with Tibet, like the classic *Lost Horizon* (1937), the dreadful musical remake (1973), *Storm Over Tibet* (1952), Hammer film's *Abominable Snowman of the Himalayas* (1957), and *The Golden Child* (1986), Tibet or the Tibet-like settings are straightforward fantasy lands, like Oz or Tatooine.

Jokey asides and references to Tibet occur now and then in other films, mostly comedies, and are, of course, as expected, unvaryingly

---

1. Based on the the Inaugural Lecture of the Modern Tibetan Studies Forum at Harvard, given on 8 October 1997. The concluding observations on the film, *Seven Years in Tibet*, are a subsequent addition.

clichéd. Tibet is either a kind of ultimate spiritual hideaway, as in *The Millionairess* (1960), *The Razor's Edge* (1984) and *Ace Ventura: When Nature Calls* (1995), or a repository of magical power as in *The Road to Hongkong* (1962) and *The Shadow* (1994).

This "magic and mystery" stereotype of Tibet had, of course, an earlier, though still peripheral, manifestation in popular Western literature. George Orwell in an essay discussing the books of his childhood, mentions "*Dr. Nikola*, Guy Boothby's exciting Tibetan thrillers". He unfortunately tells us nothing further except that a real visit to Central Asia or Tibet would in comparison probably be a letdown.

One of the best known references to Tibet (or more specifically to a Tibetan) in Victorian literature is in Rudyard Kipling's *Kim*. The innocent, kindly yet wise Teshoo Lama, Kim's benefactor and companion both on the Grand Trunk road and the road of life is probably Kipling's most generous and enlightened depiction of an Asian. *Kim* is also his richest and most mature work. Nirad Chaudhiri, the controversial Indian writer and ultimate autodidact, considered *Kim*, *pace* Edward Said, to be the best novel about British India.

Sir Arthur Conan Doyle, an ardent spiritualist, could not, of course, resist the spell of Tibet. In 1894 when he wanted to revive the Sherlock Holmes series for *The Strand Magazine* — he had killed off the great detective two years earlier — he has Holmes explain to an astounded Dr. Watson what had happened during the intervening period: "I travelled for two years in Tibet, therefore and amused myself by visiting Lhassa, and spending some days with the head Lama. You may have read of the remarkable explorations of a Norwegian named Sigerson, but I am sure that it never occurred to you that you were receiving news of your friend."

Tibet is also the setting for a little-known sequel to one of H. Rider Haggard's most well-known works, *She*. Once an immensely popular writer, Rider Haggard has, unlike Conan Doyle or Kipling, completely fallen out of favour with modern readers. He is though, still highly regarded in Russia and China. "She" or Ayesha, whom her native subjects somewhat resignedly address as "She Who Must be Obeyed" is the ruler/divinity of a lost civilisation in Africa. She is not only bewitchingly beautiful but has been kept young throughout five centuries by regular dips in the "Fire of Life". For the sake of her English explorer lover she overdoes the "Fire of Life" immersions and perishes. In the sequel *Ayesha, The Return of She*, which I mentioned earlier, Rider Haggard resurrects this Jungian *anima* figure at a monastery in Tibet where she is, once more, worshipped by benighted natives — this time Tibetans.

This fascination in the West for a land of magic and mystery in the heart of Asia may have its origins in medieval European legends of a lost Christian kingdom somewhere beyond Europe and the Islamic world, ruled by the mysterious priest-king Prester John. The significant presence of Nestorian Christians in China and Central Asia (possibly even Tibet) during the Middle Ages certainly contributed to this legend. This heretical Christian sect was quite successful in these distant lands, converting the Kerait Mongols and possibly some other tribes to Christianity. In the mid-twelfth century a papal ambassador was sent by Alexander III to Prester John. It vanished without a trace.

Aside from the Nestorian connection, this story of a Christian kingdom in High Asia could have arisen from some external similarities between Tibetan Buddhist church rituals and Roman Catholic ones: for instance in the burning of incense (especially in hand-held, chain-suspended censors favoured by both churches), the confessional, liturgical music, the sprinkling of holy water and even in something as humble as the blessing of fields by village priests. But the most obvious of resemblances between the two churches are, of course, in their respective monastic systems and in the institutions of their priest-kings, the dalai lamas and the popes.

An early Jesuit traveller to Tibet, Ippolito Desideri, though certainly opposed to Buddhism in the doctrinal sense, wrote positively about the Tibetan church and indeed quite admiringly of the morality, piety and faith of the Tibetan people. In contrast, the works of pioneering British experts on "Lamaism", like L. A. Waddell, are undisguisedly hostile. It is a sneaking suspicion of mine that these points of correspondence to Catholicism, rather than the outright "pagan" aspects of Tibetan Buddhism are what might have provoked this subliminal Calvinistic (or C of E) type of reaction. Simplistic, constipated and arrogant Victorian notions of "reason and progress" (fairly similar to Communist Chinese views) probably also contributed to this hostility.

This bring us to the fact that the Tibetan stereotype has not been static, and sometimes varied depending on the political climate. Around the time of the Younghusband expedition (1904), British accounts of Tibet play up the general backwardness of the country, the dirt, the ignorance of the peasantry and the fanaticism of the monks, at the expense of the usual romance, adventure and mystery. To an extent it resembles Communist Chinese propaganda, and propaganda is what it was: a contrived moral justification for the armed invasion of a peaceful neighbouring country. Once Tibetans had properly acceded to imperial supremacy though, reportage on Tibet in the West, especially in Britain, seems to take on a more congenial tone. This, of course, also had to do with the relative increase in information on Tibet and the writings of sympathetic political officers as Sir Charles Bell. But the fantastic, magical elements never quite disappeared.

The negative stereotype of Tibet re-emerged in the West in the sixties and seventies when the intellectual climate was one of near unquestioning admiration for Communist China and Maoism.

That Tibet held a place in the imagination of the Victorian public seems to be indicated in a passage from H. G. Wells *The History of Mr. Polly*. Alfred Polly is the archetypal English "Everyman" of his period: lower middle class, in trade, respectable and repressed. Polly escapes the mediocrity and frustrations of his petit bourgeois life by reading, a favourite book of his being the second volume of the travels of Abbé Huc and Gabet to China and Tibet:

> He followed those two sweet souls from their lessons in Thibetan under Sandura the Bearded (who called them donkeys, to their infinite benefit, and stole their store of butter) through a hundred misadventures to the very heart of Lhasa, and it was a thirst in him that was never quenched to find the other volume...

Abbé Huc's account of the remarkable journey he made with his superior Father Gabet from 1844 to 1846, across the border regions of the Chinese Empire up to Tibet, which was published in 1850 under the title *Souvenirs d'un voyage dans la Tartarie et le Thibet*, enjoyed an enormous success both with general readers and among literary circles in France. Simon Leys tells us that half a century later Leon Bloy noted in his journal that reading Huc remained for him "a supreme resource" whenever he felt that he was "dying of boredom". Fifty years earlier, his old master Barbey d'Aurevilly had been one of the enthusiastic critics who applauded the first publication of the book. Readers ignored the informative — and hence, factual — side of the book, to focus upon its extraordinary aspects. His amazing stories were taken for pure products of imagination. The book was given to children to read in the same fashion as they were given Jules Verne's novels. An English translation by William Hazlitt, *Travels in Tartary, Thibet and China*, was published in 1851.

This Gallic fascination for Tibet gained further impetus early this century with the writings of Madame Alexandra David-Neel who, like Huc, had somehow actually managed to make the incredible journey to Lhasa. Her accounts were also, like the good Abbé's, not lacking in the marvellous and the bizarre. The influence of such works could probably account for the slightly odd turn in the conversation that the Mexican poet Octavio Paz had with the mad surrealist poet Antonin Artaud when they first met in 1947 at Saint-Germain des Pres. Paz tells us that Artaud bemoaned the ruining of Tibet by progress and industrialisation. Later in the evening Artaud "went on talking excitedly about Tibet".

But *the* book that truly ensured Tibet's magical image for all time was *Lost Horizon* by James Hilton. Published during the period between the two World Wars, it appears then to have had a fairly profound impact on a generation that had gone through a war unprecedented for the scale of human slaughter. In the immediate post-war period, many in Britain and Europe turned for solace to beliefs like Theosophy and spiritualism. *Lost Horizon*, the book, and subsequently the film, also appeared when the first warning rumblings of World War II were beginning to be heard, and so probably contributed to its millenarian atmosphere.

And the name "Shangri-La" has found a place in the English language as a catchword for a secret haven of peace and spirituality lost to mankind. Camp David, the country retreat of the presidents of the United States was initially named "Shangri-La" by FDR himself.

This fascination for Tibet in the West is not without a sinister obverse. The Nazis were intrigued by the theory of Tibet being the possible site of the original Aryan homeland, and even by the somewhat odd notion that the Tibetans themselves were a lost Aryan tribe. Heinrich Himmler dispatched an expedition (largely sponsored by the SS) to Tibet in 1939 under Captain Shafer, ostensibly as a scientific expedition, but with secret instructions to locate the Aryan homeland.

Getting back to the matter of Tibet in popular literature; since the publication of *Lost Horizon* the Shangri-La image of Tibet has been revived, fairly regularly, in other novels and stories, one of the best being the Rose of Tibet by Lionel Richardson, and in less successful efforts as Derek Lambert's *The Kites of War*, and Gil Zeff's Tibet.[2]

One of the most original and unusual works of fiction on Tibet is a collection of short stories by Pierre de la Terre, entitled *Tales of the Dalai Lama*. Arthur C. Clarke's "The Nine Million Names of God", the story of a computer programmer making a disturbing discovery in a Tibetan monastery, is an eerie science fiction yarn with a *Twilight Zone* twist at the end.

Most comic books dealing with Tibet seem to be published either in France, Belgium or the Netherlands, and somewhat removed from my rather limited Anglophone purview. The few I have seen, though, appear to be of high quality. Of course everyone has enjoyed Herge's *Tintin in Tibet*, but I am informed that a French series, *The Adventures of Jonathan*[3] is also excellent. The one English comic book on Tibet that I know of, *The Black Pearl*, is a "ripping" good read. It is a well-researched and tight action story of Khampa

---

2. Other fictional works on Tibet more recently encountered: *The Rainbow Annals* by Grania Davis and *The Flame and the Fury* by John Brennand, both lent to me by my friend Tashi Tsering. *Om: The Secret of Ahbor Valley* by Talbot Mundy was discovered at the Strand in New York. An Indian writer, R. P. Bambi (who also taught at the Tibetan Refugee School at Dalhousie) is the author of two novels, *The Crusaders of Tibet* and *The Bombers of Kyithang*. The former seems to have been the inspiration for a similar novel, *Lama* by Frederick Hyde Chambers.

3. Some months after the publication of this essay in the *Tibetan Review*, I received a set of these delightful comic books (signed by the author) from M. Hubert Declear of Kathmandu.

guerillas in Mustang taking on the Red army, aided by the female James Bond of the sixties, Modesty Blaise.

The most consistently popular writer on Tibet is probably Lobsang Rampa, actually an English plumber, Cyril Hoskins. Though his many works: *The Third Eye, Doctor from Lhasa, The Cave of the Ancients, Living with the Lama*, etc., belong, properly, in the category of fiction (Hoskins claimed they were based on recollections of his previous existence in Tibet) — they were regarded, till fairly recently, by quite a few in the West as the authentic testimonies of a Tibetan spiritual master.

One would presume that these days with the opening up of Tibet to tourism, and the Dalai Lama himself being completely accessible to Westerners — what with his many visits and lectures in the West — that the "rampaesque" fantasies of Tibet would have been replaced by a more down-to-earth appreciation of the country and its problems. But an examination of the many new travel books on Tibet and the numerous New Age-type works on Tibetan religion and "culture" (invariably with an introduction by the Dalai Lama himself), leaves one with the uncomfortable feeling that nothing substantial has changed in the West's perception of Tibet since the days when books such as *The Third Eye* and *Lost Horizon* constituted the bulk of available literature on Tibet.

One indicator of this seems to be the quality of the attention and sympathy Tibetans receive internationally, which is at present considerable. But somehow it all never quite translates into hard political support for the Tibetan cause. Often it seems that the very reason Tibet attracts so many people in the first place is what makes this attention so inconsequential.

Tibet's appeal to the West stems primarily from some variation or the other of the "Shangri-La" story — of the hidden kingdom of ancient learning and lost wisdom, deep in the heart of Asia, and it is the powerful mythic elements in this perspective that seem to interject a dreamlike quality into Western awareness of the Tibetan situation, making it appear less immediate, real or consequential than other conflicts and crises around the globe. The discomforting realisation of China's immense size and power — especially economic power — could also be an unconscious factor in the reluctance of many to see Tibet in its reality.

The Shangri-La fantasy has, of course, primarily to do with the emotional needs of certain people in the West. It should therefore come as no surprise that in nearly all works of imagination about Tibet, the country and people come across merely as the *mise en scène* for the personal drama of white people. In Hilton's *Lost Horizon*, the protagonist, Conway, is English. The head Lama is European, as are most of the top brass of Shangri-La. The Tibetans are essentially superstitious peasants and labourers, hewers of wood and drawers of water — coolies — for the white elite of Shangri-La. The intermediary between the white elite and the native Tibetans is, appropriately enough, a Chinese, who acts as the major-domo of the Shangri-La Monastery.

Tibetans by and large do not seem to consider such condescending characterisations of their country and culture objectionable. In fact, although they may not be accurate or altogether flattering, these depictions of Tibet are considered good publicity for the Tibetan cause. In a limited sense they are, but in every such representation, where Tibetans or their land and culture serve only as a background or foil to the more important business of the white protagonist, there is an inherent and the underlying premise that Tibet is only relevant if it serves the purposes or needs of the West.

Conrad's novel *Heart of Darkness* can be read as an attack on Belgian colonial exploitation and subjugation of the Congo. Yet Chinua Achebe, the distinguished Nigerian novelist, assailed *Heart of Darkness* as racist. In *Culture and Imperialism*, Edward Said tells us that Achebe believes that *Heart of Darkness* is an example of the Western habit of setting up Africa "as a foil to Europe, a place of negations … in comparison with which Europe's own state of spiritual grace will be manifest". Conrad, obsessed with the black skin of Africans, had as his real purpose the desire to comfort Europeans in their sense of superiority. *Heart of Darkness* projects the image of Africa as "the other world", the antithesis of Europe and therefore of civilization, a place where man's vaunted intelligence and refinement are finally mocked by triumphant bestiality.

Tibet is seen as the "antithesis" of the West not so much in the sense of a "darker" civilization, but rather in the matter of corporeality. The West, whatever its failings is real. Tibet, however wonderful is a dream; whether of a long-lost golden age or millenarian fantasy, still merely a dream.

It is this dream-like "Shangri-La" quality of Tibet, most observed in the medieval flavour of its society and culture, and in its strange esoteric religion, which Westerners find most attractive. From tourists to academics this is the feature of Tibet which is focused on, to the exclusion of other aspects of Tibetan life or culture, no matter how important they may be to the Tibetans themselves.

One of the best examples of this can be seen in the works of Galen Rowell. Photograph after splendid photograph — hundreds of them — in calendars, posters and coffee-table books extol the out-of-the-world beauty of Tibet and the innocence and spirituality of its happy people. Practically no allusion is made to the holocaust Tibet has undergone and the foreign oppression and servitude its unhappy people endure even now.

The desire to maintain the cultural purity of such Shangri-La societies as Tibet and Ladakh, or certain Amazon Indian tribes, seems to imply cocooning them from the realities of the outside world, especially from technology, commerce and even politics. Development for such societies is only deemed appropriate when it is non-military, non-industrial, and environmentally friendly. Such considerations are probably well meant and sincere, but they very often ignore that society's own changing history, its role, however humble, in geo-political strategies, and even the desires of the people of that society who may be seeking change, for whatever reasons of their own.

For instance, in a controversial article[4] the anthropologist Melvyn Goldstein advocated his solution to the Tibetan question, whereby the Chinese would retain political, military and economic control over Tibet, but would allow Tibetans to exist within "cultural reservations". It is difficult to see anyone seriously advocating such a solution to the Palestinian question, or the problems in Northern Ireland or Bosnia, or anywhere else in the real world for that matter, and not being dismissed outright as an arrogant, condescending advocate of old fashioned imperialism.

When Claude Lévi-Strauss said that "anthropology was the handmaiden of colonialism", he was probably not looking as far ahead to the kind of "New Age" colonialism that the few surviving ancient or primitive cultures left in this world have to put up with, but the connection he postulated to anthropology still seems to hold good.

Helena Norberg-Hodge, in her book *Ancient Futures*, celebrates the traditional Ladakhi way of life and excoriates the tourism and development that she feels is destroying the ecological balance and social harmony of this "Little Tibet". What such advocacy conveniently ignores is the harsh geo-political climate in which such an

---

4. "The Dragon and the Snowlion: The Tibetan Question in the Twentieth Century", *China Briefing*, 1990, New York, Asia Society, 1990. Reprinted in *Tibetan Review*, March 1991.

essentially frail society exists. In this case, it is not so much the strength of the traditional Ladakhi culture but rather the Indian army, the progressive political system of the Indian Republic, and probably even exposure to Western tourism, which have allowed Ladakh to retain its identity and a considerable part of its old way of life. Just across the border, inside Tibet, a culture unprotected by a modern army and antagonistic to change and progress, has suffered near extinction.

Calling on people in underdeveloped societies to live passive, traditional and ecologically correct lifestyles — and not emulate the wasteful lifestyles of people in Western consumer societies — is no doubt laudable, but somehow does not sit too well coming from someone who most probably owns an SUV or has running hot and cold water in his or her home.

Slavenka Drakulic, the East European feminist writer, in her book *How We Survived Communism and Even Laughed*, describes her reaction to Fidel Castro's statement on TV saying that he would not let every Cuban have a car on ecological grounds. "As Castro uttered that sentence, I shivered with cold. At that very moment I detected for the first time in his words a frightening totalitarian idea in ecology. He was asking his people to give up a better standard of living, even before they had tasted it, in order to save the planet, to renounce in advance something that was glorified as the idea of progress. It seemed to me that asking for post-consumer ecological consciousness in a poor, pre-consumer society was nothing but the act of the totalitarian mind."

Though the "Shangri-La" stereotype is a Western creation, Tibetans, especially the refugees, are gradually succumbing to a similar fantasy idea of their lost country. This shift in perspective is somewhat self-conscious in those aware of its strong selling-point in the West, but in ordinary refugee society the change is more subtle, as life in exile takes on the routines of permanence and the collective goal of returning to Tibet becomes an increasingly distant dream.

The promotion of the image of pre-'59 Tibet as the land of peace, harmony and spirituality is one of the main tasks of the Tibetan leadership in exile. Among other things, this endeavour has unfortunately required a certain amount of rewriting of Tibetan history, especially modern history. One such revision is in the playing down of the role of the armed uprising against the Chinese since 1956 and the fostering of the fiction that the popular resistance against the Chinese was non-violent and led, Gandhian-style, by the Dalai Lama.

The Western viewpoint before which the Tibetan leadership strives to maintain a positive image, is essentially a New Age one, and many policy decisions made by the Tibetan government-in-exile in the last decade reflect this. The national struggle for an independent Tibet has been replaced by a squishy agenda of environmental, pacifistic, spiritual, and "universal" concerns that have little or nothing to do with Tibet's real problems. The Dalai Lama's recent statements that Tibetan independence was not as important as the task of preserving Tibetan Buddhist culture reflects, in a sense, not just His Holiness' frustration at Beijing's intransigence on the Tibetan issue but the influence of his Western followers for whom the problems of Tibet, the nation of the Tibetans, is nowhere as relevant or important as that of Tibet, the repository of a secret wisdom to save a materialistic and self-destructive West.

The propagation of the Shangri-La myth of Tibet, whether by the West or by the Tibetans themselves, has not gone entirely unquestioned nor unchallenged. Tsering Shakya in "The Myth of Shangri-La", *Lungta* (special issue on Tibetan writers), and Donald S. Lopez Jr. in "New Age Orientalism: The Case of Tibet",

Tricycle: The Buddhist Review, Spring 1994, provide an impressive study of the myth and its negative effect on the understanding of the real country and its problems.

In two lectures, "Orientalism and the Dalai Lamas" and "Ethno-Nationalism and the Tibetan Issue" which he gave at the Amnye Machen Institute on 13 October 1994 and 31 January 1995 respectively, Professor Elliot Sperling introduced a historical and diametric perspective to the accepted view of the institution of the dalai lamas and the Tibetan Buddhist church (and doctrine) as being inherently pacifistic. Last May an international symposium, "Mythos Tibet", was organised by the University of Bonn, where a good beginning was made in deconstructing the Shangri-La fantasy. This article (and the Harvard lecture) grew out of my own modest contribution to the proceedings of the conference.

At the conclusion of his article Donald Lopez contends that for Westerners to indulge in the Shangri-La fantasy of Tibet is "to deny Tibet its history, to exclude Tibet from a real word of which it has always been a part, and to deny Tibetans their role as agents participating in the creation of a contested quotidian reality."

However hopeless their cause, or marginal their survival at present, Tibetans must live their own reality and resist being lured into ethereal and marginal (though often financially profitable) roles for the fantasies of the West.

*

At the beginning of this article I mentioned that *Seven Years in Tibet* was the first feature film where Tibet was represented as a real place. Having finally seen the film, I must say that, though certainly well intentioned, the movie continues to perpetuate the fantasy stereotype of Tibet, and in fact adds some new features to the myth. *Seven Years in Tibet* is not a good film, but it is doing fairly well at the box office, probably because of the general sympathy for Tibetans in the West. In an otherwise caustic review (*The New Yorker*, 17 December 1990), Pauline Kael tells us why a similar film, *Dances with Wolves*, did so well with the American public: "They (Kevin Costner and associates) are trying to show the last years of the Sioux as an independent nation from the Sioux point of view. And it's that sympathy for the Indians that (I think) the audience is responding to."

My main objection to *Seven Years in Tibet* was that, unlike the book, it reduces Tibet to mere background for the personal drama of a white man. I don't think it would be unfair to say that the Heinrich Harrer character in the film spends most of his seven years in Tibet in ostentatious soul-searching and grief for the son he has abandoned in Austria. The sense of wonder and high adventure that the book conveyed is sacrificed to this overwrought and essentially unconvincing melodrama.

Nearly every Tibetan in the film seems to be a potential Dharma teacher with such cringe-making lines as "you Westerners prize achievement, we in Tibet value harmony". The young Dalai Lama does it, of course, but when aristocrats, tailors and what-not pitch in with their own pseudo-spiritual observations it is a painful experience. Probably the most ridiculous scene in the film (for Tibetan viewers at least) was the one of Tibetan labourers and monks frantically rescuing earthworms from a building site, and the entire Namgyal Monastery performing *pujas* for the worms' spiritual benefit. ("In past life, this innocent worm your mother, your father. Please no more hurting!")

To underscore the pacifistic nature of the Tibetans, the Tibetan army is depicted as a motley bunch dressed in a variety of ragged chubas and cast-off uniforms, topped with the occasional British army surplus helmet. The Tibetan army was, admittedly, not as powerful and impressive an institution as the church, but the soldiers wore proper uniforms and were equipped with standard issue Lee Enfield rifles. In fact, this modern army created by the Thirteenth Dalai Lama had roundly defeated an invading Chinese army in 1918. In the movie some Tibetan soldiers are even shown using bows and arrows against the Chinese invasion force!

Aside from the initial violence of the invasion, the Chinese in the film are represented as being neither particularly oppressive nor threatening. Harrer wanders around Chinese-occupied Lhasa even more freely than a present-day tourist. When he roughs up the collaborator Ngabo Ngawang Jigme, Ngabo's Chinese guards make no attempt to stop him. In reality, Harrer had wisely left Tibet before the Communist forces had arrived. Westerners who hadn't, like Robert Ford and Geoffrey Bull, were immediately arrested, accused of being imperialist spies, and subjected to severe "struggle" and "brainwashing". They were also given stiff prison sentences. Those were the early years of the Cold War and the Korean War, when Red China was viewed with fear and hostility in the West. Nothing of this atmosphere is conveyed in the film.

It would be foolish, probably even unfair, to expect historical accuracy in a Hollywood movie, but if the film makers were going to reinterpret events and show Harrer in Tibet after the Communist invasion, why not then use the opportunity to communicate to the audience the uniquely inhuman qualities of Chinese Communist oppression: the denunciations, public struggles, executions, etc., and maybe also the Tibetan Resistance.

For instance, in real life Harrer's friend Tsarong took part in the Lhasa Uprising. After the Uprising was crushed, Tsarong was imprisoned and died in prison the night before he was to be publicly humiliated. In the film he is shown leaving Lhasa with his furniture and household goods perched precariously on the back of yaks and mules. Admittedly, mention is made of Chinese atrocities, but only at the end of the film in a scrolled message just before the credits.

Jean Renoir once told Satyajit Ray, "You don't have to show many things in a film, but you have to be very careful to show only the right things". The makers of *Seven Years* have, in the main, been unable to do this, but in some things like the impressive replication of old Lhasa in the Andes, and the costumes, they have succeeded fairly well. The casting of the Bhutanese boy Jamyang Wangchuk as the young Dalai Lama is inspired. The young actor's natural charm and spontaneity make even his awful dialogue lines not too unbearable.

I have been told that, in a typically misguided display of devotion to the Dalai Lama, Tibetan actors and extras on location in Argentina protested about the casting of a Bhutanese national as His Holiness. I hope this account is not true but if it is, someone there should have told the protesters that this perceived act of *lèse majesté* pales to insignificance when we look back in Tibetan history and learn to our horror that a Mongol and a Monpa child were selected as actual dalai lamas — the fourth and the sixth respectively.

January 1998
Tibetan Review

Scholar and Patriot
Tethong Sonam Tomjor (1924–1997)

TETHONG SONAM TOMJOR WANGCHUK was that rarity in the Tibetan world: a traditional scholar and a genuine modernist. Well-versed in Tibetan history, religion and medicine, he was a gifted classical Chinese scholar and widely read in Western history and literature. He died on 18 October 1997 at Dharamshala. He was seventy-three. He never held high office and published little or nothing, but for those who knew him intimately, the opportunity to listen to his numerous discourses and stories were uplifting and enlightening experiences in the poverty, isolation and intellectual bleakness of Dharamshala in the sixties and seventies.

Sonam Tomjor was an informed and entertaining raconteur. He would hold forth on such far-ranging topics as the calligraphy of Tang Taitsung, the possibility of the great Chinese poet Li Po (Li Bai) being the illegitimate son of a minor Tibetan embassy official in Changan, Ataturk's modernisation of Turkey, the influence of Fabian Socialism on Churchill's social policies, and Tibetan oracles and protective deities, about which he had a fund of strange and often irreverently funny stories.

In his discussions on Tibetan history he always had the telling anecdote that gave life and immediacy to his words. I am sure that even those not intellectually inclined will remember him for his fund of ghost stories. Quite a few of these were from the great Chinese collection of supernatural tales, *Liao Tai Chi Yi*, but most were original Tibetan stories of ghosts, witches and oracles that, unfortunately, no one then thought of recording.

Sonam Tomjor was born in 1924 in Lhasa to Tethong Gyurme Gyatso and Dolma Tsering (*née* Rong Dikiling). When he was just a year old he was taken to Kham where his father, who was governor of Derge (later governor general of Eastern Tibet) was campaigning against the Chinese. His early education was at the hands of his parents and family retainers. His more formal studies were under Lama Gelek, the abbot of a monastery in Derge. He also started to learn Chinese then.

Returning to Lhasa at the age of eight, Sonam Tomjor was enrolled at the small Yukhang School. Simultaneously, he began to take English lessons at an informal school set up by Babu Gompo-la of Sikkim. He resumed his Chinese studies under the tutelage of Lao Si-la (?), the son of a former Manchu official in Lhasa, who also tutored other aristocrat children. Later, he received weekly English lessons from Hugh Richardson, the British representative in Lhasa. Two Mongols, Sogpo Geshe Gongarkyap and Horkhang Geshe Chodrak, instructed him in Buddhist philosophy.

Sonam Tomjor joined government service at the age of sixteen, but continued his scholarly pursuits, in the main, with his close friend Gendun Choephel, the Amdowa scholar who was the principal intellectual influence on his life. Sonam Tomjor later served as a major (*rupon*) in the Guards regiment.

In 1949 he obtained a transfer to the staff of the Tibet Trade Mission in Kalimpong. In that small frontier town he came into contact with such Western scholars as Prince Peter of Greece and Denmark, George Roerich, Rene de Nebesky Wojkowitz, Herbert V. Guenther and also Reverend Tharchin, the editor and publisher of the *Tibet Mirror*, who had been a good friend of his father's.

Sonam Tomjor was a patriot and constantly felt the loss of his country, unfortunately to a point where it affected his physical and emotional well-being. He detested Mao Zedong and Chinese Communism and it was from him I first learnt that the Chairman's poetry (then praised by all Western China experts) was actually quite mediocre.

Sonam Tomjor had great respect for Fabian Socialism — and Bernard Shaw and the Webbs. He admired H. G. Wells, and attempted (somewhat unsuccessfully) to encourage Tibetans to read Wells' *The Outline of History*. He was not a great reader of novels, though he enjoyed Dickens tremendously. Once commenting on the universality of Dickens' characters he said it was funny how even in Lhasa in the old days he would sometimes come across a Uriah Heep or a Mrs. Plumblechook. He also liked reciting the quatrains of Omar Khayyam's *Rubaiyat*.

After the Communist occupation, the Chinese authorities in Tibet requested him to return to Tibet to be the principal of their new school in Lhasa. He declined the offer and instead worked with such Tibetan *émigré* leaders as the former Prime Minister Lukhangwa, Gyalo Thondup, Tsipon Shakabpa, and others who were continuing the freedom struggle in India. When the Dalai Lama came into exile in 1950, Sonam Tomjor sold his home in Kalimpong and left for Mussoorie to serve His Holiness. He taught at Mussoorie school and was the first Principal of the Tibetan school at Simla. But his perennial depression made him unable to continue in government service.

Yet his guidance and example were influential in directing his brother T. C. Tethong (at present *kalon*), and his sons Tenzin Gyeche (private secretary to the Dalai Lama) and Tenzing Namgyal (former Kashag chairman) into serving the Tibetan exile government during its difficult years. Among other young Tibetans in Dharamshala then, who looked up to him as a mentor and friend, were Sonam Topgyal (now Kashag chairman) and Lodi G. Gyari (the Dalai Lama's envoy in Washington DC).

Though not directly involved, Sonam Tomjor was an intellectual influence in the formation of the Tibetan Youth Congress. I know for certain that he was inspirational in the naming of the organisation. He insisted on the word "Congress" which he felt had a great tradition behind it, as in the American Continental Congress, the Indian National Congress and the African National Congress. He advised against the term "League" which he felt was ill-omened as in the League of Nations, or uninspiring, as in the Muslim League and the Gorkha League.

When I first started to work for the Tibetan community in exile in the mid-sixties, I was a callow teenager with enthusiasm and idealism but little else. My uncle Sonam Tomjor opened my eyes to the complexity and depth of Tibet's history and the wonder and richness of its civilization. It is my hope that his notes will be properly preserved by his heirs and will see publication in the near future.

Sonam Tomjor is survived by four sons: Tenzin Gyeche, Tenzing Namgyal, Kunga Namgyal and Phuntsok Namgyal. His former wife, Sonam Peldon of Samdrup Phodrang, lives in Dharamshala.

January 1998
Tibetan Review

Shadow Tibet
Images of Contemporary Reality[1]

ONE RESULT of the partial opening up of Tibet to tourism has been the proliferation of photographic representations of the country and people in books, magazines, posters, calendars, postcards, T-shirts and, of course, coffee-table books. The images are usually vibrant with colour and nearly always focus on the out-of-the-world aspects of the country: the magnificent landscape, the awesome Potala Palace (under a rainbow, in moonlight and so on), the wildlife, architecture, and, of course, the smiling people: monks in red woollen robes, rosy-cheeked children, wrinkled grannies, nomads in heavy sheep-skin, picturesque folk-dancers, tough Khampas with long braided hair, and cowled pilgrims who seem to have stepped straight out of the pages of the *Canterbury Tales*.

---

1. This piece was the introduction to a catalogue for an exhibition of the photographs of Manuel Bauer, "Shadow Tibet", organised by Amnye Machen Institute from 17 February to 8 September 1995. The exhibition, which opened in New Delhi, toured all Tibetans centres and settlements in India and Nepal.

However aesthetically pleasing, all these recent images of Tibet are inadequate, sometimes even inaccurate, representations of the contemporary reality of Tibet. Of course, one cannot in all fairness start tossing around charges of deliberate deception. The camera, in this case, has lied not so much by artifice or fakery but by selection — the process of selection probably being influenced as much by the photographer's romantic fantasies of Tibet as by the unfamiliar and overwhelming experience of his or her visit to this previously forbidden land.

When Susan Sontag made the point that "photography inevitably entails a certain patronising of reality" she could well have been talking about the works of such romantic photographers of Tibet as Galen Rowell, who is arguably the best in this genre. In the introduction to his book *My Tibet*, Rowell defends his particular outlook with this admonition: "To dwell on the agony the Chinese have imposed upon his (the Dalai Lama's) land is to lose most of the essence of his being and his message to the world."

In spite of such spiritual constraints, Rowell and others do, once in a while, make some tentative concessions to reality: in a picture or two of PLA personnel strolling around Lhasa, or the ruins of a monastery destroyed during the Cultural Revolution. But even these few images lack the capacity to disturb, much less move one to outrage. In fact, the ruins of temples and monasteries in some photographs seem as romantic and far-away-in-time as the ruins of the Acropolis or the Parthenon. "The way photography inexorably beautifies" Susan Sontag observed in her collection of essays, *On Photography*, "has not been entirely overlooked and has troubled those moralists who were hooked on photography."

One of these "moralists", the German littérateur and philosopher, Walter Benjamen, in an address delivered in Paris in 1934, at the Institute for the Study of Fascism, observed that the camera:

Is now incapable of photographing a tenement or a rubbish-heap without transfiguring it. Not to mention a river dam or an electrical cable factory: in front of these, photography can only say, 'How beautiful.' ... It has succeeded in turning abject poverty itself, by handling it in a modish, technically perfect way, into an object of enjoyment.

The Amnye Machen Institute (AMI) has organised this exhibition of the work of Manuel Bauer to provide a reality counterpoint to the prevailing visual representations of Tibet. Manuel Bauer is one of the few photographers of conscience who has willed himself to look under the picturesque surface and colour of tourist Tibet and record the disturbing reality of the country today. Of course, Bauer's vision is as personal as that of any other photographer's, but he has at least attempted to forego romantic stereotypes and, as far as that is possible, to see things from the victim's point of view.

In stark black and white, Bauer's powerful images reveal a land ravaged by unchecked exploitation, pollution, and unregulated industrialisation; and a people victim to disease, poverty, alcoholism, unemployment, racism, sexual degradation, cultural devaluation, predatory capitalism and Stalinist control. More disturbing are the indications — underlying the whole exhibition — of the sinicization of the people, and the vague, yet ominous suggestion of the approaching end of the Tibetan race.

Many will be troubled by these harsh uncompromising representations and some may question whether instead of contributing to an understanding of Tibet, these might cause undue despair. Yet Bauer's work comes across as a far more effective wake-up call for the plight of Tibet than the standard idealised images of grinning monks and smiling grannies.

On first viewing Manuel Bauer's photographs, the work of another Swiss photographer, Werner Bischof, came to mind, especially

Bischof's striking and troubling black and white images of famine in India, which I had seen in *Life* magazine many years ago. But the undercurrent of suppressed moral outrage running through Bauer's pictures was perhaps more suggestive of the work of the late W. Eugene Smith, especially Smith's photographs taken in 1971–72 of the inhabitants of the Japanese fishing villages around Minamata Bay, many of whom were crippled and slowly dying of methyl-mercury poisoning. Even through such terrible images of disease, deformity and death — especially his Pieta-like masterpiece, *Tomoko Uemura in Her Bath* — Smith succeeded in making a powerful case for justice and human dignity.

The primary goal of this exhibition has been to inform and enlighten Tibetans in exile of the true situation inside Tibet. The exhibition has travelled to the main settlements and centres of Tibetans in India and Nepal. A parallel exhibition is taking place in Switzerland.

17 February 1998
Amnye Machen Institute

Rite of Freedom
The Life and Sacrifice of Thupten Ngodup

AFTER THE CREMATION of Thupten Ngodup, when the emotional crowd had finally marched back to McLeod Ganj, a few of us went to pay a visit to his house. It was a brief walk from the cremation-ground by the mountain stream, through a rhododendron, oak and chil[1] forest to the Tsechokling Monastery estate where Thupten Ngodup's little hut was located.

It was very small, about eight by six feet, and no more than six feet high. On two sides of the hut, just below a couple of large, low windows were flower-beds blooming with wine-red snapdragons and yellow pansies with dark patchy centres. In front of the hut was a carpet-size lawn with a young juniper growing in the middle. He had planted a neat hedge around the place, and had attempted, with a not overwhelming degree of success, to trim the top of one side of the hedge into the shape of a bird.

---

1. Chil or chir pine, *Pinus roxburghii*, a large Himalayan pine tree with thick fissured bark and bright green, needle-like leaves.

The Japanese poet/painter Buson in his illustrations for the poet Basho's travel diary, *The Narrow Road to the Deep North*, has this whimsical little sketch of a priest sitting in a tiny wayside hut in the midst of a small garden.

> Even the woodpeckers
> Have left it untouched
> This tiny cottage
> In a summer grove

The battered corrugated-tin roof (weighted down with large stones) notwithstanding, Thupten Ngodup's shack suggested, in an unexpected sort of way, the quality of "refined poverty" that Taoist sages and Japanese tea-masters of yore are said to have cultivated in their dwellings; a quality which, surprisingly enough, one comes across, now and then, in the humble abodes of solitary monks and meditators around Dharamshala.

The first thing one noticed on entering Thupten Ngodup's hut was his altar, which had at least four photographs of the Dalai Lama, two small Tibetan flags, and various other pictures of *bodhisattvas* and protective deities. In front was stacked, *en échelon*, a row of small brass bowls for the customary water offering. His bed, below the altar, was neatly made, and a pair of trousers and a shirt, both crisply ironed, hung on a plastic hanger on the wall. A "Free Tibet" baseball cap hung on the same nail. A small table and a comfortable deck-chair completed the furnishing. The wall opposite the bed constituted his kitchen. There he had rigged up a few rows of makeshift shelves on which his stove, pots and pans, buckets and plastic containers were arranged.

In the corner of a shelf were three large cartons of "27" *bidis*, which he smoked regularly. Besides the *bidis* were a few empty rum bottles — army issue. A bottle of Bachelor Deluxe whisky was half empty. He had probably treated himself to this more expensive drink before leaving for Delhi to join the hunger strike.

By all accounts, Thupten Ngodup seems to have been a light-hearted person who enjoyed an occasional drink and game of cards, particularly a game called "*sip*" he had picked up while in the force. He and some of his ex-army buddies regularly gathered below the Om Restaurant for a daily game. He was also fond of the Tibetan domino game, *bakchen*. Though certainly not a rich man, he apparently had no pressing money problems. He had some savings in the bank and made a comfortable living as a chef for the annual picnics and banquets hosted by various organisations and offices in Dharamshala, and also by baking Tibetan New Year cakes (*khapsay*) during the season.

He seems to have been a conscientious worker. The English writer, Patrick French, who met Ngodup in 1986 at the Tsechokling Monastery, mentioned in a recent article in the Indian magazine, *Outlook*, (18 May 1998) that Ngodup was always "anxious, maybe too anxious, in an ex-military sort of way, to provide perfect service". Patrick helped Ngodup draw up a menu for a meal service for Western tourists staying in the guest rooms of the monastery "tea, coffee, *thukpa, shabalay, momo*..."

On the 27 April at around six o'clock in the morning, when the Delhi police pulled their second surprise raid on the site of the Tibetan Youth Congress (TYC) organised "Hunger Strike Unto Death" to haul off the three remaining hunger strikers, this ordinary, good-humoured man did something that has since shaken Tibetan society in a fairly fundamental way. He avoided the police dragnet — one gets a glimpse of him slipping past the police in the video shot by Choyang Tharchin of the Department of Information and International Relations (DIIR) — and made his way to the public toilet. He opened a plastic container of gasoline, which he must have hidden there earlier, and dowsed himself thoroughly. Then he struck a match or flicked a lighter.

    Someone who was there told me that he probably did not come out immediately from the toilet and must have deliberately remained a moment or two inside to ensure that he was well lit. That, of course, is conjecture. When he came out he was, quite literally, an inferno. The DIIR video makes that horrifyingly clear. We see him charging out to the area before the hunger strikers tent, causing chaos in the ranks of the police as well as the Tibetans there. A very English female voice — off camera — screams, "Oh my God!, Oh my God!", again and again. With that and other screams and shouts, it is impossible to hear what the burning man is saying. According to someone there, he shouted "*Bod Gyal lo!*" or "Victory to Tibet!". Others heard him crying "*Bod Rangzen!*" or "Independence for Tibet!". He also shouted "Long live His Holiness the Dalai Lama!". How on earth he managed to shout anything, much less run about as he did is a mystery to me. Every breath he took must have caused live flames to rush into his lungs and sear the air sacs and lining.

    The burning man then appears to pause and hold up both hands together in a position of prayer. At this point the fire seems terribly intense and the cameraman later told me that he could distinctly hear popping sounds as bits of flesh burst from Thupten Ngodup's body. The cameraman was so shaken that he found it difficult to hold his camera steady. Then policemen and Tibetan bystanders beat at the flames with rugs and gunny-sacks, and finally, pushing Thupten Ngodup to the ground, stifled the blaze.

    Ngodup was rushed to the Ram Manohar Lohia hospital. The doctors there declared that he had nearly hundred per cent burns and there was no hope of him surviving. On being asked whether the patient could feel any pain the doctor replied in the affirmative, explaining that the burns were largely first degree and most nerve endings were functional. But Thupten Ngodup, though conscious, was silent.

The Dalai Lama visited him next day in the evening. Thupten Ngodup made an attempt to rise but was gently pushed back. He held up his bandaged hands together in respect. His Holiness asked him if he could hear him. Thupten Ngodup nodded. The Dalai Lama told the conscious man that he should not harbour any feeling of hatred towards the Chinese, and that his act had created an unprecedented awareness of the Tibetan cause. Later that night, in a barely audible whisper, he asked for a sweet to suck, then a little later, he asked the TYC leader attending, to take out the sweet from his mouth and give him a sip of water. He then asked about the six hunger strikers who had been arrested by the police. On hearing that they were in hospital and alright, he sighed and said that he was very happy. He passed away at 0:15 A.M. on 29 April.

*

Just a few weeks before Thupten Ngodup's self-immolation, I was having a heated argument with a self-styled environmental expert on Tibet (of Indian origin) who was justifying the activities of his and other foreign "experts" and "advisors" (who since the late eighties have battened themselves on the Dalai Lama's court with the tact and sensitivity of lampreys) by pointing out how Tibetans in exile were incapable of any effort or sacrifice. In fact, another "expert" had told me earlier in New York that the Dalai Lama had no choice other than to give up independence because the Tibetans in exile did not have the courage and commitment to continue the struggle for independence.

Well, Thupten Ngodup has effectively nailed that lie. Exile Tibetans, whatever their other failings, seem quite prepared to die for their country. The courage and endurance of the six hunger strikers who maintained their fast for forty-nine days before being forcibly dragged away by the Delhi police clearly demonstrate this as well. We must also bear in mind that about a hundred Tibetans had signed up with the Tibetan Youth Congress to carry on the strike when the first six should die.

This is by no means the first time that Tibetans in exile have embarked on such a campaign. In 1988, the TYC launched a "Hunger-Strike-Unto-Death" which only came to a halt when the Dalai Lama personally wrote (over the head of the TYC leaders) to each of the eight hunger strikers, ordering them to give up their fast. I recollect another TYC- led hunger strike in 1977, in which I participated in a small way, and I find myself still deeply impressed by the spirit of all the Tibetans who were there — not only the actual hunger strikers, who were indomitable, but even the thousands of supporters who came to Delhi from every part of India and Nepal to do their bit for the cause. There have been other such campaigns, like the National Democracy Movement led hunger strike in New York. It must be admitted, though, that these campaigns have varied greatly in effectiveness, and it should also be said, their integrity.

We are, of course, not talking here of the exiles who went on suicide missions inside Tibet, or the many secret agents, Mustang guerrillas and others who, in one way or another, gave up comfort, security and even their lives, for Tibetan independence. Thupten Ngodup, as a young man, was one of many such Tibetans who sought to free his nation through force of arms.

I talked to Samten, a storekeeper at McLeod Ganj, who signed up with Thupten Ngodup on 1 October 1963 to enlist in establishment 22, a joint CIA and Indian army run Tibetan special force. Samten and Ngodup were together in the same (Sixteen) company, the same mess and the same barracks for thirteen years. After their basic training, they trained as paratroopers and successfully completed the required number of jumps and received their "wings". They were then posted to various sectors on the Indo-Tibetan border till November 1971 when, with great secrecy, their company was taken to a jumping-off point in North-Eastern India, code name "camping ground".

The war for the liberation of Bangladesh had started, and the immense rivers and their myriad tributaries radiating across Bangladesh were slowing down the massive Indian advance from the west. With the approval of the Dalai Lama, the Tibetan force was launched through the virtually impenetrable jungles of the Mizo Hills across South-Eastern Bangladesh to capture the port city of Chittagong, thereby threatening the rear of the Pakistani army.

Crossing into Bangladesh, Sixteen company ran into enemy fire in the Chakma hills. Two men were killed and two wounded when they captured a hill held by Pakistani forces. Another company, Fifteen company, was less lucky in its mission and suffered heavy casualties when attacking an enemy-held hill. Having cleared Pakistani forces out of the hill tracts, the Tibetans proceeded southward to the city of Rangamati, which they took from the Pakistanis. They also blew up the large railway bridge outside the city, to prevent Pakistani armour from counter-attacking.

While on detail on the bridge, Samten and Thupten Ngodup saw, in the river below, hundreds of corpses, particularly skulls, of Bengalis who had, a month or so earlier, been hanged along the side of the bridge by Pakistani soldiers. By the time Sixteen company got to Chittagong the Pakistanis had surrendered. After a couple of weeks in the city, the Tibetan troops were flown back to their base in Chakrata.

Finally, in 1976, the two friends split up. Samten joined a regular unit, while Thupten stayed on in the special guerrilla force. Thupten Ngodup got his discharge in 1983.

Samten remembers Thupten as tough, decisive, and extremely healthy, and has no memory of him ever being sick, even for a single day. Though Thupten never aspired to leadership, he was an enthusiastic soldier, always volunteering to make tea, carry heavy loads and do other chores for the squad. He never missed out on any of his training courses, and strangely enough never took a day's leave from the army in his entire twenty years of service. The Tibetan soldiers were paid very little, but, according to Samten, Thupten was not materialistic and thought little of saving. Thupten does not seem to have been a particularly religious man either. Samten does not remember him reciting mantras or doing any special practice. But he was honest, upright and a good companion, though not much of a conversationalist. He talked little of his past in Tibet, even to his closest friends.

All we know is that Thupten Ngodup was born in 1938 in the village of Gyatso Shar in Tsang province. He is said to have some relatives there still. He was of peasant stock and seems to have joined the Tashilhunpo Monastery as a boy. After the Lhasa Uprising Thupten fled from Shigatse to India through Lachen-Lachung in Northern Sikkim. With other refugees he worked as a coolie on a road gang in Bomdila, and after a year moved to the Lugsung Samdupling Tibetan Settlement in Bylakuppe. He remained there till joining the army in 1963.

After his discharge, Thupten Ngodup came to Dharamshala where he worked as a cook for Tsechokling Monastery. The monastery gave him a small plot of land to build his hut, conditional on its return after his death. In Dharamshala another ex-serviceman, Tenzin, became his good friend and the two of them often shared a meal or a cup of tea. Tenzin also remembers Thupten as a very healthy man, who ate moderately but liked his meals to be well prepared. He was a cheerful (*nangwa-kyipu*), positive thinking man, who enjoyed life and made it a point not to miss any football matches or the shows at the Tibetan Children's Village or the Tibetan Institute of Performing Arts. He and Tenzin would also take long walks around Dharamshala, always ending up at a tea stall. Tenzin tried, unsuccessfully, to get him to be a little more religious. Like others who knew Thupten, Tenzin told me that he was a quiet man who never discussed his past.

Thupten only seems to have lost his cheerfulness when Tenzin or others talked of becoming old or giving up. He would insist that it was silly to think that way and Tibetans would certainly return one day to a free Tibet. Though not politically inclined, he unfailingly attended all demonstrations, candle-light vigils or meetings for Tibet. He took part in the first Peace March in 1995 and seems to have been disappointed by the outcome. The goal of the Peace March, which was initially Tibet, was later switched to Delhi; but halfway to Delhi, at Ambala, the march-leaders hustled everyone onto buses, claiming that they had to meet the Dalai Lama in Delhi. Thupten returned to Dharamshala and told Tenzin of his disappointment. He wryly remarked that there had been a lot of talk of great achievements, especially by the leaders of the march, but aside from the sympathy of Indian people on the route, he was not sure if anything had been gained. Nevertheless, Thupten volunteered for the next Peace March, which doesn't seems to have inspired him any more than the first.

Finally, this April, when Thupten Ngodup learnt about the Tibetan Youth Congress organised "Hunger Strike Unto Death" in Delhi he came over to Tenzin's house and, over a cup of tea, told him that he was going to join the hunger strike. Tenzin admits to teasing him a bit and asking him what he could do to change the political situation. Thupten was unusually emphatic in his reply, saying that there would be definite results this time. He said that though the Dalai Lama had achieved much, the people had not done enough, and unless they did they would grow old and die in India and that would be the end of everything.

He asked Tenzin not to tell anyone that he had joined the hunger strike. He also asked Tenzin to be his guarantor, since the TYC required one of all volunteers. Tenzin accompanied him to the Youth Congress Office where he signed the guarantee document. After completing the formalities, Thupten donated five hundred rupees to the Youth Congress. The vice-president declined the money, but Thupten insisted, saying that money was necessary for the struggle. Before leaving Dharamshala, he entrusted the key of his hut to Tenzin and instructed his friend that on hearing of his death, he should sell his pots, pans and the few bits of furniture in the house and donate the money to the Tibetan Youth Congress. He insisted that every rupee was important to the freedom struggle.

Once in Delhi Thupten Ngodup was assigned to the next group of hunger strikers to replace the first group when its members should finally die. Characteristically, he busied himself cleaning up the hunger strike grounds and helping to bathe, massage and otherwise take care of the hunger strikers, who were by now emaciated and weak.

On the 23 April, around noon, a correspondent for the Norwegian-sponsored Voice of Tibet radio station interviewed him. I have reproduced the main part of his statement, editing it for repetitions and disjointedness, and have also left out the interviewer's questions. A couple of important passages have not only been translated verbatim but the Tibetan original (in transliteration) has been provided within parenthesis:

> I joined the Hunger Strike because I am a Tibetan and I have a duty to perform ... No, there is no fear in my heart at all. When I met the six hunger strikers I felt very happy. It is now nearly forty years since we lost our country and much of our culture and religion has

been destroyed. Inside Tibet and all over the world much has been done for the struggle.

The Dalai Lama has tried so very hard to implement his peaceful Middle Path programme, and has attempted to communicate with the Chinese. But this work has achieved no results. Therefore the situation has become desperate. These six people, led by the Youth Congress, have responded to this urgent situation by undertaking the Hunger Strike, and this has made me very happy. (*Gyalwa Rinpoche kyi tsenme shiwae umae lam la-ya dinde chik betsoe nangchen gyami la drewa masongnae shul yog ray. Lay-ga di la nuba thon yog ma ray. Di song yin tsang, dha ni zadrag yin tsang mi droog di shunue u tri-jay zadrag la tay, zalchi ngogoe la pheba dila nga rang pe gabo chung.*)

The six "do not have a hair of doubt or hesitation" (*thetsom pu chik minduk*) about giving up their lives. I am of the same determination. I do not have a hair of doubt or hesitation about giving up my life. This is my stand ... When my turn comes to go on hunger strike I have decided to make it more effective. Many Tibetans are now determined to go on the hunger strike unto death. Many people I know personally want to join the hunger strike. In my own case, I have decided not to accept any kind of massage treatment or drink any water. The Tibetan situation has become desperate ... I am giving up my life to bring about peace and freedom to my unhappy people ... I have one hundred per cent confidence that the people inside Tibet will not only continue the struggle but will intensify it. They will never sit back and not struggle.

Five days after giving this interview Thupten Ngodup immolated himself.

After his death, some official and support-group periodicals carried what was claimed to be a quote from Thupten Ngodup's last statement: "I have full faith in the 'Middle Way Approach' of His Holiness the Dalai Lama and it is very important for all Tibetans to think this way." It is possible that at some earlier point in time he may have supported the Dalai Lama's Middle Path approach, but just five days before his death he was so certain that this had failed that he had not hesitated to say so on the radio.

So what's going on? I think that Thupten Ngodup like most Tibetans revere His Holiness so much that they can never quite bring themselves to openly contradict him. Yet their native good sense forces them, in extreme circumstances, to act in contravention to the Dalai Lama's wishes. For instance, in March 1959, Tibetans in Lhasa city seemed to have realised that the Dalai Lama's policy of trusting the Chinese and co-operating with them, whatever the cost, had not only undermined the nation, but even compromised and endangered the life of His Holiness himself. Defying his explicit instructions, they took up arms to defend his sacred person and restore the honour of the Tibetan nation. Thupten Ngodup's self-immolation, as well as the action of the hunger strikers, seems to derive from very much the same sort of desperate reasoning.

Pacifist New Age notions to the contrary, giving up one's life for one's country and one's beliefs has always been considered an admirable, indeed a magnificent act, by Tibetans. In the early eleventh century, when the Buddhist King of Western Tibet, Lha Lama Yeshey Wo was captured by the Muslim King Qarlog and held for ransom, his nephew tried to raise a large amount of gold as ransom. But the King told his nephew that he should not give the Muslim King even a speck of brass and that he was prepared to die for the Dharma. He urged his nephew to use the gold to invite great Buddhist teachers from India. Yeshey Wo died in prison. Thupten Ngodup may have heard this story and others like it as a young monk.

In 1966, just before the Cultural Revolution, in Drapchi prison in Lhasa, a CIA trained Tibetan agent, Trede Tashi Gyaltsen, a native of Gyantse, went on hunger strike. The first time around he was not successful. The Chinese guards force-fed him and injected him with some unknown medication. But a month later he tried again and this time, in spite of every effort by the prison administration, he starved himself to death. A comrade of his, who was with him in prison, assured me that Tashi's decision was not actuated by despair, but that it was a deliberate political act of defiance against the Chinese.

However much admiration and respect have been expressed for Thupten Ngodup's self-immolation in the Tibetan community, it, as well as the hunger strike, has not gone entirely uncensured, especially by some Westerners. One creepy missionary type in Dharamshala, who runs a New Age newsletter for cover, has been doing dirt on Thupten Ngodup's memory, telling young Tibetans that Thupten Ngodup probably acted as he did from alcoholic depression. This is probably as mean-spirited and despicable as anyone can get.

But to return to the fundamental question of self-sacrifice, I feel compelled to point out to the orange-juice-sucking, tear-in-the-eye pacifist crowd that their basic contention that people should not die or be killed for a cause is monstrously false. Life is undeniably precious, but if it has to lived at the price of appeasing tyranny, or serenely and unconcernedly accommodating injustice and evil, then a spiritual death, far worse than any physical death, must eventually and assuredly result.

Moreover, the struggle for Tibet's independence is not just an issue of territory or nationalism but has a more universal and moral dimension. It is, in the final reckoning, a fight for justice and truth; not truth as an abstraction but as a living principle to guide the lives of brave men and women. Gandhi, whose writings I sometimes turn to for answers on such questions, is clear about this and on the issue of sacrifice as well. In the 22 September 1942 issue of *Young India* he wrote: "Abstract truth has no value, unless it incarnates in human beings who represent it by proving their readiness to die for it."

In the annals of political struggles not too many people have chosen a fiery death for their beliefs, but it does appear, nonetheless, to be generally effective. Sometimes the results have been swift and dramatic. In June 1963, Thich Quang Duc set fire to himself in Saigon to draw world attention to the repression of Buddhists by the Catholic president of Vietnam, Ngo Dinh Diem. A wave of protest swept through the whole population, carrying off in its wake the government of President Diem, which fell on 1 November 1963.

It may be some years before Thupten Ngodup's dream will be realised, but I think that, like the aspirations of the young Czech student, Jan Palach, who burnt himself to death in 1969 in Prague to protest the Soviet invasion, it will come about eventually. As Patrick French in the conclusion of his article writes, "Today the Soviet empire has been dismantled, but Jan Palach lives on".

In his last photograph taken before the hunger striker's tent in Delhi, Thupten Ngodup is smiling. One cannot altogether presume to know what was going on in his mind but he certainly looks cheerful and confident. There is no hint of anger or fanaticism (or alcoholic depression) in that smile. He was a simple man (he only read Tibetan haltingly), but when I look at his photograph I feel I am seeing the calm happy face of someone who has discovered a fundamental truth about life; something that has always eluded our leadership, but which traditionally Tibetans have regarded as basic to any major undertaking, especially the effective practice of the Dharma — *thak choego ray*, you have to make a decision and act on it.

(To everyone at TYC Centrex, especially Yangchen Dolkar-la, thank you for your co-operation. Thanks also to Choyang-la, Topden-la and Tenzing Damdul-la of the DIIR. To Gyen Tenzing and Gyen Samten-la also, many thanks)

6 August 1998
World Tibet Network News

Bungled Bombing
Letter to the Editor

THE RAGE OF THE CHINESE at the NATO bombing of their embassy in Belgrade [17 May 1999], in contrast to their seeming resignation to the greater carnage and tyranny of their own leaders, brought to mind an observation of this century's greatest Chinese writer, Lu Xun:

> Of course, whether we are massacred by our own people, or we are massacred by foreigners, does not amount to exactly the same thing. Thus for instance, if a man slaps his own face, he will not feel insulted, whereas if someone else slaps him, he will feel angry. However, when a man is so cretinous that he can slap his own face, he fully deserves to be slapped by any passerby.

14 June 1999
Time Magazine

Silent Struggle
Tsongkha Lhamo Tsering (1924–1999)

WHEN I FIRST ARRIVED at the Resistance headquarters at Kelsang Phug in Mustang in July 1971, I was somewhat taken aback to come across a library. Granted, it was not much of a library. It only had a few books and some Tibetan magazines like *Sheja* and *Tibetan Freedom*, but I had assumed I would be hunkering down in a rough bunker or a tent, stripping down my rifle to while away the time. So the library came as a pleasant surprise.

It was the brainchild of Lhamo Tsering. He had even designed the small building and laid out the flowerbeds outside. The compound was surrounded by a wooden fence that also served as a backrest for the low benches where we sometimes sat in the evenings drinking black tea, admiring the plants and looking up at the disconcertingly close face of the giant Nilgiri range.

The Resistance journal, *Gotok* ("Understand") was another of Lhamo Tsering's ideas. The editor was a sharp young fellow from Tsum called Damdul, whose snub nose and spiky hair bought to mind the Artful Dodger. My own contribution to the journal was picking up stories from the BBC World Service and sometimes doing a piece. The magazine was mimeographed, or, as the Tibetans called it, "oil printed" (*num-par*). The Gestetner machine would sit out in the blazing sun for an hour or two and when the rollers and works were nearly too hot to touch we would crank out the voice of the Resistance. The heat made the viscous ink flow nice and even and we got perfect results every time.

Lhamo Tsering had also set up a school for the younger soldiers of the Resistance. The headmaster, Thondup Gyalpo, who was an ex-sergeant (*shengo*) from the Guards regiment of the old Tibetan army, kept the fairly wild young nomad and Khampa men on their toes. I gave classes in arithmetic, English and conversational Nepali. Occasionally I would hold forth on the various liberation movements that were shaking the world at that time, and which the men enjoyed hearing about.

One day in the library, I picked up an English translation of Sun Tzu's *Art of War*, with an appendix of selections from Mao Zedong's writings on guerilla warfare. The margins and borders of nearly every page were heavy with neat pencilled annotations in Chinese, English and Tibetan. I found it somewhat reassuring that our chief of operations — for that was roughly Lhamo Tsering's role in the organisation — was someone who, at least intellectually, worked at his job. He worked at it in other ways too. He would be up an hour earlier before anyone else and have finished his exercises and his morning run by the time everyone else turned out for PT — when he would join them for another round of exercises. He was a soft-spoken person and I never heard him raise his voice at anyone. He was polite to the point of formality with his officers, agents and the common soldier.

Thinking back, I realise I owed Lhamo Tsering for the opportunity to join the Resistance. As a boy I had tried to enlist a couple of times and had failed. I once even got to meet Gyalo Thondup, the Dalai Lama's older brother, who was the overall kingpin of the Resistance, but in an undefined *eminence grise* sort of way. I went to his Delhi house in the posh neighbourhood of Golf Links and begged him to let me join. But he laughed at my naiveté and packed me off home.

A couple of years later I met Lhamo Tsering in Dharamshala. He accepted my services as a matter of course, and even commended me on my *simshuk* (patriotism). I didn't know that Lhamo Tsering was at the time neck-deep in problems: with the withdrawal of American support for the Resistance and the abrupt departure of his boss Gyalo Thondup for Hong Kong. He probably didn't need an additional headache in the form of an enthusiastic but totally unprepared rookie like me. I benefited from his thoughtfulness in other ways. He regularly sent me *Time* and other magazines through our courier. I was just a volunteer, like everyone else up at Mustang, but he must have felt that coming from a relatively privileged educational background, I was going to get bored up in the mountains. I wrote to thank him and also described my positive impressions of the camp, the men and the whole set-up. Years later, going through his papers, I was touched to see my old letter carefully filed away in a volume of documents from that period.

The men, without exception, had tremendous respect for him, more, I think, than for any other living Resistance leader, even the Dalai Lama's brother. Of course, he had his detractors. Earlier a small breakaway faction of the Mustang group had left with the former Commander, Baba Heshe, which split the whole "Four Rivers, Six Ranges" organisation in the exile world. The faction that supported Heshe, among other accusations, charged Lhamo Tsering with being Chinese. They based their accusation on the fact that members of the Dalai Lama's family, when speaking among themselves in their native Xining dialect, called Lhamo Tsering by the Chinese name (Bei Xiansheng) he had been given when he first attended a Chinese school.

Lhamo Tsering was born in 1924 in the village of Sina Nagatsang near Kumbum Monastery in Amdo, then under the Chinese Muslim (Hui) warlord, Ma Bufang. Nagatsang was close by Taktser, the Dalai Lama's birthplace. Chinese immigration had, since Ming times, asserted itself in those parts of Amdo, and Nagatsang had over fifty Chinese families to two Tibetan. Till the age of eight Lhamo Tsering was a monk at Kumbum Monastery, when he began attending the local Chinese primary school in the nearby village of Rusar. On finishing primary, school he went to the Teacher's Training School in Xining city and graduated from there.

The end of his schooling in Xining coincided with the Sino-Japanese war and he was briefly conscripted into the Youth Volunteer Force of the Nationalist Chinese Army. Before he saw action, the war came to an end. He then went to the Institute for Frontier Minorities in Nanjing to pursue further studies. There, in 1945, he met the Dalai Lama's older brother, Gyalo Thondup, who had also come to study in Nanjing. Lhamo Tsering became Gyalo Thondup's assistant and close companion.

In 1949, Communist forces were taking China's major cities one by one. Lhamo Tsering and Gyalo Thondup escaped from Nanjing to Shanghai. Gyalo Thondup then departed for Hong Kong and left Lhamo Tsering behind to collect a bank transfer. But the money didn't arrive on time, and Communist troops surrounded Shanghai. Lhamo Tsering once told me of his experiences at that time. His vivid description of the period stirred in me boyhood memories of poring over photographs (probably Cartier Bresson's) in an old *Life* magazine, of Shanghai's last days: panic-stricken Chinese men in double-breasted suits or traditional long gowns topped with fedoras, women in Anna May Wong *cheongsams* and cloche hats desperately pushing and shoving each other to get to the closed door of a Shanghai bank; bedraggled Kuomintang officers and their mountains of possessions alongside other desperate refugees at the railway station, waiting for a train that would probably never come; and of course the inevitable abandoned baby by the tracks. Lhamo Tsering narrowly managed to escape Shanghai before the city fell. He and another Tibetan forced a local fisherman to row them out beyond the harbour to the open sea where a last ship bound for Hong Kong picked them up.

Lhamo Tsering settled in Kalimpong, the Indian frontier town and centre for the wool trade with Tibet. In February 1952, he accompanied Gyalo Thondup to Lhasa. This was Lhamo Tsering's first trip to the Tibetan capital. Here he was able to observe and experience first-hand the implications of the Communist Chinese invasion of Tibet. After four months, Gyalo Thondup and Lhamo Tsering managed to leave Lhasa and returned to India. On 6 August 1954, Gyalo Thondup, along with Tsipon W. D. Shakabpa and Jamyangkyil Khenchung, founded the Tibetan Welfare Association in Kalimpong. Lhamo Tsering was its main administrator. The objectives of the Tibetan Welfare Association were to oppose the Chinese occupation, to publicise internationally the Tibetan situation, and to initiate underground movements inside their homeland.

In 1956, the CIA decided to help the Tibetan Resistance movement. Their main contact was Gyalo Thondup. In July 1958, Lhamo Tsering secretly led a group of eleven Tibetans to America. They were trained first at a secret camp in Virginia, and then at the newly reactivated Camp Hale in Colorado. Lhamo Tsering was also trained separately in Washington DC in intelligence tradecraft. The Americans did not at first tell the Tibetans where they were being trained but Lhamo Tsering managed to find out. He told me in an interview in 1991 how he had done it: "We were not told where the camp was. It was not a very mountainous area but it was well forested ... I managed to find out through helping out in the kitchen. Our supplies were purchased in the city and delivered to our cook every day, along with the bills and receipts. One day I took a quick peek at a receipt. Below the name of the store were the words, 'Richmond, VA.' We were in Virginia."

Following his return to India in August 1959, Lhamo Tsering created and headed an office for intelligence operations in Darjeeling. Its main function was to liaise between the CIA and the various Resistance operations that were being launched from India and Nepal. These included radio teams that were being parachuted into Tibet; radio teams that went overland; and the Mustang Resistance Force that was started in Northern Nepal in mid-1960. The ailing leader of the "Four Rivers, Six Ranges" Force and the undisputed leader of the resistance movement, Gompo Tashi Andrugtsang (1905–64) was then convalescing in Darjeeling. He passed on to Lhamo Tsering the old battle standard of the "Four Rivers, Six Ranges", first flown in June 1958 when the force set up base at Driguthang in Lhoka district. The old man also gave Lhamo Tsering his own Browning automatic pistol and sixty rounds of ammunition. He also entrusted to him his personal seal, made when the desperate Tibetan government at Lhuntse Dzong in March 1959 gave him a *dzasak* title and appointed him Commander-in-chief of all Tibetan military forces.

From 1964 to 1974, the activities of the Darjeeling office were expanded and a tripartite office was created which had its base in New Delhi. Lhamo Tsering headed the Tibetan section of this office. The main operations of this office included the Mustang Resistance Force and the intelligence gathering missions inside Tibet. With a new era of Sino-American relationship heralded by Nixon's visit to China, the CIA terminated their support of the Resistance in 1969. The Chinese began to put pressure on the Nepalese government to do something about the Tibetan guerrillas in Nepal.

In 1974, Lhamo Tsering was arrested in Nepal and used as a bargaining chip by the Nepalese government in its efforts to disarm the Mustang guerrillas. But he refused to co-operate and managed to send a message to the guerrillas to disregard his capture. Finally, the Dalai Lama sent a message to the guerrillas asking them to give up their weapons. Following the surrender of the guerrillas, Lhamo Tsering was imprisoned in Nepal for seven years. In Kathmandu Central Jail, Lhamo Tsering and six other Tibetans were housed together in one large cell. There was a real possibility of demoralisation, especially since they were left pretty much alone by the authorities and liquor was freely available through the prison Mafia. In the same interview, in 1991, he told me of his prison experiences:

> I said to the others that it would be difficult to survive if we didn't organise ourselves. I suggested that we kept strictly to an active and productive routine every day without fail. The others agreed. I wrote down the routine and pinned it up on our cell wall. It went like this: We got up at six and then held a prayer service. After that we exercised till eight when we had our breakfast. From nine we had classes in English, Hindi and Nepali. Teachers were no problem. The jail was crowded with lawyers and teachers from the banned Congress Party and other dissident political groups. In our jail there were more than one hundred such people. The previous prime minister of Nepal was in our jail for some time.[1]

---

1. The jail also housed Westerners: druggies, hippies and backpackers, who had run afoul of Nepalese law. One such, Jeff Long, wrote of his time in Kathmandu jail with the Mustang group in *The Rocky Mountain Magazine*, entitled "Going After Wangdu; the Search for a Tibetan Guerrilla Leads to Colorado's Secret CIA Camp".

After lunch we played volleyball till tea time at three, after which you could do as you pleased. Little Tashi used to fly kites. He was from Lhasa and had a passion and the skill for the sport. Ngagtruk and Pega were great chess players, and also very religious. They meditated a lot and both managed to recite the "Praises to Tara" over hundred thousand times. The rest of us weren't that spiritual. Our speciality was humour. Rakra was tremendously funny and had an inexhaustible fund of hilarious stories and jokes. But Chatreng Gyurme was even better at making up strange tales. He made them all up in his head, and they were weird. Our jailers and the Nepalese prisoners were puzzled by the constant laughter that would come from our cell.

So we kept ourselves busy and were never bored. In fact, I never seemed to have enough time for my own writing and reading. One of the books I did read at the time was Leon Uris's *Exodus*. I was deeply impressed and moved by the courage and sacrifice of the Jews in their struggle to create an independent nation. We managed to keep up this routine till the day we left that jail — and we stayed healthy and mentally disciplined. The consequences of not doing so were only too clear in the Central Jail. There were many suicides.

Our education programme was a great success. Everyone became quite proficient in Nepali and Hindi except for me. I sadly lack the gift for languages. We shared our food and tea with our Nepali teachers. They did everything they could to help us, advising us on legal matters, drafting our petitions and helping to prepare our defence. Since many of these lawyers and dissident politicians had friends in the various government offices, they even managed to get some documents concerning our case copied and smuggled into prison.

One day, the jailed leader of the Nepalese Communist Party, Manmohan Adhikari[2] dropped by to talk to us. He had to apply for

---

2. With Nepal becoming a democracy in the 1990s the Communist Party became a major force in Nepalese politics and Adhakari even served as Prime Minister for a time. He died on 26 April 1999.

high level clearance from the Home Ministry for the visit, which surprisingly, they gave him. Adhikari told us he hadn't come to discuss ideology or Communism, as we all had different views on this. He said that fundamentally we were all brothers in this world. He advised us that if we did no more than hope for clemency, we could be in jail for the rest of our lives. He suggested various ways in which we could try to advance our case and stressed that we were not to overlook even the slightest advantage or the most insignificant contact we had outside. He then went on to tell us not to pay too much attention to Nepali government propaganda about "Khampa bandits" and "atrocities". We were to remember that what we had done was for the sake of our country and people. In times of war unfortunate things happened, but that was life, and we should not become disheartened. Before he left he said he had a personal request to make of us: that we keep in good spirits, good health and not lose hope.

We stuck to our routine till the last day of our jail term. We were released in December 1980.

Lhamo Tsering was back in harness after a short seven-month break. Though his former work had been of vital national importance, his role had not exactly been a recognisedly official one, and he was generally known as "Yabshi Drunyik-la" or honourable secretary to the Dalai Lama's family. This time he worked directly in the Central Tibetan Administration (CTA) of the Dalai Lama. From 10 April 1981 until 1 October 1985, he was additional general secretary of the Department of Security (CTA). From 1986 until 1993, he was a member of the Advisory Board of the Department of Security (CTA). From 9 August 1993 until 3 June 1996, he was elected minister of the Department of Security.

I am not privy to Tibetan government intelligence secrets, and Lhamo Tsering's activities of this period will most likely remain classified for years to come, but he was probably running agents inside Tibet again. I got a hint of this from a newcomer from Tibet whom

I had befriended and taught English at Bir school. This young Khampa, whom I suspected had been recruited, always spoke of Lhamo Tsering with respect bordering on awe. There was a general feeling among those who knew him closely that Lhamo Tsering was never quite the same man after coming out of prison, but it was nice to see that he could still inspire the kind of loyalty in his agents as before.

After his release, Lhamo Tsering also started work on a detailed history of the Resistance movement that he had been intimately involved in. The entire twelve volume series, entitled *Resistance*, is being published by Amnye Machen Institute (AMI), Dharamshala. The first volume, *The Early Political Activities of Gyalo Thondup, Older Brother of H. H. the Dalai Lama and the Beginnings of My Political Involvement, 1945–1959*, was published in 1992. The second volume, *The Secret Operations into Tibet: 1957–1962*, was published in 1998.

Future volumes will include a five-part account of the Mustang Resistance Force; a two-part account of underground organisations inside Tibet; a four-part account of the underground organisations and intelligence-monitoring units set up inside Tibet; and finally, an account of the resettlement programme of the former guerrillas of the Mustang Resistance Force. These books cover the entire period from 1945 to 1988. All the volumes have already been written, and are being edited by the director of AMI, Tashi Tsering.

After a long illness, Lhamo Tsering died in New Delhi on 9 January 1999. He is survived by his wife Tashi Dolma, a son, Tenzing Sonam, daughters: Dolma, Diki Yangzom, Tenzing Chounzom, and an adopted daughter, Tsering Yangzom.

Somehow I seem to have left this till the end. Probably I wasn't sure how it would play, or how the reader might respond to an account of yet another aspect of Lhamo Tsering's integrity. But at a time when cynicism is widespread, and corruption has made considerable inroads into our church and society, it may reassure people to know that Lhamo Tsering was honest and conscientious, almost to a fault. Even when he was minister for Security he would travel to Delhi by public bus, to the frustration of his family who were worried for his safety. In his long career, hundreds of thousands of dollars of secret funds passed through his hands, without there ever being the suggestion that even a penny of it had been misused. He retired poor. He did not own a house or a car and his wife fleshed out his very inadequate pension with petty trade.

Though Lhamo Tsering was the complete professional, and the most meticulous and organised person I have known, there has been the occasional remark on his seeming lack of requisite ruthlessness for the job. And it must be admitted that there was an ambivalence — something of the George Smiley about him. But, on the other hand, his modesty and concern for others were among the qualities that elicited the loyalty and dedication of his many agents and fighters.

At the height of the Cultural Revolution, when intelligence from China was near non-existent, and — as an old hand informed me — "not a sparrow could move from one village to another without an official permit", Lhamo Tsering managed to place (and nurture for years) a high-level agent in Lhasa itself.

I was in the Resistance for only a short while and can make no claim to camaraderie or shared experiences with Lhamo Tsering, but I think I speak on behalf of all the common soldiers of Mustang, when I say that it was a privilege to have known him, and an honour to have served under him.

1999
Tibetan Review

Body-Snatchers
Enduring Phobias and Superstitions in Tibetan Society (Part 1)

ON A GREY MORNING during the monsoon of 1976, the small town of McLeod Ganj, or at least the Tibetan part of it, experienced a curious upheaval. The event had everyone out in the narrow bus-stand, which is also the surrogate town square, and where every New Year's day the Toepa (Western Tibetan) men and women perform their Navaho-like round dances, shuffling and stamping their feet to the dull beat of a single drum. That morning the crowd at the bus-stand was not in a celebratory mood; the women were howling with all the zeal of professional Chinese mourners, while the men were running around bellowing like lunatics.

The cause of the disturbance was not physical, like an earthquake (which the area is somewhat prone to), nor social or political, like the communal riot we had some years ago. A psychologist might say that it originated from "the dark, inaccessible part" (to borrow from Freud's definition of the id) of the Tibetan mind. The only parallel I can draw, off hand, is the "dancing mania" that gripped a number of towns and villages in medieval Europe after the Black Death.

One of the most widespread and persistent of phobias that Tibetans have had in the past about travelling to "the great Indian plains" (*gya-thang* or *gya-ding*) was of being abducted and having their "human-oil" (*mi-num*) squeezed out of them. The extraction process was explained to me by a *geshe* (doctor of divinity) from Drepung Monastery, when the two of us arrived at the North Indian city of Siliguri from Kalimpong. Geshe L... was a heavily-built man of around fifty years of age, quite learned, in the traditional sense, yet fairly open-minded as well.

As we boarded a cycle-rickshaw and were pedalled away to the New Jalpaiguri railway station by a skinny, hollow-cheeked rickshaw-wallah, Geshe-la appeared ill-at-ease. He turned to me and asked whether I had heard of any "human oil" squeezers operating in the town. I insisted that those old stories were absurd and completely without foundation. But he was not reassured, and seemed to regard my attitude not only as frivolous but dangerously naive as well. Geshe-la patiently explained it all to me.

It appeared that in most cases of human oil abductions, the victim was first rendered helpless by a drug slipped into a drink or a cigarette. He or she was then taken to some lonely warehouse or shed where he or she was stripped naked and hung upside down from the rafters over a low fire. Gradually, the body would begin to drip fat — in the manner of a roasting pig — which was collected in a pan underneath, and later bottled, or whatever.

I came to understand from an uncle of mine that the human oil scare had been especially prevalent among Tibetans during World War II. At that time, an unprecedented number of Tibetan merchants, traders and muleteers travelled to India to buy consumer goods to sell — at huge profits, incidentally — in South-Western China, where the beleaguered Nationalist government was holding out against the Japanese. The belief among Tibetans then seemed to be that human oil was a vital ingredient in a miracle-drug the Allies had discovered for healing battle wounds. An interesting cachet to this story was that in the interests of the war effort there was an official policy of turning a blind eye to such abductions.

Even after settling down in India as refugees, Tibetans never quite lost their fear of human oil extractors and one would, now and again, hear references to it in conversations with older Tibetans. The story gained a surprising revival in Dharamshala around the time of Mrs. Gandhi's "Emergency". Whether the unhealthy political climate of repression and rumours contributed to the revival is debatable, but the subsequent events in Dharamshala seemed somehow not out of place in the nervous mood of the country at the time.

In McLeod Ganj, deliberations and speculations on the human oil issue emanated, on the whole, from three different sources. The opinion at Crazy Horse's (Samdup's) Noodle Palace favoured the conclusion that India's new aircraft carrier was fuelled by human oil. The nuclear option prevailed at the Kokonor Restaurant, where there was a clear consensus on the theory that human oil had been the critical factor in the success of India's then recent, and first, nuclear test. The conversation at the Last Chance Tea Shop was the least imaginative, never rising beyond hesitant conjectures on human oil being the fuel for India's *namdru*, or aeroplanes.

Around that time, Mrs. Gandhi's somewhat draconian Family Planning programme was being implemented, and stories were rife of entire Indian communities being forcibly sterilised by over-zealous officials trying to meet birth control quotas. In the Tibetan exile society these got mixed up with the older human oil story, and contributed to a growing paranoia about officially abetted abductions. Rumours about kidnappings not only began to proliferate but sprouted details that were quite specific and authentic sounding. One was that the abductors always arrived in a jeep flying a red flag, which was, of course, the signal for the police and local officials to look the other way.

Then, one day, a small disturbance occurred just outside McLeod Ganj, which in a way was a harbinger of the "curious upheaval" I mentioned at the beginning of this piece. A monk taking a walk from the town to the Tibetan Children's Village (TCV) encountered a group of Indians on the road. At this time of the year, Dharamshala is filled with yatris, pilgrims, visiting Hindu holy sites around the area. These pilgrims generally wear red headbands or carry red flags as tokens of their faith. This particular group of Indians on the McLeod–TCV road started to shout and whistle (in the noisy exuberant way of Indian pilgrims) to some of their friends on the road below. The monk, who was somewhat corpulent, suspected the worst and fled back to McLeod Ganj, where his breathless account of red flags and near abduction immediately circulated around the town, sending a frisson of apprehension through it.

Two days later, on a somewhat overcast day, I was hanging about the bus stand at the air-gun stall that once stood just by the intersection of the two roads, one leading to the Tibetan Children's Village and the other to the nearby village of Forsyth Bazaar — which then continues on to Lower Dharamshala. The stall owner and I were having a chat when a few Tibetans from Forsyth Bazaar walked by. They were hailed by a McLeod Ganj Tibetan. The subsequent conversation went something like this:

McLeod Tibetan: Hey! Where are you all going?

Forsyth Tibetan 1: We're going back to Phosa Baza (Forsyth Bazaar).

McLeod Tibetan (*gravely*): You'd better be careful. People are being grabbed and taken away these days, just like that. There's this jeep with a red flag that comes along, and then there's nothing you can do about it.

FORSYTH TIBETAN 1: We heard something like that.

FORSYTH TILETAN 2 (*worried*): We'd better rush back, our children are alone at home.

MCLEOD TIBETAN: You do that. Someone told me that there was a jeep full of Indians this morning at Phosa Baza. He thinks the jeep may have had a red flag stuck in the front.

The group from Forsyth Bazaar quickly walked away down the road. The McLeod Tibetan hurried towards the main street. I couldn't swear it was him but the next minute there was this outcry "Where's our children?". Another voice pitched in, "The children have been taken!" It was absolute chaos after that.

In a surprisingly short time, the bus-stand was filled with panic-stricken Tibetans. The women were the noisiest, screaming at the men to do something, and crying and howling as if it were judgement day. The men rushed around shouting threats and curses. I remember one man in particular, a self-important but simple fellow whom a friend of mine had rather facetiously named *dhonchoe* (an official term for the Dalai Lama's representative), since he loved bustling about in public gatherings, looking busy and important. That day he was running up and down the main street brandishing a long and wicked-looking Tibetan dagger, all the while shouting ferociously: "Where are they? Where are they?"

A few female hippies were in the crowd with some old *amalas*. All of them were weeping copiously. One old granny was holding a yappy little Apso that was adding its share to the general cacophony. A rather brainless German girl I knew spotted me and came over howling, "Save the children! Save them!"

I'm afraid I laughed out aloud. Some people in the crowd turned on me. "How can you laugh? … Our children … abducted … etc."

I tried to explain how mistaken they were but got nowhere. Fortunately there was a timely distraction; someone had the sense enough to suggest that they check the local day-school where the very young children of McLeod Ganj studied. Everybody surged down the street to the small two-room school. The old monk teacher was rudely woken up from his nap. He had given the kids the day off and most of them had gone off to play. Finally, the children were rounded up. In fact, quite a few of them had been in the crowd all along, shouting and enjoying themselves.

The older children attended the Tibetan Children's Village (TCV) school some miles away. One of the self-appointed leaders of the crowd, a local politician of unbelievable shallowness of intellect and character, then led everyone to the Tibetan Women's Handicraft Centre which had a telephone. The TCV principal was called and the demand made for an immediate inspection to see if any McLeod Ganj students were missing. After a lengthy altercation, the principal managed to persuade the caller that all the children were present and accounted for. But our representative wasn't done yet. He began to make noisy demands that the TCV provide motor transport and escort for the town children when they returned home after school. But the principal terminated the conversation at that point.

That evening a large escort of parents, all armed to the teeth, brought their children home from school. A duty roster was drawn up and for the next few days, two or three McLeod men, armed with knives and cudgels, accompanied the town children on their way to and from school. After some time the men got tired of this task, or it probably dawned on them that there had never been a threat in the first place, for the escort was discontinued and the children went about their own way to school, free and unattended as usual.

*

I did not then regard this incident as being of any significance. I thought such shortcomings in our society would gradually disappear with education and entry into the modern world. That was twenty years ago. Every year since then we seem to be going backwards. In his opening statement at the famous Scopes "Monkey" trial in Tennessee in 1925, Clarence Darrow warned: "We are marching backwards to the glorious age of the sixteenth century when bigots lighted faggots to burn men who dared to bring any intelligence and enlightment and culture to the human mind." We aren't burning people in Dharamshala yet but the evidence shows we are moving in that direction.

In 1996 a man was set upon by a McLeod Ganj mob. Only the timely arrival of the Indian police saved him from something worse than the beating he received. His crime? While taking shelter from a heavy downpour (it was monsoon time again) he had jokingly remarked that even the Dalai Lama was helpless against the Dharamshala rains. An old *amala* overheard him and raised the alarm. Last monsoon too (1998) we had another little "upheaval". Holidaying tourists leaving the Mc'llo beer-bar late one night were treated to the sight of sleepy-eyed Tibetans in various states of *déshabillé* (but armed with knives and cudgels) wandering confusedly about the streets of McLeod Ganj. They had been roused from their slumber to fight off a supposed invasion of Shugden worshippers.

It is not an original observation that traditional societies disrupted by the advance of modern industrial and technological culture, or some other traumatic change, invariably seek recourse in magic, superstition and fundamentalism for a solution. Every such threatened community probably goes about it in its own distinctive way, but sometimes interesting coincidences occur.

When the writer, Nicholas Shakespeare, was travelling in the town of Ayacucho in Peru in 1987 he came across a widespread belief among the Indian population surprisingly similar to the Tibetan human oil fear. The Indians believed that "human grease" was rendered from Indian victims by a sinister character known as a *pistaco*. In fact, Shakespeare himself seems to have been suspected by the locals of being a *pistaco* and suffered some bad moments without quite understanding why.

Finally, in the local paper *Ahora!*, he read an article "Ayacucho lives in terror", and from it he learned that "a *pistaco* was a tall white foreigner who slept by day, drank a lot of milk and carried a long white knife under his coat. He used the knife to cut up Indians. He chopped off heads and limbs, and kept their trunks for the human grease with which he oiled his machines. Europe's industrial revolution had been lubricated with the lard made from helpless Indians. So had the Vietnam and Korean wars. The space shuttle Challenger, he learned, had blown up because it lacked this 'aceite humano'." ("In Pursuit of Guzman", in *The Best of Granta Travel*)

Shakespeare also learned what happened to the last white man who visited Ayacucho. "He was set on by a crowd. His head was crushed by stones, because you cannot shoot a *pistaco*, and his eyes were pulled out by hand. His body was dragged through the town until the bones showed." He had only been a commercial traveller.

In a reference to *pistaco*, from as early as 1571, it is mentioned that the Indians believed that an ointment from the bodies of the Indians had been sent for from Spain to cure a disease for which there was no medicine there. A university lecturer told Shakespeare that the myth was the Indian way of explaining the Spanish domination, and that the present manifestation was not organized but spontaneous: the community, under fire from both the military and Sendero (the Maoist, Shining Path guerrillas), had turned against all.

On the other side of the globe, another group of similarly threatened people tries to understand the relentless advance of modern technological materialism through the inadequate medium of a traditional world view. Eric Hansen ("Stranger in the Forest") when walking across Borneo, was mistaken for a *bali saleng*, or a collector of blood offerings for coastal construction projects. A *bali saleng* has a special set of spring-powered shoes that enables him to jump four metres in the air and ten metres away in a single leap. He can spring through the air to cover long distances quickly and capture people by surprise. After tying up his victim with strips of rattan, he takes the blood from the wrist or the foot with a small knife and a rubber pump. Hansen was attacked by villagers in the jungle and nearly killed. Only when they searched his pack for spring-powered shoes or a rubber pump and didn't find them, was he reluctantly released.

September 1999
High Asia Journal

Oracle Bones
Random Speculations on China's Future[1]

ALL CONJECTURE ON THE FUTURE of China by even the most far-seeing of experts involves, of necessity, tremendous simplifications. It would appear that the human intellect is simply not equipped to deal with the unimaginable complexities of a nation that is not only the world's largest in terms of population, but also the oldest, in terms of a continuous history. The fact that it is the world's last major totalitarian power compounds the intellectual disorientation of those trying to understand that country — and divine the direction in which it is headed.

Having an understanding of China based in the main on random reading (in translation) of Chinese histories, novels and folktales, it would perhaps be best if I were to observe the injunction that Wittgenstein laid down near the end of *Tractatus*, that: "Of those things of which he cannot speak man must remain silent."

---

1. Based on a paper presented at the Conference on Sino-Tibetan Relations, 5–6 October 1992, at Washington DC.

But this would probably not go down too well with the organisers of this conference. So, for someone with such crippling limitations, I feel it would put the least strain on my own credibility and also the credulity of the listener, if I were to restrict my discourse to a less exacting and unquantifiable area of Chinese studies where, if nothing else, empathy could perhaps prove more discerning than expertise.

This untidy, elusive realm, not too often featuring in discussions on the future of China is, for want of a better word, the psychological one. To even begin to probe this, especially as it relates to people on a collective level, as in a nation, I feel that it is imperative to understand the cultural values of that society. And this I feel is most accessible, even for the not-so-expert, through the national literature.

Isaiah Berlin observed that one of the most reliable criteria for grasping the intellectual and moral vitality of a nation was the quality of its literature.[2] This yardstick is particularly applicable to China, since it is a nation with the oldest continuous literary tradition in the world. I am probably influenced in the choice of this criteria by the fact that I am a writer of sorts, but I am convinced that an appreciation of contemporary Chinese literature, even in translation, and even by someone so ignorant of the subject as myself, would permit us a glimpse of the inner health of the nation. Furthermore, a comparison with the evolution of literature in the Soviet Union should provide some clues as to the divergence in the paths of these two nations in the last few decades, and maybe reveal something of their futures.

Seven years before the Chinese Communist Party took power,

---

2. Isaiah Berlin, 1979, "The Hedgehog and the Fox". In *Russian Thinkers*, London: Penguin Books.

Mao Zedong had decided on the fate of writers in China with his "Talks at the Yanan Forum On Literature and Arts",[2] in 1942. With the outbreak of the war with Japan in 1937, many leftist intellectuals and patriotic students left their universities and homes to join the Communists at their headquarters at Yanan. Among these were nationally famous writers such as Zhou Yang, Ding Ling and Xiao Jun, the young Manchu writer who was a *protégé* of Lu Xun. But soon these writers were discovering that all was not as Communist propaganda had represented at Yanan, and that many cadres were insensitive, corrupt and enjoyed a range of special privileges denied to the ranks.

Gradually, the intellectuals began to question these anomalies, especially in the pages of the Yanan paper, *Liberation Daily*, edited by Ding Ling, who stimulated such debate with criticism of her own on the lack of sexual equality in Yanan. Of these critics probably the most acerbic was Wang Shiwei, a translator and writer of fiction, who, in a two-part essay "Wild Lily", denounced the selfishness of some leaders, the suppression of free speech, and the alienation of young people from the Party.[3] Initially these critics had been encouraged by Mao's own "Rectification Campaign" where he had singled out for condemnation: bureaucratism, dogmatism, sectarianism, and a failure to cherish the masses. The Yanan intellectuals accepted this campaign at its face value and failed to see it as a political ploy to destroy "the right opportunist" tendency led by the CCP's main Stalinist, Wang Ming, and to strengthen Mao's own position as Party Leader.[4]

---

2. Mao Zedong, 1985, *Selected Works Vol. III* Beijing: People's Publishing House.

3. Gregor Benton, 1982, "Writers and the Party: The Ordeal of Wang Shiwei, Yanan 1942" In *Wild Lilies*, Poisonous Weeds, edited by Gregor Benton. London: Pluto Press.

4. Merle Goldman, 1967, *Literary Dissent in Communist China*, Cambridge, Mass.

The writers in their own campaign of criticism received much support, especially from young people in Yanan. The Party leadership, surprised at the force of the criticisms and the unexpected support for the critics, decided to clamp down hard on the writers. The Party fired its opening guns with Mao's famous "Talks On Arts and Letters",5 the main thesis of which was the need to subordinate art and literature to political requirements. These talks were the main turning-point in CCP cultural policy. All the writers were criticised, "struggled" and underwent thought reform. Most, including Ding Ling, disavowed their earlier views, and many gave up writing altogether. Only Wang Shiwei stuck to his guns. He was tried as a "Trotskyist" spy, and eventually executed in 1947.

In Russia, on the other hand, the magnificent flowering of Russian literature and poetry in the 1890s, far from being arrested by the Bolshevik revolution, continued to derive vitality and inspiration from the vision of a new socialist world. Despite the conservative tastes of the Bolshevik leadership, anything that could be represented as a "slap in the face" to bourgeois taste was approved and encouraged; and this opened the way to a great outpouring of excited manifestos and audacious, controversial, often highly gifted experiments in all the arts and in criticism, which in due course was to make a powerful impact on the West.6

Some of the most original among the poets whose works survived the revolution were Alexander Blok, Andrey Bely, Vyacheslav Ivanov, Valery Bryusov, and in the next generation Mayakovsky,

---

5. Mao's talk was presented as his original doctrine but, according to Merle Goldman, much of it could have been translated from the speeches of the Soviet literary czar, Andrei Zhdanov.

6. Isaiah Berlin, 1982, "Meetings with Russian Writers". In *Personal Impressions*, Oxford: Oxford University Press.

Osip Mandel'shtam, Anna Akhmatova and Boris Pasternak; among painters Benois, Chagall, Kandinsky, Soutine, Bakst, Goncharova, Malevich, Tatlin, Lissitsky and Roerich (who not only painted those Martian landscape-like depictions of Shambala that annoy certain Tibetan aesthetes, but also created the sets for the first production of Stravinsky's Firebird); novelists as Aleksey Tolstoy, Babel and Pil'nyak; and the pioneering movie-makers Pudovkin, Meyerhold, Vakhtangov, Tairov, and the incomparable Eisenstein.

Under Stalin this genuine movement of revolutionary creativity was crushed by the dead weight of state-controlled orthodoxy. Mayakovsky committed suicide, others were shot or imprisoned.[7] But eventually Stalin called an end to this terror, and with the advent of World War II and the German invasion, poets and writers, even those not approved of by the Party, and whose works had been unpublished or banned, began to receive public accolade. Their works were widely read, learnt by heart, quoted by soldiers, officers and even political commissars.

After the war and till the end of their lives, such poets as Pasternak and Anna Akhmatova remained heroic figures in the eyes of the Russian people, and vast audiences packed halls to hear them read their works. In the bleakness of the Russian political landscape all throughout these years it cannot be doubted that it was the power and integrity of such poets, writers and artists, and in later years of such writers as Solzhenitsyn, Leonid Borodin, Yury Dombrovsky, Andrei Bitov and others, that preserved the essential humanity and hope of the Russian people.

After the establishment of the People's Republic of China all the

---

7. For the best account of the life of the intelligentsia during this period see Nadezhda Mandelstam's memoirs. *Hope Against Hope* and *Hope Abandoned*, London: Collins Harvill.

leading figures of modern Chinese literature fell into almost total silence and sterility;[8] Lao She, Mao Dun and others producing only a few trite occasional pieces, or works of Communist propaganda. Ding Ling's novel *The Sun Rises Over the Sanggan River* (*Taiyang zhaozai Sangganhe shang*) was a propaganda paean to the brutal Land Reform campaign and received the 1952 Stalin Prize for literature. In the wake of this success Ding Ling became a powerful literary functionary, even taking part in the anti-intellectual campaigns of the early 1950s, and having a hand in more purges of intellectuals than party norms required.[9] There has been some marginal writing of value from dissidents such as the *Li-Yi-Zhe Manifesto*, and the short stories of Chen Jo-hsi of the Cultural Revolution,[10] written after the writer was allowed to leave China. She wrote nothing while she lived in the PRC for seven years.

After the fall of the "Gang of Four", manifestos and magazines, published unofficially but openly, called for a variety of political and social reforms. Short stories exposing the horrors of the recent past, and poems in praise of freedom and democracy featured in these publications, though most could not avoid the clichéd stridency and melodrama of official propaganda writing. The exception was the work in *Today*, edited by Bei Dao[11] and Mang Ke, though the magazine was proscribed in 1980.

---

8. For a quick sampling of writing in the PRC during this period (accompanied by a very naive but sympathetic analysis) see: Kai-Yu Hsu, 1976, *The Chinese Literary Scene*, London Penguin Books.

9. Jonathan Mirsky, 26 October 1989, "Stories From the Ice Age", *The New York Review of Books*.

10. Chen Jo-hsi, 1979, *The Execution of Mayor Yin and Other Stories from the Great Proletarian Cultural Revolution*, Bloomington: Indiana University Press.

11. Bei Dao, 1989, *Waves*, Translated by Bonnie MacDougall and Susette Cooke. London: Sceptre.

The category of writing about the horrors of the Cultural Revolution known as "wound literature" (*shang-hen wenxue*) has continued, as it does not altogether contradict the official line. But even though this does seem to be an improvement on the past, I feel that in literary terms it is a deception. It is not only a literature of self-pity, but essentially serves as a prop to official dogma, which seeks to lay the blame for all of China's past horrors solely on the Cultural Revolution. For the writer, such a literary form, consciously or unconsciously, limits examination of the past to what is convenient in terms getting along with authority or demonstrating some misguided sense of patriotism.

One question Chinese writers never seem to ask is who the victims of the Cultural Revolution really were, and whether these victims themselves had not in some way been involved in, or been responsible for, the sufferings and deaths of millions of people prior to the Cultural Revolution — or had at least been party to condoning it? Milan Kundera provides a partial answer to this question: "When I was a boy, I used to idealize the people who returned from political imprisonment. Then I discovered that most of the victims were former oppressors. The dialectics of the executioner and his victim are very complicated. To be a victim is often the best training for an executioner."

A book that came out last year, *Wild Swans: Three Daughters of China*, though written in English, provides a case in point. Written by Jung Chang, a Chinese woman now living in Britain, it describes the horrors of the Cultural Revolution in which her parents were caught up as victims, especially her father, an important Communist official, who was hounded to insanity and eventual death. Though the description of this period is presented with conviction and accuracy, the earlier period of her father's role in the guerrilla war against the Kuomintang is straight out of a Revolutionary opera like *Shachiapang*, replete with wicked landlords and *e-ba* "ferocious despots".

Of course, a girl's idealisation of her father is understandable, but some of her statements do not square with facts. She talks of the peasants' ferocious desire for vengeance against landlords, and the efforts by Communist cadres like her father to restrain the people from killing all landlords; and how because of her father's intercession the Party ordered that Land Reforms be conducted without undue violence.

The truth is, of course, somewhat different. The late Lazlo Ladany, editor of *China News Analysis* and "the most exact and consistently correct observer of the political and social scene in the PRC"[12] has clearly pointed out that the Party insisted on the Land Reforms being a "violent struggle":

> The procedure was the same everywhere. The first step was to arouse the masses against the landlords. It might have been thought that the peasants, if given a free hand, would seize the land, but this did not happen. The peasants obviously became suspicious when they saw that huge numbers of Party cadres and even soldiers had been sent to stir up anger against the landlords. In Guangdong province alone, 62,000 Party officials and soldiers were sent to the villages to mobilise the peasants. This was done on the instructions of the Party Central Committee's South China Bureau. The peasants had to be disciplined into discontent and revolt against the landowners.

A report presented to the Military-Political Committee of Central-South described the difficulty of "arousing the masses". Many peasants were reluctant to act; in some places they sympathised with the persecuted landowners.[13]

---

12. Jurgen Domes, in a preface to Laszlo Ladany's *Law and Legality in China*, University of Hawaii Press, Honolulu, 1992.

13. Laszlo Ladany, *The Communist Party of China and Marxism 1921–1985. A Self Portrait*, 1988, Hoover Institution Press, California.

The Land Reform campaigns were not only extremely bloody and "an extremely violent struggle which reached every corner of the country" but "a lesson in terror" as well. Liu Binyan, the well-known dissident and former reporter of *The People's Daily*, provides a firsthand account of the land reform in his autobiography, *A Higher Kind of Truth*; which confirms Ladany's researched report. No official figures have ever been released of the victims but a pamphlet circulated internally thirty years later, in 1980, stated that the number of landlords and *kulaks* had fallen by 10.5 million.[14] This may or may not be indicative of the exact number of those killed during the land reform, but it gives us a substantial idea of the magnitude and ferocity of the campaign.

What if the daughter of a Nazi official had written a book extolling her father's role in benevolent Nazi programmes to deal with the problems of socialists, gypsies and Jews? What if the happy tone of her account only changed to one of grief and outrage when the SS tortured and executed her father for, let us say, involvement in the army bomb plot against Hitler?

Nowhere, too, in all the recent and past literature that has come out of China has there been any sense of national shame or sense of responsibility for the crimes committed by the Chinese on neighbouring people like the Tibetans and Uighurs. "We did not know" is the common answer to this, "the Communists kept us ignorant". But the Chinese in Taiwan and elsewhere in the free world knew what was happening in Tibet. Why the silence?

The only Chinese in the West to write about Tibet has been Han Suyin, and her book is far more demeaning and mendacious of the

---

14. Kan-pu hsueh-hsi ts'an-k'ao (Cadres Study Material), People's Broadcasting House, no. 1. 1980, (for internal circulation only). From *Law and Legality in China*, by Laszlo Ladany, University of Hawaii Press, Honolulu. 1992.

Tibetan people and issue than official Communist propaganda.[15] According to Han Suyin, Tibetans were so incredibly backward that Tibetan farmers used "wooden ploughs, not iron tipped, for iron was not only expensive but 'malefic'. I noticed that the ploughs were now iron-tipped, and instead of pushing them (as was done before when the yaks pushed the plough forward with their lowered heads, surely a most inefficient way of making a furrow not more than four inches deep) the yaks were now pulling the plough. This was already innovation."

Furthermore, when there was a modicum of freedom in the PRC for magazines and newspapers to publish original observations, what did Chinese writers come out with? I quote from a translation of Jigme Ngapo's article that appeared in the *Center Daily News* in October 1987.[16] "I have read the story by Ma Jian ("Show the Coating on Your Tongue or All Void") originally published in *People's Literature*, and reproduced in a Hong Kong magazine. It is disgusting. The author uses rumours about Tibet and mixes them with elements of his imagination, producing a nauseating picture. The story is not the first of its kind to attack the Tibetan people." The editor of this magazine was dismissed for publishing this story as well as for an editorial of his own. But according to Ngapo, this did not reflect a new sensitivity on the part of the authorities to give justice to the Tibetan people, but was based on its anti-bourgeois campaign which was at its peak around the time (February 1987). In this article Jigme Ngapo also comments on the attitudes of Chinese students, even those in universities in the United States, towards Tibetans and their aspirations. "They want independence? Give them a good lesson!"

---

15. Han Suyin, 1979, *Lhasa, The Open City*. London: Triad Panther Books.
16. Translated and reprinted in *Lungta*, no. 6. Geneva.

I read Ma Jian's story translated somewhat differently as "Stick Out Your Furry Tongue, or Fuck-all",[17] and was not impressed. His ignorance of Tibetan religion and customs, about which he writes so blithely, makes Lobsang Rampa seem erudite and profound in comparison. Though Ma seems to regard himself as modern and artistic, his attitude to Tibet is no different from that of all other Chinese, past and present — condescending and exploitative. What is most striking about Ma Jian's writing is its self-conscious artiness; as if he had gone about highlighting passages of his story with different coloured marker-pens, signifying "dadaism", "surrealism", "magical realism", or whatever.

Another writer with similar *avant-garde* aspirations is the officially approved Tibetan author Zhaxi Dawa (Tashi Dawa), who claims he does not write in Tibetan as his message is too sophisticated for non-Chinese reading Tibetans. I have been told by Tibetans from Lhasa that he not only cannot read or write Tibetan, but cannot speak it either. *In Tibet: Soul Tied to a Leather Buckle*,[18] his ostentatiously magical-realist novella is essentially a vehicle for the recapitulation of age-old Chinese racist calumnies about Tibet: about people barely more civilised than beasts, clinging superstitiously to a dark and savage religion. It is no wonder that this essentially trite, posturing and derivative piece of writing should have become a great hit with the Chinese some years ago.

No work by any author from China — or, for that matter, a Chinese writer anywhere on the globe — has in any way dealt intelligently or sensitively with Tibet — with its people, religion, history and customs. On the whole they have been uniformly and

---

17. 1988, Geremie Barme & John Minford, *Seeds of Fire; Chinese Voices of Conscience*, Hill and Wang, New York.

18. ibid.

offensively racist, often with an ill-concealed vein of hostility towards even the mildest of Tibetan aspirations for freedom.

In 1863, when Russia was choking the life out of Poland, the liberal socialist writer Alexander Herzen cried "I am ashamed to be Russian".[19] Tolstoy, in a story, "What For?" (1906) gives a sympathetic presentation of Poles involved in the insurrection of 1830–31.[20] Though it must be pointed out that the ultra-nationalist Dostoyevsky, and also Pushkin could hardly be said to have been sympathetic to Polish aspirations.

Even a wretched Russian *zek* in a concentration camp in the nineteen fifties admitted to shame at Stalin's oppression of other peoples. Such were the feelings of Alexander Solzhenitsyn when the tenth anniversary of the "liberation" of the Baltic States was celebrated at his prison camp:

> I found the Estonians and Lithuanians particularly congenial. Although I was no better off than they were, they made me feel ashamed, as though I were the one who had put them inside. Unspoiled, hard-working, true to their word, unassuming — what had they done to be ground in the same mill as ourselves? They had harmed no one, lived a quiet, orderly life, and a more moral life than ours — and now they were to blame because we were hungry, because they lived cheek by jowl with us and stood in our path to the sea.[21]

We also know that Andrei Sakharov and other Russians suffered official reprisals when they openly protested the Russian invasion of

---

19. Alexander I. Solzhenitsyn, 1979, *The Gulag Archipelago*. Translated by Harry Willetts. New York: Perennial Library.

20. Ronald Hingley, 1967, *Russian Writers and Society, 1825–1904*, World Universal Library, McGraw Hill, New York.

21. ibid.

Czechoslovakia in 1968.22 We must also remember the demonstration by Moscow students against the Russian action in Hungary in 1956, which was sharply put down by Khrushchev.

On 18 September 1990, Alexander Solzhenitsyn, in the *Komsomolskaya Pravda* and the *Literaturnaya Gazeta* made a plea to the Russian people and leaders to give up the empire, to let the Baltic Republics, Armenia, Georgia, Moldavia, and the Central Asian Republics that so desired, secede. He was convinced that clinging to the empire prevented the regeneration of Russia itself and the upliftment of her people. "We have no need for the empire, for it destroys us," Solzhenitsyn said.23

A Chinese, to whom I pointed this out, retorted that Solzhenitsyn had spoken less out of conviction than convenience, for by 1990 it was quite obvious that the Soviet Union was going to break up one way or the other. But a reading of Solzhenitsyn's earlier works easily dispels any such doubts as to his integrity. His massive and monumental work on the Soviet concentration camp system, *The Gulag Archipelago*, was begun in 1958 and finished in the mid-sixties; though only published in 1973. In the book, he talks of meetings in the camps with Ukrainian nationalist prisoners many of whom had sided with Nazi Germany against Russia. He has this to say of their dreams:

> Why are we so exasperated by Ukrainian nationalism ... why does their desire to secede annoy us so much? Can't we part with the Odessa beaches? Or the fruit of Circassia? For me this is a painful subject. Russia and the Ukraine are united in my blood, my heart,

---

22. George Bailey, 1989, *The Making of Andrei Sakharov*. London: Allen Lane the Penguin Press.

23. Alexander Solzhenitsyn, 1991, *Rebuilding Russia*. translated by Alexis Klimoff. London: Harvill.

my thoughts. But from friendly contact with Ukrainians in the camps over a long period I have learned how sore they feel. Our generation cannot avoid paying for the mistakes of generations before it.

Nothing is easier than stamping your foot and shouting: "That's mine!" It is immeasurably harder to proclaim: "You may live as you please" ... We must prove our greatness as a nation not by the vastness of our territory, not by the number of peoples under our tutelage, but by the grandeur of our actions. And by the depth of our tilth in the lands that remain when those who do not wish to live with us are gone.

It is my conviction that Solzhenitsyn's observations about the Soviet empire and the solutions he advocates are equally applicable to the Chinese empire. In China, more than anywhere else, the nexus of imperial triumph on the one hand and repression and cultural regression on the other has been a long and enduring one. In fact Qin Shihuang, founder of the first Chinese empire, also has the distinction of being the architect of the first totalitarian system of government in the history of humankind.

On the other hand, China's feudal age, the Spring and Autumn Period (*Chun Qiu*), 770–476 B.C., and the Period of the Warring States (*Zhan Guo*), 475–221 B.C., when China was split into many disparate states, small duchies and kingdoms, was the most glorious age in the history of Chinese thought. It was a period when ethical and philosophical systems like Confucianism, Taoism and others arose which have exercised a lasting influence on the culture of the Far East, similar to the influence of classical Greece on European civilisation.

The Song dynasty is unique in Chinese history, not only for its conscious renunciation of imperialism, but also for the consistent humanity and efficiency of its rule. Song rule was based on general acquiescence and constitutional rule to an extent never achieved in Chinese history. It never made any attempt to extend its borders beyond the Great Wall, and was never threatened by internal rebellions of any importance. In the opinions of many, Chinese civilisation reached its apogee in these years, and in later centuries never recovered the level to which the Song had attained.

In modern cultural development, especially literature, China can look back to the 1920s and 1930s, certainly not as a period of imperial advancement — rather the reverse — but nevertheless as an era whose creative dynamism has not been equalled since. In 1924, the eminent German Sinologist Richard Wilhelm observed: "Chinese intellectual life today is at the forefront of our epoch. Its leading lights in the arts and sciences are working together in the most thorough manner on the universal problems of our age in the technical, scientific, philosophic and artistic spheres."[24]

All this has been noted and discussed before by Sinologues such as Simon Leys who, in an article, asked the question: "What if, unhappily, there is some necessary link in China between political ineptitude and cultural flowering? The former always seems to be the atrocious price of the latter, and conversely the re-establishment of imperial order usually goes with a dramatic intellectual impoverishment."[25]

Bertrand Russell, who visited China in the early 1920s, though accepting this intimate relationship between cultural and political questions in China, was in no doubt as to which was crucial, even for the development of the other: "For my part, I think the cultural questions are the most important, both for China and for mankind; if these could be solved, I would accept with more or less equanimity any political or economic system which ministered to that end."[26]

---

24. Richard Wilhelm, 1924, *Aus Zeit und Leben: Abschied von China*, Beijinger Abende.
25. Simon Leys, 1979, *Broken Images*. New York: Saint Martin's Press
26. Bertrand Russell, 1922, *The Problem of China*, London.

Rabindranath Tagore, when he visited China in 1924, also had a message for the Chinese people. The major thrust of it was that China's hope lay in man's eagerness to seek freedom from "the servitude of the fetish of hugeness, the non-human".27 Though his lectures were well attended by the public he also drew taunts and protests. Chinese reacting to their own hurt racial pride found it "particularly distasteful in being preached to by an Indian, even if he had won the Nobel Prize".28 His message of love and humanity was jeered at, even by the writer Mao Dun, who suggested in an article "a much better slogan" to Tagore's appeal. "Reply to our enemies' machine guns with Chinese machine guns; answer their cannons with our cannons."29

The maintenance of empires and colonies by force is not only culturally and spiritually demoralising to the tyrant, but potentially a source of considerable political upheaval within the oppressor state itself. According to a study of viceregal government in Sichuan under the Zhao brothers, Zhao Erfeng and Zhao Erxun, the province overextended itself by the imposition of direct Chinese rule into Eastern Tibet, and the invasion of Tibet proper in 1909, which among other factors like tax rises in the province caused the rebellion of September 1911 in Sichuan. This in turn caused the Wuchang Uprising, bringing about the downfall of the Manchu Empire and the formation of the Republic. Of course, the fall of the dynasty had other and more underlying causes, but the Sichuan revolution, caused in part by Chinese overextension in Tibet, was, in the words of the author of this study, "the fuse of the double ten revolution and part of its explosive force".30

27. 1981 Jonathan D. Spence, *The Gate of Heavenly Peace; The Chinese and Their Revolution 1895–1980*, Viking, USA.

28. ibid.

29. ibid.

30. S. A. M. Adshead, 1984, *Province and Politics in late Imperial China. Viceregal government in Szechwan, 1898–1911*. Scandinavian Institute of Asian Studies Monograph Series. London and Malmo: Curzon Press.

Empires, when maintained by force and intimidation, without even partial consent of the subject peoples — which wasn't always the case in such empires as the Roman or the British — can, I am convinced, only lead to the brutalisation and degeneration of the ruling nation itself. Whatever apparatus of repression one devises to control one's colonies: informers, the secret police, thought control, a brutal army, can also be easily turned against one's own people. Political violence is a two-edged sword.

In Britain, the democratic rights of the people have considerably eroded over the past years by the insistence of the Conservative government in dealing with the question of Northern Ireland in a harsh and undemocratic manner. The long-standing reputation of the British legal system and the reputation of its police force have been extensively damaged over the past couple of decades by its overreaction to the threat of the IRA. So, too, in India with the violence in the Punjab and Kashmir. Now, if problems of this magnitude affect mature democracies when dealing with separatist movements, how can democracy possibly begin to take root in China, when even the fledgling Chinese democracy movements-in-exile are not only unwilling to give up a square inch of the empire, but are even demanding more territory — Taiwan, the Spratleys *et al*. And of course, the Chinese empire can only be maintained by employing the entire apparatus of repression and control; for without it, Tibetans, Uighurs and others would not hesitate to rise up violently for their freedom.

I think those Chinese who desire democracy and peace for their country should take their lead from General Charles de Gaulle's reversal of policy towards French colonies in North Africa. Emotionally, de Gaulle was committed to the greatness of France, but he was a realist enough to see that not only were France's military efforts to hold on to its colonies becoming an economic drain on

France, but that the brutality involved was demoralising an army that he loved, and promoting a very dangerous neo-fascist movement that threatened French democracy.[31] Against tremendous opposition, he decisively divested France of Algeria and other colonies. That decision brought about ruin, suffering, and dislocation to many thousands of French colons who had settled for generations in Algeria. De Gaulle's decision also brought about considerable danger to his own life and virtual civil war in France itself; but history has shown that the General was right.

It is now vital for intelligent and right-thinking Chinese to put aside misplaced ideas of face and patriotism, and seriously consider the liability of empire, not only for the cultural and spiritual regeneration of the Chinese people but for the birth of democracy in China as well. It is not enough for the Chinese to reluctantly acquiesce to Tibetan demands for independence. They must actively participate in the dismemberment of the Chinese empire and the unshackling of subject nations, before their own individual freedoms can be truly realised.

November 1999
Tibetan Review

---

31. Philip M. Williams and Martin Harrison, 1973, *Politics and Society in de Gaulle's Republic*. New York: Doubleday Anchor.

Return of the Referendum

LIKE THE CHILDREN OF ISRAEL wandering through the desert to the Promised Land, we Tibetans have often been diverted from our goal by "golden calves" and false gods of one kind or another: genuine autonomy, truth insistence, zone of peace, constructive engagement, associate status, middle path, etc. None of these much vaunted, dazzling solutions to the Tibetan problem have ever came close to approaching realization. They failed because they were not based on even a minimal study of Chinese history and politics, nor an understanding of modern totalitarian and authoritarian systems, nor for that matter, an appreciation of the hard-ball nature of global politics. Looking back, these proposals leave behind a strong impression that they were devised primarily to appeal to the West, as non-nationalistic, world-peace oriented, environmentally friendly, and most important of all, non-disruptive of the West's economic interests in China.

The latest of such false gods doing the rounds within the Tibet support community is the "Referendum Proposal" that made its debut as a WTN article some months ago, and is being promoted vigorously by the Committee of 100 for Tibet. On close inspection this proposal seems to be a reworking of an earlier referendum scheme that the Tibetan government launched some years ago. That earlier scheme called for a referendum throughout the Tibetan world to make a choice between, essentially, "Independence", and the Dalai Lama's "Middle Way Approach" which required the giving up of Tibetan independence and living in an autonomous Tibet under Chinese sovereignty. In order to downplay the stark contrast between these two choices — and muddy the water as it were — two other quite irrelevant options were added. These were "Self-determination" and Samdhong Rinpoche's recondite doctrine of "Truth Insistence".

After the first announcement of the referendum scheme it may have dawned on the authorities that such an exercise could not be conducted inside occupied Tibet, for a further announcement was made that the referendum would be confined to the exile world. Right from the start it was clear that the whole point of the exercise was to whip up public support for the Dalai Lama's "Middle Way Approach". A gesture of impartiality was demonstrated by the organizing of a debate in Dharamshala. But when teams of Tibetan members of Parliament and government officials toured the Tibetan settlements and communities-in-exile to announce the terms of the referendum, it was made clear to the public, in not very subtle ways, that failure to vote for the "Middle Way" would be tantamount to showing disloyalty to the Dalai Lama.

The Tibetan community was thrown into controversy and confusion. The Tibetan Youth Congress was the only organization that came out clearly and unequivocally for independence and started a campaign, with posters and public discussions, to voice their conviction. The Congress was vilified by nearly all the corrupt, reactionary organizations that dominate Tibetan politics, and whose stock-in-trade are noisy, hysterical and aggressive (but also calculatedly self-serving) displays of loyalty to the Dalai Lama. A community already divided by a fierce and violent religious controversy was now being politically divided in much the same fashion.

The general public was, without question, strongly attached to the cause of independence but at the same time did not want to disappoint the Dalai Lama, or at least be seen in opposition to His wishes. It was a traumatic, confusing and extremely divisive period for Tibetans. Even within families the referendum caused much bitterness and discord. Finally a plebiscite of sorts was conducted, but the results were never made public. Instead the government-in-exile issued a statement declaring that it was not quite the right time for a referendum yet, and the whole sorry debacle was brushed under the already lumpy carpet of our recent history.

The present call for a referendum does give the impression of being an attempt to reintroduce the former scheme in a fresh way, this time by roping in the Tibet support groups around the world to endorse what the Tibetan public failed to do. That the object of the exercise is still to promote the Dalai Lama's "Middle Way Approach" can be gauged in the statement of his special envoy, Lodi Gyari in an article in the latest *Tibetan Bulletin* (May–June 2000) where in a tacit endorsement of the Referendum Proposal as a lever to persuade the Chinese to have a dialogue with the Dalai Lama, Gyari writes, "If the result of such a referendum affirms China's claim that the Tibetans are happy and contented, then His Holiness the Dalai will be the happiest person of all."

Even if this present Referendum Proposal were completely sincere and did not contain a hidden agenda, I feel that its promotion would further divide the Tibetan community and divert effort and resources from the real goal of carry on the struggle for Tibetan freedom.

The revival of the referendum scheme was probably inspired by events in East Timor last year, with the UN supervised plebiscite bringing about the freedom of the East Timorese people. Yet however uplifting this historic event it is important to note some major differences in the circumstances that led to the referendum in East Timor, and the current situation in Tibet.

Indonesia was in a state of economic collapse and near anarchy. The old repressive regime had been thrown out and totally discredited. China's economy hasn't collapsed. Party control is total and absolutely repressive. This is not to say that events won't change, but it clearly hasn't yet.

The United Nations had never recognized Indonesia's takeover of East Timor and had condemned the Indonesian government for its repression of the East Timorese people. The UN does not question China's sovereignty over Tibet. In fact the UN is so submissive to China that it regularly objects to the presence of the Dalai Lama or any other Tibetan in events organized under its auspices, and further goes out of its way to ensure that references to Tibet and the Dalai Lama do not appear in its publications — or anything related to it.

We must bear in mind that even with the advantages mentioned above, East Timor paid a terrible price in terms of its people massacred (in the many tens of thousands) tortured and raped. I should also mention the looting and destruction of thousands of buildings and homes, and the near-complete leveling of East Timor's capital city, Dilli. All these outrages took place after the referendum. The UN displayed an unfortunate and bewildering disinclination (or inability) to protect the people of East Timor from the wrath of militant groups loyal to Indonesia, until quite late into the events.

If we take the figures issued by the Tibetan government-in-exile of Chinese population transfer into Tibet, holding a referendum inside Tibet now would be fraught with uncertainties, even if we were absolutely sure that every Tibetan voted for independence. Furthermore pressure from the UN or the World Community for referendum in Tibet (if it ever did come) could easily provoke the Chinese to accelerate their population transfer timetable in order to present a fait accompli.

But let us look on the bright side of things. Let us suppose that we could be sure that a referendum in Tibet would reveal to the world that Tibetans did not want to live under Chinese rule. Would the Chinese allow such a referendum if there was even a remote chance of such an outcome? This is where the logic of the referendum advocates completely escapes me. I just don't understand why the Chinese, who have made it absolutely and brutally plain that they are not in the least interested in the Dalai Lama's surrender of Tibetan sovereignty and his proposal for "genuine autonomy", should want to consider a more dangerous option like referendum where "independence" would have to be a choice. (Or maybe we are talking here of a referendum where no reference to independence or "Free Tibet" is contemplated).

Furthermore I don't see how world leaders and governments who are unwilling or unable (even in the slightest way) to persuade China to accept the Dalai Lama's absolutely tame proposals for negotiations, could persuade China to accept a more dangerous and uncertain option.

I am certainly not against the idea of referendums per se, and it is quite possible that in the eventuality of a collapse of Chinese power in Tibet and the presence of even limited Tibetan control over the country we might be able to conduct a genuinely free and fair referendum under the supervision of the UN or a respected international agency, and also protect ourselves against a Chinese backlash. But clearly we should only call for a referendum when we have the wherewithal to ensure its success and not to have it backfire on us and become the final nail driven into the coffin of Tibetan sovereignty.

For those who feel that a referendum is important in order to ascertain what the people inside Tibet want, I would ask them to spare a little time to listen directly to the voices of the Tibetan people inside Tibet and not to those interpreting them in the West. The word "Rangzen" is the most constant and powerful refrain in nearly all protest documents that have come out from Tibet in the last twenty odd years, whether it be lengthy petitions to the United Nations, humble scraps of paper surreptitiously passed on to tourists, or wall posters hurriedly pasted up in the night (sometimes upside down) on the walls of Lhasa city. The cry of the suicide bomber in Lhasa last year was also "Rangzen". In fact, every political demonstration and protest has had as its fundamental demand, independence for Tibet; followed by a demand for human rights, and expressions of loyalty to the Dalai Lama as the sovereign of Tibet. Hundreds of such posters, leaflets, pamphlets and manifestos have made their way out of Tibet and in not a single one of them has there ever been a demand for autonomy, dialogue, or for that matter, referendum.

More than through paper ballots, Tibetans inside Tibet have declared their aspirations in a far more demanding and dangerous referendum. Braving incarceration, torture and execution they have, in the streets, monasteries and prison-cells of Tibet, raised their voices for "Rangzen". The direction for the Tibetan struggle is clear. It is up to us to take our own first steps on that hard road and not try to persuade oneself and others to adopt easier routes, which may appear safe, politically correct, undemanding and even personally advantageous, but which will eventually lead our people and nation to darkness and extinction.

*

This article was also posted on the Tibet Support Group List and elicited much discussion. Some replies to questions raised.

In his refutation G writes: "In true democracy there are no thoughts of 'ensuring' success." Does G think that China is a democracy and that China will respect the rules if the UN tells them to do so? The UN will do as it's told by China. Let's just review recent events when His Holiness the Dalai Lama was not invited to the Millennium World Peace Summit of Religious and Spiritual Leaders because China did not approve of it.

It may have escaped G's notice but most Tibetans are living in one of the most repressive states in the world, and the situation is worsening daily. If a referendum were held under present circumstances one could be near certain that China would win a landslide victory. It has a lot of experience in organizing such happenings. Communist Party candidates regularly gain 99.99% of the votes in elections to the National Congress in China. And who's going to call on State Security personnel — stuffing ballot boxes or terrorizing Tibetan voters — to cease and desist? The UN, the USA, Great Britain, Canada? I seriously doubt it.

When one is conducting a referendum or an election within it is, of course, imperative that there should be a philosophy of accepting defeat gracefully and not just "winning at all costs". But within one doesn't have to go to prison or get shot because one has lost a referendum or an election. But unfortunately not everyone in this world is privileged to live in a democracy as G does. Remember how East Timorese were massacred even though they won the referendum.

G says that even if the referendum is lost it shouldn't really matter, "Simply another day, another vote, another chance" is his philosophical refrain. The loss of a referendum in Tibet would not only provide the final legitimization of China's take-over of Tibet, but could well be the death knell of Tibetan civilization. It could possibly trigger a horrendous persecution, if not massacre, of Tibetans who voted or campaigned for freedom.

But of course if a disaster like that happened it wouldn't be anyone's fault, not least of all G's and other proponents of referendum. So what if nobody took the trouble to think the whole thing out properly. Their motivations were pure. So, don't get too upset about it. Just chalk the whole thing up to experience, pack up your "Satyagraha" in your old kit-bag, and move on to causes anew. "Simply another day, another chance."

*

F says that the Committee of 100 for Tibet's referendum campaign is different from the Tibetan government referendum scheme which was primarily to poll Tibetans outside Tibet. Wrong. The first announcement made by the Tibetan government clearly indicated that they intended to poll people inside Tibet too. Even some harebrained schemes were proposed of sending pollsters secretly to Tibet. Only when the impossibility of the scheme really sunk home did it become limited to the exile population.

F further remarks "The distinction is that the 1995 referendum was intended to decide the strategy or path that was to be followed in the Tibet movement;" Nothing of the sort. Does everyone remember the four options of this earlier referendum. One was "Independence". For the life of me, does that sound like a strategy? Or more precisely, a goal. Fred adds that "the current referendum is to let the Tibetan people determine the destination, or the goal, or the outcome of the movement."

I would like to suggest that the Tibetan people have already determined what they want. Are our memories so short that we

RETURN OF THE REFERENDUM | 251

forget the many demonstrations since 1987, all over Tibet, where Tibetans had only had one demand "Rangzen". Is it necessary to ask these people again if they really meant what they said when they risked their lives by calling for an independent Tibet.

I also did not take the Lodi Gyari quote out of context as F maintains. Lodi Gyari though not expressing immediate support for the referendum did write that it would be the proper solution if the Chinese did not respond to the Dalai Lama's offer of negotiation; something I clearly stated. Of course, Gyari threatening to unleash "referendum" on the Chinese if they did not respond to the Dalai Lama's overtures, is the height of absurdity.

As for the claim that I have not provided an answer as to how Tibetan independence can be attained, I would like to plead guilty. I do not have a blueprint on how to liberate Tibet. If the reader has a copy of my Rangzen Charter he will know that I propose a broad strategy of Direct Economic Action (at least in the free world) to destabilize China, and weaken its hold on Tibet. But that's as far as it goes for the present. I am not a prophet or the medium for a Tibetan oracle. Anyway how do you think revolutions and freedom struggles work? Do you think Nelson Mandela had a complete plan of action in prison on how he was going to bring down apartheid? Do you think George Washington, shivering in Valley Forge, with a rag-tag army decimated by desertion and disease, knew exactly how he was going to beat the Brits?

All you can do when the odds are stacked against you is to hang on to your goal like grim death, and keep on fighting regardless of all the attractive comfortable alternatives that well intentioned but essentially anaemic souls, try to make you accept in the name of good sense, peace and understanding.

If the Committee for 100 had existed in 1770s America and had managed to push for a referendum then, there would be no United

States of America today. Only fourty per cent of Americans supported the revolution. The rest of the colonists were essentially loyal to their sovereign, His Majesty King George III. Thank God for firebrands, dreamers and fanatics like Tom Paine, Jefferson, and Patrick Henry.

*

E says "Yes, Tibetans have for several years sought negotiations and nothing has come about, but political strength building takes time." I would like to correct E. The Dalai Lama tried negotiations from 1950 to 1959, for about ten years, and failed completely.

The more recent initiative was undertaken around the late seventies, which would make this present futile exercise over twenty (not "several") years old. All in all, over thirty years of hoping we could negotiate a deal with the Chinese. When will we ever learn?

9 August 2000
World Tibet Network News

Acme of Obscenity
Tom Grunfeld and *The Making of Modern Tibet*

THEY SAY THAT no book is all bad. You wouldn't think so at first, judging by the reviews of Joan Collins' last offering. Still, I suppose if one really looked at the whole thing in a less literary, more egalitarian and somewhat dispassionate light, even the out-and-out hate literature and racist tracts produced by white-supremacist groups, or the propaganda material generated by the Ministry of Truth in Beijing, serve to inform us of a definite point of view, no matter how distorted, hateful or ugly, of certain groups of people in this world. So at least in that narrow sense it could be said to fulfill a function.

But in the hate/propaganda genre there is a sub-class of publications which, through their authors' skill in providing a superficial gloss of scholarship or objectivity to their work, renders them capable of great mischief. Chief among these is, without doubt, *The Protocols of the Learned Elders of Zion*, a document put together by the Okhrana, the tsarist secret police, purporting to be the report of a series of twenty-four meetings held by Jewish leaders and Freemasons in Basel, Switzerland in 1897, to make plans to take over the world. It was translated into practically every European language, also Arabic, and its effect has been poisonous in the extreme.

Mother India (1927), by American journalist Katherine Mayo, is a work that purports to be one of genuine concern for the welfare of the Indian people. It is a mishmash of the usual indictments of Indian society: the caste system, child marriage and so on, topped off with such spurious and outrageous charges as that Indian mothers regularly masturbated their sons "to make them more manly." It is essentially a racist tract serving to confirm long-held prejudices of white people against Indians, and, in essence, making out the case that Indians were an exhausted race of sexual degenerates morally unfit to rule themselves. This message was grasped eagerly in Britain where *Mother India* received enthusiastic press reviews. The book's success in the USA did considerable damage to the Indian cause there, which till then had been gaining in support and sympathy.

Tom Grunfeld's, *The Making of Modern Tibet* (Zed Books, 1987) is a work that is more in line with Mayo's book than with *The Protocols*. Grunfeld doesn't exactly accuse Tibetan mothers of masturbating their sons, but he does claim that "babies were not washed as they emerged from the womb but sometimes licked by the mother" — like animals. He offers neither source nor citation for this amazing fabrication. He goes on to specify that Tibetans were cruel, dirty, ignorant, syphilitic (90% of the population suffering from venereal diseases according to Grunfeld) sexual degenerates who were observed making love on rooftops in full public view.

Why make such outrageous accusation, you may ask? What purpose does such ridiculous abuse serve? But these are not random insults Grunfeld is hurling, but essential components of his greater design — to expose Tibetans as barbaric, subhuman, even bestial, thereby justifying Chinese rule in Tibet as necessary and civilizing. It is particularly galling for any Tibetan even to have to deny such charges, coming from a propagandist for a country where till very recently, ritual cannibalism of the most gruesome kind was practiced to honour Chairman Mao (*Scarlet Memorial: Tales of Cannibalism in Modern China,* Zheng Yi, Westview Press, 1996)

The first clue I got of Grunfeld's closet racism was on the cover of his book. It shows a Tibetan man sitting cross-legged on what appears to be an oversized garbage can. He is wearing an old sheepskin robe incongruously topped off with a large Mao cap adorned with a star in the front. He also has a wide grin plastered on his face. It reminded me of those racist postcards once said to be sold in stores in the American South, the kind where a happy black man is sitting on a barrel with a big slice of watermelon (or a banjo) in his hands and a wide grin on his face. Another image that came to mind was that of the stereotypical cartoon depiction of an African tribal chief: a fat black man with lips like a jelly doughnut, wearing a grass skirt, a bone ornament inserted through his nose and a shiny top hat perched rakishly on his head.

Grunfeld's other efforts to establish that pre-invasion Tibet was a corrupt, cruel and degenerate country relies heavily on a very discredited device — selective quotations wrenched from context. For instance, though Grunfeld has to admit that Chinese propaganda about Tibetans practicing human sacrifices is without evidence, he goes on to write that "The most convincing clue we have comes from Sir Charles Bell. Bell wrote that he once visited a spot on the Tibet-Bhutan border where he saw a *stupa* called Bang-kar Bi-tse cho-ten that contained the bodies of an eight year old boy and girl 'who had been slain for the purpose' of some religious ritual."

What Grunfeld omits to tell us is that Bell is talking about events of the distant past, as he clearly mentions that the stupa had been built "many years ago." Furthermore it is evident that Bell intended the story as folklore, as an old tale that someone else had told him, and not as an eyewitness account. We can confidently assume that Bell did not tear apart the stupa (in the manner of the Chinese Communists) to check for the corpses. Bell also immediately follows up the sentence about the two bodies with this line: "Scenting the corpses and blood a demon took possession of the chö-ten", bearing out the fictional nature of his account. (*Tibet Past and Present*, p. 80). Charles Bell also writes that the area in question (Dromo) had been a stronghold of the old pre-Buddhist faith, Bon. This, in all probability, makes the stupa in question an old Bon one, and not the usual Buddhist stupa that is the familiar feature of the Tibetan landscape.

Furthermore the charges against the Bon religion of human sacrifices and black magic is to a very large extent based on Buddhist clerical misrepresentations of a once successfully competing religion. A bit like Christian propaganda about pre-Christian "pagan" religions. No scientifically acceptable evidence has, to this day, been unearthed (even by Chinese academics) that savage rituals and practices of the kind that prevailed in pre-Columbian Central and South America ever existed in Tibet, even in remote antiquity.

If an American tourist at Stonehenge, on being told by locals that virgins were once sacrificed there, used that bit of information to claim that human sacrifice was an accepted practice in modern Britain, he would probably be regarded as a candidate for the funny house. But such methodology is fairly standard throughout Grunfeld's book.

Grunfeld also uses Bell's statement that "slavery was not unknown in the Chumbi valley" to imply that slavery was a standard institution throughout Tibet. Once again Grunfeld does not include Bell's subsequent remarks that the institution was then on the wane and that "only a dozen or two [slaves] remained"; and that "the slavery in the Chumbi valley was of a very mild type." (*Tibet Past and Present*, p. 79).

Grunfeld further completely fails to mention that Bell made these observations in 1905 when, as assistant to Claude White, he was posted in the Chumbi valley. This was at a time when slavery and bondage of a very cruel, inhuman and completely legal kind was universal throughout China, and also prevalent in large parts of the British Empire in the legalized form of "indentured labour."

If we adopt Grunfeld's cavalier style of stretching events of 1905 to fit anywhere before 1959 (when the Chinese Communists took full control of Tibet, and which is Grunfeld's cut-off date for "Tibet As It Used To Be") we could probably overlook the fact that slavery ended in the United States in 1863 and compare it to what was going on in Tibet in 1905. We should also bear in mind that the "very mild kind of slavery" of "a dozen or two people" can hardly stand comparison with the slavery practised in the USA where, for example, in South Carolina sixty-four per cent of the population were slaves, and where every manner of torture and cruelty were inflicted on them, and where well into modern times such people could be "lynched" for the most trivial of reasons.

Even the few instances of "mild" slavery that Charles Bell reported in 1905 probably disappeared in the following years, for later accounts of Western travellers and even such long term European residents of Tibet as Heinrich Harrer, Peter Aufschnaiter and Hugh Richardson, make no mention of any such practice. What ensured its disappearance is almost certainly the Great Thirteenth Dalai Lama's reform and modernization programs, which despite some failures in such areas as modern education, managed to take unprecedented and far-reaching steps to protect the rights of the most humble Tibetan peasant and nomad against exploitation and official corruption.

Perhaps it should be mentioned here that in 1913 the Thirteenth Dalai Lama officially banned capital punishment and other forms of "cruel and unusual" punishments; possibly making Tibet one of the first countries in the world to do so. Switzerland abolished capital punishment in 1937; Britain in 1965 and France guillotined its last criminal in 1981. In the United States, especially Texas, even being underage or mentally retarded is no guarantee of not being sent to the "chair", or whatever is on offer.

In China, right now, they are going at it as if there were no tomorrow. An "execution frenzy" was how an Amnesty International press release of 6 July 2001, termed it. The press release went on to state that "More people were executed in China in the last three months than in the rest of the world for the last three years." 1,781 executions and 2,960 death sentences passed in three months. Yet, according to Amnesty these statistics are likely to be far below the actual number.

The Thirteenth Dalai Lama even turned down his cabinet's recommendation to execute his former regent and accomplices who had conspired to assassinate him. There is a possibility that the main conspirator, the Nyaktrul sorcerer, was secretly murdered in his cell by an overzealous official, but there is no evidence of any higher official involvement. Even the few instances in which this law was breached serves to demonstrate the fullness of Tibetan commitment to the Great Thirteenth's ideals. In 1924 when a soldier died under punishment, the Commander-in-chief of the Tibetan army, a man who had personally saved the Dalai Lama's life, was permanently relieved of his duties.

Not only is there no record of executions after 1913, but the one recorded case of a "cruel and unusual" punishment serves to demonstrate how deeply the law had taken root in Tibetan life. Some years after the death of the Thirteenth Dalai Lama, the official, Lungshar, attempted a coup d'état. On its failure many in the government wanted him executed but the old law stood in their way. So Lungshar was sentenced to the lesser punishment of having his eyes removed. The operation was badly botched. Such punishments had for so long fallen into desuetude that, according to Melvin Goldstein, the class of people who in the past had carried out executions and such punishments "told the government that they were only able to do it because their parents had told them how it was done."

But, to get back to the issue of slavery, let us put matters in perspective. Surely Grunfeld is aware of the Laogai camps in China where millions of wretched inmates, are, as we speak, toiling in unimaginably horrendous conditions, at what can only be described as slave labour. Even in "normal" Chinese society today slavery is not only prevalent but increasing, according to a report in the *Far Eastern Economic Review*, a Hong Kong based journal, entitled "Toil and Trouble: Slavery is on the rise in China as number of poor migrants increases. Beijing appears unwilling and unable to prevent it", by Bruce Gilley, 16 August 2001.

When making his very selective quotations of Sir Charles Bell, Grunfeld takes care to establish Bell's *bona fides* as a British colonial official and "a renowned Tibet scholar". But then Grunfeld completely fails to inform his readers that Charles Bell's main contention in all his books was that Tibet was an independent nation — culturally and historically distinct from China. While pointing out that Tibetans and Chinese were racially distinct, Bell took pains to point out a number of singular differences:

> The two races differ strongly in many qualities which have their roots deep down in the characters of the two nations ... Firstly, the Tibetans are deeply religious ... The Tibetan government is truthful. It can be slow, obstinate and secretive in dealing with foreigners, but it has a strong regard for truth. But the Chinese authorities from time to time made statements which were deliberately untrue ... The Chinese are far more cruel than the Tibetans are. When they tried to conquer areas in Tibet, they used to put to death what

prisoners of war they captured, although the only offence of these was fighting in defence of their homeland. The Tibetans, when they captured Chinese prisoners of war, used simply to send them back to China. The Chinese treat the granting of a favour merely as a step towards asking for another ... The Tibetans do not treat favours in this way. They have a national memory of things for which they are grateful ... Many other examples of the differences dividing these two nations could be given ... For instance, the status of women in Tibet is higher than China; the kinder treatment of animals; and the more orderly government." (*Portrait of the Dalai Lama*, pp. 353–354.)

Grunfeld's wrenching quotations out of context even extends to a few quotes from my *Horseman in the Snow*. To discredit Bell's and others' observations that women in Tibet were treated on a basis more equal to that of men than in neighbouring China, Grunfeld triumphantly pulls out this line from my book, "A man's wealth was, first and foremost, measured through the number of sons he had." Once again Grunfeld fails to include the subsequent sentences which read: "It was a matter of survival. Strong hardy sons were needed in every family to work and to fight bandits and settle feuds." And why was it so? Why was this area so violent and lawless? Because it was under Chinese administration. In that part of Tibet administered by the Dalai Lama's government "where law and order prevailed" as my informant emphatically states in the same book, the social status of women was higher, and certainly in advance of contemporary China with its foot-binding and child concubinage, and even present-day China with it's mind-numbing and sickening statistics on female infanticide.

Grunfeld uses a similar trick in order to allege that descriptions of the typical Tibetan diet of tsampa, butter tea, meat and vegetables were exaggerated and that "a survey made in 1940 in Eastern Tibet came to a somewhat different conclusion. It found that thirty-eight per cent of the households never got any tea but either collected herbs that grew wild or drank 'white tea', boiled water. It found that fifty-one per cent could not afford to use butter, and that seventy-five per cent of the households were forced at times to resort to eating grass cooked with cow bones and mixed with oat or pea flower."

Once again Grunfeld neglects to inform us that the survey was made in a long-held and Chinese administered area of Tibet, where the rapacity of Chinese officials ensured not just the poverty of the population but often its starvation as well. Grunfeld's notes at the end of his book exposes his deception. The source is *Frontier Land Systems in Southwestern China*, by Chen Han-seng, 1949.

In 1916 an American missionary with experience in Chinese administered Eastern Tibet wrote: "There is no method of torture known that is not practised in here on these Tibetans, slicing, boiling, tearing asunder and all ... To sum up what China is doing here in Eastern Tibet, the main things are collecting taxes, robbing, oppressing, confiscating and allowing her representatives to burn and loot and steal."

This observation is mentioned in *Travels of a Consular Officer in Eastern Tibet*, by Eric Teichman of the British Consular Service in China who, on the request of the Chinese government travelled extensively through Eastern Tibet in 1918, to conclude an armistice between warring Tibetan and Chinese forces. In his book he observes that the areas of Eastern Tibet administered by the Tibetan government were peaceful, orderly, well administered and contrasted dramatically with the lawlessness, poverty and misrule in Chinese administered areas. Teichman also cites similar observations by other European travellers who had travelled to both areas.

Grunfeld's chapter on early Tibetan history is absolutely disingenuous. While relating Songtsen Gampo's marriage to the Chinese princess as an "enlightened" move on the Tibetan's emperor's part, concurring with standard Chinese propaganda that Tibetans were eagerly seeking "superior" Chinese culture, he is completely silent on the fact that the princess was in fact a tribute, a prize wrested from the Chinese emperor's hand after the Tibetans had soundly defeated a Chinese army in battle.

Grunfeld mentions without qualification (and again without sources) that the Chinese princess "is credited with having introduced into Tibet the use of butter, tea, cheese, barley, beer, medical knowledge, and astrology." If butter, cheese, and barley, which are the staple food items of the Tibetans, did not exist in Tibet before the arrival of the Chinese princess, what does Grunfeld suppose Tibetans ate? Grass perhaps, which would, in a sense, support Grunfeld's other contention that Tibetan women licked their newborn babies clean, thus confirming the subhuman, perhaps bovine, nature of the Tibetan people.

Far from introducing such products to Tibet, the Chinese traditionally never ate cheese, butter and milk, and well into modern times regarded dairy products as somewhat disgusting. It is amazing that a person who nowadays refers to himself as "a historian on China", should lack such basic knowledge about traditional Chinese diet.

And this is perhaps where mention should be made of the fact that Grunfeld most probably does not read or even speak Chinese, since in his work he provides no primary Chinese sources. Furthermore, it is more than obvious that Grunfeld does not speak or read even basic Tibetan. Not a single Tibetan source is cited in his book. In fact his "history" relies on often outdated secondary literature, and does not even utilize the significant body of scientific and scholarly articles and monographs that have appeared (in English and other European languages) over the last twenty-five years or so.

Though problematic, linguistic inability might not, under

certain circumstances, prove so absolutely crippling in conducting research on Tibetan history. Alastair Lamb's *Tibet, China & India 1914–1950*, derived largely from official British archival sources, is a significant contribution to our knowledge of modern Tibetan history. Also use of translators, long term contact with Tibetan scholars and close association with the Tibetan community could also compensate in part for lack of language skills, as Warren Smith's discerning *Tibetan Nation* demonstrates.

Grunfeld has no dealings whatsoever either with Tibetans in exile or those inside Tibet, though he has made a couple of visits to Tibet, one just recently. He does occasionally attend seminars and lectures on Tibet in New York City, where he sits at the rear of the hall with a newspaper or magazine held up before his face. During breaks he has been known to pour out, to anyone willing to listen, woeful accounts of Tibetan mistrust and hostility towards him.

Grunfeld is patently dishonest in not owning up to his ignorance of the Tibetan and Chinese languages. He skirts the issue in the introduction to his book by claiming that he was aware that he had not drawn on Tibetan and Chinese sources, but that getting his book published took priority. He also has the shameless effrontery of justifying this with a quote from Hugh Trevor-Roper: "All researchers reach a point of diminishing returns where to continue without publishing only postpones the inevitable."

On another occasion he fobs off his ignorance of Tibetan and Chinese with this blatantly false declaration: "Chinese, Tibetan and Nepali sources are not very plentiful, on the whole, and not readily accessible even if one has the necessary language skills." (*Bulletin of Concerned Asian Scholars*, IX. 1, 1977: 59) Granted, Nepali sources may not be plentiful, but at the same time they are not as vital as Chinese and certainly Tibetan sources are in studying Tibetan history. And Tibetan sources are undeniably plentiful. They are also completely accessible to Grunfeld in New York City. Thanks to a US Library of Congress program, under the PL 480 program, from the mid-sixties onwards, copies of many thousands of volumes of basic, primary materials for historical research on Tibet were made freely available at such institutes as Columbia University or the New York Public Library — to anyone with "the necessary language skills" to read them.

Grunfeld even seems to lack the smattering of basic Tibetan that tourists to Tibet or hippies in Dharamshala manage to pick up during their stay. For instance in the introduction to his book he translates the Tibetan name for Tibet *Bod* (or *P'oyul*) as "the land of snows" which is laughably pathetic. *Bod* absolutely does not mean "land of snows". Tibetans do sometimes refer to their country as *Gangchen Jong* or "land of the great snows" in the same way an Irishman might refer to his country as the Emerald Isle. Grunfeld's book is so rife with such elementary mistakes that I think it serves no purpose to go on pointing them all out. The task could be more suitably performed at a Tibetan school perhaps, where children could compete with each other to spot all the many howlers.

Such being the case, I would be justified in asking Grunfeld the same question that Nirad Choudhuri (the great Bengali scholar and writer) asked of Katherine Mayo: why she, "who on the face of it, had neither the qualification nor any business to write on India", undertook her project. Mayo's book was suspected by many Indians of being inspired, if not commissioned by British officials in India. Even Gandhi was goaded to write, "We in India are accustomed to interested publication patronized — 'patronized' is accepted as an elegant synonym for 'subsidized' — by the government ... I hope Miss Mayo will not take offence if she comes under the shadow of such suspicion."

In 1971, Manoranjan Jha, came out with a book *Katherine Mayo and India*, which provided extensive documentary evidence to show that British authorities in India from the highest to the lowest ranks had indeed not only actively helped Mayo but had supplied much of the scandalous details. According to Mayo's papers now at Yale University, John Coatman, Director of Public Information to the government of India, had provided her with such salacious tidbits as that Indian men often practised sodomy on their own sons.

Like Mayo, Grunfeld claims that his work is honest, objective and motivated by genuine concern; and like Mayo, Grunfeld takes up a posture of martyrdom when attacked by critics. But the fact of the matter is that like Mayo, Grunfeld is a hypocrite and racist, and also the agent (probably less unwitting than Mayo) of a tyrannical imperial power.

Grunfeld was a member of the "US China People's Friendship Society" which Simon Leys has pointed out has nothing so much to do with friendship among peoples, as with serving the will of the Chinese Communist Party. He was also on the staff of *New China*, the propaganda vehicle of the Society, and was also a contributor. In 1975, before the Cultural Revolution had ended, when everything in Tibet was reduced to rubble and misery by this campaign's violence and madness, Grunfeld wrote an article, "Tibet: Myth and Realities," for *New China*. In it he unreservedly declared that extensive modern education, widespread healthcare, scientific agriculture, industry, commerce, and indigenous cultural life were flourishing in Tibet. Even Chinese officialdom later admitted that Tibet had suffered terribly and conditions had gotten far worse that what was supposed to have prevailed in pre-1950 Tibet.

Grunfeld was also a member of the Committee of Concerned Asian Scholars, a now discredited organization of left-wing Mao-worshipping Western academics who subscribed unquestioningly to the belief that Mao and the Communist Party of China had not only solved the problems of China but those of humankind as well; and that Communist China should be regarded as a model not just for developing nations, but also the United States.

When, at a meeting with Zhou Enlai a group of Concerned Asian Scholars sought to extol China's many achievements, the premier, irritated by their infatuation with the Cultural Revolution, cut them short by saying that much remained to be done. The deputy foreign-minister Chao Guanhua, complained about such adulation from the West with this objection "They used to write that everything in China was wrong. Now they write that everything in China is right." Steven Mosher in *China Mispercieved* exclaims in amazement: "This must surely rank as one of the wonders of the global village: Beijing's master image-makers giving lessons in balance and objectivity to American journalists." (And scholars.)

But is Grunfeld connected more directly to the Chinese government or the Communist Party — in some covert manner, perhaps? A revelation by a longtime friend of his indicates that he probably is. In his book *China Live: Two Decades in the Heart of the Dragon*, CNN Hong Kong bureau chief, Mike Chinoy writes that following the 1987 demonstrations in Lhasa, CNN's attempts to get permission to visit the Tibetan capital were constantly rejected by Chinese authorities. But in the summer of 1988 "Tibetan historian Tom Grunfeld, a longtime friend and fellow CCAS (Committee of Concerned Asian Scholars) activist from the 1970s with good access to senior Chinese officials responsible for the territory, was allowed to visit Lhasa, where he lobbied on our behalf. Two months later, we were thrilled to receive a telex from the Lhasa *waiban* inviting CNN to Tibet".

There are only so many ways one acquires such clout, such impressive *guanxi*, in the PRC. One thing we can be sure about is that Grunfeld doesn't have a spare million dollars to invest in China.

Earlier on, I dealt at such length on Grunfeld's equivocations on early Tibetan history and old Tibetan society that I now feel obliged to emphasize to the reader that the bulk of Grunfeld's book deals with Tibet after the Chinese Communist invasion. It is also here, in a presentation comparable only to Houdini's amazing trick of making a live elephant disappear on stage, Grunfeld performs a *tour de force*. He manages to write his entire account of this period without once referring to any famine either in Tibet or China, and does not even make a remote allusion to the Great Famine. A famine which is now generally acknowledged to be the greatest in human history, where thirty to sixty million people died and where starving people boiled and ate their own children.

Furthermore this famine was not an act of nature, but occurred as result of Mao's megalomaniac programs and the Party's complete indifference to human life and suffering. To Grunfeld, all this never happened. Instead he regales us with heady accounts of steady progress and reforms from the first instance the Chinese took power in Tibet. A summary of these amazing accomplishments is presented in his article in New China, "a decade earlier mutual aid teams were formed, then agricultural cooperatives, and finally, in 1965–66, people's communes. Mechanization has begun and experimental agricultural stations have developed more resilient, higher-yield grains as well as strains of tobacco, tea, sugar beets, and a dozen vegetables, which can grow readily in the climate of the 'Roof of the World'. Innovations such as insecticides, chemical fertilizers, irrigation, and veterinary medicine have been introduced into a land that hardly even know of their existence ... In short the lot of the Tibetan people has improved immeasurably."

Another black hole in Grunfeld's account is the imprisoning of hundreds of thousands of Tibetans in Forced Labour Camps, and also the mass killing of Tibetans by the Chinese. Grunfeld is absolutely silent on this. China's leading official Tibetan figure, the Panchen Lama, in his address to the Tibet Autonomous Region Standing Committee Meeting of the National People's Congress held in Beijing on 28 March 1987, clearly stated that in his native Amdo (Qinghai) "there were between three to four thousand villages and towns, each having between three to four thousand families with four to five thousand people. From each town and village, about eight hundred to one thousand people were imprisoned. Out of this, at least three to four hundred people of them died in prison". Nearly half the prison population.

At the same meeting the Panchen lama also provided specific instances of mass killings in his area. This is what he said: "If there was a film made on all the atrocities perpetrated in Qinghai province, it would shock the viewers. In Golok area, many people were killed and their dead bodies were rolled down the hill into a big ditch. The soldiers told the family members and relatives of the dead people that they should all celebrate since the rebels had been wiped out. They were even forced to dance on the dead bodies. Soon after, they were also massacred with machine guns. They were all buried there".

Grunfeld's silence on this issue makes his book the equivalent of a history of the American South with no mention of slavery, or a history of modern Germany without any reference to the Holocaust. Which raises the question, is Grunfeld's book comparable to the works of revisionist historians as David Irving who claim that the holocaust had never happened, that the gas chambers had never existed, but were invented for British propaganda purposes and then picked up by Jews to extort German and American finance for Israel?

First of all David Irving is a real historian, whose works have been published by major publishers in Sweden, Germany and Macmillan in Britain, and not like Grunfeld's "history" which was published by Zed Books in London, probably some left-wing propaganda setup. Also Irving is a fluent linguist and speaks and writes German like a native. In fact his knowledge of German language, history and culture is so exceptional that he was able to expose the phoney "Hitler Diaries" that the German magazine *Stern* had purchased and which had been publicly endorsed not only by a number of German experts but even by Hugh Trevor Roper, whom Grunfeld quotes to prop up one of his numerous falsehoods.

Also David Irving is no hypocrite or the cat's paw of a brutal dictatorial regime as Grunfeld is. No matter how distasteful and abhorrent his views, David Irving is at least open and straightforward about them. He does not pretend that he has nothing to do with neo-nazi groups, and in fact openly lectures at large gatherings in Germany where he is greeted with enthusiastic "Seig Heil's." More than anything he does not pretend to be the disinterested friend of the Jews. And to credit the man, Irving does not retail mediaeval anti-Semitic vilification, like the kind that Jews poisoned wells and performed secret rituals with the blood of murdered Christian babies. Nor does he repeat racist slurs about Jews being dirty, miserly, treacherous or sub-human. All of which Grunfeld enthusiastically does, in the Tibetan context.

But I find myself unable to go on any further. I must come up for air — pull my head out of the open sewer that is Tom Grunfeld's *The Making of Modern Tibet*. If the printed word could physically emit a stink, then this book would reek not only of dung and putrefaction but the charnel house as well. All the usual words of condemnation: scurrilous, disgusting, abominable, are inadequate to censure the man and his work.

Once again, as I have done many times in the past, I am obliged to touch on the wisdom and incisiveness of Lu Xun for an adequate concluding description of this deeply disturbing hate-tract and its perverted author. And modern China's preeminent humanist and writer, a man with a lifetime experience of skewering tyrants and their toadies on his mobi, his writing brush, does not disappoint. With his withering dismissal of the writings of Zhang Shizhao — one of the more unredeemably disgusting intellectual whores in the world of Chinese letters — as the "acme of obscenity", Lu Xun allows me conclude this piece.

30 August 2001
World Tibet Network News

Ian Buruma–Jamyang Norbu: an Exchange

4 October 2001, *New York Review of Books*

To the editors:

Ian Buruma in his article "Tibet Disenchanted" (20 July 2000) states that "Muslims had been persecuted in the past by Tibetans who wanted to keep Tibet 'pure', that is purely Buddhist."

Nowhere in Tibetan history is anything remotely of the kind indicated. Muslims were a very small and peaceful minority in the Tibet of the past, mainly merchants settled in Lhasa and other major towns. Most of them were from Kashmir and Ladakh and came to Tibet during the reign of the fifth Dalai Lama. A history of their community published some years ago in Srinagar (Kashmir) relates how the fifth welcomed them and gave them land within the city to build their mosque and burial ground. Most Muslims in Tibet owned successful business and in fact one of them started the first cinema hall in Tibet.

Most of them now live as refugees in Kashmir and the Middle East. They still take extraordinary pride in their Tibetan heritage and their many contributions to Tibetan culture, in the way of cuisine, elegant conversation and music.

Quite a few of their educated young men worked for the Tibetan government-in-exile and some still do. There was also a small community of Chinese Muslims (Hui) who had their own mosque, and who ran the butcher shops. Not only is there no record of the persecution of Muslims in Tibetan history, but even in the few accounts by Muslim scholars nothing of the kind is hinted at.

In recent years, as a part of the Chinese population transfer program, there has been a large influx of Chinese Muslims from Gansu and Qinghai into Tibet, which has caused real hostility to break out between the two communities.

It is a pity that certain Western intellectuals writing on Tibet (one being Orville Schell), try to make up for their ignorance of Tibetan language, history and culture, by calling attention to the fact that they, unlike Richard Gere or other celebrity Buddhists, haven't been taken in by the Dalai Lama's charms or the current craze for Tibet. They usually demonstrate this in their writings by exaggerating the failings of the old Tibetan church and society, or in Ian Buruma's case by insinuating that Tibetans were just as intolerant and violent as those suppressing them.

Jamyang Norbu

*

Jamyang Norbu would be quite right to criticize me if I had said that Tibetans were just as intolerant and violent as those suppressing them. However, that is not what I said. Quite evidently, they are not. I quoted a Tibetan Muslim who had told me that his father had suffered some persecution by Tibetan zealots. He was unclear about when this happened. But he added that things have been better for Muslims since the Communists took over in Tibet.

It is hard to assess the accuracy of such statements, but it is certainly not implausible. Trouble between Tibetans and Muslims goes way back at least to the early twentieth century, when there were wars in eastern Tibet between Tibetans and Chinese Muslims. And most Tibetans I have spoken to agree that Muslims were never regarded as fully Tibetan. In the tradition of all colonial powers, the Chinese often cultivated the minority as a way of controlling the majority. Muslims in Tibet were promoted to high positions, and so forth. This led to widespread resentment among Tibetan Buddhists, especially in the early years of the revolution. In 1959, for example, a mosque was burned down in Lhasa, because Muslims were accused of collaborating with the Chinese.

Ian Buruma

*

I think that a single confusion in terminology could be the source of the misunderstanding between Ian Buruma and myself. What I, and other Tibetans mean by Tibetan Muslims are the descendents of those who originally came to Tibet from Kashmir and Ladakh around the fifteenth century and who settled permanently in Tibet, mainly in Lhasa. Except for those imprisoned by the Chinese military authorities for participating in the 1959 uprising, nearly all Tibetan Muslims left Tibet after 1959 and resettled in Kashmir.

The people who Ian Buruma calls Tibetan Muslims appear to be Hui residents in Tibet, who originally came from Gansu and Qinghai. Tibetans always referred to them as Chinese Muslims and that is, incidently how all Hui, mostly those with the Chinese surnames of Ma (horse) are referred to generally in scholarship, whether they lived in Lanzhou or Lhasa.

Quite a few of them were permanent residents in Tibet, and even in the old days their relations with Tibetans were often strained. During the fighting in 1911 when Tibet managed to free itself of

Manchu rule, the Hui community in Lhasa threw in its lot with the Manchus. In the fighting in Eastern Tibet from 1956 onwards, the Communists used Hui cavalry (formerly troopers of the Chinese Muslim warlord of Qinghai, Ma Bufang) against resistance fighters. Tibetans did not regard Huis so much as collaborators, but as simply Chinese. And indeed the Hui, even those born in Tibet, who spoke the language and some of whom may have married Tibetan women, regarded themselves as essentially Chinese.

The fact that Tibetans invariably got along fine with their own Muslim community and with Muslim Uighurs of East Turkestan would indicate that Tibetan animosity against the Hui was more the product of political than religious friction.

In the violent uprising of 1959 the Chinese Muslim mosque was only one of many buildings destroyed in Lhasa, largely by Chinese artillery fire. The old Medical School on the Iron Hill opposite the Potala was completely levelled. The Chinese Muslim Mosque could have been burnt down by Tibetans as Ian Buruma mentions, though there is no evidence to support this. But as the building was being held by Chinese troops and armed Hui supporters, its destruction was probably not so much an act of religious intolerance, as one of military necessity. Ian Buruma should also know that the other mosque in Lhasa, the Tibetan Muslim one, did not suffer any damage.

I may have probably been somewhat precipitate in holding Ian Buruma to task, the way I did in my first letter. The whole subject is a fairly obscure one, with little documentation, and it would be unfair to expect any non-Tibetan, even such an accomplished scholar and writer as Ian Buruma to be spot-on with his information and conclusions.

Jamyang Norbu
(This reply was not published)

The Tibet–China Visit
According to Peanuts

ECLECTIC THOUGH THE SMALL WORLD of Tibetans and Tibet supporters appears to be, I am not sure that it holds all that many fans of the late Charles Schulz and his wonderful comic strip, *Peanuts*. Yet if there are any, might I ask them to cast their mind back to one well-known strip that is often repeated, though with novel variations each time, that together have served me as a parable of sorts on the congenital inability of the Tibetan leadership to learn from hard, even painful, experience.

That particular collection of strips tells essentially one story, which goes something like this: Lucy tries to persuade a reluctant Charlie Brown to take a running kick at a football that she is holding down on the ground with her finger, in the manner of the American game. Charlie Brown is understandably suspicious as he has done Lucy's bidding many times before and she has never failed to yank the ball away at the last moment. But Lucy persists and wears down his resistance. For the clincher she asks him "Look at my eyes Charlie Brown. Aren't these eyes you can trust?"

Eventually, good old Charlie Brown agrees. Giving it all he's got — tongue sticking out of the side of his mouth — he races towards the ball. Lucy, of course, pulls it away at the last moment. Charlie Brown flies in the air and falls flat on his back. In the concluding frame Lucy bends over the dazed and supine Charlie Brown and says "Isn't trust a wonderful thing, Charlie Brown."

I must confess to the fact that I had made an earlier reference to *Peanuts* in an article I wrote in 1994. That article also followed a Gyalo Thondup visit to China, which was also closely followed by a Tibetan government delegation, much in the way of recent events; for, the phenomenon of the Tibet–China visit by the Dalai Lama's envoys, along with the accompanying hope and hype, is certainly not a new thing. In fact it has happened so many times before that I could probably just recycle an old piece I had written on the first visit, again and again, without anyone really noticing. But I want to assure the reader that I'm not going to do that. I will just quote one short passage from the old article to make my point, and reveal how the *Peanuts* reference first started.

> Whenever the Tibetan issue has received any substantial attention in the world, be it with the demonstrations in Lhasa or the awarding of the Nobel Peace Prize to the Dalai Lama, the Chinese have nearly always succeeded in side-tracking international concern by making titillating press announcements soon after the event, declaring their willingness to sit down and talk with the Dalai Lama or his representatives. Those sympathetic to Tibet naturally heave a huge sigh of relief on hearing this, and the situation is then effectively defused. At Dharamshala a delegation to Beijing is announced and fierce intrigues are conducted by various political factions to get their man on the team. It all comes to nothing, of course. Once in a while, though, the delegation does actually get to go to Beijing. They invariably return to Dharamshala in a daze, with a look on their faces not unlike that on Charlie Brown's when he is lying flat on his back..."
> etc. ("The Heart of the Matter", *Tibetan Review*, March 1994)

So what is Beijing's reason this time for inviting Gyalo Thondup, and after him the official team of Lodi Gyari *et al*? Of course for anyone with a smidgen of intelligence it is a given that Beijing has no intention of negotiating with the Dalai Lama or anyone from the government-in-exile. About a week ago the historian Tsering Shakya and I were interviewed by Radio Free Asia on this subject and invariably asked what Beijing's motives could be for extending the invitations.

Tsering answered that one main reason probably had to do with Jiang Zemin's forthcoming visit to the United States. Jiang's previous visits to Europe and America had been completely ruined by the huge, noisy and well-publicized demonstrations organised by Tibetans and Tibet supporters. The magnitude of the opposition to Jiang's visit had prompted President Clinton to tell Jiang that he should talk to the Dalai Lama, a request that Clinton repeated on his own trip to Beijing. So this time around if any American president, or anyone else for that matter, should ask Jiang that he should talk to the Dalai Lama, Jiang could quite conveniently reply that he was actually doing so, and so play down the issue.

Not only do I think that Tsering is dead right, but I also fear that the Tibet–China visit with all the hopes it has raised and the confusion it has created among Tibetans and supporters, will do more harm than ever to activism on behalf of Tibet. I know for a fact that, already, a major SFT campaign has been completely derailed by the Tibet visit. I have also heard vague but unsettling rumours of impending orders from Dharamshala to all Tibetans and Tibet support groups not too protest Jiang's forthcoming coming visit to the USA.

That China's real purpose behind the invitations was not to open genuine negotiations could be ascertained from the way Beijing had, all along, played down the trip as a private visit and repeated that its policy on the Dalai Lama had not changed. In a statement issued to AFP (28 September 2002) after the envoys had returned to Dharamshala, Lodi Gyari, the chief envoy, said that they had "frank exchanges of views" with officials in Beijing, who stood by China's refusal to open dialogue with the Dalai Lama. Gyari also added "They reiterated the known position of the Chinese government on dialogue with His Holiness the Dalai Lama."

If you go through the reports and statements and carefully edit out — preferably with a thick black marker — all the tremendous circumlocutions, the exhilarating expressions of soaring (but absolutely unsupported) hope and the hyper-inflated rhetoric about "landmark visit", "frank exchanges" "a new chapter in China-Tibet relations" what remains is the cold hard nub of the fact that the Chinese refused to consider any kind of dialogue on Tibet.

Of course Gyari wants to return to Beijing: "We are fully aware that this task cannot be completed during a single visit," he said. You bet it can't. But is it just possible that the Chinese officials might have casually said "Come again" or "Come again next year." Something of the kind may possibly have been said, for on the envoy's return to Dharamshala, the Tibetan government-in-exile, in a statement to AP (28 September 2002) "expressed hope that they could begin negotiations for greater autonomy from China by July". Even if the Chinese had made it perfectly clear that they were never going to negotiate, but that the envoys were welcome to visit next July anyway — we have to ask ourselves, why July?

China's leadership will be undergoing a fundamental change beginning this November, and a new generation, the fourth generation (Mao's generation being the first) will take power. According to Zong Hairen (the pseudonym for a party insider) whose book on the subject, *Disidai* (*The Fourth Generation*), will be published this November by a US based Chinese language publisher, the leadership change will not merely be of one or two leaders but of the entire top strata. Appointments to military and government posts will not be final until March 2003, when the National People's Congress meets to formalize them. So by July a spanking new regime ought to be in place in Beijing, and I seriously doubt if it will have any time to spare for a pointless meeting, the invitation to which the previous administration may have vaguely extended to the Dalai Lama's envoys, in order to prevent "splittists" from spoiling the former president's last official visit to America.

What really upset me, made me burn with shame for the feeble-mindedness and snivelling pusillanimity of our leaders and "diplomats", is that we were not even the victims of some kind of fiendishly cunning Fu Manchu conspiracy, but were taken in, hook line and sinker, by such a cheap, obvious and feeble trick. More and more our leaders appear to be responding to a kind of Pavlovian conditioning. All that Beijing has to do these days, it seems, is to snap its fingers, and the Dalai Lama's brother and other Tibetan envoys will come a running, no questions asked.

This declaration of *dan xiang si* or "one sided love" (as the Chinese put it so nicely) by the Tibetan leadership is so wretchedly pathetic that it veers on the edge of masochism. For instance, the AP report of 28 September, stated that "The Tibetan government-in-exile said on Saturday that its envoys had been treated as equals for the first time by Chinese officials". How wonderful for them! So how were the previous delegations treated? Did their members have to perform full *kowtows* before the Chinese officials? Did they have to kiss Chinese bums?

Traditional Chinese opinions of "barbarian officials" coming to Changan or Beijing to pay "tribute" to the emperor have invariably been low, if not openly disdainful. Of course this attitude is rooted in racist, sinocentric and quite unwarranted ideas of Chinese cultural superiority. Tibetan ministers such as the great Gar Tongtsen Yulsung stood out in the Tang court for his brilliance, astuteness and diplomatic skills. Another Tibetan minister astonished the emperor of China with his profound knowledge of Chinese language and literature.

But to be fair to the Chinese there were probably some among the many Tibetan, Mongols, Uighur or Khalka officials visiting the Chinese capital who were not only ignorant, obsequious or even self-serving (tribute missions were great opportunities for advancement and for trade) who probably deserved the epithet "barbarian official". Whether our present envoys to Beijing will be viewed in a similarly disdainful way by Tibetan public opinion will depend on whether they are perceived to have sold out or not. If they carry out Beijing's bidding and recommend that the government-in-exile halt all demonstrations and protests during Jiang's forthcoming US visit, then history will certainly condemn them in far harsher terms.

I would request all Tibetans, friends and activists not to lose heart over this recent debacle, and pull out all the stops when Jiang Zemin comes into town. Let us have earsplitting slogan-shouting, monster rallies, dynamic demonstrations, rotten tomatoes, tear-gas, police charges, all on such an unprecedented scale that old Jiang will learn that even if he could fool or compromise some of our leaders, the Tibetan people and their stouthearted friends will never... never, never, never... give up the fight for Tibetan independence and justice.

30 September 2002
World Tibet Network News

After the Dalai Lama

THE DALAI LAMA AT SIXTY-SEVEN is fortunately a healthy man, probably healthier and (on average) slightly younger than his chain-smoking adversaries in Beijing. Yet in recent years, discussions on life after the Dalai Lama has been fairly widespread among Tibetans, especially after Beijing, apparently convinced that the Tibetan question would just disappear with his passing, announced that it would never negotiate with him.

Most Tibetans have a deep and natural faith in their leader, and would no doubt view his death as a traumatic blow. But Tibetans are psychologically prepared for this eventuality, and for reasons beyond the fact that "impermanence" is an article of their faith. Tibetans' confidence in the future rests on their own religious and political traditions, which are more enduring than their devotion to a single man. Constitutional provisions are already in place, in the event of His Holiness's death, for the election of a three-person council of regency, one of it's duties being to oversee the long and arcane process of searching for his reincarnation.

Yet, in truth, the absence of the Dalai Lama would not altogether be a bad thing for the Tibetan struggle. Yes, His Holiness is the draw for much of the international publicity showered on the Tibetan cause, but this attention does little to advance Tibetan national interests. Most leaders and politicians in the developed world assuage their consciences by praising the man and his noble mission, all the while ignoring the Tibetan question in their policies. It is as if by being personally nice to His Holiness they hope to make up for their empty encouragement of his belief, that by surrendering independence he might arrive at an accommodation with Chinese leaders. Many Tibetans already question the wisdom of this path. His departure, a few are convinced, would shake Tibetan society out of such comforting delusions.

The Dalai Lama's presence in Tibetan political life is somewhat like the giant Banyan tree, whose shade is pleasant but under which little grows. Tibetan ministers give the appearance of being no more than messenger boys, and members of Parliament fall over each other in their eagerness to agree with him. The Dalai Lama himself has remarked upon the dilemma of his omniscient leadership, but has done little to resolve it. His absence might be just the thing that allows mature democratic institutions to take root. To be sure, without His Holiness's presence there is danger of dissension within refugee society. But exiled Tibetans already have a half-century of experience in the rough-and-tumble of India's robust democracy. Surely they are ready for their own.

The transformation of Dharamshala's court politics into a genuinely democratic forum would have a profound impact on Tibet's struggle for freedom. At the moment, Tibetans' faith in the Dalai Lama is as strong as their resentment of Chinese rule, but little else is clear. The success of the democratic experiment in exile would represent a sincere hope for Tibet's political future. It would also be the best rebuttal of Beijing's propaganda that Tibetan independence would equal a return to theocratic feudalism.

Tibetans genuinely love the Dalai Lama, but his lofty ideas on world peace and universal compassion probably find more enthusiastic subscribers in California than in Tibet. Tibetans most wish to witness two events: a free Tibet and the Dalai Lama once again seated on his golden throne in the Potala Palace. There is no doubt — at least to this observer — that given half a chance, they are prepared to do whatever necessary to realize this dream.

Unfortunately, there seems to be an underlying conceptual dissonance between the leader and his people. Take for example the annual Tenth of March rally in Dharamshala commemorating the 1959 Tibetan Uprising. In his last few speeches on this occasion the Dalai Lama carefully explained why relinquishing independence and accepting autonomy within China was the best hope for preserving Tibetan culture. The Tibetans in the crowd listened respectfully. But after His Holiness concluded, they marched away waving national flags and lustily shouting, "Independence for Tibet" — as if they hadn't heard a word he said. It is worth recalling that in March 1959 Tibetans respectfully disobeyed the Dalai Lama's many appeals not to take up arms against the Chinese occupation army.

Still, it may be too early to speculate on a post-Dalai Lama period. He has assured Tibetans that he intends to live to a ripe old age and even joked that he might turn out to be "quite a handful, a real feisty old geezer" (*porto lagpae khyoktse*). With so much energy and spirit, perhaps he can begin to accomplish in life what many fear can happen only after his death.

Fall–Winter 2002
Newsweek International (Special Edition on China)

Back to the Future
Enduring Phobias and Superstitions in Tibetan Society (Part 2)

In Satyajit Ray's film, *Ganashatru*, an adaptation of Ibsen's play, *Enemy of the People*, a doctor discovers that leaking sewers are contaminating a water source which is regarded as holy, and which attracts large number of pilgrims. The doctor concerned by the sudden rise of water borne diseases tries to warn the town people of this danger. But the mayor and others, with a vested interest in the pilgrimage site, attack the doctor for what they see as his anti-Hindu views, and soon with all manner of demagogic rabble-rousing tactics turn the entire town against him.

For the few Tibetans who fancy themselves as rational and progressive, and further suffer from the need to express such views, life in the Tibetan community in Dharamshala often takes on much of the absurdities, frustrations and hazards as those faced by Ray's doctor/hero. Even on such a basic issue as public health it is easy to put oneself in a false position by merely doing the sensible thing. In 1983 there was a nasty outbreak of rabies in Dharamshala. At the Tibetan Children's Village over a dozen children were bitten by rabid dogs and two boys died. I was director of the Tibetan Institute of

Performing Arts (TIPA) at the time and, despite opposition, had all the dogs around the area removed somewhere far away. In spite of my efforts a woman whose husband worked at TIPA was bitten by a stray. I wanted her to get rabies shots immediately but her husband insisted on her being treated by a shaman. There was little I could do except rail against the futility of shamans and oracles. The woman died, of course, and it was a horrible lingering death. But that in no way seemed to convince the husband, or his friends and relatives, that they had done anything wrong. All it did was add to my reputation as an "unbeliever", which eventually got me into the kind of hot water that Ray's doctor experienced.

I am no advocate of Victorian style rationality and progress, and I certainly do not see myself as shepherding the ignorant masses out of their superstitious darkness onto the sunlit path of empirical facts. Yet in the exile Tibetan world even a moderately progressive position runs up not only against the conservatism of the older generation and the church, but often against the whimsies of Western "Dharma types" enamoured with everything "traditional" or "mystical" in the Tibetan world. The advantage for Westerners in love with shamans, spiritual healing and what not, is that unlike the natives, if things go wrong they can fall back on the technology, wealth and security of the Western world.

Of course, even in the so-called developed world, irrational beliefs still persist — as Miss Cleo the TV psychic, and the UFO phenomenon demonstrates, at least on one level. Then we have fundamentalist Christians attempting to replace education on evolution in American classrooms with "creationism". The latest version of "creationism", stripped of the more awkward bits (God creating the universe in six days and resting on the seventh) and renamed "Intelligent Design", is being promoted as a Christian but scientific challenge to evolution — but I digress.

Bernard Shaw in his introduction to Saint Joan went so far as to declare that modern man was as credulous as someone from the Middle Ages. Shaw was exaggerating (Orwell points this out in one of his "As I Please" columns for the *Tribune*) but he did have a point. Still, even if modern man is not all that wonderfully rational a being as was hoped he would be become by such pioneering promoters of reason and science as H. G. Wells, he is, nonetheless, miles ahead of the average Tibetan in this respect.

Nearly every traveller to old Tibet, even the friendliest, has unfailingly commented on how auguries and magical beliefs dominated the lives of the people. Such observations, in books and documents from around the period of the Younghusband expedition (Waddell, Landon, Candler *et al*), are more pronounced and hostile, with Tibetans being described as a brutish people mired in ignorance and exploited by a degenerate and xenophobic priestly class. But it is not an uncommon practise to demonize those you are going to subjugate or massacre. Chinese propaganda about old Tibet being a backward barbaric society under the yoke of a "man eating" ruling class, is qualitatively no different from British publications of the Younghusband expedition era. Just a couple of years ago Beijing once again revived its 1960s and 1970s style vilification of the Dalai Lama "charging him with having used human heads, intestines and skin in sacrificial offering."

This kind of crude propaganda, of course, needs no refutation. And it does seem particularly thick coming from a country where ritual cannibalism was being enthusiastically practised in the 1960s (one ate the liver of the class enemy to show ones devotion to Chairman Mao), and where the national belief prevailed that the pedestrian quotations of a power-mad dictator who never brushed his teeth or washed his genitals (according to his personal physician) could inspire cabbages to remarkable feats of spontaneous growth. Even now, at public executions in China, spectators rush to dip steamed buns in the fresh blood of victims, in the belief that the consumption of such blood is a powerful tonic. But that's all by the by.

When Tibetans first came into exile the catastrophic turn of events back home were still immediate and traumatic enough to convince even the most blinkered among them that they had to drop the more reactionary aspects of their culture and learn from the outside world. I have dealt with this in a couple of articles before so perhaps it is not necessary to recount once again the somewhat muddled experiments in democracy, science and modernisation that took place in the Tibetan refugee community in our first decade of exile.

But besides our own rocklike conservatism, there were other obstacles on our road to modernisation. Even in exile the Dalai Lama and the refugees lived in considerable intellectual isolation from the rest of the world, and in a sense, even from the rest of India. Dharamshala had few visitors except for hippies lured there by Tibetan esoterica or the local hashish. Furthermore, the town was an exhausting twelve-hour bus journey from Delhi. Many Tibetan settlements were located in remote and inaccessible parts of India and Nepal.

Though a number of Indian intellectuals and national figures of that period did meet the Dalai Lama, it does not appear that there was any attempt to maintain some regular dialogue with them. It is a real pity. Such leaders as Jayaprakash Narayan, Acharya Kripalani, and the journalist and writer Frank Moraes were not only enthusiastic supporters of the Tibetan cause, but men of considerable experience, wisdom and democratic vision, who could have made a valuable contribution to His Holiness's political education.

We must remember that the Dalai Lama was then in his formative years, politically speaking at least, and that the only formal political or civic education he had received till then was a Chinese Communist one — one of his teachers being Liu Keping of the Nationalities Affairs Commission. But once in exile, His Holiness's initial enthusiasm, even to study English, gradually appears to have dimmed as administrative, but predominantly religious, routine once again took over his life.

The Dalai Lama also faced considerable humiliation and obstacles in attempting to travel outside India. Most countries refused him a visa outright. Yet the impetus of modernism was strong enough in the Dalai Lama, at least in those early years, for him to speak out against the conservatism and materialism of the old Tibetan church. He also took the initiative in discouraging a number of traditional practises and superstitions. But these were unfortunately only symbolic (as in not wearing silk robes) or short-lived.

In 1964 an actor at the Tibetan Institute of Performing Arts (TIPA) was possessed by a spirit. The possession seems to have been genuine enough. Three separate eyewitnesses gave me identical accounts of how the possessed man ran himself through with a long dagger (one eyewitness even remembered seeing the tip of the blade sticking out from the man's back). He was not only unharmed by this performance, but was not marked by even a small scar. Such paranormal feats by Tibetan and Mongol oracles have been reported from early times by such travellers as Marco Polo and the Lazarist priest, Abbé Huc. More recent accounts by Nebesky Wojkowitz and Joseph Rock describe personal encounters with Tibetan oracles who twisted steel broadswords into spirals.

But getting back to our TIPA story; after his somewhat dramatic prelude with the dagger the possessed man proclaimed that he was the mountain god, Nyechenthangla (of the Trans-Himalayan Range) and blessed all those present. He finally came out of his trance and fell in a dead faint. The matter was reported to the Religious

Department of the exile government and probably to the Dalai Lama as well.

Some days later the mediums of one of the state oracles came to TIPA accompanied by his monk servitors. The monks performed the invocatory rituals and the medium went into a trance, at which moment the Nyechenthangla deity spontaneously possessed the actor again. The state oracle greeted his fellow deity by touching foreheads, and from what I was informed, passed on to him instructions from the Dalai Lama. These were that since Tibet was on its way to becoming a modern country, the business of gods and spirits possessing human mediums could not be permitted anymore — or words to that effect. The two state oracles were, however, exempt from the decree.

There was definitely a new-wine-in-old-bottles quality to most of the modernisation efforts of the period.

I was a child of six in Kalimpong, when I was dragged before a terrifying red-faced oracle to receive his blessing. Childhood terror evolved to fascination as I grew up and heard numerous stories of the supernatural marvels of Tibet. Especially fascinating were accounts of the state oracle, which for a history buff like myself had the added appeal of a romantic connection to ancient Greece and Rome — to seers like the Pythoness at Delphi and the Sibyl of Cumae. The whole business was, however, hard to square with our supposed goal of creating a modern Tibet. It was even more difficult to ignore the state oracle's dismal track record of failed prophecies.

Just before the British invasion of 1904, the Tibetan government consulted the state oracle in Lhasa. The oracle declared that the "enemies of the Dharma" (*ten-dra*) would be soundly defeated by a "heavenly army" (*lha-mak*) which he would personally lead. The Tibetans were, of course, overwhelmingly defeated, around seven hundred peasant levies being massacred in a couple of hours at the hot springs near Guru. The British marched into Lhasa on the third of August 1904.

The next year during the New Year celebrations in Lhasa, when the state oracle came charging out of the Jokhang Temple in full trance, as was the annual custom, the exasperated citizens of Lhasa are reported to have booed the god — the women flapping their aprons, and the men shouting "Hey-le! Hey-le!" or "Shame on you!".

The death of the Thirteenth Dalai Lama can definitely be attributed to a wrong medicine forced on his Holiness by the state oracle. The case has been fairly well documented and there seems to be no doubt that, at the very least, the state oracle's action was a criminal blunder[1].

In an article, "Tibetan Oracles", in the *Tibet Journal*, Summer 1979, Prince Peter of Greece and Denmark mentions another fatal intervention by the state oracle in a crucial moment in our history:

> During the flight of the Dalai Lama to Dromo (Yadong) in the Chumbi Valley at the time of the invasion of Tibet by the Chinese in 1950, the Nechung Oracle was consulted repeatedly as to what course of action the Tibetan ruler should take. Should he take refuge in India or should he stay in Tibet? Twice the oracle said that he should stay in Tibet despite attempts by the government to get him to say the contrary. It is said that it was eventually discovered that he had been bribed to deliver his message by the pro-Chinese monks of Sera...

The Dalai Lama himself recalls in his autobiography, *Compassion in Exile*, that when he was considering not returning to Tibet at the end of his 1956 visit to India, he consulted the Nechung and Gadong oracles:

---

1. See Heather Stoddard, "The Death of the Thirteenth Dalai Lama", *Lungta*, No 7, or Sir Charles Bell, *Portrait of the Dalai Lama*, Collins, London, 1946.

> Lukhangwa (the prime minister relieved of office due to Chinese pressure, and then living in Kalimpong) came in during one of the consultations, at which the oracle grew angry, telling him to remain outside. It was as if the oracle knew that Lukhangwa had made up his mind (to try and stop the Dalai Lama from returning to Tibet). But Lukhangwa ignored him and sat down all the same. Afterwards, he came up to me and said, 'When men become desperate they consult the gods. And when the gods become desperate, they tell lies.'"

In exile, despite the initial fervour of modernisation, Tibetans, because of the very uncertainty of their predicament, soon became caught up in the thrall of prophecies and auguries. One year, I think it was in the early sixties, there was a report in the Tibetan language newspaper *Tibetan Freedom* that a bird had been sighted at the Tibetan school in Happy Valley, Mussoorie, cooing "*Bhod rangzen thop*", or "Tibet will gain its independence", over and over again. Everyone became terribly excited.

The state oracle would also regularly deliver prophecies that Tibet would be free the next year, or the year after that, and so on. Now and then he would be more circumspect and suggest that a major international change would take place in the near future, which would benefit Tibet. On a few occasions he was even emboldened enough to claim that his "heavenly army" was poised to do its stuff against the Chinese. What is mind-boggling in retrospect is the absolute faith of the public and even the Dalai Lama in these predictions that never even came remotely close to being realised.

The Dalai Lama also invested much time, energy and resources in the performance of magical torgya rituals, to defeat China. These were elaborate and portentous affairs that usually concluded with the dramatic burning or the destruction of an effigy, giving McLeod Ganj wags the opportunity to make jokes about the Tibetan atom bomb.

Select Western guests of the Tibetan government were treated to performances of the oracle and they were invariably impressed by the mysterious rituals and the dramatic physical changes the medium displayed when going into a trance. Photographs and accounts of the oracle began to appear in a number of books and magazines. The Tibetan government's English language journal, *Tibetan Bulletin*, once featured an interview with the medium. In the cover of the same issue they had the photograph of a fully costumed oracle in a dramatic martial-arts kind of stance, that to my profane eyes, seemed more inspired by Bruce Lee than any Buddhist deity.

Chö-Yang, the glossy full-colour journal of the Religious Department (and the Norbulingka Institute), edited by Western Buddhists, also came out with chatty interviews with the medium and reports on the oracle's lifestyle. Somehow, all that this exposure and publicity seemed to do was strip away the mystery and exclusivity of an ancient institution and turn it into another spectacle for novelty seeking Westerners.

In this unhealthy climate of fashionable and profitable spiritualism, some unhappy and troubled young women, especially newcomers from Tibet, began to claim they were possessed by this or that deity, sometimes with unfortunate consequences. In another of Ray's films, *Devi*, a young bride comes to believe she is the manifestation of the Mother Goddess, and her father-in-law, obsessed with her delusion, brings tragedy to her home.

Right now there is a glut of oracles in Dharamshala. Over and above the two state oracles there is the deity Dorjee Yudonma, one of the twelve Tenma goddesses, whose medium is a mild looking old *amala*. There is also the oracle Lamo Tsangba, a local protective deity of Lhasa. His medium is a somewhat corpulent gentleman who was a trombone player in the Chinese military orchestra in Lhasa.

Then there are the five Tsering-chenga mountain goddesses (of the Everest range) whose collective medium is a fruity young woman from Eastern Tibet. She was very much *en vogue* some years ago, even pronouncing on the arrangements for a welcome ceremony for the Dalai Lama on his return from a US tour. She selected the songs that TIPA artistes were to sing on the occasion, and also their costumes. On a more sinister note, she twice attended services at the main temple in Dharamshala, and, in the style of the witch Gagool, in *King Solomon's Mines*, proceeded to "smell out" those monks, nuns and lamas, who, in contravention of the Dalai Lama's orders, were secretly propitiating the deity, Dorgee Shugden.

Which brings us to the pre-eminent spiritual, or more accurately, "spiritualist", controversy in the Tibetan world. A few years ago when this affair first blew up, it was covered fairly widely in major international newspapers, magazines and television programmes, but the initial hue and cry has, thankfully, died down somewhat, though it always seems to be threatening to resurface. It has created, for the first time ever, an open and vocal opposition to the Dalai Lama from within his own people. The controversy has also been the cause of a terrible triple murder in Dharamshala, and numerous other fights, purges, and one full scale riot.

It would be impossible to discuss the affair in just an article and I am not going to try. The entire business is so convoluted and, frankly, so depressing that I find it requires all my will power to just focus my mind on it for more than a minute or two. Furthermore the polemics on the subject — including the diatribes of Western supporters on either side — are so brainless and so ferociously partisan that any appeal to good sense and even common humanity would probably be lost on them. It is not my usual belief but I think that in this case the old wives' homily "least said soonest mended" would probably apply.

This dispute has all the stupidity and viciousness that attended the pointless theological controversies in the Eastern Roman Empire under the Emperor Justinian. The entire population of Constantinople, including even such unlikely sections of society as prostitutes, chariot-drivers and street hooligans, instead of attending to their own businesses, pleasures or depravities, became intensely involved in theological disputes, such as the nature of Christ's divinity, which more often than not led to brawls, murders, massacres and the infamous Nike riot.

Beijing has been quick to capitalise on this rift in the Dalai Lama's following and to adopt a moral high tone in the matter, so perhaps they should be reminded of their own "god or ghost" controversy that attended the reform of the Beijing opera in early Maoist China. According to the late Richard Hughes of the *Far Eastern Economic Review*, "a 'moderate' Marxist school of thought sought to distinguish between 'ghosts' and 'spirits', arguing that there could surely be 'progressive spirits', and citing as an example a play (1959) which depicted the return to the modern world of an eminent ancient statesmen to read the works of Mao". The chances are excellent that these 'moderate' Marxists eventually ended up doing "Reform Through Labour" in some frozen Manchurian wasteland.

Of course, people must be allowed their beliefs no matter how ridiculous or wrong we may perceive them. I believe people have the right to worship Shugden or any other deity they want, while the Dalai Lama as a spiritual leader certainly has the right to object to this on theological grounds and ask people to refrain from such practises. But that is not the problem.

The trouble is that the Tibetan government has been inducted to implement the Dalai Lama's proscription of Shugden worship. The Tibetan government claims it has not issued any orders or appeals to people to harass or fight Shugden worshippers. Yet it has produced and distributed literature and videos demonizing Shugden worshippers. It has furthermore made no effort to discourage or condemn attacks on Shugden groups. Furthermore, His Holiness's statement that the worship of Shugden is harming his health and life (which I have a problem accepting) is definitely inflammatory, considering the kind of blind fanatical loyalty he draws from many simple Tibetans.

The Shugden supporters are, of course, are more than exaggerating when they claim that the Dalai Lama's actions are similar to China's repression of religious freedom in Tibet. Such statements belittle the genocidal tragedy that the Tibetan people have suffered under Communist Chinese occupation.

Now more than ever, Tibetans absolutely need to move away from the world of superstition, oracles and magic into the real world of the twenty-first century. There are overwhelming crises in the Tibetan world that not only require the full attention and energy of our leaders, but also an enlightened and up-to-the-minute appreciation of realities. In the matter of public health alone we are facing an emergency that borders on disaster, but to which His Holiness and the Tibetan government have paid scant attention.

In the 5 March 1997 issue of *The Journal of American Medicine*, Vol. 277, No. 9 there was a study of tuberculosis among Tibetan immigrants from India and Nepal resettled in Minnesota. The conclusion was that tuberculosis infection was "nearly universal among Tibetans settling in Minnesota." It does not require undue perspicacity to realise that the conclusions of this particular study could logically be extended to cover all Tibetans in India and Nepal. Also, why is it that so many Tibetans in exile seem to be dying of stomach cancer and that Tibetan monks in South India have some of the highest incidents of peptic ulcers in the world, as another medical study has shown?

Inside Tibet half the child population suffers from stunted growth and impaired intellectual development due to malnutrition, according to a study in *The New England Journal of Medicine*, 1 February 2000. Catriona Bass's, *Education in Tibet: Policy and Practise Since 1950* (TIN 1998) reveals that Tibetans suffer from what is probably the lowest literacy rate in the world, with as much as seventy per cent of the rural population unable to read. All these near-overwhelming problems require immediate investigation and effective response, not prayer nor prophesy.

There is a tendency these day among many of our more admiring Western friends to ascribe to the Tibetan people extraordinary qualities, not only of serenity and peacefulness, but even a special wisdom, not merely traditional but proto-scientific — a characterisation which is so flattering and advantageous that quite a few of our leaders and lamas are avidly endorsing and promoting this view. I do not intend to deny or belittle the more admirable qualities of the Tibetan people and our civilisation, and there are many, but perhaps the appeal of these have to some extent concealed the more backward and unhealthy aspects of our culture. We are frankly, a people still in the thrall of ignorance and superstition, which far from declining with the years seems to be gaining new life and impetus with foreign sponsorship and encouragement.

Among the elite, especially among lamas who have centres in the West, there is an appearance of modernism that never fails to impress their Western disciples and friends. Terms from quantum physics, cognitive science and pop psychology flow easily in their conversation, but genuine interest in science is absent. More crucially, the scientific outlook is non-existent. Tibetan lamas view science from a reverse Fritjof Capraean perspective. All they are looking for in science are possible similarities or parallels in Buddhist philosophy, essentially, it seems, to prove to themselves and their followers that they are as modern as is necessary and do not need to change.

There is, furthermore, a proclivity to seeing modern knowledge as primarily utilitarian — as techniques that could be grafted on to traditional values and institutions, which could then remain immutable. China at the end of the nineteenth century had reacted in much the same way to the challenges of the modern world, with Confucian bureaucrats espousing *Zhong xue wei ti, Xi xue wei yong* — or "Chinese learning for essence, Western learning for utility". Which is also what the Communist mandarins in Beijing are, in essence, espousing right now.

Many older Tibetans, especially geshes — like Hindu fundamentalists who go around saying that atom bombs and aeroplanes were invented by ancient Indians in Vedic times — are not shy of informing you that the Kangyur and Tengyur contain the secrets to the making of nuclear weapons, or that in the Great War of Shambala, tanks and nuclear weapons would be used. His Holiness himself, in an interview in an Italian journal, declared that he did not regard the account of Shambala as symbolic or legendary and believed that the apocalyptic events prophesied would actually come to pass.

One would expect that in Tibet itself, after so many year of Communist occupation, some modern ideas, no matter how distorted, would have taken root. It has happened with some of the youth, but with the larger section of society the years of living under Communism seems to have driven them ever more backwards to their old beliefs and ways. Because nearly everything to do with Communist Chinese ideology and rule in Tibet was so permeated with lies and half-truths, Tibetans viewed even basic information provided in Chinese educational material with suspicion and hostility. For instance, a historian friend of mine, interviewing an old monk who had been imprisoned for many years, told me that the monk refused to accept that the world was round, because he had been given this information by the Chinese. In exile these days, the more fanatical and reactionary Tibetans can be found among new-arrivals from Tibet. Yet it must be said that many of the younger new-arrivals are much better-read and more interested in modern literature and secular culture than Tibetan youth in exile.

Even Tibetans born and raised in the West do not seem to be entirely free of conservative traditional thinking. In their case the influence probably comes in a roundabout way from New Age Buddhist influences. Looking at some of the internet chat-sites and email discussion groups frequented by young Tibetans one is struck by the number of communications that are signed off with a "Peace and Love" and "Om mani padme hum". More significantly, there appears to be a near complete absence of any critical examination of Tibetan beliefs, spiritual or political, among these young people.

Probably this would be a good time as any to mention that I personally do not reject the existence of deities, ghosts and oracles. I think that what people regard as real are to a great degree conditioned by the worldview of the period they live in. When ancient Greeks believed in gods and titans they probably did exist, and not merely as pale symbols of moral qualities or forces of nature as later European readings of the Greeks mythologies and epics would have us accept, but as living powers and entities that interacted in the lives of the people.

Throughout his life Einstein worried about the striking and, to him, suspicious manner in which observed reality conformed to the laws of mathematics. Why he wondered, should the natural world be amenable to man-made rules? Could it be that we can grasp only that stratum of reality that is measurable by our limited methods.

There is a theory that material phenomena, even physical laws, are conditioned by the belief systems of the period. While if we enter the world of quantum physics even the most bizarre event that we can think of has a chance of happening. Even something like the molecules of my body falling apart and assembling again in the next room. And it can be proven mathematically. Of course it will probably take a few billions years for the event to take place, but the possibility is there. And I am going to stop right here, before I entirely succumb to the error I earlier accused Tibetan lamas of committing.

Still, whenever I read the biography of Milarepa I cannot but be convinced that the great yogi did practise black magic, and did perform those miracles described in the book; and that these weren't just allegories or parables. Yet with the same absolute conviction I know that now, in this day and age, lamas can't do these things. I do not doubt Marco Polo when he writes with amazement that Tibetan lamas levitated the Great Khan's cup to his lips. But these days lamas are patently unable to levitate anything. When they have to fly, they do it in aeroplanes, like the rest of us. The only miraculous thing being that they do it first class.

We must also bear in mind that even in the past, back in "medieval" Tibet, people were not blind to the drawbacks and limitations of oracles and prophecies. The Great Thirteenth Dalai Lama issued a directive to district officials nationwide, to investigate oracles and fortune-tellers, and make sure that they did not exploit the common people. In the Tibetan opera *Sukyi Nima*, there is a satirical scene of a drunken state oracle, repeatedly beating his long-suffering hunchback secretary, in between delivering such brainless prophecies as: "It will snow in winter" and "It will rain in summer".

Stories of fake oracles and rigged prophecies are not unusual in Tibetan folklore. One of the popular folk heroes of Central Tibet is Lama Methon Phangbo, a merry con-man who delights in hoodwinking the pious and gullible. On a more sinister note there is the story of Shagdun Sangye (Seven Day Buddha) of Ghungthang, a religious charlatan and mass murderer who promised people who undertook a seven day retreat under his guidance a complete dissolution of their corporeal self and a direct entry into nirvana. He accomplished this by dropping them into a bottomless pit normally covered by the retractable floor of his meditation cave. He was eventually exposed by the "divine madman" Drukpa Kunleg, who arranged for him to receive a poetic sort of justice. In fact such popular Tibetan saints as Drukpa Kunleg, Aku (Uncle) Tompa and even Milarepa essentially taught people to disregard appearances, ritual, superstition and even conventional thinking and to seek spiritual (and sometimes worldly) truths through good sense, direct experience and their own efforts.

Our forebears may have often been superstitious and credulous, but they did not lack common sense. And better educated people in the past were constantly given to railing against superstition, *namthok*, as being against the spirit of Buddhism.

A former resistance fighter and CIA agent, Lithang Athar Norbu (who died last year in New York City) told me this story. Shortly after the outbreak of the fighting in Eastern Tibet in 1956, a local resistance group laid siege to a Chinese garrison. The Khampa fighters did everything they could to crack its defences but failed. During deliberations among the fighters on a fresh course of action, one of their number went into a spontaneous trance, what Tibetans call *thonbe*, and announced that he was the local protective deity and that he would personally lead the charge to wipe out the "Red enemies of the Dharma" (*tendra-gyamar*).

Everyone was excited, and morale, which had dropped in the last few days, soared again. Next day at dawn, the fighters got ready for the attack. The medium, now in full godly regalia (borrowed from a nearby monastery) and armed with a sword, trembled and shook as monks performed the *chendre* or invocatory rites. As soon as the deity took possession of the medium, he rose, snarling and hissing, from his seat and climbed up on the rampart and brandished his sword in the air.

"A single shot rang out — tak-ka!" Athar told me, "and the oracle fell over backwards on the ground. Right on his forehead, dead centre, was a hole. And that was that. No, he wasn't a fake. None of us there had any doubts about the genuineness of the oracle. Perhaps it's just that their days are over, and its another sort of world now."

4 January 2003
(Unpublished)

The Incredible Weariness of Hope
Tibet, Tibet: A Personal History of a Lost Land
by Patrick French

Harper Collins Publishers India, 333 p., IRS 395

TIBET, TIBET. The title of Patrick French's latest book intrigued me. Vaguely suggestive of a biblical lament, it also hinted at a kind of patient reproach, of the sort that Sir Isaac Newton is said to have dished out to his pet dog after it knocked over a candle and set fire to his research papers ("Diamond! Diamond! Thou little knowest the mischief thou has done."). I fancied that the title could offer me a clue as to the disposition of the book itself and after going over a few chapters realized I had not been all that whimsical in my supposition.

Running through the book is an emotional undercurrent, a sense of disappointment if not disillusionment with a cause and a leader that once meant a great deal to the author. Unlike his previous books, *Younghusband* and *Liberty or Death*, both of which were remarkably well-researched and well-written historical works, *Tibet, Tibet: A Personal History of A Lost Land* is, as sub-titled, a much more personal work. As with things personal some vagueness, contradictions, doubts and denials appear in the book which though interesting in themselves as revelatory of the author's state of mind (was it Ibsen who said that when we write we sit in judgment on ourselves?) do not contribute to the fluidity of the narrative.

Patrick French's involvement with Tibet or more specifically with the Dalai Lama started as a schoolboy in England. He provides a fairly detailed account of this at the beginning of the book and adds that he gave up the Roman Catholic faith of his childhood to adopt Tibetan Buddhism. He even joined the Free Tibet Campaign in the UK and worked hard to promote the Tibetan cause in Britain. I remember seeing him, in the March of 1991 or thereabouts, dressed in crisp khadi, leading a large pro-Tibet demonstration around Trafalgar Square. Of course, he visited Dharamshala with other international activists. "We sat in the tea shops of McLeod Ganj, deliberating. Everyone tried hard to treat Richard [Gere] as if he were just another regular activist. There was a sense of momentum, that we were on the cusp of change."

This was just after the major demonstrations in Tibet and the Tiananmen Massacre, around the time when the Dalai Lama received the Nobel Peace Prize and Hollywood was commencing work on two major feature films on Tibet. The Tibet craze was going international and it seemed inevitable, at least to Tibetan leaders and Western supporters that all this enthusiasm would soon translate into a brilliant resolution of the Tibetan issue. Patrick French describes it happening, "Everything seemed to be going well. The Free Tibet Campaign was thriving. The plight of Tibet was becoming mainstream. Governments hardened their line and lobbied China over Tibetan political prisoners. Bill Clinton promoted the need for dialogue with the Dalai Lama at a historic joint press conference held with Jiang Zemin in Beijing in 1998 and broadcast live across the People's Republic of China."

A few Tibetans, beside myself, who had been involved in the

Tibetan freedom struggle since the sixties, did not share this exhilarating *frisson* of, quite frankly, unjustifiable optimism. I expressed my suspicions and misgivings publicly in my writings, but only succeeded in putting the backs up of the Tibetan leadership and some of its Western supporters. As could be anticipated by anyone with even a basic appreciation of China's cynicism, ruthlessness and sophistication in matters of "barbarian control", these exciting years for the Tibet movement soon came to an end and the ice age set in. Patrick French admits, "It took some time to realize that none of this seemed to have had the slightest effect on the Chinese government."

And why should it? Coupled with the fact that politicians, economists and business leaders in the developed world began to hail China as the ultimate investment opportunity and the market to dwarf all others, the Chinese government began to acquire friends with more political clout than Richard Gere or the Beastie Boys.

James Schlessinger, Michael Blumenthal, Alexander Haig, Richard Holbroke and especially Henry Kissinger began to actively lobby for China in Washington DC, and in turn gained guanxi access in Beijing for their corporate clients. Even former President George Bush, his national security advisor Brent Scowcroft and his trade representative Carla Hills offered themselves as trade consultants on China to corporate America. Everyone made huge sums of money. The biggest contributor to the Clinton-Gore campaign in 1992 was a shady Indonesian businessman of Chinese origin with suspicious ties to Chinese intelligence. Interestingly enough, some of these lobbyists, Richard Holbroke, California Senator Diane Feinstein and her entrepreneur husband Richard Blum (who has extensive business interests in China) have represented themselves as sympathetic to Tibetans and friendly with the Dalai Lama, largely, it would seem, for the purpose of weakening Tibetan activism against China's business interests in the USA. A classic instance of the successful application of the ancient Chinese strategy of *yiyi zhiyi* or "using barbarians to control barbarians".

China then launched a major effort to refurbish its public image. The most powerful media czar in the world, Rupert Murdoch, systematically began to present a sanitized version of China in his many newspapers and TV networks. BBC news which carried a little too much Tibet and Human Rights in China related stories was booted out of Murdoch's Star TV satellite network which covered most of Asia. Murdoch also attempted to kill the publication of Chris Patten's book on the Hong Kong handover and the efforts by Chinese authorities to undermine Patten's efforts as governor of Hong Kong to ensure some measure of democratic rule for the island. Beijing also organized a major official campaign to influence Western support for Tibet and even made partially successful overtures to Western academics on Tibet to reexamine the Tibetan issue from Beijing's point of view.

Tibetans also began to score a succession of own-goals. One of the most prominent Dharma teachers in Europe, Sogyal Rinpoche, was served with a lawsuit allegedly for seducing a student. The Dalai Lama came under attack from a section of his own Gelukpa sect for depriving them of their right to worship a deity, Dorjee Shugden, resulting in an unprecedented rejection of his leadership from a section (albeit a small one, but with noisy Western support) of his own community. Strangely enough Patrick French doesn't touch on this issue. He tells us though of the story of another Tibetan lama "Penor Rinpoche who, in the most dubious of circumstances, identified the high kicking Hollywood action hero Steven Seagal (Marked for Death, Hard to Kill) as a reincarnation of the seventeenth-century master Chundrag Dorje."

It did not help matters that the Dalai Lama himself now voiced his enthusiasm for brave new capitalist China (despite his oft expressed Marxist and socialist convictions), and offered to surrender Tibetan independence for a measure of autonomy. The world of Tibet activism was thrown into disarray. Support groups and, in fact, the Tibetan government-in-exile itself became directionless and attempted to reorient their objectives around such other issues as the environment, world peace, religious freedom, cultural preservation, human rights — everything but the previous goal of Tibetan independence.

In this atmosphere of confusion, apathy and perceived betrayal many former activists and supporters began to drift away to other causes and concerns. Some did a bit more. A prominent Tibet activist, after a trip to Tibet and confabulations with Chinese officials now spoke up openly in support of China's rule in Tibet. Others, especially Tibet-related academics joined in the fun to demonstrate that they, unlike Richard Gere and the rest of the silly buggers, had not fallen for the charms of the Dalai Lama, and had known all along that the popular notion of Tibet as an idyllic and spiritual land was entirely a Western creation now being exploited by Tibetans themselves to gain support for their spurious movement. Books purporting to deconstruct this image: *Virtual Tibet, Imagining Tibet, Demystifying Tibet,* and *Prisoners of Shangrila,* began to appear in quick succession.

With such controversy surrounding Tibet, Patrick French wanted "to see it [Tibet] unmediated by the versions or hopes of others". That was what set him on the road to Lhasa in the summer of 1999. "I wanted to move forward from the image I had created for myself during the years among exiles and campaigners."

French finds a very different Tibet from the one he had previously encountered on his first trip in 1980. This time the atmosphere throughout the country is heavy with fear, resignation and hopelessness. Yet to his surprise French discovers that defiance of Chinese rule had surprisingly not ended. The fiercest and bravest advocates of Tibetan nationalism were often extraordinarily young — in their twenties, or younger... "their devotion to Buddhism, the Dalai Lama and the idea of Tibetan nationhood was clear, absolute and impassioned." A nun Nyima tells him of the unbelievably rigorous supervision and spying in her monastery. "It was only later, looking back, that I wondered whether her courage — the very act of dissent in a totalitarian society — might be her means of psychological survival. Nadezhda Mandelstam had written that people living in a dictatorship 'are soon filled with a sense of their helplessness, in which they find an excuse for their own passivity.' Nyima, and others of her generation, were far from passive as they worked to keep the idea of Tibet alive."

In Lhasa French tells us of the inmates of the feared Drapchi prison, five nuns who were beaten to death for shouting pro-independence slogans instead of singing required patriotic songs when a European Union delegation visited the prison. Another pro-independence activist Jampal Khedrup was apparently beaten to death by a prison official. Tibetans boycotted the Minority Nationalities Games in Lhasa... "Only officials in blue blazers and white baseball caps. There was no crowd. I had come to a fantasy National Minority Games." Later he heard that a Tibetan wrapping explosives around his chest had attended the Games and managed to pull down the Chinese flag and had started to raise the Tibetan one. When policemen had tried to stop him he had attempted to detonate the explosives but it was raining and his clothes were soaked and there was no explosion.

The extent of anti-Chinese and pro-independence sentiments French encounters is surprisingly extensive. He even has a conversation with a Tibetan prostitute in Lhasa who tells him that she would never have sex with a Chinese man. French believes her, though he thinks that her decision might have more to do with traditional Tibetan prejudice against Chinese and Muslims. French even dedicates quite a few pages at the beginning and end of his book to an activist in exile, Thubten Ngodup. To draw world attention to the cause of Tibetan independence this former monk and ex-paratrooper doused his body with gasoline and set himself on fire.

But then Patrick French meets a Tibetan nomad, a semi-official functionary, Namdrub, in North-Eastern Tibet, who is certain that fighting for Tibetan freedom is absolutely hopeless, and that it made life more difficult for those who had to live under Chinese rule. This then, inexplicably, becomes the central message of French's book: that it is pointless even detrimental for Tibetans to hope or struggle for an independent Tibet and that Western supporters of Tibet would be advised not to encourage this sort of thing. In an interview with *Gulf News* French states flat out: "I think it [Tibetan freedom] is politically unrealistic, and those who believe in it are naive." And this is also the central message readers of French's book seem to derive, for instance *The Economist* (9 April 2003) reviewer endorses French's observation and adds "Tibetans working within the Chinese system have a better chance of safeguarding what is left of Tibetan identity than can any amount of righteous outrage in the West."

Tibetans have always had such unsolicited counsel proffered to them from people with a strong interest in not offending China yet desiring to be seen as caring, though realistic, on the issue of Tibet. Such disingenuous concern is probably best dealt with by a curt dismissal of the kind that a British Foreign secretary once directed at an aide. On 20 December 1961, the General Assembly of the UN, with 56 yeas, 11 nays and 29 abstentions, renewed "its call for the cessation of practices which deprive the Tibetan people of their fundamental human rights and freedoms, including their right to self-determination." Even the British voted for the resolution presumably on the orders of Lord Home, who had become impatient with his staff's petty arguments and excuses. One Whitehall aide had suggested that a UN resolution supporting Tibet's independence might make the lot of the Tibetans even harder. Home dismissed this with a curt, handwritten marginal note, "It could hardly be worse."

When Patrick French got back to Britain from Tibet he decided to step down as a director of the Free Tibet Campaign. "After all I had seen and heard in the Tibetan Autonomous Region and its borderlands, I could no longer view things with the necessary simplicity to be part of a political campaign. I doubted whether a free Tibet had any meaning without a free China."

One is tempted to ask whether French would have said the same to dissidents in Eastern Europe. Would he have cautioned Lech Walesa that a free Poland would have no meaning without a free Russia? Let us remember that freedom came to Poland first and in fact it was that initial event that precipitated the downfall of the Communist world. And let us also remember that everyone then, including the experts, did not foresee the break up of the Soviet Empire and were resigned to the possibility of the Cold War going on forever, *in saecula saeculorum*. Furthermore, for someone who quotes Nadezhda Mandelstam, French does not seem to appreciate the depths of despair and hopelessness that dissidents in Russia felt about keeping up their moral opposition to the Soviet regime, or even just maintaining their common humanity and integrity in the face of the steel and concrete permanence of their totalitarian world. I think we can conclude that Mandelstam did not choose to call her autobiography *Hope Against Hope*, as a casual afterthought.

Unlike other repressive regimes in the world today as that in Burma, North Korea, or lately in Iraq, China's has tremendous influence internationally in business, politics, media and academic circles. In fact this power is so pervasive and so subtly intimidating, that a leading American sinologist, Perry Link, of Princeton has dubbed it the "The Anaconda in the Chandelier." In an article by that title in *The New York Review of Books*, 11 April 2002, Link makes it clear how scholars, journalists, human rights lawyers, even "whistle-blowers" in the West find it daunting, sometimes impossible to write or speak in explicit contradiction of what the Beijing government has pronounced to be a "fundamental principle." One of these being the fact of Taiwan and Tibet being inalienable parts of China.

In Patrick French's case I feel that the principal, but unstated, reason for his advocacy of the abandonment of the Tibetan freedom struggle, comes from the fact that the Dalai Lama himself has called for it. Patrick French makes it clear throughout the book of his deep admiration for the Dalai Lama and often compares him favourably to those who serve him in his exile government whom he accuses of "incompetence and cupidity," which though superficially an accurate observation is not a fair one. Essentially these are people whom His Holiness has chosen to have around him, maybe not so much for their competence as for their unquestioning loyalty.

French's contention that "the Dalai lama has tried to bring democracy to the exiled government, and allow new leaders to emerge ... but has failed because of "conservative popular opinion" is essentially a pious fable that frustrated exile Tibetans repeat like a mantra to berate themselves for the crushing stasis of their society and political movement. Of course, freedom movements are not democracies, but in the Tibetan exile world there is not even an attempt at open public discussion on national policy, and certainly no room for questioning the Dalai Lama's judgment. In such a situation powerless functionaries and foreign "advisors" (whose primary criterion for selection seems to be how faithfully they can echo the Dalai Lama's views) though deserving of a swift kick in the pants, cannot be blamed for the policy failures of the paramount leader.

Patrick French has managed to insert a considerable amount of history into his account, though not all his research is well digested. Yet somehow, despite the plethora of historical information, a central and abiding feature of Tibetan history completely eludes our author. Though there have been periods of Tibetan history when China (or rather the China-based dynasties established by Mongol and Manchu conquerors) gained a measure of control over Tibet, Tibetans have somehow always somehow managed to re-assert their independence: The Mongols were thrown out in 1358 and the Manchus in 1911.

In 1904 the Thirteenth Dalai Lama fled Tibet before a British invasion force. Seeking support in Beijing from the Manchu emperor, His Holiness received a humiliating lesson in realpolitik. The Beijing correspondent for the London *Times* reported that the Dalai Lama was finished and Tibet was firmly in China's power (Chinese troops occupied Tibet in the wake of British withdrawal). The American envoy in Beijing wrote to a very interested president (Teddy Roosevelt) that he had been a witness to the end of the dalai lamas of Tibet. For seven years His Holiness was forced to wander in-exile in Mongolia, China and India. But in 1911 the Manchu dynasty fell and fighting broke out in Tibet. The next year Dalai Lama returned in triumph to Lhasa and declared his nation's independence.

Of course, history does not repeat itself in a mechanical fashion and this is not to assert that Tibetan independence is inevitable or even foreseeable in the immediate future, but Patrick French's failing is that he does not even allow for the possibility. All he does, in essence, is tell Tibetans to give up hope. Wang Lixiong, a leading Chinese writer on Tibet is less sanguine than our author about permanent Chinese control of Tibet. In an article published in

Beijing in 1999 Wang concludes "A review of history shows that whenever Chinese sovereignty over Tibet gets out of control, the prerequisite is nothing but instability in China".

The greatest of all modern Chinese writers, Lu Xun, would, I feel, probably not have advised Tibetans to curl up and die in the face of their present tragedy. He was a congenital pessimist but he had this to say on the matter of hope: "Hope can neither be affirmed nor denied. Hope is like a path in the countryside: originally there was no path — yet, as people are walking all the time in the same spot, a way appears."

1 October 2003
World Tibet Network News

Freedom Wind, Freedom Song
Dispelling Modern Myths about the Tibetan National Flag and National Anthem

RECENTLY, A TIBET SUPPORTER, arguing to get her support-group to drop the goal of Tibetan independence from their charter, was reported to have said: "the whole Tibetan independence issue is a myth. Even the flag has been copied from the Japanese."

In an enlightening but cautionary piece of writing, "The Anaconda in the Chandelier," a leading American sinologist, Perry Link, of Princeton University, makes it clear how scholars (including himself), journalists, human rights lawyers, even "whistle-blowers" in the West find it daunting, sometimes impossible to write or speak in explicit contradiction of what Beijing has pronounced to be a "fundamental principle."[1]

Since the uncompromising denial of Tibetan independence (even as a matter of historical reality) has always been one of these "fundamental principles" it should come as no surprise that a great

---

1. Link, Perry, "The Anaconda in the Chandelier". *The New York Review of Books*, 11 April 2002.

deal of academic and even general writing and opinion on Tibet should evince a mealy-mouthed quality, one that often degenerates into outright and unashamed intellectual dishonesty. Even in something as peripheral as Buddhist studies, certain scholars have been known to insist that Tibetans don't have a national identity, and that Buddhism was the only specific feature that could be said to define Tibetan identity.

Then there are others who insist that the idea of a Tibetan nation-state was the construct of British imperialism — through its representatives Sir Charles Bell, Frank Ludlow and others. For instance, the writer Patrick French, in an interview with a Dubai paper, was asked this question: "It is the British, then, who tried to create the myth of Tibetan independence?" French replied: "Certainly so. The Simla Convention of 1914, in which the British recognized Tibet, was not ratified by the Chinese. The McMahon Line drawn under the convention is an imaginary line, and it does not correspond to the international boundary."

Aside from the annoying superficiality of their grasp of Tibetan history, the detractors of Tibetan "nationalism" are evidently unaware of more recent and enlightened developments in nationalism studies. Such traditional and somewhat condescending Eurocentric views of Asian and African national identities as merely following "models" already formulated in Europe or America and imposed on, or adopted by, such colonized lands, are now, of course, regarded as exclusionary and incomplete. These outdated notions of Asian nationalism as being "imagined, or invented" have been pretty well dismissed by experts on the subject as Partha Chatterjee (*The Nation and Its Fragments*) and Prasenjit Duara (*Rescuing History from the Nation: Questioning Narratives of Modern China*) who offer us more complex and nuanced views of Asian nationalism where indigenous historical, cultural and even religious factors are no less relevant to its evolution than merely the influence or machinations of European or American colonial and imperial powers.

But let me stop here. I do not intend to go into a detailed discussion on Tibetan nationalism, at this time. I raised the issue largely to set the stage, as it were, for this defence of Tibetan nationalism's two principal symbols — the flag and the anthem.

With the subject of Tibetan independence being almost unthinkable in Beijing, and also fairly taboo in Dharamshala (as well as in the more credulous and submissive sections of the Tibetan exile world), it should come as no surprise that its two faithful symbols should have to put up with growing misrepresentation, even ridicule, as mentioned at the start of this article. Most probably the Tibet supporter (?) in question had picked up the bit about the Tibetan flag being "copied from the Japanese" out of Patrick French's last book, *Tibet, Tibet*, where the author suggests that both symbols were somehow made up "deliberately in exile, a regimental banner devised in the 1920s by a wandering Japanese man became the Tibetan national flag, and a song written by the Dalai Lama's tutor Trijang Rinpoche was adopted as Tibet's national anthem." French is flat out wrong in his assertion about the flag and only just partially right about the anthem.

THE FLAG

Let's first take up the issue of the flag. To begin with, what French and others casting doubts about the origins and authenticity of the Tibetan flag fail to appreciate is that the entire business of countries having specific "national" flags is in itself a fairly recent development, and a quite artificial one at that. An overwhelming majority of the countries in the world have only had a national flag since the

1940s or thereafter. Furthermore, few national flags have any meaningful contiguity, historical or cultural, with their nations' past. Take the tricolours of Egypt (1984), Iraq (1991), Yemen (1990), and Syria (1980). What connection do they have by way of symbol or colour to Pharaonic Egypt or the Mesopotamia of Hamurabi, and so on? Or for that matter what link of tradition or symbolism does the present day flag of Communist China (1949), or even of Nationalist China (1928), have with ancient China? Absolutely nothing, as far as one can make out. All these flags, especially the Nationalist Chinese one with its sun emblem, might as well have been designed by "a wandering Japanese man".

And let us take a look at the national flag of French's own country. The Union Jack was originally a royal flag, rather than a national flag. In fact, no law has ever been passed making it a national flag, but it has become one through usage. Its first parliamentary recognition as a national flag came in 1908, when it was declared that "the Union Jack should be regarded as the National flag." A more categorical statement was made by the Home secretary in 1933, when he stated that "the Union Flag is the National Flag."

Even the various elements of the flag, for instance the red on white English Cross of Saint George with the white on blue Scottish Cross of Saint Andrew, were only introduced in 1606 after England and Scotland were united under James VI of Scotland and I of England. The diagonal red on white Cross of Saint Patrick appeared when Ireland was joined to the United Kingdom in 1800.

In contrast the central element of the Tibetan flag, the snow lion, has far hoarier antecedents as a symbol of the Tibetan empire. The vexillologist, Professor Pierre C. Lux-Wurm, maintains that "the main features of the Tibetan flag were designed in the latter half of the seventh century A.D. by King Songtsen Gampo ... The lion emblem first displayed as a war-banner became in time the national flag. The final consolidation of Tibetan independence brought about the addition of the rising sun and the twelve stripes of red and blue, which were introduced by the thirteenth Dalai Lama" ("The Story of the Flag of Tibet", *Flag Bulletin*, Vol. XII, No. 1, Spring 1973).

In a publication of the Library of Tibetan Works and Archives, (*Tibetan National Flag*, Dharamshala, 1980) more historical details are provided of how the snow lion symbol featured on ancient Tibetan flags. "It is recorded that the regiment of Yö-ru tö had a military flag with a pair of snow-lions facing each other; that Yä-ru mä had a snow-lion with a bright upper border; that of Tzang Rulag, had a snow-lion standing upright, springing towards the sky; continuing with that tradition up to the beginning of the twentieth century, various regiments within the Tibetan army have had military flags with either a pair of snow-lions facing each other, or a snow-lion springing upwards and so forth."

This work also mentions, as does Professor Lux-Wurm, that the Thirteenth Dalai Lama himself designed the modern flag. Most other accounts repeat the same, and further state that it occurred sometime before 1920, which, if accurate, makes the Tibetan flag far older than nearly all the national flags discussed earlier, even the two Chinese ones. The Dalai Lama retained the snow lion motif but added a white mountain below six red rays of a rising sun. The last feature is probably the grounds for the charge that "a wandering Japanese man" designed the flag. In His written description of the colours and symbolisms of the flag, His Holiness mentions that the six rays of the rising sun represented the *miu dongdrug*, or the six ancestral tribes of Tibet. Obviously the Dalai Lama was attempting to symbolize the primordial origins of Tibetan nationhood, and not revealing a weakness for the trappings of Japanese militarism.

For anyone with even an elementary appreciation of Tibetan Buddhist art, the aesthetic provenance of the national flag should be fairly obvious. The abundance of bright primary colours (especially golds and reds), the profusion of symbols, the general "busyness" of the design, all somehow (quite inexplicably) coming together in a single harmonious whole, is appreciably in keeping with the principles and genius of Tibetan Buddhist art.

The Tibetan flag lacks the *wabi*, the requisite "reverence for simplicity" of Japanese aesthetics, exemplified in the single red circle on a field of white, which is the Japanese national flag, the Hinomaru. If Yasujiro Yajima, to give our "wandering Japanese man" his proper name, did design the Tibetan flag he certainly created something very un-Japanese. And I think that unlikely. The one thing we know Yajima definitely designed in Tibet are the barracks of the Guards regiment at the Norbulingka. The design is traditional Japanese, adapted to Tibetan building materials, but retaining the simplicity and bucolic functionality of Japanese architecture.

And the idea of a dalai lama taking it upon himself to design the national flag is not an incongruous one, if we make an effort to understand the personality of the Great Thirteenth. He was fond of military display and attended not just the drills and parades of his soldiers but the polo matches of his officers, even personally awarding them special medals (possibly designed by himself) for their skill in horsemanship and musketry. He was a hands-on sort of ruler and involved himself in the minutiae of administration, perhaps to a fault, as his friend and biographer Sir Charles Bell mentions. An old servitor of His Holiness told me that on learning of the "Eighteen-course Chinese Feast" (*Gyazay liu chugay*) menu of official government banquets, a scandalized Dalai Lama personally worked out a less expensive bill of fare for official luncheons and dinners, the prosaic "Six Bowls, Four Plates" (*Kadrug deshi*) which became the standard for all but the most important official functions.

Tsarong Dundul Namgyal in the biography of his illustrious

father, Tsarong Dasang Dadul, the Commander-in-chief of the modern Tibetan army, writes that the national flag was first displayed in the late spring of 1916 at the great parade near the Norbulingka when the different regiments of the modern Tibetan army first demonstrated the various military styles (British, Japanese and Russian) that they had been trained in. After reviewing the troops His Holiness subsequently chose the British model, and thereafter the Tibetan army was trained in that method. The whole city turned out to witness the display of troops, their new weapons, new uniforms and the new national flag "which had been designed and approved by His Holiness." Dundul Namgyal Tsarong also writes that "His Holiness had also given a detailed description of the Tibetan national flag, written in his own hand. Usually, official writing is carried out by the chief secretary, so when His Holiness the Dalai Lama writes something out personally, it is greatly treasured. This description was in the possession of my father until the year 1946, when it was given to the newly formed Foreign Office for preservation."2

The only existing copy (in exile) of the original design is now in the possession of the Tethong family. It was sent, sometime around 1929–30, from Lhasa to Chamdo to the headquarters of the Governor General (*domay-chikyap*) of Eastern Tibet, Tethong Gyurme Gyatso. His eldest daughter, Lobsang Diki, clearly remembers her father receiving the design and showing it to her and others. According to Lobsang Deki, the design was the size of a small hand flag (about 7" x 10") and painted on white cotton cloth. The bottom half of the cloth had a written description of the symbolisms of the various colours and design elements. Lobsang Deki recalls her father telling her that

---

2. Dundul Namgyal Tsarong, *In the Service of His Country; The Biography of Dasang Damdul Tsarong Commander General of Tibet*, Snow Lion Publications, Ithaca, 2000.

the description or praise (*toepa*) of the flag had been composed (*jatsom*) by His Holiness himself. She vaguely remembers the description being in the *umay* script, though she is not sure that the calligraphy was that of His Holiness or of a secretary. It was from this source material that the design of the first national flag in exile was established in Mussoorie in 1959. It could perhaps be mentioned that the Tethong family also has in its possession one of the older flags flown by Tibetan regiments. It is a large silk banner about five by seven feet, and depicts a single snow-lion *rampant* on a field of red.

The flag was not only carried by all the regiments of the Tibetan army, but even displayed in certain public buildings as a national flag, long before Tibetans were forced into exile. In the two-part BBC documentary on Tibet (*Tibet: The Lost Civilization* and *The Bamboo Curtain Falls*) there is a footage of the Potala from the roof of the Jokang. You can see the national flag fluttering from the top of the largest building at the foot of the Potala.

But perhaps the most significant feature of the flag, typically overlooked by its detractors, is that the Tibetan public of the past clearly regarded it as their national symbol. Furthermore, the flag seems to have stirred the same sort of patriotic emotion in them as such symbols undoubtedly do elsewhere — in times of war or great national crisis.

In 1951 the Chinese occupation authorities made demands of the Tibetan government that Tibetan regiments only display the Chinese national flag. The prime ministers Lukhangwa and Lobsang Tashi refused and the Kashag tried to arrange a compromise where the regiments could carry both national flags. Rumours of this dispute spread among the Lhasa public, and, as with such things, became more dramatized in the telling. The final story, firmly believed to this day by the general Tibetan public, is that the Chinese demanded that the Red Flag be hoisted over the Potala but that

Lukhangwa refused, declaring defiantly that as long as he lived only the national flag would be flown over the Potala. Tsering Shakya, in his history of modern Tibet (*The Dragon in the Land of Snows*) tells us that both prime-ministers became "folk-heroes to the masses" over this incident.

In a couple of interviews with former Tibetan military personnel I was told that when the Tibetan regiments were finally ordered to carry the Red flag on their parades the soldiers shortened the pole for the Red Flag, and marched with the national flag raised higher, annoying the Chinese occupation authorities even further.

It should also be remembered that, subsequently, Tibetans braved imprisonment, torture and even execution for the flag. Just this year Radio Free Asia aired a report on a young monk, Choeden Rinzin of Ganden Monastery who was arrested for possessing a flag of Tibet. Last year in August 2003 activists in Lhasa raised the national flag from a high radio tower.[3] Even from a remote corner of the Tibetan world, two men Lungtok and Choejor were arrested in January 1997 for pasting wall posters in the street of Gade County in Golok "Tibetan Autonomous Prefecture" and for displaying the national flag.

On 21 February 1997, at a public demonstration in Malho County in Qinghai province, the Tibetan National flag was raised and independence posters displayed in the main market place. In the very first pro-independence demonstration in Lhasa on 27 September 1987, many protesters carried small homemade national flags. The demonstration was put down with great brutality by Chinese state-security forces. All those later arrested were accused of carrying the prohibited "snow mountain and lion" national flag of Tibet.

---

3. Patrick French in *Tibet, Tibet*, tells us that a Tibetan protester at the 1999 National Minority Games in Lhasa managed to pull down the Chinese flag from its pole and started to raise the Tibetan flag in its place before he was arrested

THE NATIONAL ANTHEM

In Michael Curtiz's great war romance, *Casablanca*, there is a corny but nonetheless moving scene in Rick's Café Americain, when roused by a provocative rendition of the Deutschland Uber Alles by partying Nazi officers, the French and other customers led by the Czech Resistance hero, Victor Laszlo (Paul Reid), defiantly sing the Marseillaise. Yvonne (Madeleine Le Beau), a pretty French coquette, drinking with the Germans, and flirting with the chief Gestapo officer Major Strasser (Conrad Veidt), has a turn of conscience and, with tears streaming down her cheeks, joins in the singing of the French national anthem.

A leading Tibet expert in the United States, Professor Elliot Sperling of Indiana University argues that visitors to present day Tibet, including Tibet experts, encountering a population going about its daily business and not expressing open defiance of Chinese occupation, and then concluding that Tibetans are satisfied with the status quo, invariably fail to take into account the realities of life under Communist Chinese rule.[4] They further fail to take into account, what Professor Sperling has termed the "Yvonne factor" of dormant or suppressed Tibetan nationalism, which could be galvanized by a crisis or some unusual event, as it happened in 1979 with the first visit of the Dalai Lama's representatives and in 1987 by the Dalai Lama's speech to the US Congress — or perhaps, sometime in the

---

4. Vaclav Havel has eloquently spoken of the double personae that people living under coercive and repressive regimes adopt with regard to their intellectual, social and political behaviour (see Timothy Garton Ash, "Eastern Europe: the Year of Truth", *New York Review of Books*, 15 February 1990). It is this forced adjustment to coercion that led observers so astray in predicting popular sentiment in a number of places (perhaps most notably the outcome of Nicaragua's 1990 election).Put bluntly, a state that penalises people for holding 'wrong' opinions is ill equipped to

foreseeable future, by a lone voice singing the Tibetan national anthem at a Communist Party rally in Lhasa.

The current Tibetan national anthem was written in exile, and the lyrics composed by the Dalai Lama's junior tutor as Patrick French states — but that is not the whole story. First of all the lyrics of the anthem were written specifically for the national anthem and were not just some song written by him and adapted for the purpose, as French seems to suggest. Furthermore, the Dalai Lama's junior tutor was requested to write the lyrics not because of his official or spiritual position but because he was considered to be the leading poet in the classical *snyen-ngag* style (based on the Sanskrit *kaviya* tradition).

So, much in the way as poet laureates of new nations are sometimes commissioned to write the lyrics of the national anthem — as Rabindranath Tagore wrote the verses of the *Jana Gana Mana* — Trijang Rinpoche also composed the lines of our national anthem. Many of the lyrics of the new songs composed in the sixties and sung at Tibetan schools and the Tibetan Institute of Performing Arts, were written by Trijang Rinpoche. The Dalai Lama's senior tutor, Yonzin Ling Rinpoche, also wrote a number of songs at the time.

I am not a great fan of classical *snyen-ngag* poetry, as I find its stylised conventions and ornamental language somewhat contrived, but my opinions count for absolutely nothing in this debate as I am

take an accurate reading of those opinions, and may likely poison the atmosphere for such investigations. In 1979 the Chinese authorities were stunned by the overwhelming emotional reception accorded the Dalai Lama's emissaries when they arrived in Lhasa. So too, the authorities appear to have actually believed, at some level, that only a "handful" of Tibetans supported "separatism", until the depth of the problem forced the authorities to take repressive measures well beyond a basic restoration of order.

far from being any kind of expert on Tibetan poetry or Tibetan literature for that matter. Still, the limitations of stylised classical verse for evoking the kind of immediate passions essential to a proper national anthem, seem evident in the translations of the first few lines of the Tibetan national anthem:

> *sishe pende dogu junwi ter*
> *tubten sampel norbu onang bar*
> *tendro nordzin gyache kyongwi gon*
> *trinle kyi rolsto gye*
> *dorje khamsu tenpe*
> *chokun chamtse kyong*
> *namkho gawa gyaden u pang gungla beg*
> *puntso deshi nga-thang gye*
> *pojong cholkha sum gyi kyonla deoden sarpe khyap* ...

The source of temporal and spiritual wealth of joy and boundless benefits,
The wish-fulfilling jewel of the Buddha's teaching, blazes forth radiant light.
The all-protecting patron of the doctrine and of all sentient beings,
By his actions stretches forth his influence like an ocean.
By his eternal vajra-nature
His compassion and loving care extends to beings everywhere.
May the celestially appointed government achieve the heights of glory
And increase its fourfold influence and prosperity.
May a golden age of happiness spread across the three provinces of Tibet ...5

Few Tibetans are aware that Tibet had an older national anthem dating back to the eighteenth century. Sir Charles Bell calls it Tibet's

---

5. Transliteration and translation from the website of the Office of Tibet, New York.

"national hymn", and remarks how in just a few lines it captures the essence of the Tibetan land and spirit.

> *Ghang ri rawe kor we shingkham di*
> *Phen thang dewa ma loe jungwae ne*
> *Chenrezig wa Tenzin Gyatso yin*
> *Shelpal se thae bhardu*
> *Ten gyur chik*

> Circled by ramparts of snow-mountains,
> This sacred realm,
> This wellspring of all benefits and happiness
> Tenzin Gyatso, bodhisattva of Compassion.
> May his reign endure
> Till the end of all existence

The eminent Tibetan scholar, Tashi Tsering citing the historical work *Bka' blon rtogs brjod*, says that this verse was composed by the Tibetan ruler, Pholhanas, (in 1745–46) in praise of the Seventh Dalai Lama.[5]

I am, admittedly, hugely biased in the matter, but I cannot help but feel how the delicate simplicity and humanity of this verse probably has no equal in the genre, especially when one has to take into account the fact that most other national anthems usually express sentiments that are either boastful, chauvinistic, or outright militant. Take for instance this verse from the British national anthem, *God Save the Queen*:

---

5. My translation.

6. Tashi Tsering, "Reflections on Thang stong rgyal po as the founder of the a lce lha mo tradition of Tibetan performing arts", *The Singing Mask: Echoes of Tibetan Opera, Lungta*, Winter 2001, No 15, eds. Isabelle Henrion-Dourcy and Tashi Tsering.

> O Lord our God arise,
> Scatter her enemies,
> And make them fall:
> Confound their politics,
> Frustrate their knavish tricks,
> On Thee our hopes we fix:
> God save us all.

Or this relentless us-against-everyone-else paean to xenophobia and violence, from the People's Republic of China:

> Arise, ye who refuse to be slaves!
> With our flesh and blood, let us build our new Great Wall!
> The Chinese nation faces its greatest danger.
> From each one the urgent call for action comes forth.
> Arise! Arise! Arise!
> Millions with but one heart,
> Braving the enemy's fire.
> March on!
> Braving the enemy's fire.
> March on! March on! March on!

The only national anthem that, to my mind, shares the simplicity and poetry of the Tibetan national hymn is the Japanese *Kimi Gayo*.

> *Kimi ga yo wa,*
> *Chiyo ni,*
> *Hachiyo ni,*
> *Sazare ishi no,*
> *Iwao to narite,*
> *Koke no musu made.*

> May the emperor's reign,
> Continue for a thousand,
> Eight thousand generations;
> Until the pebbles,
> Grow into boulders,
> Lush with moss

The words of the Japanese anthem are actually from a waka style poem from Japan's Heian Period, about one thousand years ago. It was an Englishman, J. W. Fenton, who urged Japan to adopt this verse for a national anthem, and he wrote the original music for it in 1869. A German bandmaster, Franz Eckert, who established the military band of the Imperial Guards, later revised it into its present form. It was formally adopted as a national anthem in 1888.

It should be noted that in old Tibet the "national hymn", *Ghang Ri Rawe*, actually served pretty much the same purpose as a national anthem. It was recited at the end of most government functions (*zego*), or at the conclusion of daily prayer services in monasteries and religious gatherings. In fact many individual Tibetans conclude their own personal devotions with this patriotic hymn that describes the essential features of the Tibetan landscape and wishes their sovereign a long life.

The hymn is also mandatory at every opera performance, and is sung during the introductory ceremony. It is one of the most beautiful arias in Tibetan opera. But of course it requires a trained voice to sing it in that manner. Even in exile the hymn is recited daily at all schools, monasteries and institutions.

So why didn't Tibetans just retain this old hymn as a modern national anthem? Probably it was just a case of overlooking the obvious. In Japan it required an outsider to point out the eminent suitability of the old waka verse for a national anthem. If Sir Charles Bell had raised the issue as J. W. Fenton had done, or, more to the point, if the old Tibetan government had been as receptive to new ideas and advice as the Meiji leadership were, we might, at the very least be now singing a shorter and more lucid national anthem.

Also in the early years of exile in Dharamshala there was "new broom" spirit, when the Dalai Lama and the Tibetan government wanted everything new and modern, and so, of course, we had to have a new national anthem, as we had to have new nationalistic songs and new historico-musical dramas and propaganda plays (the old lhamo opera went out of official favour for some years).

But the "new" anthem is now over forty-five years old and seems to have acquired, over time, the requisite soul-stirring quality of the genre. I may have quibbled earlier on about the limitations of classical *snyen-ngag* poetry, but I am prepared to admit that I do succumb, sometimes, to the emotional call of the national anthem. I first analysed these feelings when I was a young volunteer at Mustang and we sang the national anthem every morning after our callisthenics and military drill. An excerpt from a work in progress:

> In spite of our martial demonstrations we (our platoon of about thirty men) were not an impressive lot. We varied in age from a white-haired ancient of seventy odd years to two little boys (the product of a liaison of one of our men with a local Lopa woman). We also wore no uniforms as such, except for homemade forage caps and anoraks that we stitched ourselves out of cotton khaki fabric. Some men wore shirts made of camouflage parachute nylon, and odds and ends of Chinese uniforms. Footwear varied from traditional Tibetan boots, to Chinese canvas sneakers. The few lucky ones had vibram-soled army boots bought at Pokhara and Butwal from British Gurkha soldiers on leave. But the informality of our attire didn't bother me. I felt about it much as Orwell probably did the turnout of his comrades at the Lenin barracks in Barcelona during the Spanish Civil War. '...the mashed forage caps and ragtag, hand-me-down uniforms gave the men a grizzled courageous look you see in embattled legionnaires — a kind of sloppiness that seemed indistinguishable from hard won experience.'"
>
> "Following the PT and drill we would line up in formation, stand to attention and holding a salute, sing the national anthem. We sang it badly. No one had really mastered the tune, and the obscurely literary, symbol-steeped lyrics were barked out in plain honest staccato Khampa accents. The old man in front of me had his large prayer wheel, or rather its long wooden handle, stuck

down the back of his shirt collar, while he stood rigidly to attention belting out words he probably didn't understand. The whole thing seemed faintly ridiculous. I had come from a somewhat elitist educational background where it was considered the done thing to sneer at established beliefs. But up at Mustang, the national anthem touched something in me. In a safe civilized life patriotic demonstrations may seem silly, but when you know that your survival depended to a large part on the strength of the collective belief in what you were fighting for, then the symbols of that belief: the national flag, the national anthem (though badly sung), took on meaning and substance — and became deeply moving."

20 May 2004
www.phayul.com

Tibetan Flag in 1934 *National Geographic*

A FEW DAYS AFTER the appearance of my essay "Freedom Wind, Freedom Song" on World Tibet Network News and Phayul.com, I received an email from an old friend, Tendar-la, formerly an official from the Department of Information and International Relations (DIIR), now at the Office of Tibet, New York. He wrote to tell me that the DIIR had, some years ago, obtained a very old issue of the *National Geographic* magazine, which carried a reference to the Tibetan flag. I managed to get a photocopy of the issue (volume LXVI, number 3, September 1934) and flipped to the main article, "Flags of the World" by Gilbert Grosvenor and William J. Showalter. And there it was on page 383, the national flag of Tibet, looking exactly as it does these days. It was between the flags of Switzerland and Turkey. The description was straightforward: "TIBET: With its towering mountain of snow, before which stand two lions fighting for a flaming gem, the flag of Tibet is one of the most distinctive of the East." Most probably the National Geographic Society had obtained the Tibetan flag from Tsarong Dasang Dadul, the Commander-in-chief of the modern Tibetan army and a member of the Geographic Society.

There was no particular mention that the Tibetan flag was a new one or that Tibet was a new entry in their list. The editors had, in the case of some other countries, made qualifications where necessary. In the case of the German flag the editors had been careful to mention that that the Swastika flag of Nazi Germany had been adopted just a year earlier as the German national flag by a special decree of the Chancellor, Adolf Hitler. A special reference was also made in the case of Manchukuo (or Manchutikuo): "The Kingdom of Manchutikuo came into being just in time to permit a flag to find its proper place in our plates."

It should be mentioned that in the case of such entries as Cambodia and Annam, there were clear mentions in each case that these countries were the protectorates of France, or in the cases of Lebanon and Syria that they were under French mandate. Even the old flag of Korea, (then Chosen) was grouped together with Japan, and mention made that the Japanese flag had replaced this old Korean flag. No such qualifications were made in the Tibetan case. I am not in any way citing these factoids to make Tibetan readers feel good, but to bring forward the observation that change is a condition of history. Going through the list and seeing the flags of nations that don't exist anymore, gave one the feeling of what the Japanese call *mono no aware*, melancholy at the realization of the fleeting quality of human existence. Who even remembers a kingdom of Danzig, or even the state of Manchukuo, both of whose flags the magazine carried? These nations are now "history" in the most terminal sense.

On the other hand the *National Geographic* did not carry the flags of India, the Philippines, Israel, Ireland, Libya, Singapore, Indonesia, Burma, Nepal (Nepal's present flag was only adopted on

12 December 1962), Malaysia, Mongolia, Bhutan and many other present day nations. Even Australia and Canada do not rate separate entries as nations but are grouped together under the British Empire. The magazine listed seventy-seven independent countries in 1934. Right now we have 191 member states in the United Nations, and every so many years some new nation is inducted. Could Tibet be the 192nd or the 193rd or even the 200th free nation to join the United Nations?

My good friend Lhasang Tsering is an inspiring speaker, as those of you who have seen the documentary film *Cry of the Snow Lion* will know. Now and then he ends his talks with this interesting observation. "Tibetans, as Buddhists, believe that all phenomenon, everything, is impermanent. Why should we have to believe that only China's occupation of Tibet is permanent?" Why indeed?

4 September 2004
World Tibet Network News